2/16

Off Balance

Ballet Theatre Chronicles, Book 1

Terez Mertes Rose

Published in the United States
Classical Girl Press - www.theclassicalgirl.com
Cover design by James T. Egan, BookFly Design, LLC
Formatting by Polgarus Studio

ISBN-13 978-0-9860934-0-1
ISBN (ebook) 978-0-9860934-1-8

For Peter and Jonathan, with love and gratitude

"The only way to make sense out of change is to plunge into it, move with it, and join the dance."

— Alan W. Watts

Prologue

Spring Season 1997

On Saturday night Alice Willoughby's world, her glittering soloist's career, came apart with a single misstep executed in front of 2000 spectators at San Francisco's California Civic Theater. Rendered careless by fatigue, she'd prepped wrong and the next step into an arabesque en pointe proved to be her last. A curious pop sounded, her knee gave out and she fell to the black, slip-resistant marley floor. She heaved herself to sitting, adrenaline surging through her, stunned by the realization that she couldn't get up any further. Her left knee simply wouldn't cooperate. The pain was like an explosion, obscuring everything but the mantra drummed into her after twenty years of ballet.

The show must go on.

Without breaking character.

Ben, her partner that night, immediately caught on to the situation. He made his way over to her, via a series of grand-jeté leaps to give the illusion that they were still dancing, that her fall had merely been part of the ballet.

Time slowed to a psychotropic-hued crawl. She seemed to be watching herself, her brain whirring uselessly, her limbs dumbly splayed out. Her gaze swung to the right, past the blazing stage lights, where she saw the other dancers now crowding the wings, jaws slack in horror. April, the ballet mistress, was standing in the middle wing, crying out, "She's down! She's not getting up!"

The voices sounded tinny and yet piercingly clear, as if transmitted through a long metal tube. Although the audience heard only the orchestra, she could hear the stage manager calling out to April, "What are they doing? Do we end? Lighting's asking me," and April's, "She's hurt, someone get Lorraine back here," and the stage manager's tense voice saying into his headpiece, "I don't *know* what they're doing, Larry, okay?"

"We'll wing it," Ben called out through the corner of his mouth, like a ventriloquist. "Give us sixty seconds."

He swooped behind Alice and helped her rise from her sitting position onto her good leg. Somehow, in spite of the state of shock she'd descended into, she managed to shift her bad leg behind her and strike a pose, swaying like a drunken corps de ballet dancer, yet raising her arms to a grace-laden fourth arabesque position, arms at ninety degrees.

This shouldn't be happening, her mind kept crying out.

It couldn't be happening.

But it was.

They improvised through the last minute of their pas de deux variation, the third-to-last movement of the ballet, Ben murmuring cues to her every time his back was to the audience. He'd lift Alice lyrically and set her down a few steps later. She'd hold the pose as he executed a series of movements, here a stylized lunge, there a few steps into a sharp, clean, triple pirouette. Gone for her, the fast-paced, rigorous choreography, but she still had full control of her upper-body presentation, employing expressive hand and arm movements until Ben returned to haul her to another part of the stage.

"Can you do the big lift?" he panted in her ear thirty seconds later.

She was trembling with spent adrenaline, losing energy fast. "Have to," she said through gritted teeth, never dropping her serene stage smile. It was their final departure from the stage, the last thing the audience would remember. It couldn't be half-assed.

"Okay, hang tight," he murmured. Placing one hand on her right hip and the other under the thigh of her bad leg, he hoisted her high above him.

The pain of it took her breath away. Sweat, and now tears, stung her eyes as she arched back, gaze high, arms in high fifth. She pressed her good leg up against the maimed one, as a human splint. She knew she must be cutting a sorry figure, and yet even this seemed to encompass the mood of the ballet.

Tomorrow's Lament was its name. Fitting, that.

She kept her expression regal, her arms high, as Ben wafted her offstage. The conductor of the orchestra, alerted to the plan change, allowed the music to grow softer before subsiding, thirty-two measures early, on a haunting note.

Perfect silence, as the stage faded to black.

The audience seemed to take one great, collective inhale before they burst into applause, cheers and calls of "*brava*," which grew louder as Ben eased her down backstage.

"Oh, Alice," the other dancers cried, crowding around her, reaching out to touch her arm, her knee. The assistant stage manager whisked over a chair and she slid into it.

"Oh, Alice," April cried, hurrying to her side.

"Oh, Alice," Lorraine, the physical therapist said, shaking her head as she probed at Alice's knee, her ankle.

Ben returned from his solo curtain call as the audience roared their approval. "Alice, they want *you*," he said, half-laughing, half-crying.

"They can't have her." Lorraine sounded grim. "She's not going anywhere."

They'd been the pas de deux couple for the third movement. A trio of dancers stood waiting to take the stage for the fourth movement, which would be followed by the finale, an ensemble movement. Alice, however, was done for the night. Even now, they were summoning a substitute dancer to the wings, to don Alice's costume and replace her for the finale.

The applause hadn't stopped. The dancers in position to go on next had to wait as the stage manager cued Ben for another curtain call. When he appeared, the audience exploded into louder applause, over which could be heard shouts and clamors. For Alice.

"Damn," said the stage manager, observing the scene on his monitor. "They really do want her."

They were calling for her. Begging. It was a childhood dream come true.

Except for the pain.

So began the euphoria—the thrill of having turned an onstage accident into a triumph, the glow of so much attention—a high so deeply intertwined with the pain that it was difficult to know where one ended and the other began. Until the euphoria faded and the pain didn't.

Until the other dancers returned to company class on Monday morning and Alice returned to the hospital for surgery.

Until a new cast list was posted for the next performance that didn't include Alice's name. Nor would it, for some time to come.

It wasn't until two weeks later, however, that reality finally sank in. She was at the medical clinic for a follow-up appointment with the orthopedic surgeon. Earlier in the day, she'd buoyed herself with the idea of taking college classes, something deemed unnecessary, even preposterous seven years earlier, upon high school graduation. She'd wanted only to be a soloist with San Francisco's renowned West Coast Ballet Theatre. But now, soloist position on hold, she recognized the importance of a temporary diversion. Further, it would serve to wake up that analyzing, information-seeking part of her brain, dormant since school days.

"Don't think," Balanchine used to tell his New York City Ballet dancers. "Don't analyze. Just dance, dear."

She endured the doctor's appointment with its disappointing news and decided that, yes, college classes were a must. She'd drop by San Francisco State's admissions office that very afternoon.

As she crutched her way toward the clinic's exit, she spied a vending machine. It sold, among other high-caloric, low-nutrition snacks, Snickers bars.

When was the last time she'd allowed herself a Snickers, just for the hell of it?

She fed the machine a five-dollar bill and pressed the correlating button. The familiar brown-wrapped bar thunked down. Afterward her fingers hovered over the return-change button. She thought about the doctor's words, his "hmm, usually we like to see better progress around now," as he'd studied X-rays of her leg, showing the ankle fracture—a bonus injury she'd discovered only later—and the knee's torn ligaments. Something inside her gave an uneasy flicker.

In an adjacent trash bin, someone had thrown out a banana peel, but had missed getting it all the way in. It hung there now, two yellow limbs clinging to the exterior. It looked like a starfish, determined to climb out of the refuse pit, a quixotic, ill-fated endeavor if there ever was one. She studied the peel, this little blot of stubborn, misguided optimism against this huge landscape of antiseptic order and barely masked unwellness.

That was her. That speckled banana peel, whose too-sweet aroma carried over, competing with the iodine and ammonia smells. Reality engulfed her, like a big bucket of water. She was screwed. She would have staggered if she hadn't already been on crutches.

Five miles away, her colleagues had just finished company class. They'd be leaving the studio together, leotards saturated with sweat, dance bags slung over their shoulders, griping about last-minute casting changes, aching joints, wondering aloud if there were time for a catnap between rehearsals and the evening's seven o'clock theater call. For them it was just another day. And here she stood, alone, bad news percolating through her, seeing the glacial, uncaring nature of the world as if for the first time.

No wonder Balanchine didn't like his dancers to think.

The Snickers bar lay in the trough of the vending machine, the credit balance displayed in glowing red numbers on the machine's face. In a frenzy, she began punching the designated number, three times in rapid succession. Down came more Snickers bars, one clunking after another, a satisfying *thunk, thunk, thunk.*

Grabbing them all, she shoved them into her backpack and made her way clumsily over to a padded bench in the corner. After she got herself and her encased leg situated, she tore open the first Snickers and took a bite. The flavors exploded in her mouth, alongside the recognition that she now had the freedom to eat this. She would not be wearing any skintight, paunch-exposing costumes any time soon.

Three more bites finished the first bar and she started right in on the second. The shock of the pleasure was like great sex after a year of celibacy. The chocolate and caramel, the mysterious "nougat" and peanuts. The sugar. The hint of saltiness providing complexity. A sigh escaped as something intractable inside her yielded to the pleasure.

She hesitated over the third one. Somehow it penetrated her stimulus-fogged mind that this was not about sensory gratification anymore. If she decided to eat more, it was because she understood somehow, deep down, that she would not dance onstage again.

"It's not over," the orthopedic surgeon had encouraged her, following his "this isn't looking good" analysis. "All professional dancers have setbacks." He'd offered stories of dancers who'd suffered broken limbs, torn ligaments, crushed feet, coming back to lead roles. Her friends—all dancers, because who had time to cultivate any other kind of friendships?—had tried to feed her the same kind of pep talks.

She unwrapped the third bar.

How did she know it was over?

She just knew.

She began to cry, she who never cried, above all in public. Since her earliest years, such a display had been taboo. She remembered her mother, back when she was alive and hadn't yet taken sick: the indomitable Deborah Whittier Willoughby, marching the six-year-old Alice right out of a ballet class, scolding her the entire way to the car. Alice had been crying, upset because her rival had been chosen to play the lead daisy in the recital.

Deborah had been unforgiving. "And in front of everyone," she'd hissed. "You're a Willoughby. Shame on you."

But Deborah was not here now, which struck her, even fourteen years after her death, as one more thing to cry about. Instead it was Alice, her loss, and the remaining Snickers bars. She held up the third one and sank her teeth into it. She continued to cry, softly, as she ate, helpless to stop either act. It was exquisite pleasure and agony at once, swirled together like soft-serve ice cream that came out half chocolate, half vanilla.

It was over, then.

Chapter 1 – Alice's New Life

Fall Season 2005

The new soloist for the West Coast Ballet Theatre arrived on the first Friday in August and by Friday afternoon the buzz of gossip and speculation had risen to the organization's administrative level. Alice heard two girls enter the ladies' room talking, as she huddled in a faux-suede armchair on the lounge side, clutching a letter addressed to Alice Willoughby, associate director of development, and contemplating the terrible news contained within.

The girls turned right, toward the sinks, without looking in the direction of the lounge. "But how could you have not seen her?" one of them was asking in a high, girlish voice. "She was here last spring for those two days, for her audition."

"That must have been the week I was so sick and missed company class a few times. But nobody made a fuss about her at the time."

"Because we all thought she was auditioning for the frickin' *corps*, not for a soloist position."

"What's she like?"

Alice leaned forward and caught the girls' reflection in the corner floor-to-ceiling mirror. Ballet dancers. If the leotards and tights hadn't given them away, the hair, slicked back and corralled into a bun high on the backs of their heads, would have. High-voice was a pretty, dark-haired girl who hoisted herself onto the Formica counter before replying.

"Oh, God. She's a perfect nightmare."

"Skinny?"

"Well, duh."

"How are her legs?"

High-voice sighed. "Up to her armpits."

"Feet?"

"Banana arches."

"Extensions?"

"Effortless. Obscene."

"Bitch," the other girl muttered.

"No kidding." High-voice twisted around to study her face in the mirror above the sinks. "And she was a soloist, in Kansas City, where they only have a thirty-five-week contract. You'd think corps de ballet here with us, right?"

"Totally!"

"Oh, why did Anders change his mind? A soloist. God."

"Wonder who she slept with to make *that* happen?" The other girl gazed around, scanning the room, the textured beige walls, as if the answer might be written there. Instead she caught sight of Alice's reflection in the corner mirror. She stared, horrified, then gave her friend a nudge.

"Poor Gabrielle," High-voice was saying. "She was so sure she'd get the... Ow! Why are you poking me, Charlotte?" She caught sight of Alice, as well, and her next words trailed off.

Alice approached them, setting the letter on the counter to wash her hands. "Well, hello there," she drawled. "Bet you're glad to see I'm not the new girl."

She could sense their relief, mingled with embarrassment. "It was just that..." High-voice began, but Alice waved away her words.

"Don't worry, I understand." She soaped her hands, meeting their eyes in the mirror. "I've been around for a long time. I've seen and heard it all."

The girls smiled, relaxed. She guessed they were corps dancers, the lowest level on the hierarchy, who'd taken company class earlier, not bothering to change from their skimpy leotards and tights. In that peculiar way dancers had of wandering publicly, confidently, in a state of near-undress, they made Alice feel like the anomaly, overdressed in her business attire, bursting with flesh next to their quivering whippet thinness, their dance-ness.

A pang shot through her, not unlike the twinges of pain her knee still gave her. She drew herself taller and allowed a note of chilliness to enter her voice as she reached for a paper towel. "What brings you girls to the administrative level?"

They reacted accordingly, eyes wide, laced with unease. "It's all right to use this restroom, isn't it?" one girl asked.

"Of course. What a silly question!"

"The other restroom was so crowded," the other added. "Last day of the school's summer intensive, all those kids acting hyper and emotional."

"Yes, indeed." Alice paused to scrutinize her bobbed chestnut hair in the mirror, smooth it into place. "And of course the company members are returning in full force this week, right?"

They both nodded eagerly. "Oh, *everyone's* here now," High-voice exclaimed.

"So it would seem. Even the new girl."

Before they could stutter another apology, she turned, picked up the offending letter and headed toward the door. "Have a nice day," she called over her shoulder.

As for her, thanks to the news she now had to share with her boss, her day was screwed.

The opportunity to discuss the bad news came up quicker than expected. She encountered Gil striding down the hallway just as she was returning to their offices. "Alice," he exclaimed, "that's no expression for a Friday afternoon."

He flashed her a grin, looking like a kid, which was no great stretch as he was still in his twenties. He was the boy wonder of the WCBT: a surprise hire for director of development three years earlier at the tender age of twenty-six, uncommonly successful at his job, a master of charm and persuasion. He still had the high coloring of a boy, as well—cherry lips, smooth complexion, his wide blue eyes an unlikely match with his glossy black hair. Office eye-candy. He knew this and cheerfully exploited it whenever it suited his needs.

"Why the down face?"

On impulse she thrust the letter at him. "Here's something that might kill your TGIF glow. From the Prescott Foundation."

She watched his expression as he scanned the letter. When he winced, she knew he'd gotten to the part about the foundation's regret in being unable to match the previous three years' contributions of $200,000, but they were pleased to award the West Coast Ballet Theatre $10,000 for the following year.

He finished the letter and looked up at her. "Well, shit," he said.

"I'm so sorry," she muttered. "I should have seen this coming."

Gil shook his head. "Don't beat yourself up. I didn't see it coming either. I had lunch with one of the board members a few weeks back and he led me to believe we were still in good standing. And we are, really. It says here that they look forward to returning to a bigger award next year."

She was too disheartened to offer further reply.

He studied the letter again and flipped it over, just as she'd done, as if hoping to find a *Just kidding!* postscript on the back. He sighed. "The worst part is that I have a meeting on Monday morning with Charlie and the board of directors. Things were looking so good for next year. This is going to put us way under forecast."

"Can you pretend like we haven't gotten the letter yet?"

Gil shook his head. "They might have copied Charlie Stanton."

"How about we sort of stretch the truth on the proposals that are out, the ones I'm almost sure will be a go?"

"No. The best thing at this point would be to come up with a new lead. A strong one."

"By Monday?"

"Sure."

"Well, gee." She consulted her watch. "Two o'clock. That gives you roughly three working hours."

He smiled. "I've had bigger challenges thrown at me."

Something in her began to feel the tiniest bit better. "Okay, boss. Let me know if I can help."

"I will. Don't go anywhere."

He set to work immediately. Over the next ninety minutes, she overheard him on the phone, networking with friends, business associates, service personnel, local receptionists—anyone who might serve as a point of contact for reeling in a bigger fish. He regularly checked with the city's hotel concierges to find out what group was in the hotel, who'd stopped in the lounge for a drink. Today that avenue paid off. She heard him speaking more enthusiastically and after he hung up he emitted a loud whoop.

Moments later he was at Alice's office door, shrugging into his suit jacket, clutching his BlackBerry and keys. "Let's go," he said.

She looked up from the report she was editing. "You did it? Like that?"

"It's big, Alice. Big, big, big." He grinned at her, then made shooing motions with his hands. "Come on, already. I can't guarantee how long he'll be there."

"Where? Who?"

"The lounge at the Ritz-Carlton. The who? Only Andy Redgrave."

Her mouth formed a silent O.

He chuckled. "Yes. My sentiments exactly."

"I'm ready."

"Then let's do it."

The Redgrave Foundation, like its eponymous billionaire founder, was notoriously elusive and difficult to conduct business with. But its allure was irresistible: five million dollars of its considerable funds reserved for the California arts annually. Last year the San Francisco Symphony had received $1.2 million. The WCBT had received a form rejection.

Gil's plan now, he told Alice as he drove, was to wander in, strike up a conversation with Andy and bring up the name of a friend of a friend he'd dug up. Andy was a theater person—Gil's former domain, where he still had influential friends. This mutual friend was a sure connection, Gil insisted.

"So why am I here?" Alice asked.

"Well, you'll be Plan B."

"What is Plan B?"

"That part I haven't figured out yet."

She clutched the door handle tighter. "Jesus, Gil. I don't know about this."

"Trust me here," he said as they pulled up along the Ritz-Carlton's front drive. As a team of valets hurried over to their car, Alice drew in a deep breath. She had to trust him; there were no other options at this point.

The lobby was predictably opulent, replete with chandeliers, marble floors, elaborate vases of flowers. Half a dozen staff members stood at attention, poised to offer immediate assistance to guests. Alice took a seat on a cream brocade settee just outside the lounge as Gil went on in. A few seconds later she picked up his soothing baritone. A murmur of conversation followed and, to Alice's relief, a rumble of laughter. She waited another minute, rose and entered the lounge.

Gil spotted her and waved. Beside him sat Andy Redgrave. Early forties, Alice guessed, lean, receding silvery-blond hair, elegant in a fitted charcoal suit, looking every inch the powerful billionaire player. He was not handsome in the same way Gil was; his face was too angular, but it served to highlight his posh bearing, the arresting nature of his pale blue eyes.

Gil made the introductions. Alice accepted Andy's offer to join them for a drink, a glass of white wine the server produced even before she could settle into her high-backed leather chair. Sipping her wine, she listened to the others talk. The two men across from Andy remained largely silent, listening to Gil recount an anecdote about Gil and Andy's mutual friend.

"So, we both know Joel," Andy said afterward. "I've just learned Alice is your associate. But I didn't catch what organization you two work for."

He hadn't told Andy yet. She couldn't believe it. Her toes curled in fearful anticipation.

"The West Coast Ballet Theatre Association." Gil offered Andy his most winning smile.

"In what capacity?"

"Oh. That would be development."

Andy's own smile faded. "I hope you're not here to try and talk business."

"Not in the least," Gil assured him. "We know your organization's submission guidelines."

"Good. Because otherwise I'd feel compelled to ask you to leave."

"I can fully appreciate that." Gil kept his tone confident, but Alice saw behind his eyes the first flicker of insecurity.

It was time for Plan B.

Fast.

"Actually," Alice blurted out, "Gil and I are here to settle a bet. He didn't believe me when I told him my great-great-grandfather and yours might have done business together."

Gil stared at her, baffled.

Andy looked her way as well. "Your great-great-grandfather. And he would be...?"

"Elijah Whittier."

"Ah. Railroads."

Alice nodded.

Andy cocked his head at her. "What did you say your last name was?"

"Willoughby."

"As in James Willoughby?"

"No. Thomas."

"I don't know the name."

"Neither did my mother's family." Alice offered him a conspiratorial grin. "But she married him anyway."

The corners of Andy's mouth lifted as he raised his highball glass and took a sip of his scotch. "Well, Gil," he said after he'd set the drink down. "It would appear you lost the bet. So what do you owe your associate?"

"A drink." Gil's eyes latched onto Alice's, transmitting pure, unadulterated gratitude. "A big one."

Gil hadn't conceded the game, however. He worked the conversation back to Chicago, to the mutual friend, mentioning how he'd helped Joel's brother create and run the Haberdasher Street Repertory Theatre.

"Good troupe they've got there in residence right now," Andy commented.

"Agreed."

"Who do you think is the better actor, Bryce Hamlin or Hodge O'Connor?"

"It depends on whether you're talking about the dramatic roles or all-around versatility. Or sex appeal."

"Which do you think most lends itself to an actor's success?"

"Oh, sex appeal," Gil said. "Face it. Sex sells."

Alice winced.

Andy, as well, looked taken aback, even disdainful. "Sex…"

"Sex," Gil repeated. "An unmistakable facet of life. And what's theater if not an elaboration of the core stimulus that drives us? A vicarious release of all those subconscious desires every human carries down in them. Desire for power. For sex. For domination. Being dominated."

Silence. Alice saw the account flash before their eyes and disappear. She hardly dared look in Gil's direction. But when she stole a glance a moment later, he was smiling, calm, regarding Andy expectantly.

Andy sat back in his leather armchair, his hands coming together to form a steeple. "I think that's a provocative perspective."

"Good theater is nothing if not provocative. Art in general. As it should be."

Andy mulled over this without replying. He reached for his glass, took a sip of his scotch and glanced at his Rolex. Alice's spirits sank. They'd been dismissed. Andy confirmed this when he stood a moment later. The two men accompanying him scrambled to their feet as well.

"I'm afraid we must take our leave," Andy said.

Gil rose and thrust out his hand, undaunted. "It was a pleasure to meet you. And if you talk to Joel, tell him Gil Sheridan sends his regards."

Andy shook Gil's hand but paused, mid-shake. His other hand swung around to sandwich Gil's hand. The Cadillac of handshakes: the two-handed grip.

"I'm having a private party in a month's time, at my Hillsborough home. Maybe I'll send a few invitations your way."

"We would certainly appreciate that," Gil replied without missing a beat. "It would be a pleasure to spend more time discussing, uh, theater with you." He gave Andy's hand one last vigorous pump before Andy released it.

"I'll give it some thought," Andy said. "We'll be in touch."

Had that been an official invitation or not? Over the next twenty minutes, on the way back to the WCBT offices, Gil and Alice speculated over this. Gil thought yes. Alice wasn't so sure. She told Gil he'd been too shocking, too overt about the sex-and-domination business. He told her quite the contrary, that if they received invitations, it would be because he'd gotten Andy's attention over that.

She shook her head as they entered the lobby. "It was my reference to the great-great-grandfathers. Otherwise he would have asked us to leave. I mean, did you see how cold his eyes had grown?"

"I would have come up with some way to save us. And hey, I didn't know Marianne was a Whittier."

She hesitated. "She's not."

"So, you lied."

"I did not. Maybe Marianne's not my birth mother."

"Nice try. Except that I've heard you call her 'my mom' a hundred times."

"I'm serious. Deborah Whittier is. Was."

He stopped and regarded her in surprise. "You *are* serious."

She nodded.

"You never told me any of this."

"Why should I have? I was a kid when she died and my father remarried. It's all ancient history."

"Sure, okay." He resumed their walk toward the elevators. "Point is, your diversion worked. Thank you. And now I think we're in, Alice."

"Well. Time will tell if we sufficiently impressed him."

"We did. He ended with 'We'll be in touch,' didn't he?"

"That could mean anything."

"Regardless, I'm calling this a lead. A strong one." He chuckled to himself. "Charlie Stanton's going to be over the moon. He's been trying to make inroads with the Redgrave Foundation for years. It drives him nuts that the symphony gets all the funding."

The elevator door pinged and slid open to reveal a young woman, clearly a dancer, standing inside. She had the perfect dancer's body, Alice noted, thin and delicate but not starved-looking, appealing angles and planes to her face and shoulders. She was sweetly pretty rather than beautiful, with pale, unblemished skin, light brown hair pulled back into a bun, and full pink lips.

Paperwork poked out of the girl's dance bag and Alice realized this must be the new hire, the soloist the girls in the bathroom had been gossiping about. She looked nervous, her hazel eyes wide with unease, the look of someone forced onto a roller-coaster ride, anticipating that first giant dip.

"Were you getting out?" Alice asked.

"Oh," the girl said. "Oh. Right."

A tango of sorts ensued as the girl tried to get off the elevator, only to step right in front of Gil, back up and step right in front of Alice. She next tried stepping to Gil's left, just as he shifted in that direction.

He began to chuckle. "Shall we dance?" he asked.

She didn't smile back. She looked as if she were ready to cry. "Sorry," she whispered, and shot between them.

Bemused, they stepped onto the elevator, followed by three other people who blocked their view of the girl. Even after the doors slid closed, however, Alice could still feel the girl's presence, that frozen, anticipatory moment among the three of them.

Gil was conspicuously silent on the ride up to the fourth floor. Alice glanced over at him out of the corner of her eye. He looked confused. Unmoored.

He was not thinking about Andy Redgrave, she realized. He was thinking about that girl.

A prickle stirred the hairs at the back of her neck. She understood, in a way she couldn't put into words, that the dancers she'd encountered earlier had every reason to feel threatened by the new girl.

Unfathomably, so did she.

Chapter 2 – The New Hire

Lana couldn't find a place at the barre for company class. It was like a game of musical chairs, or something from a bad dream. Two weeks into the game, each day still felt like her first, nerve-wracking and awkward. She darted around the studio, searching, her panic growing. She spied an opening along the main barre affixed to the wall, paralleling the floor-to-ceiling mirrors, but a petite Asian-American woman wearing cutoff sweats and a frayed red sweater over her leotard frowned when Lana asked if she could squeeze in.

"There's really not enough room," she told Lana.

Of course there was, Lana wanted to argue. The woman could take one step back and make room. But instead of arguing, Lana smiled weakly and backed away.

She saw another space along the other wall, beside the window, but even before she could get up to the barre, a muscled blonde man was shaking his head. "That's Katrina's spot," he told her.

Katrina was a senior principal. Royalty.

Lana swallowed, nodded and turned away. She noticed two dancers bringing another portable barre to the center. She scurried after them and the moment the barre was down, planted her hand firmly on a middle spot.

Two corps de ballet dancers had claimed similar spots on the other side of the barre. They cast glances her way, which she ignored. She couldn't keep getting bumped from spot to spot. But this time no one challenged her. As she warmed up, she studied the dancer across from her out of the corner of her eye. She was pretty, with velvety brown eyes and thick lashes like something out of a Maybelline advertisement. She looked confident and happy, the kind of person you saw and instantly wanted to be, rather than your own inhibited, ever-worrying self. She caught Lana's glance and broadened her smile.

"Settling into San Francisco?" she asked. Her voice was high, sweet-sounding.

"Oh. Yes, thanks." Lana said, clutching onto the barre.

"That's good."

She could think of nothing else to say. The girl turned back to her friend and the two resumed conversation.

Another dancer approached, looking for a spot, and Lana gestured to the place in front of her, taking a step back to make room. The woman was one of the other dancers in *Arpeggio*, the ballet that Lana was scheduled to rehearse for the spring repertory season. She saw Lana, smiled and hurried over. "Thanks," she murmured. "It's crowded today."

"It is," Lana agreed, and some of the tightness inside her eased.

The rehearsals for future programs, beginning to appear on the daily rehearsal sheet, were starting to make Lana feel like she belonged here. Over the last two weeks, most attention had been focused on the two programs the company would perform on their October ten-day West Coast tour. The first program incorporated works from last year's season. Lana, as a newcomer soloist, wouldn't play much part in that program. Only one role, dancing within the corps in Balanchine's *Serenade*, not even soloist work.

Three-quarters of Program II had been cast with nothing yet for Lana. There'd been an afternoon audition session with the choreographer's representative from Paris who would stage *Autumn Souvenir*, but no casting news. It had a demi-soloist trio, though. She knew she was under consideration there; the stager, standing alongside Mr. Gunst, had singled her out to dance a sixteen-count solo passage.

And now there was *Arpeggio*. Five days ago, Lana's name had been posted alongside seven others. As a soloist. Upon seeing this, a wave of dizzying relief had passed over her.

It would all be okay. It was as promised, after all.

The situation had carried with it the hazy, unsubstantial nature of a dream ever since last spring, when she'd received the phone call from Anders Gunst, artistic director of the West Coast Ballet Theatre. She'd been speechless to hear from him, his interest in the audition tape she'd sent as little more than a dare to herself, something to keep her from sinking into despair. He'd invited her out to San Francisco and she'd spent two days in the WCBT studios, which had culminated in a contract offer. Initially, just for the corps de ballet, as she would have expected, but a month later, a call, with news that was even better.

Inconceivably better.

The same could not be said for her new life here in San Francisco. It had been wrenching to leave her native Kansas City, her family. Worse than she'd expected. Mom had been so emotional, creeping in late to huddle on the bed with her that last night. Lana could feel her silently weeping, the sobs shaking her body. But when Lana reached over to comfort her, Mom pushed her hand away roughly, rolled off Lana's bed and left the room without a word. The next morning as Lana and her father were leaving the house for the airport, Mom came out into the front yard, still in her robe.

She looked at Lana, locking her red-rimmed eyes onto Lana's like a laser. "You just remember that you can come home any time," she said, sounding fierce, even angry. "Don't let anyone make you believe there's any sort of shame in that. We're your family and we love you more than anyone else possibly could. Don't you forget that."

Mom's hands gripped Lana's arms so hard she later found bruises there that melted into little blue and yellowing finger points on either arm. Then Mom had dashed inside, leaving Lana to finish the terrible task of saying goodbye to her little brothers, six-year-old twins. Luke, her special one, was sobbing, begging her not to go, and she was the one tearing herself loose, tears making her stumble blindly toward the car as Dad, from the driver's seat, called out for Annabel to stop sulking, get over here and take care of your little brothers.

Annabel, fifteen months Lana's junior, had given Lana a hug goodbye, because they were a family that got along, Mom had snarled to Annabel. Lana had seen the resentment, the coldness in the back of her sister's eyes, however, even as she was saying, "Goodbye, we'll miss you, good luck in your new job, new city. Wish I were the one going." The last bit, at least, had been sincere and heartfelt.

Gone, all of this, and her old ballet company, the only worlds she'd ever known. She felt lonely and alienated beyond words here. At least there was *Arpeggio* now, a thawing from some of the other dancers, like the one in front of her. Rumor had it more casting for Program II was close to being decided and would be posted soon. That would make two ballets, two sets of closer association with other company members, in addition to the corps de ballet role. It would be a good start.

The din in the studio grew louder, sleepy dancers waking up both their minds and bodies. "Who's teaching?" called out a guy with a light Spanish accent, stretched on the floor in the front splits. He pivoted himself effortlessly via side splits into the other side.

"Gunst is at a meeting. Curtis, maybe?" someone answered.

"Oh, God," another guy said as he bent over his leg at the barre. "I'm not ready for Curtis this morning."

But instead it was Ben, Anders' assistant and the youngest of three ballet masters, well-liked, who strode in, called out for the accompanist to give him something smooth and flowing for pliés, but not too slow. Everyone took their places, left hand on barre, and class began. The dancers were layered in sweatpants and tops, leg warmers, layers that came off as bodies warmed up. Beneath, lay the basics: black tights and white tee-shirt for men, a thin-strapped leotard for the women, pink or black tights, or both.

They worked their way through tendu, degagé, rond de jambe, développé and grand battement. Those with mirror access regarded their reflections critically, checking posture, alignment, turnout. Lana relaxed into her efforts. Physical struggle, the tensing of muscles, pushing them, challenging herself, was far and away the easiest part these days of being a ballet professional.

A lyrical adagio followed barre, in the center of the room. A pirouette turn combination. A petit allegro combination of quick, fast jumps to sharpen footwork. Finally the group moved diagonally across the floor in small groups for the grand allegro. Class ended, as all ballet classes did, with a graceful reverence bow to the teacher. Afterward all the dancers clapped, relaxed, and began chattering again.

Gradually the news filtered in: a new rehearsal list was up, finally incorporating casting for the entire Program II. In a matter of seconds, the room had cleared.

Lana joined the others crowded around the bulletin board. Bare, sweaty shoulders bumped as everyone pressed closer to seek out their names on the list. The final choices for Program II produced a different reaction than the other rehearsal sheets had. Lana felt it instantly in the air.

"Oh. My. God," she heard one of the dancers mutter. Jaws agape. Frowns directed her way. Lana peered closer at the list, baffled. Yes, she was on there, in the ballet *Autumn Souvenir,* with Javier, a principal dancer. Javier, the Cuban-born powerhouse she'd read about in *Dance Magazine* over the past five years. There were three names beneath theirs—the demi-soloist trio—and below that, a list of eight corps dancer names. Alongside that, the list repeated itself with new names for the leads. A second cast.

Which meant she was first cast. With the female lead.

Oh, God.

"I don't believe it," one dancer muttered. "A new dancer, not even a principal, and she gets this?"

The pretty dancer with the velvety brown eyes spied Lana nearby and gave her friend a nudge. "Shhh, Charlotte."

Lana ducked her head, pretending to be interested in checking her watch as she edged her way out of the group. Elation battled with a sickening sense of dismay. The dismay won, powered by the indignation she could feel radiating off the other dancers. She made herself go numb inside, a protective measure she'd learned long ago that kept things from hurting too much.

So, there it was, over before it had even happened, the friendships, the welcoming nature. She'd been cast in a plum role in a plum ballet, her first month in her prestigious new job. And for this, she would pay.

The following Sunday was her twenty-second birthday, a day so lonely and devoid of joy she wanted to curl up into a ball and weep. An earlier call home, the phone passed from Mom to Luke, to Dad, to her other siblings, had only served to sharpen her loneliness. Afterward she'd looked around the room, a dank, dimly lit "furnished" studio that was cheap and centrally located but otherwise wholly unredeeming. From her sagging twin bed she'd studied the cheap framed picture adorning a scuffed wall, the nearby kitchen table that listed to one side. A *tap-tap* from the leaking kitchen faucet played counterpoint to the wheezing drone of the ancient refrigerator until the compressor choked and died with a shudder. In the newfound semi-silence she could hear the low rumble of traffic from outside, a few shouted obscenities from the liquor store down below.

It was the most depressing place she'd ever lived in.

She had to get out.

But her ensuing "escape" to Fisherman's Wharf provided little respite from her gloom. Throngs of chattering visitors milled about, streaming in and out of shops while seagulls careened overhead, swooping to pick up popcorn and bread crusts. The briny tang from the bay cut through the aroma of frying hamburgers and fresh seafood on display. She made her way over to the Marina Green, a long expanse of lawn that paralleled the bay. There, she studied the sparkling water, the sailboats that dotted the bay, the Golden Gate Bridge. It was the prettiest day possible, sunny, tiny nubs of clouds scudding across the blue sky, a cool breeze teasing the wisps of hair that had escaped her ponytail. She should have felt so happy. But she didn't. Today it felt physically impossible.

Then she saw the beautiful man from the WCBT.

She'd been so ashamed, that Friday afternoon over three weeks ago, stumbling out of the elevator into him and the woman. It only made it worse that he was so good looking. He'd caught her staring, which had made her blush and feel like the world's biggest hayseed. Not to mention the clumsiest dancer on the premises.

And here he was now. He was wearing shorts and a tee-shirt, and had apparently just completed a jog, slowing his walk down to a stop. He lifted his hands over his head, clasping hands behind, and looked around with a satisfied smile.

She turned around swiftly and began to walk the other way, not noticing the scenery anymore, focusing on making space between the two of them. She wasn't up for further awkwardness, not today. She stopped and faced the bay, faking interest in an approaching ferry, crowded with people milling around on the deck and inside.

A minute later, deciding she was safe, she turned around.

He was right there.

"I recognize you," he called out to her. "From a few weeks back. You were coming out of the elevator at the Ballet Theatre building as I was getting on. You're the new hire."

Surprise rendered her mute. When she found her voice, her reply came out like a squeak. "I am."

He took a step closer and thrust out his hand. "Well, hello, and welcome. I'm Gil Sheridan. I'm the director of development there."

She shook his hand. It was warm, with a firm grip. "I'm Lana Kessler. I'm a dancer."

"Yes, I kind of figured that part. Well, Lana Kessler. It's a pleasure to meet you."

He asked her where she lived, how she was enjoying San Francisco, the usual array of questions, but, unlike the dancers, he seemed genuinely interested in her replies. He was easy to talk to, she realized. Soon she found herself admitting it was her birthday.

He was delighted. "So, what are your big plans today?"

"Oh, I have no plans." She kept her voice light.

"What about your friends?"

"I have no friends."

She'd intended for this to sound equally light, a witty admission of a minor foible, but the reality of the statement swept in and overwhelmed her. She was alone and friendless on her twenty-second birthday. She fixed her gaze on the bobbing boats in the nearby harbor, willing herself not to cry, not in front of this beautiful man.

"Well, I'm sorry," he said, and he did indeed sound grave, contrite. "I'm afraid I'm not going to let you be alone today."

She was so moved, so grateful for his words that she couldn't speak. They stood there in silence, looking at the boats until she felt composed enough to try again. "I don't mind being alone. It's actually a nice change," she said. "I'm from a big family, with most of them still there, in a too-small house."

"How many kids?"

"Six." Seven, actually, if you included Baby John, but only Mom counted that way anymore.

"Is your family Catholic?"

She offered him a wry smile. "How did you guess?"

He grinned. "Mine is, too. I'm the seventh of seven kids."

She couldn't believe it. She stared at him, waiting for him to laugh and tell her he was just kidding. "I didn't think big Catholic families were a California thing," she said.

"What makes you think I'm from California?"

She bit her lip. "I'm sorry. You just seem so…" She moved her hands, trying to encompass in them his glamour, his polished looks. She realized she was making an idiot of herself.

"I'm a Chicago boy, born and bred."

"No! I can't believe this! I'm from the Midwest too. Kansas City."

"Kansas City? Oh, that's great. I love Kansas City. The Country Club Plaza, Westport, Crown Center."

"Yes!" This was just getting better and better.

The commonalities between the two of them continued. He loved barbeque as much as she did. He'd tried both Arthur Bryant's and Gate's Barbeque and could weigh the merits of the two different sauces. They laughed about the logistical impossibility of eating out as a whole family in any restaurant, the burden on their mothers to cook for so many people night after night.

"Mothers, now that's a different subject entirely," Gil said. "Is yours as baffling and difficult to deal with as mine?"

She stopped smiling. "I don't know what you mean."

"You know, just being irrational. Emotional. Judging you by harsh standards."

"No. Not in the least."

Gil looked startled, then unsure. "Oh. Sorry. Then never mind."

She felt obliged to explain at least some of it. "She's had a hard life, my mom. I mean, sure, sometimes she seems irrational, emotional. But it's because she's overworked and overwhelmed. My youngest brothers are six-year-old twins."

"Wow, twins at the tail end."

She nodded. "They're a lot of work. One of them has some development issues, so he needs extra attention and encouragement in order to get things right. That was sort of my job."

"You're a good daughter."

"It's not that. We're a close family, we take care of each other." A lump filled her throat at the thought of them, getting along now without her. "But why do you say that about your own mom?"

"Oh, nothing."

"No, really. I want to know."

He hesitated. "Well, it's just that I'm out of favor with her right now."

"Why?"

His shoulders rose and fell. "Inappropriate lifestyle, inappropriate friends, inappropriate attitude toward the family beliefs. Super conservative. I told her I thought Catholicism was just a load of guilt-ridden, brainwashing hooey, and she went ballistic. And when she heard about some other stuff happening in my life around that time that I was stupid enough to share, she freaked. Told me I was no son of hers. Five years later and she still holds it and my life choices against me. Never mind that I'm the kid who sends money home to help out whenever it's needed."

The story appalled her. Was the mother that irrational or was Gil Sheridan someone to steer clear of? What had he done? Maybe they didn't have that much in common, after all.

"Gil, I'm sorry. That sounds awful."

He blinked at her and began to laugh. "Whoa, where on earth did all that wash up from? Sorry to bore you with my tales of woe."

"You didn't bore me. I care about family-related stuff."

"Yeah, well, that's all in the past. Bye, bye, Chicago and the family; hello, San Francisco. This is home now, where I fit in, and I love it."

She wasn't sure if this last bit made her like him more or less.

His cell phone trilled and he cast her an apologetic glance.

"Oh, please, take the call," she said.

She pretended to study the scenery as he talked.

"What, you mean he's in town? Now? That would be great. No, nothing planned today. It's as if it stayed open just to meet up with him. ... A late lunch? Of course I can make that happen. La Bahia at two-thirty, got it. Bet we can stretch it out into happy hour. Okay, see you soon."

He disconnected and regarded Lana, stricken, as if just reminded of her presence.

So much for her birthday company.

"I'll call him right back," Gil said. "I'm sorry, what was I thinking?"

He began to punch numbers on his phone, but Lana stopped him.

"No. Please. Really, this has been great, but I think I just want to head back to my place for a rest anyway. The crazy past few weeks, and all."

He didn't look convinced. "I don't like going back on my promises."

"It's no big deal."

"Tell you what. Let me show you around one afternoon next weekend, to make up for this."

"Really, that's not necessary."

"It would be my pleasure. My girlfriend spends most weekends in New York. She keeps an apartment there too, so usually it's just me here, entertaining myself."

She hesitated, biting her lower lip again.

"I'm not going to take no for an answer here," he said.

He wasn't. She sensed he was a person used to getting what he wanted. She agreed finally, but refused his invitation to drive her home. When he headed off alone, five minutes later, she watched him, taking in his toned body, the confident stride, the smile on his face, the way people reacted positively to him. She watched until he receded into the distance and traffic swallowed him up.

She stayed right there for a few minutes longer, feeling the last of his presence waft away. The high of meeting such a man battled with the low of having him leave. She would tuck the memory of their conversation into her pocket, to pull out once she was back in her dank, lonely studio. This man, who'd recognized *her,* who was insisting they go out together again.

Question: Did the high produced merit the low that was settling back into her spirits?

She'd have all night to figure that one out.

Chapter 3 – The Prospect

The invitations arrived on Monday morning, three weeks and three days after their meeting with Andy Redgrave. They were encased within a heavy, square, cream envelope, hand-addressed to Alice and Gil. Andrew Redgrave, the invitation read, requested their presence at his Hillsborough home on Saturday evening to join him in a soirée celebrating the recent acquisition of an 1872 Renoir painting and a 1684 Stradivarius cello. Evening entertainment would include catering by La Folie and a brief recital featuring international cellist phenomenon Matthew Nakamura.

Gil was sitting in a chair across from Alice, studying his own invitation.

"This is big," he said in a reverent tone. "This is really big."

"A serious lead, just like you promised. I wouldn't have thought it possible."

He wagged a finger at her. "That'll teach you to mistrust my skills."

They studied their invitations for another long moment. "This will open the door there in a major way," Gil said. "Do you know how much we could ask from the Redgrave Foundation?"

She hardly dared say it out loud. "Fifty thousand? A hundred?"

"Double that. Hell, I'm going to say 250K."

More than the amount they'd lost from the Prescott Foundation.

It would save them.

"And I'll tell you what, Alice," Gil continued. "We'll get it. Go ahead and start up on that proposal right now, for $250,000. I'm going to work him. I'm going to carefully, meticulously reel Mr. Andy Redgrave in, and he'll never know what snared him."

Grinning, he stretched himself out luxuriously in his chair, looking beautiful and carefree and carnal, like a centerfold model, a mental image she'd never been able to fully erase since his admission that he'd once posed nude for a porn magazine. The easiest 10K he'd ever made, he'd boasted, although he declined to elaborate, saying it had been a long time ago, another Gil. She sensed he harbored a rather colorful past. But she agreed with him that the past held little bearing on the present. Look at her life, after all. Devoting every waking moment to a craft she revered beyond all else, for two decades, until a chance slip destroyed that career in one night.

He sat up suddenly. "Hey," he began, but hesitated.

"Yes?"

"Change of subject. Remember that dancer we bumped into, as we were getting onto the elevator, the afternoon we met Andy?"

I knew it! a voice inside her screamed. *I knew she'd be trouble.*

"Yes." She kept her voice calm. "What about her?"

"Well, I ran into her yesterday. On the Marina Green."

She waited for more, but he only ducked his head and chuckled to himself.

"You ran into her," she said. "Goodness. That sounds painful. Did you apologize?"

"Oh, stop it. You know what I mean."

"Fine, boss. You met the new dancer. And this clearly was

followed by something auspicious, otherwise you wouldn't be here now, stumbling over words."

"All right. So I met her, we spent some time talking, she's just the sweetest, cutest thing you could imagine. And now, well, I need your help."

"Help, how?" She had an uneasy feeling that whatever it was, she didn't want to participate.

He looked down at his invitation as if it were a cue card that might provide the words eluding him. "Well, I'd like you to go down there. Check her out in company class."

"Why?" she protested.

"I want to know what she's like. How she dances, and such."

"Why me?!"

"Because there's no one here in this office who fits in as seamlessly downstairs as you do."

"Gil, that was eight years ago. I don't do that anymore. I haven't been down there in so long, it would make me uncomfortable." She'd maintained contact only with Ben, now Anders' assistant, partly because injuries had forced him, too, to switch from performing to administration. He understood how it was. They saw each other and chatted at WCBT functions. That was as far as connection to the "down there" world went. She aimed to keep it that way.

"C'mon, Alice, be a sport."

"The answer is, forget it."

"Seriously."

"No."

"You know, maybe this isn't just a 'fetch me a coffee while you're in the café' kind of request." A note of steeliness had crept into his voice.

Alice stared. "Are you're trying to tell me this is something that, as my boss, you're commanding me to do?"

An unfamiliar awkwardness filled the room. The two of them warily regarded each other but then, as if on cue, they both shrugged and laughed.

"Of course it's not a command," Gil said. "It's a favor. What, you think I'd fire you if you said no?"

"Well, I just didn't know, that's all." She kept her tone light, friendly, the way you were supposed to address a strange, snarling dog. "So. It means that much to you?"

"It does."

A knot of tension worked its way up between her shoulder blades. She looked at his hopeful face and sighed. "Fine. I'll do it. Ten minutes, though, and that's it."

"That would be great. I really appreciate it."

"You'd better," she grumbled.

Lana was the girl's name. She was good. Alice saw that immediately, watching through the studio's large picture window as the company members worked their way through an adagio. She had perfect turnout, a lovely upper-body port de bras, good pirouette preparation with her passé leg shooting up high and clean, right to the knee as she began turning. A double—no, wait, a triple—which she ended cleanly without hopping out of it. There was a naturalness to her, an innate musicality and attention to detail, the way she finished each movement down to the tips of her toes, her fingers, the proper angle of her head.

Anders Gunst, artistic director, was teaching that day, and she assessed him as well. In the thirteen years since he'd hired her, the year of his arrival, he'd changed very little. Medium height, still the toned physique of an Olympic-level athlete, dressed casually in dark jeans and a pullover shirt, but nothing casual about his energy, his authority. He'd been a force of nature since the day he walked through the WCBT's doors, and had remained so. He was now having Lana demonstrate the pirouette combination, poor girl. Likely it was intended to shake up the others, push them from their comfort zones, make them reconsider long-held notions of épaulement and placement, because there was indeed something in the way the new girl moved. Fresh, unaffected, but hungry as well. Usually it was what you saw in the Vaganova-trained dancers, those elite, envied little Russian girls absorbed into the craft at age ten and given a merciless training. The loneliness and discipline and absolute lack of coddling combined with sublime natural talent produced a perfect artistry with a razor edge.

Apparently this Lana girl had trained and danced professionally in Kansas City alone. What on earth had she been doing there, hidden away for so long? She should have been shopped out to the coasts years earlier, in her training years. The WCBT would have snapped her up at any time. Alice knew what Anders loved: strong technique and artistry, complexity and a commanding presence, but purity as well, which this Lana had.

Following petit allegro jumps in the center, the group took a thirty-two-count combination across the floor. Alice recognized some of the senior members and noted that both Katrina and Delores from her own days were there. They, like Alice, were in their mid-thirties, and they looked it, all sinew and bones and haggard morning faces. Ballet did not wear well on the female body, particularly for lifelong corps members like Delores, whose body took on double the workload of the principals with a fraction of the glory. The younger girls appeared dewy and fresh in comparison, and none more so than the new girl.

Lana was in the penultimate trio of dancers to go across the floor. She took off with a sauté arabesque and proceeded to dance without reserve, as if her career depended on this very combination, this moment. It was mesmerizing to watch her, so lyrical and clean, yet so powerful. At the end of the combination, however, another dancer stepped the wrong way and crashed into Lana, shattering her concentration. It was surely an accident, but Alice saw a few of the watching females exchange catty grins.

A bolt of recognition shot through her as one of the smirking dancers turned her head and spotted Alice. It was the pretty dark-haired girl who'd been gossiping in the administrative level restroom. For an instant their eyes locked. Alice saw uncertainty come over the girl, once again caught in the act of mocking the new soloist. Then coolness flooded her features. She straightened, raised her brows in a lofty manner and turned her back on Alice.

The message came across loud and clear.

You are a nobody here, on my turf. Only dancers, talented ones, belong here.

The barb hit its mark far better than the girl could have imagined. Alice's hands balled into fists. What the hell *was* she doing there? Satisfying some whim of Gil's only to be mocked as some stuffed-shirt administrator, a moose among gazelles?

She wished, not for the first time, she were anywhere but there. An instant later, she decided she was done being there. She turned and left, taking long impatient strides down the hall. She'd make her report to Gil and tell him to leave her the hell out of this loop. She had real work to do.

On her way home from work that evening, she stopped at her favorite mostly-outside-her-budget wine store to buy a premium bottle of wine. Tonight she wanted to celebrate: five months since she and Niles had begun dating. Things were going so well with him, it frightened her. She told herself she'd play it cool around him, not draw attention to the five-month business so much as celebrate the fact that one year ago this week the two of them had met, introduced by their friends, Montserrat and Carter. Theirs had been a cozy, friendly foursome that met regularly for dinners, lively affairs abounding with good food, wine and conversation, which they all enjoyed. Between her and Niles had been simply the warmth of a growing friendship. No sparks, no problem. She'd always succeeded best with friendships like these; serious relationships for her were tricky, messy and ultimately short-lived. And yet, in the end, getting romantically involved with Niles had become one of the best things to happen to her, right there alongside Gil plucking her out of administrative obscurity three years earlier to make her his associate.

Even as friends, she'd loved the way Niles would ponder her thoughtfully, his brown hair, pulled back into a ponytail, lending a rebel air to his otherwise serious, businessman's demeanor. Very Silicon Valley. His blue-grey eyes, fringed by a smudge of thick lashes, would study her for a long moment before replying. He did this now, as a form of seduction, and it never failed to make the back of her knees grow weak.

She couldn't get enough of him. Miraculously, he seemed to feel the same, reaching for her the minute they were together behind closed doors. The last time he'd come over to her place, they hadn't even made it to the bedroom. They'd clung to each other in the entryway, clothing items falling by the wayside until they were naked, supine on the carpeted stairs, limbs intertwined, straining against one another while Odette, her cat, circled warily before coming to rest on a stray article of clothing.

A delicious shiver passed through her. She couldn't wait to see him tonight. He was coming up for the evening even though his work pressures were heating up, with an important project checkpoint approaching. She told him fine, they'd get right down to business in that case. She visualized greeting him, slipping her hands under his shirt to feel the hot silkiness of his skin, pressing herself along the length of him, her mouth working a trail up his neck.

"Well, hello, Alice Willoughby, whose great-great-grandfather was a Whittier."

Shaken from her erotic reverie, she looked up to see a pair of pale blue eyes fixed on hers. Andy Redgrave. She couldn't believe it.

"Hello," she stuttered. "What a surprise to see you again so soon."

"Quite the surprise," he agreed.

She reached up to nervously tuck an errant chestnut strand of hair behind her ear. "Gil and I received the invitations to your party this morning."

"Good. I was going to ask about that."

"We're both looking forward to it."

"Oh, I imagine your boss is. Another lead for the books."

This was a man who cut through the bullshit.

"I don't know what you mean," she tried.

He smiled, which was a good sign. "I sense it wasn't the grand coincidence you and he played it out to be, that afternoon at the Ritz. My guess is you two didn't approach me to settle your bet. But that's all right, because your credentials passed my test."

She wondered if "your" meant hers, or hers and Gil's. A moment later he clarified.

"I must say, if you'd been lying about the great-great-grandfather business you wouldn't have gotten the invitations."

Stellar prospect or not, she had her pride. She drew herself taller. "And why would I have been lying to you about such a thing?" she asked in a cooler voice.

"Oh, you'd be surprised at what people will try in order to get and keep my attention."

"With all due respect, sir, it's hard to get anything but a generic 'no thanks' response through your foundation's existing channel of submitting proposals. Gil felt more creative measures needed to be taken."

"Gil's a live wire," Andy said.

"He is. He's also very committed to his work and the accounts he brings in."

"Well. I imagine he'll enjoy Saturday's gathering."

"I will too. You've really got Matthew Nakamura performing?"

"I do indeed."

"I'm looking forward to that. I've met him; he's a friend of a friend. In fact, I was wondering if she might be performing with him that night."

"Who is your friend?"

"Montserrat Benes-Fortray. Violinist. She performs in a trio with Matthew from time to time."

He looked impressed. "Well, you have some talented friends. Yes, she and Jukka Laksonen are accompanying Matthew in his program."

She was thrilled. "Really? Oh, that's wonderful. Now I'm sure to enjoy myself."

"Because otherwise it would have been insufferably dull."

Her face grew hot. "I'm sorry, that came out wrong. It's just that I'm a classical music buff, so seeing Matthew and Montserrat perform is a big deal."

"I understand. I'm a classical music person myself."

Which made sense, given his $1.2 million grant to the San Francisco Symphony.

"Do you attend the symphony?" he asked.

"Oh, yes, season subscriber. I can't get enough of it."

"What about the ballet?"

"Oh, that." She gave a wave of her hand. "I much prefer the symphony."

His pale eyes assessed her. "You're trying to persuade me to channel some of my foundation's funds into an organization you work for but don't yourself support?"

She felt the faint stirrings of fear. He was a tricky, unreadable man. Even now she couldn't tell whether he was joking, or whether there was something menacing behind those eyes.

Before she could churn out the appropriate groveling reply, the store manager hurried out from the back office. "Mr. Redgrave, hello! Please forgive me, I was on the phone."

"It's no problem," Andy said.

"I found the wines you were looking for. Shall we go to my office?"

He nodded and turned to Alice. "Looking forward to seeing you on Saturday."

She gulped. "Mr. Redgrave?" she said in a low voice.

"Please." A small frown crossed his face. "Andy."

"Andy. Please forgive me for what I just said. It came out all wrong. I hope you don't judge Gil and the West Coast Ballet Theatre harshly for my lack of tact."

He shook his head. "Don't think anything of it."

Right.

The manager was waiting for Andy, smiling at Alice in a puzzled fashion. "I'll see you Saturday," Andy repeated.

"Great. I look forward to it." Alice put on her bright, professional smile and nodded.

After he'd left, she stared unseeingly at the array of Cabernet

Sauvignon bottles in front of her. Gil would kill her if she'd done anything to jeopardize his new lead. What had she been thinking, in speaking to a billionaire prospect so candidly?

The chime of her phone interrupted her churning thoughts. She glanced at the number and immediately felt better.

"Hello, you," she said into the phone. "You've arrived?"

"I have," Niles said. "Your couch feels very good. Where are you?"

She visualized him stretched on her couch, his long body relaxing, probably for the first time that day. "I'm just at the wine store, picking up a bottle," she said.

"It must be heavy. Your voice sounds strained."

She chuckled and squeezed her eyes shut. "Oh God, it's been a strange day, just one thing after the other. I'm ready for it to end."

"Well. The good news is it has." His voice had a pleasing timbre, still a hint of the London accent he'd never lost in his twenty years in the U.S. "So get yourself right home."

Relief and a silken sense of peace flowed through her. This was her reality, this friend-turned-lover waiting for her at her home, the place she loved the most. This was what mattered in her life. Not Andy Redgrave, not the new dancer who had Gil so dazzled.

"I'll be right home to you," she said, relishing the way "home" and "you" sounded together. "As fast as I can."

Chapter 4 – Gil

The homesickness hit the hardest in the afternoon. The fact that she had it at all, at twenty-two, was absurd. Homesickness was a given in most dancers' training, leaving home from age fourteen, sixteen, to pursue the best training possible. The people you danced with, worked alongside daily, became your family, your tribe. Here, Lana was the anomaly; her training had always been local and she'd remained living at home, with family. She was the only professional ballet dancer she knew who'd had such a cloistered upbringing. One who actively participated in her family life, to boot. She was miserably aware of the barrier it seemed to put up between her and her peers, but Mom had always needed the help, and Lana's siblings were not the type to offer it. There'd never been a question about which came first, her career or her family. That was how the Kessler family worked.

Further struggle that felt equally absurd: she was having trouble keeping busy all day long. It was not a problem she'd ever experienced, or imagined, in her entire life. There'd only been the initial *Autumn Souvenir* rehearsal because the stager in charge of their production, who'd teach them all the ballet steps and nuances, was still finishing up staging work in Seattle. He'd be in Seattle all week, but he'd scheduled a rehearsal for the following

Sunday. In the meantime, her weekday rehearsal schedule was all the more sparse, only two assigned roles among three programs. She had every late afternoon free, a bitter irony, given that was the time slot, back home, she'd fought to have, usually unsuccessfully, in order to help Mom. Witching hour. Brutal for moms, she'd been told. So whenever possible, she'd squeezed in time with the twins, sending Mom off to rest while she sat reading to the boys, their small bodies pressed on either side of her, their wriggling for once stopped. In truth, she'd relished this quiet time, the comforting warmth of their bodies, the sweet puppy smell of their silky hair. Mom would reappear ninety minutes later and start dinner amid the clank of pans, the ensuing sizzle of onions and aroma of browning meat filling the air. Scott, still in high school, would burst in, shouting that he was starved, when was dinner, followed by Annabel, who would wander into the kitchen to either gossip or bicker with Mom, depending on their respective moods. Lana would slip out shortly thereafter, off to the theater, or to seek out some quiet time of her own.

Which she now had, every single day. To go from that overcrowded life and years as an in-demand dancer, to this. Who would have thought being a soloist in a bigger company would be so agonizingly lonely?

The ballet school's late afternoon advanced class was open to any WCBT member looking for yet another workout for the day. Ideal for dancers recovering from injuries, it also helped out new soloists who weren't cast in enough ballets to fill their days with rehearsals until six o'clock and were frantic to keep dancing rather than return to a lonely, too-quiet evening in an ugly, uninviting place.

Tonight, to her surprise, she saw two other dancers in the class, as well. She commented on this to the friendlier one, Sergei, after class.

"This is because it is pizza insanity night," Sergei told her, by way of explanation.

She angled her head at Sergei, wondering if she'd misunderstood him. He was Russian, but spoke very good English. Usually.

"Pizza insanity?" she repeated.

Sergei nodded. "It is quite a tradition, actually. A group of us go to Giovanni's and eat pizza. We do this insanity to celebrate trying to get back into shape after July's laziness." He laughed at Lana's expression. "Yes, I know. It sounds strange. But it is a tradition. Anders will even—how do you say this?—foot the bill."

He regarded her in affected surprise. "What, you did not hear of this? I thought everyone knew."

She swallowed her hurt. "Maybe it's because there's not a lot of new people here this year, that it didn't need to get advertised. Besides the apprentices, there's just those two corps dancers and me."

"Well, of course you are invited. You really must go."

It was either pizza insanity or the grey, depressing silence of her studio apartment. Even so, she hesitated. Sergei smiled and patted her arm.

"Yes, come on. We will go together."

When she stepped into the back room of Giovanni's pizzeria and saw all the others, three-quarters of the company, there was a palpable pause. Faces froze in surprise, even dismay, at the sight of her. Lana wanted to turn and run out of there, back to her crummy little apartment. But she was there, Sergei was behind her, bumping her forward, and everyone remembered their manners, telling Lana hi, glad you could make it, finding open spots for her and Sergei at the table.

To her relief, the servers appeared a minute later with the pizzas, a half-dozen of them, and laid them in the center of the three tables pushed together. Lana's presence was forgotten as the male dancers tore into the pizzas, grabbing piping hot slices and biting into them before they could hit the plate. The melted cheese stretched, beckoned seductively. The females reacted differently, some regarding the pizza with unease, distrust. They seemed to relax when the servers returned with three enormous bowls of salad.

Lana was one of the fortunate ones: naturally slim, with a high metabolism. She was careful, however, to follow the other women and take just one slice of pizza, loading the rest of her plate with salad. She didn't need this issue, as well, to set her apart.

It was entertaining to watch the others. One of the younger girls, a petite Russian, took little mouse bites of her slice. She shut her eyes as she chewed, ever so slowly, a dreamy smile playing on her lips. Opening her eyes, she issued a little sigh, as if in sorrow that she was one bite closer to being done. Next to her, an older dancer, fuller-figured than the rest, had loaded her plate with so much salad there was no room for a pizza slice. She squeezed the juice out of a lemon wedge onto the salad and commenced eating with a virtuous smile. Three bites and the smile faded. She doggedly plowed through her salad as she watched the men wolf down their second and third slices. Finally she set her fork down. "This is bullshit," she muttered to herself. "Utter bullshit." Finally she leaned over and grabbed her own slice of pizza. Plopping back down on her chair, she hesitated before taking a defiant bite. She nodded, as to herself, and took a second bite, her shoulders relaxing.

Courtney, the pretty dark-haired dancer Lana had admired in

company class, had peeled back her cheese and laid it on the side of her plate before taking a bite of the denuded pizza. "Trade you," said her friend, sitting across from her, "I'm doing protein and not carbs this month."

Boyd, a corps dancer with golden, surfer-dude good looks, watched their exchange of cheese and crust with exaggerated amusement.

"You ladies," he said. "All of you. You're gorgeous. You look great just the way you are. And you know you'll burn everything off, now that we're working all day again."

The protein-eater, a girl named Charlotte, shook her head. "I'm not easing up until I get back to pre-layoff weight."

"What, you didn't work out all July?"

"I was trying to give my left hamstring extra healing time. And it was family this, family that, all month long. Two weddings and an anniversary party. All these big sit-down meals and relatives pushing me to eat, eat. Casseroles. Mashed potatoes and gravy. God. It's no wonder America has an obesity problem."

"You'll be fine in no time," Boyd said. "Especially with classes like today's."

The comment elicited groans and rolled eyes.

"God, Anders was brutal," the salad-eater said.

"I thought I was going to die after that sixty-four-count jump combination," Courtney said. "And did you notice the way he smiled through it all? Positively evil."

Boyd nodded, grimaced. "What a bastard he can be."

The others continued discussing the class, but Boyd had turned to Courtney. "Did I see you afterward, in the café with Gil?" he asked.

"You did." She smiled. "He owed me a Diet Coke."

Gil.

They were talking about Gil. She strained to listen in.

"We had this little bet going," Courtney was saying to Boyd. "I won, he was paying up."

"You had a big grin on your face. Was he making a pass at you?"

"No way," someone cut in, and now everyone was listening, as if the mention of Gil's name had the same charmed effect on everyone. "Gil's not a flirter with the talent, not in that way."

"God," one of the guys breathed, "what I'd give for an hour alone with Gil. I could teach him a thing or two about flirting with the talent."

"Oh, trust me," Courtney said, "Gil flirts. But he and I are just friends."

To Lana's shock, Boyd turned to her next. "And how about Gil and *you*, Lana?" He seemed pleased by her panicked reaction. "Min-jun says he saw you two on Monday night, having dinner together at Primavera's. What are the chances of that?"

His innocent smile didn't seem all that innocent.

Everyone had grown silent, waiting for Lana's reply. She paused to fortify her response with a gulp of Diet Coke, which went down too fast and made her cough. "It was nothing," she said once she'd regained her breath. "He saw me leaving on Monday evening and offered me a ride to my place."

"I thought I heard you say you lived nearby," Charlotte said.

"I do, and that's what I told him, but it was the end of a long day."

"And he has a nice car," someone else commented slyly.

He did, a sleek, red Audi TT Roadster. When she'd slipped into the seat and shut the door behind her, encapsulating her in Gil's more luxurious world, it had felt like a dream.

"So he offered to drive you home and took you to dinner

instead?" Boyd asked.

"It was his idea, I was just keeping him company," she stammered. "He was killing time before going to pick up his girlfriend from the airport."

"Ah, Julia. The famous Julia." Boyd raised his beer cup as if in a toast.

"She's gorgeous," Courtney said. "Have you seen her?"

Lana gave a reluctant nod. She'd seen both Gil and Julia on Wednesday evening; they'd all been leaving the building around the same time. Julia was a thin, coldly beautiful woman in silk trousers and an expensive-looking blouse, her shimmering gold hair in a cut that set off her cheekbones, her wide blue eyes. She had a commanding presence and an authoritative voice as she declared that she'd been simply *pining* for a good cioppino. Lana had stood there, dance bag now heavy on her shoulder, and watched them sail out the double doors, never once looking her way. Julia looked older than Gil, she'd decided uncharitably. Much older.

"But Gil and I are just friends," Lana said to the others, realizing too late that she was parroting Courtney's comment.

"Oh, that Gil," Boyd said. "He so gets around. Makes a new friend every day." The innuendo hidden within his words made everyone laugh. Lana forced herself to join in.

Saturday was Lana's afternoon with Gil, which he still insisted on doing even though he'd paid off his rain-check obligation with Monday's dinner. He drove them over the Bay Bridge and up into the Oakland Hills, to a regional park with glorious views of the San Francisco skyline, the bay, sparkling in the sunlight, and around them, the rolling, golden hills of the East Bay. They strolled along the redwood-studded trails, talking about everything and nothing, inhaling the pine-baked smell of the warm air, the shimmering dried grasses around them issuing a soft *ssshhhh*. It felt like paradise.

Time passed too quickly. The sun was beginning its descent as they returned to the car. Gil told Lana about his plans for the evening: a party, but business related. Some suit with deep pockets named Andy Redgrave he was trying to woo. She, of course, had no plans for the night, just the confines of her lonely prison cell of a studio.

Correction. She had a phone date. With her mother.

She'd called Mom the previous night, pouring out her loneliness, which Mom alone seemed to want to hear about. When she confessed her dread of another lonely, solitary Saturday night, Mom had grown animated.

"Tell you what. I'll be your date. I'll call you, once the boys are off to bed and your dad's watching TV. How does that sound?"

A phone date with her mother sounded almost as lonely and pathetic as sitting alone in her studio, but Mom seemed pleased by the idea. Her voice quivered with purpose as she decided aloud that she'd pour herself a glass of wine and commandeer the bedroom, so Lana could have her undivided attention.

Lana had learned to reward these infrequent bursts of motivation and euphoria on Mom's part with complete agreement and enthusiasm. She could almost see her mother right then, her thin body straightened out of its customary fatigue-induced slouch, her tired eyes brightening at the prospect of this change of routine and the chance to play hero to her homesick daughter at the same time.

Lana forced excitement into her voice as she agreed yes, that would be the perfect solution, and yes, seven-thirty her time would be great. She'd be home. No plans whatsoever.

Gil noticed her gloom now as they drove back toward San Francisco.

"You're awfully quiet. What's up?"

It took a moment for her to sum it up in a non-self-pitying manner. "I guess I haven't fully adjusted to life out here yet."

"You miss Kansas City." It was a statement, not a question.

Lana gave a small nod in reply and silence once again filled the car. There was nothing more to be said, after all. Kansas City was no longer her home.

A moment later Gil sat up straighter. "I just thought of something. We have enough time to squeeze it in. You want a taste of Kansas City and I'm going to get it for you." He swung over three lanes and took the next highway exit for downtown Oakland.

"What is it?" she kept asking, but he only laughed, shook his head and said it was a surprise.

Once on city streets, however, his destination proved elusive. Gil, his voice growing terse, said he'd find it. After several more turns and city blocks, he did. He stopped the car on what appeared to be a residential corner and pointed.

Lana looked around. "What am I supposed to be seeing?"

"That little shop there, across the street."

"That's a shop? What do they sell?"

"Barbeque. Barbeque that could pass for Kansas City barbeque."

It was indeed a storefront, she saw now, next to a liquor store and what appeared to be a closed-up nail salon. The shop was small, with a line of people snaking out of it and along the sidewalk, waiting to buy ribs, the only thing they sold.

They left the car and joined the line. When it was their turn, Gil ordered a half-slab of ribs from the cook-cashier-owner, whose dark-skinned face was sweaty and irritable-looking. He took their money without a word and a moment later thrust a newspaper-wrapped parcel at them. Gil took the parcel and steered her out of the shop, back toward the car. Inside the car he displayed their booty: smoked ribs atop the requisite slice of white sandwich bread, two tiny cups of spicy-sweet barbeque sauce alongside it all.

"I tried to ask for extra barbeque sauce once," Gil said. "I thought he was going to pull out a shotgun."

Lana chuckled and accepted the rib Gil had pulled off for her. It tasted incredible, every bit as good as Kansas City barbeque. The meat was smoked tender, the pork salty and tangy on the outside.

"Thank you," Lana said after they'd wolfed down all the ribs, mopping up the last of the sauce with the white bread. "This was the greatest. A real taste of home."

"I'm glad you enjoyed it."

"You're amazing. You can make anything happen, can't you?"

"I can. And don't you forget it." He gave her a playful nudge.

They licked their fingers to get the last bits of flavor and Lana noticed aloud that Gil had barbeque sauce on his face. He tried to take it off with the tip of his tongue.

"Did I get it?"

She chuckled and shook her head.

"How about now?"

"Missed again."

"Fine." He positioned his face toward her. "You wipe it off."

She reached out and wiped it off his smooth face with her finger.

"Give me that sauce," Gil said, catching her hand and popping her finger into his mouth. Her fingertip was enveloped by the hot, moist environment, the soft tugging action as he sucked. For a moment she was paralyzed—in shock, in pleasure, at the frank eroticism of the gesture. She snatched her hand away. Gil seemed unfazed as he smacked his lips, smiled, looked down at his watch.

"Okay, time to hit the road."

But the road did not cooperate; Gil couldn't find the highway. They were in a dodgy neighborhood, Lana could tell. What alarmed her was not what she saw, so much as what she didn't see. No cats or dogs, no people on their porch or strolling down the sidewalks, and then she realized there were no sidewalks at all. No lawns. Just houses, plain clapboard structures with iron grates over the small front windows. Patches of dirt where grass should have been. A beat-up Pontiac parked on the street, glass missing from the windows. A car further down missing its wheels.

The tension inside the car increased, particularly when Gil rounded a corner and a moment later a trio of young men appeared, just as Gil shifted gears wrong and his Roadster choked and died. The trio approached as Gil tried too hastily to start the car back up. One man was white, comically underdeveloped, like a kid playing dress-up. Another looked like a little bit of everything: Asian, Hispanic, African-American. The third was a muscular African-American in a red stocking cap. They were all wearing oversized jackets and baggy pants. The underdeveloped one was carrying a thick metal pipe.

Lana heard a *click* as Gil locked the doors. He managed to start the Audi back up. By now, however, it was impossible to ignore, or even drive around the approaching group. Two of them stood in front of the car while the third one rapped on Gil's window. Reluctantly, Gil lowered the window a crack.

"Some trouble there?" the guy in the stocking cap drawled.

As Gil stuttered a reply, the guy took in the car's interior. His eyes settled on Lana. "That your girlfriend?" he asked Gil.

She could feel Gil's fear. Her own heart was hammering. But Gil offered him a relaxed smile.

"No, she's a friend. She's new to the area, from Kansas City. I'm showing her around."

"Kansas City?" Stocking Cap peered closer at Lana, who nodded. His dark, broad face broke into a smile, exposing a gold tooth. "My cousin. He's living there."

"Really? What a coincidence." Lana's voice cracked. "Do you know where?"

"Somewhere's near downtown."

"I know that area. That's close to where I worked."

"She's a ballet dancer," Gil added. "A really good one."

"You're a ballerina?" Stocking Cap studied her with new respect. "You serious?"

Lana nodded. "I was with the Kansas City Ballet. And here, I'm with the West Coast Ballet Theatre."

"It's a dance company in San Francisco," Gil added, and the guy frowned at him.

"I know that. What, you think I'm stupid or something?"

"No, of course not. Sorry."

Stocking Cap ignored Gil, but smiled more warmly at Lana. "A ballerina. Isn't that something?" His friends, now behind him, began to mumble and he turned toward them and said that this here was a ballerina and she knew where his cousin lived.

He swung back toward Lana. "You wear those little skirts? Those pointy shoes?"

"All that stuff," Lana assured him.

He beamed. It was surreal.

"And you know what?" she said. "I'm really late for returning to the studios now, and we're not sure about how to get back on the highway. Could you maybe help us?"

"Sure. Your man here just needs to take a right turn at the next intersection. Go three blocks. Take a left. It's not marked for the highway but just take it and a block later, there's the entrance, on your right."

He ignored Gil's babbled thanks, but smiled at Lana. "You take care, miss," he told her.

"Thanks. And thanks so much for your help."

His gold tooth gleamed as he grinned and nodded. He stepped away from the car, motioning for his friends to move as well. Gil put the car into gear and quickly drove off, leaving the trio behind. He said nothing as they followed the directions to the highway. Only when they were on the entrance ramp and heading toward the Bay Bridge did Gil exhale, a deep, shuddering noise.

"Jesus," he said, and fell silent. He clutched the steering wheel, his knuckles white. "That was so irresponsible of me. I'm so sorry."

"I'm fine. It's all okay."

"No, it isn't."

She could tell by the set of his jaw just how upset he was.

"Gil," she tried again. "I'm fine."

It wasn't until she laid a hand on his thigh, however, that he looked at her. "I'm okay," she said more softly.

He tried to smile. "Thank you. You're the greatest. Julia, boy, she'd be all over me right now, just freaking out."

"I'm no Julia."

"No. You're not." He reached down and covered her hand with his. One tight squeeze, held an extra few seconds, then he released it, focusing on the road. She brought her hand back to her lap, feeling it throb with the residual heat of his skin.

They said no more until they'd crossed the bay. Gil glanced at the clock on the console and took the exit for Fisherman's Wharf. "Damn. I'm playing it close. Is it okay if we stop at my place first, before I drop you off? I can change in a matter of minutes."

"You can drop me off anywhere and I'll take a bus."

He shook his head. "Not an option. This is door-to-door service. Besides, you'll love the view from my apartment. You've got to see it."

"All right. If it's not a hassle."

His apartment building was a pristine white structure that looked all the more expensive in its efforts to not look fancy. They entered the marble foyer, took an elevator to the third level and entered another richly appointed foyer. When he ushered her into his apartment, she saw the scene, a floor-to-ceiling window view of the San Francisco Bay and the Golden Gate Bridge. A cry of delight escaped her. Gil smiled at her reaction.

"What did I tell you? Now, if you'll excuse me, I'll go change and we'll be out of here in five minutes."

She stood there, mesmerized, until she heard him call out for her. She followed the sound of his voice into the bathroom. It was a beautiful, elegant bathroom, all marble and chrome and soft lighting. He was leaning over, peering into the mirror, shirtless. He turned to her, pointing to his chest.

"How on earth did I get barbeque sauce *here?*"

She came over and saw it on his collarbone, right in the vee where his shirt had opened to expose skin. "Can't go wasting that sauce," she said, in a mock-gruff voice. Hardly believing her own daring, she leaned in, resting her hands on his bare chest for balance, and licked the tiny sweet-spicy spot. Retaliation for the finger-sucking business. Or perhaps reward.

It was his turn to be paralyzed. She felt his hands drop to her hips as a low groan escaped him. She pulled back to meet his eyes; his hands on her hips tightened, and that was it. His mouth clamped down onto hers as her arms snaked around his neck. He hoisted her up onto the bathroom counter. There was a percussive clatter of a decorative tissue box tumbling and a water glass toppling, which they both ignored. Instead she tucked her legs around his, drawing him closer as they kissed. She found herself making little noises in the back of her throat, both shocked by her aggression and hungry, so hungry, for this contact. Starved.

Seconds passed. Minutes. Finally Gil gave another groan, a reluctant one this time, and pulled away from her.

She found her voice. "You need to leave."

"I do."

"I'm taking a bus from here."

"No, you're not." He stepped away and whisked a clean shirt out of his closet. "I'm driving you. In fact," he said, looking back over at her, where she was still seated on the counter, "I don't think I'm going to let you leave me at all."

She hesitated. "What is that supposed to mean?"

"Come with me. To the party."

The lurch of joy his words brought almost knocked her over. "Oh, I can't. This is business for you, you said."

"So what? It's being there that is such a big deal." He buttoned his shirt in silence and gave a decisive nod. "I got it. Alice will be with us. I'll take the four-seater and we'll arrive as a threesome. Anyone asks, you're Alice's friend. Okay?"

"Alice?"

"My associate. The woman I was with, that day we bumped into you at the elevator."

An image of an attractive, impatient woman with Julia-like elegance flashed through her mind. "But...won't she mind?"

"She's my employee. She'll do what I say."

She hesitated, uneasy. But now Gil was approaching, drawing her off the counter and into his arms.

"Please say yes," he murmured. "This was too short. And this way we'll be together afterward. Just in case I can persuade you to come back here with me."

It was a proposition she couldn't resist.

"You're sure it won't be a problem?"

"I'm sure," he said.

"Okay, it's a deal."

Chapter 5 – The Party

It wasn't until Alice looked up from the front steps she was descending that she noticed Gil was not alone in his car. She hesitated, squinted. The passenger front door of his BMW flew open and out stepped the girl. The little dancer. Alice couldn't fucking believe it. She'd thought she'd known Gil's parameters on what he considered appropriate.

Apparently not.

The girl looked nervous, hand still clutching the door. Alice made her way down the last few steps, trying to decide what to scream at Gil first.

"Alice, this is Lana," Gil called out through the open door. "We're all going together."

Alice drew a steadying breath. Manners won over and she offered the girl a polite nod and a handshake. "Nice to meet you."

"Likewise," Lana said, giving a self-conscious tug to the hem of her dress as she edged away from Alice. "I'm just going to go sit in back."

Alice sized up the girl's dress. It was ill-fitting, all pink and flowery. It made Lana look fifteen years old and very Midwestern. Alice turned to Gil, who was smiling at her from the driver's seat with an *I know what I'm doing and let's not forget who the boss is* set to his jaw.

"Gil," she said, "she can't wear that dress over to Andy's."

Lana froze. Gil's confident expression faded. He eyed Lana and a moment later nodded in reluctance.

"Can she wear something of yours?" he asked Alice, who began to laugh.

"I weigh just maybe a little more than she does. Like thirty-five pounds. The baggy look isn't going to cut it."

Lana, still standing on the driveway, looked afraid to get into the car. Alice could see that the issue embarrassed her. Too bad. She peered down at Lana's shoes. Hopeless as well.

"What size shoe do you wear?" she asked.

"Um, seven?"

They were in luck in that department, at least. She sighed. "I'll be right back," she told them.

Back inside her house, in her bedroom closet, she grabbed the box holding the size seven black and gold stiletto Ferragamos she'd bought last year. She'd known even at the time that they probably wouldn't ever fit her oversized feet but the price had been so good she'd bought them anyway, thinking that perhaps for some lucky event, her feet would shrink a half-size.

She riffled through her jewelry box; she knew without having looked at Lana's jewelry that she'd be wearing the wrong thing. She retrieved a thin gold chain with a small gold and diamond pendant affixed. Matching earrings. The ensemble was discreet and tasteful. It would make no statement.

Back in the car, Lana now huddled silently in back, Alice told Gil their first stop was the Macy's on the way out of the city. No one spoke on the drive across town. When they pulled into the mall parking lot, Alice told Gil that he'd join them inside at Macy's as well. It was not a request.

Gil nodded, meeker now. After they parked he followed Alice, who strode toward the front double doors. Inside, she moved with purpose, not even bothering to see if Gil and Lana were following. She stopped by an evening attire department, swiveled around and sized up Lana.

"Just a simple black dress, I'm thinking," she said and without waiting for a reply, plunged into a nearby section of dresses on racks. She peered over at Gil for the first time since they'd left the car.

"You. Wait right here in this department. Don't go wandering off to look at ties. I'll be furious with you if we get to the party late and I miss hearing Montserrat and Matthew perform."

Gil made an elaborate "at your service" bow and headed over to a nearby armchair. Lana looked at the dresses and fingered a silky peach-colored dress.

"Maybe this?" she asked Alice, holding it up to show her.

Alice shook her head. "Looks tacky." She ignored Lana's hurt look, just as she ignored the scrunched-up face a moment later when Alice held up three black sheath dresses.

"They look like something you'd wear to a funeral," Lana said.

"This is what we want. Trust me. Go try these on."

She stood outside the dressing room door, waiting while Lana changed. The first dress did not suit Lana's body; it gaped at the hips and her flat chest and Lana looked uncomfortable. But the second dress was a marvel. The silken fabric seemed to melt into her body, highlighting her angles, her long legs. It made her look both sophisticated and seductively innocent.

"Try it with the shoes," Alice said. "You brought them in, right?"

Lana nodded and a moment later, walked out of the dressing room. "Hey," she exclaimed. "These shoes are more comfortable than they look."

And they looked good. So did Lana. She glided over to the three-way mirror at the far end of the dressing room, studied herself and fell silent. She turned to face Alice, a stunned expression on her face.

Alice couldn't hide her smile. "I do believe that works."

Lana looked down at the price tag and paled. "I can't buy this," she cried. "It's five hundred dollars."

"Marked down from nine hundred. A steal. And you're not buying it." Alice's smile broadened. "Gil is going to."

"No! That's impossible."

Alice grew impatient. "Look, Lana. This is big, tonight. It's worth potentially a quarter of a million dollars. If Gil wants to stage our show this way, fine. But he's going to pay for the right costume." She looked down at her watch. "Come on. We're out of time."

Lana scowled at her but Alice scowled right back. A moment later Lana's shoulders dropped and she gave a little nod.

Dancers, Alice thought irritably. They were good at taking direction, at least.

The party took place in Hillsborough, tucked into the foothills of the coastal mountain range paralleling Highway 280. Andy Redgrave's home was impressive, more of a mansion than a house, the white sandstone exterior making it look like an Italian villa. A team of valet parking attendants hurried to open Gil's car doors and take his keys. At the massive carved-oak front door a sharply attractive woman with a professional demeanor greeted them, checking Gil and Alice's names off the invitation list before directing them into the two-story entryway. The last of the evening's light glowed through the windows while strategically placed track lighting illuminated the high ceilings and the rest of the room.

"Showtime," Gil murmured to Alice, who nodded. Lana nervously chewed her lower lip.

"Maybe this dress was the right call," she said to Alice.

"It was."

She'd harbored anxiety that Lana, even with the dress, would stand out as a liability, but that wasn't proving to be the case. Lana comported herself well, moving through the entryway like the graceful dancer she was, taking in the statues, the marble floors, the staircase's elaborate carved molding in a sweetly nervous, deferential manner. Gil excused himself to go hunt down Andy, and Lana stayed close to Alice as they entered the living room. When an announcement circulated that the musicians were going to perform shortly, they made their way to a salon where several dozen padded folding chairs had been set up to face a platform in the front of the room.

Alice claimed three seats but as she was searching around for Gil, she turned to see, instead, Andy Redgrave.

"Hello, Alice," he said in that cool way of his. "Glad you could make it. Gil here, as well?"

"Actually, he's looking for you."

"Well. Here I am."

Tonight Andy was dressed more casually, in a pin-striped button-down oxford shirt and navy trousers, simple elegance that probably had cost a thousand dollars. He was more tanned than when Alice had last seen him; probably a day out on the yacht. The tan highlighted his blond hair and pale blue eyes. He looked handsome and all-powerful, like an Old Testament angel tossed down to earth, thrown into contemporary clothes and told to "act mortal but not too much."

She introduced Andy to Lana. "Lana's a soloist with the company," Alice added as they shook hands.

Andy turned back to regard Alice in amusement. "Do you always bring your product with you on a sales pitch?"

Alice assumed a breezy confidence she didn't feel. "Only when they'll agree to climb into my briefcase. But this is pleasure tonight, not business. Lana's, um, my friend."

"Well, I hope you ladies enjoy the performance. Alice, I know you will. This is going to be the highlight of your evening, I think you mentioned."

This time she was prepared. "Oh, no, Andy. The highlight will be when you grace us with more of your presence."

He smiled. "Gil's been coaching you."

He left to greet another guest. Lana and Alice settled into seats, Alice glancing around anxiously until Gil reappeared.

"Where did you go for so long?" Alice hissed as he took the seat next to Lana.

"I told you. I was looking for Andy."

"He was here. Right here."

"So. You chatted?"

"Of course."

"And you said Lana was your friend?"

"Yes."

She was somewhat heartened by the fact that he looked worried. He would be taking tonight seriously, after all, in spite of Lana's presence. Not until the track lights dimmed and the three musicians strode out to the platform, however, did she begin to relax.

Applause broke out, particularly at the sight of Matthew.

"Hey," Lana whispered as the musicians arranged their music on their stands. "That looks like the guy from the American

Express commercial. The musician they did a documentary on last year."

"That's because it's him," Alice whispered back.

Lana's eyes widened. "Oh. Oh!"

Alice kept her own eyes focused on the violinist, her friend Montserrat. She was attired in a long black evening dress that added drama and height to her petite frame. Her dark hair was held back with a gold clip, her honey-brown eyes serious as she studied the open page of music before twisting around to murmur something to the pianist. Matthew rose to greet the audience.

Matthew was a warm, boyishly handsome Japanese-American, a concert hall favorite for years. He shared a few details about the Stradivarius, Andy's new acquisition, that he was playing tonight, which would thereafter be loaned out to a deserving San Francisco-based cellist. He gave a quick rundown on the pieces the trio would be performing. Once he'd finished and returned to his spot, the lights in the back of the room dimmed further. The pianist and Montserrat watched Matthew, who, once his cello was tuned, met their eyes, gave a quick little lift of his chin, and they began.

The first piece was a favorite of Alice's—one of Saint Saens' piano trios, a lively, engaging crowd-pleaser from the Romantic era, the melody continually passed around from instrument to instrument. Most of the listeners, Alice sensed, were focused on Matthew and the Stradivarius. The cello's allure was undeniable. It roared, it purred, it vibrated with intensity and warmth. Alice's focus, however, remained on her friend and her instrument, the golden antique perfection of her Vuillaume, which could sound sweet and angelic one moment, husky and imploring the next.

This form of artistry was a mystery to Alice, just as Montserrat herself was, even after knowing her for six years. She didn't like to talk about her past; Alice knew only that she'd had an unconventional youth, shuttled around Europe by actor parents, and that she'd always had to work very hard for her craft, six to eight hours of daily practice, even now. The violin, she'd told Alice, wasn't something you learned once, and coasted along after that. It was a lifelong, consuming endeavor.

Alice, habituated to creating art through her body, pondered the implications of being a professional musician. You had to take good care of an instrument, true, but you could store it away and relax. You could break your leg and still the instrument would play sweetly. If the instrument were destroyed, you could get a replacement, although Montserrat had told Alice her violin, an 1862 J.B. Vuillaume worth $120,000, was irreplaceable to her.

Following the Saint Saens, the trio performed a lively, syncopated tango, the violin singing in staccato double-stop bursts, almost like an accordion, the cello sounding jazzy and sexy. For the final piece, Matthew played unaccompanied Bach, the famous "Prelude" from his Cello Suite No. 1 in G Major. The sound was rich, deep and pure, the aural equivalent of a fine old Cognac. Even Alice had to admit it was a showstopper. The other listeners, classical music fans or not, were all riveted. Lana gave a little gasp when he'd finished and they were all clapping.

"I've never heard anything like that before," she exclaimed to Alice.

"No, I'm sure you haven't. Not this close up, certainly."

"And you said these musicians are friends of yours?"

"Montserrat is, and I know Matthew through her."

"And he's so famous. Wow."

"It couldn't have been cheap to engage him."

"How much do you think he makes?"

"For tonight's performance, probably around 40K."

"Forty thousand *dollars?*" Lana's voice rose to a squeak.

Alice grinned. "Welcome to the major leagues. Imagine what he gets for a big concert."

Gil leaned over, his eyes glowing. "Alice. Introduce me to him later?"

The double doors leading to the living room were opened. In wafted irresistible smells of roasted meat, garlic in melted butter, baked pastry puffs. The caterers had set up a buffet while the guests had been listening to the music. Alice's stomach growled, as if on command. Time to indulge, courtesy of Andy Redgrave.

An hour later, Alice, pleasantly sated and buzzed, left her conversation with Montserrat and a now restless Lana to seek out a bathroom. The two on the first floor appeared to be occupied, so she trudged up the carpeted staircase to the second level. Before she got to the bathroom, however, she spied Gil at the other end of the hallway, preparing to shut the door of the room he was in. He looked surprised to see her there.

"I know someone who wants to see you," she called out in a singsong fashion, but his eyes sent out a warning. "Matthew Nakamura," she improvised. "Remember I was going to introduce the two of you?'

The relief on his face was palpable. A moment later Andy appeared behind him. "Is she cool with this?" he murmured to Gil.

Gil hesitated. "Of course."

"Then come join us, Alice."

She tried to read Gil's expression, but Andy was studying her at the same time. It reminded her of the trapped way she'd felt when they'd talked at the liquor store. But Andy was smiling at her now, and Gil was here.

She flashed Andy a smile. "I'd love to."

The master bedroom was spacious, opulent, the bed off in its own section and a living room setup closer to the door. Gil locked the door as Andy returned to his spot on the sofa, beckoning Alice to sit in the armchair across from him. Between them was a glass table, on which sat a delicately filigreed mirror holding a small mound of cocaine.

Gil joined them, sitting next to Andy, who cut the powder with a razor and arranged three neat lines before offering Gil a rolled-up bill. A real $100 bill from the looks of it, she noted in amusement. Her partying friends, back in her less responsible years, could never manage more than a twenty-dollar bill. The three of them each took a turn and sat back, sniffling, basking in the conspiratorial air, the camaraderie such an act always seemed to bring.

The euphoria set in. The teeth-grinding and chattering.

"I loved the recital," Alice gushed. "Just loved it. That's a beautiful Strad you've acquired, Andy. And that unaccompanied Bach Matthew played at the end? It really showed off the cello's sound."

"It did. It really did," he exclaimed.

Andy on cocaine, it appeared, was a lot more friendly. He asked her how she'd liked the program, the order, how the acoustics were from her spot, which piece she'd enjoyed the most.

"Oh, I'd have to say the Saint Saens."

"Very good, you remembered the composer."

"Of course." She gave him a coyly flirtatious look. "I told you I was a classical music person. I love that piano trio. Actually, I like all of Saint Saens's work."

"So do I. The cello concerto?"

"Definitely. And his third violin concerto. The second movement is like a slice of heaven."

"It's sublime," he agreed. "Then there's his organ symphony."

"Yes. And the *Rondo Capriccioso. Danse Macabre. Carnival of the Animals.*" She wrinkled her nose. "Well, in truth, I only like the cello solo."

"'The Swan.'"

"That's it."

"I'm just now exploring his chamber music," he said. "It intrigues me. It's like Fauré's, only not."

"I know just what you mean. You know Fauré was one of Saint Saens's students."

"No, I didn't know that." He looked pleased. "But it makes sense."

"And later, Fauré taught Ravel. All those French composers—Ravel, Debussy, Poulenc—they all have a similar yet distinct sound."

Gil, catching Alice's eye, gave her a little *good job* nod. He himself knew nothing about classical music and Alice could almost see his thoughts whirring. *Become classical music aficionado so as to impress prospective billionaire donors.*

"Speaking of French sound," Andy said to Alice, "how do you like your friend's Vuillaume?"

It was a curious question. Granted, he'd just bought a million-dollar antique stringed instrument, but few people knew anything about violins beyond the famous makers, Stradivarius, Gagliano, Amati, Guarneri and a handful of other Italian luthiers.

"You know the maker of Montserrat's violin." She raised one eyebrow at Andy. "I'm impressed."

He acknowledged this with a bob of his head.

She was glad she knew enough about J.B. Vuillaume's instruments to respond with eloquence. "It's got a powerful sound, like most Vuillaumes, but at the same time, it produces a warm, rich tone. Of course, that's Montserrat's skill coming into play. It never fails to amaze me when I hear her play, how many different voices she can draw out of that instrument. She told me she's been offered the loan of a Stradivarius a few different times in the past, but that the tone never appealed to her as much as what she could produce on the Vuillaume."

He nodded thoughtfully. "She is truly an artist well-matched to her instrument."

A moment later he returned his attention to the cocaine mound. Alice declined seconds; she was wired enough. After he and Gil each had another line they grew too agitated to sit, so the three of them stood in a huddle of sorts, chattering like parakeets.

Gil, sniffling and laughing, told a vaguely off-color joke about a man who arrives at his friend's house, sits with the friend's wife while they both wait for her husband to return, and persuades the wife to show him her breasts by offering to give her two one-hundred-dollar bills, one for each breast peek. She does, and he does. Afterward, the man announces he can't wait any longer, and leaves.

"When the husband arrives home," Gil told them, "the wife tells him his friend stopped by, but was behaving strangely. The husband mulls this over and says, 'Yes, but did he drop off the two hundred bucks he owed me?'"

They all laughed. Andy glanced inquiringly over at Alice, who waved away his concern.

"I'm used to Gil's jokes. I can beat him any day."

"Oh, just try," Gil scoffed.

Alice pondered this. "Okay," she said a moment later, "here's one for you. One afternoon a little girl comes home from school and tells her mother that someone on the playground just informed her where babies came from. Her mother smiles, squats down to her level and asks her daughter what she learned. 'Well,' the little girl says, 'the Mommy and Daddy take off all of their clothes, and the Daddy's thingee sort of stands up, and then Mommy puts it in her mouth, and then it sort of explodes, and that's how you get babies.'

"And the mother chuckles and says, 'Oh, honey. That's not how you get babies. That's how you get *jewelry*.'"

The silence that greeted her punch line was terrible. Just as Alice was deciding she'd blown it with him, Andy burst into loud, wheezing laughter. Gil joined in and so did Alice. Andy slung his arms over their shoulders and they all drew closer, foreheads touching.

"Do you know?" Andy said, "I'm thinking I'd like to do some business with you two and your organization."

The moment exploded into euphoria as the three of them stood there, arms around each other. She felt the heat of Andy's arm against her shoulders, Gil's around her waist, the energy and heat radiating from their bodies. They were all as carefree and happy as college kids right then. They were the Three Musketeers. They were Beautiful People, exploring life's boundaries, and Alice discovered that when you were a billionaire player, the horizons stretched very far indeed.

Andy straightened first. He asked Alice to reach over and grab the wine bottle on the table behind her. She brought it over, they all retrieved their glasses and Andy poured.

They raised a toast, not to business, but to life, to friends. New friends, Andy clarified. Special friends. His arm was back around Gil's shoulders. Gil's arm was around Andy's waist, as if supporting Andy, who was indeed swaying a bit. A moment later Andy's glass tilted and red wine sloshed out of the glass and onto the snowy carpet.

"Whoops," Andy said, "guess it's time to replace the carpet." He and Gil found this hilarious, laughing and leaning into one another. Andy rested his head against Gil's. He murmured something Alice couldn't quite catch, that made Gil laugh more.

Andy exhaled, a happy little sigh. The hand resting on Gil's shoulder slid down and began to caress Gil's upper arm, a tiny back-and-forth motion with the fingers, discreet but unmistakable in its intent.

Alice recognized the gesture with a visceral jolt. It was precisely the way Niles had seduced her, five months earlier.

Gil was still laughing, but his expression had grown alert. His gaze caught Alice's and hung on.

Her breath caught. This was going in the wrong direction fast. Gil needed her help.

What can I do? her eyes radioed.

The insecurity faded from Gil's expression.

Leave us, he radioed back.

She stood there, frozen, until Gil gave an impatient little nudge with his chin in the direction of the door.

So she left, as unobtrusively as possible.

He was the boss, after all.

Chapter 6 – Cinderella

This was the most amazing night of Lana's life.

It was the Cinderella story come to life. The new gown, poof. The slippers, poof. The Prince Charming, the grand party—check, and check. Granted, her fairy godmother had been a little on the grouchy side, but Lana didn't begrudge Alice this. Gil, after all, had sprung this on her. But in spite of that, Alice had been kind enough to give Lana a pair of her brand new shoes. Lana had seen shoes like these before in fancy department stores. They'd cost over three hundred dollars. Alice had told her she could keep them. Along with the dress. She couldn't believe it. Even Cinderella hadn't gotten that kind of bargain.

She'd stayed close to Alice for the first part of the evening, but when Alice disappeared she felt comfortable enough to wander around the house by herself. All around her was luxury atop luxury. The leather furniture was plush and soft to the touch like the finest gloves. The tables and lamps looked like contemporary art. One entire wall of the massive living room was composed of glass, revealing the San Francisco Bay far below and the twinkling lights of the houses on the hills surrounding the water.

There was a library, looking like something out of *Masterpiece Theatre*, with a real Renoir on the wall. Next door, a formal dining room. One sumptuous room after another, and this was only the first floor. Just as Lana began to feel overwhelmed—she hadn't seen Gil for over half an hour, nor was Alice anywhere to be found—Montserrat spied her and motioned for her to join her back in the main room. The dessert pastries had been laid out, an eye-popping assortment of treats as elegant and pretty as artwork. Montserrat offered to pick them out an assortment to try.

Once they'd found seats in a corner of the living room, Montserrat pointed out each pastry and told Lana their name in French. Even Lana, with her inexperienced ear, could tell it was an authentic French accent. It was no surprise, really. If Alice were one of the most elegant, cosmopolitan women she'd ever spent an evening with, Montserrat was one step up in sophistication. An established soloist, playing to crowded concert halls all around the world, buddying up with people like Matthew Nakamura. No surprise that she spoke French. Maybe she owned a villa there.

There were pinky-sized chocolate éclairs. *Petits-fours*, which Montserrat told her meant "small ovens." Lemon tarts in a thin, delicate pastry shell with a shiny lemon glaze, topped with a tiny dollop of whipped cream and the teeniest bit of lemon rind. Little fruit tarts that looked like miniature works of art, held in place by the sheerest glaze. Miniature chocolate mousses in edible chocolate cups. *Petite choux chantilly*—tiny overloaded cream puffs.

Montserrat cut a rectangular *millefeuille* in half, its flaky pastry alternating with cream, topped by a thin glaze of white frosting and calligraphy-like chocolate swirls.

"That looks like something I got from a bakery once," Lana said, "but it was called a Napoleon."

"That's the generic name for it here in the U.S. I have a hunch, though, that the one you had didn't taste like this."

Lana took a tentative bite. The flavors invaded her mouth all at once: the buttery, paper-thin crunch of the pastry, the delicate intensity of the whipped cream, the haunting semi-sweetness. Montserrat smiled at Lana's expression, her delight.

"Why does it taste so different?" Lana asked.

"French pastry makers are masters of subtlety. Not too much sugar, flaky pastry that doesn't soak up filling. High-quality butter and cream, never a vegetable oil replacement."

"It's incredible."

"All of these are going to be." Montserrat smiled as she cut into a second pastry.

Lana couldn't believe how kind Montserrat was being to her. So easy to talk to. "You speak French really well, it sounds like," she offered shyly.

"It's because my parents and I lived in Paris on and off when I was growing up."

"Wow. That must have been glamorous."

"Not particularly. It was just one of the many places we lived in those years."

"You moved around a lot?"

"Lots. You?"

"Oh, gosh, no. Kansas City. That's the only place I've ever lived."

"Really? I used to dream about having a life like that. Stability. What about your family? Tell me it was one of those big, cozy families."

"Big is right. There's eight of us, including my mom and dad."

Mom. Her phone date.

She stared at Montserrat in helpless dismay.

"What's wrong?" Montserrat asked.

"I just remembered my mom was going to call and I promised I'd be there for us to talk. But I left my purse in the car." She hadn't needed Alice to tell her its tacky, oversized vinyl-ness would have been out of place here.

"Uh, oh. No purse, no call, huh?"

"Right."

She studied the plate of pastries with a growing sense of horror. How could she have forgotten? How would Mom react to this? With anger, or, far worse, a lapse into one of her dark moods? What a screw up on Lana's part.

"Do you want to borrow my phone and call her now?" Montserrat asked.

She hesitated, shook her head. Better to not call at all than try and explain why she was at this party, among this elegant, privileged group. She'd just have to live with the consequences tomorrow when she called Mom to apologize.

"Wow," Montserrat said, studying her. "You and your family *are* close."

"We are."

"Tell me what it was like, growing up in a big family like that."

But she didn't want to talk about her family, that sloppier, more chaotic world, to this exotic creature. Briefly she considered lying, but knew she'd never be able to keep it up.

"It was, um, crowded. Loving. But nothing like this. Not even remotely."

She kept her eyes trained on the éclair. It was a moment before Montserrat spoke again.

"You know, a humble upbringing is nothing to be ashamed of."

Easy for someone like her to say. She lifted her eyes to Montserrat, whose expression was warm and empathetic. For whatever reason, she sensed she could trust this woman.

"Everyone here seems so accomplished, so privileged," she said in a low voice. "I just want to fit in. I look at them, at people like

Alice, and I wish I could be like them."

"But you *are* like Alice. You two have a lot in common, with the ballet business."

"Well, we're both employees of the West Coast Ballet Theatre, if that's what you mean. But she's an administrator."

"Now, maybe. But she was once a dancer in the company."

Surely she'd misheard. "The West Coast Ballet Theatre?"

"None other. She danced with them for six years."

"Omigod. What happened?"

"She had an accident, an injury that ended things for her. I didn't know her at the time, so I can't tell you much more. You should ask her. Except that she might... Well, speak of the devil." Montserrat's tone changed as Alice appeared in front of them.

"Ooh, good," she said, plopping down next to Montserrat on the couch. "Snackies." She reached over and plucked one of the chocolate mousse cups and popped it into her mouth.

Lana was having trouble processing the fact that this associate of Gil's, this cool, controlled woman, had once been a dancer like herself. She knew she'd fumble with her words and say the wrong thing if she tried to bring it up right then, so instead she asked Alice if she'd seen Gil.

Alice frowned and Lana immediately regretted saying anything.

"I just left him. We were talking shop with Andy. Gil's getting closer to a deal, so please, don't bother him right now, Lana. Okay?"

"Oh. Sure."

She swallowed her hurt, reminding herself that this was a business event for them, after all. Alice and Montserrat began talking about a dinner party at Montserrat's on Monday night, how someone named Niles was expected to be there too, no excuses about his being too busy with work. They talked about

Montserrat's upcoming East Coast tour and the music Montserrat would be performing. Lana made her excuses a minutes later and wandered off.

Eventually she spied Gil in the kitchen, an inviting, softly lit room, all maple woodwork and sleek granite surfaces, bearing no resemblance to any kitchen she'd ever prepared meals in. He was alone, the first time she'd seen him alone all night. He saw her and waved her closer.

"You've been working the crowd," she said, and he nodded. "You look tired."

"Oh, I'm okay."

"What can I do to bring your smile back?"

The distressed look behind his eyes receded. He stepped closer, reached behind her and ran a finger from the nape of her neck, down her spine, trailing it right down to her coccyx. The intimacy of it stole her breath.

"Your dress is so beautiful," he said.

"Thank you," was all she could manage.

He was still staring. "You are so beautiful." He said this with a kind of wonder, as if he'd found a rare antique in a junk shop, worth thousands but priced to sell at five dollars. "I can't stop thinking about you."

He hesitated. "There's something I need to tell you. About me."

Her stomach clenched. Whatever he was about to say, she wasn't ready to hear it.

"Julia and I have been living together for almost three years now. But, well, we don't share a bedroom anymore. Or a bed."

Maybe this was something she was ready to hear.

"You what?" she stuttered.

He was intent, focused on her as if he were translating a phrase that must not be misinterpreted.

"It's not that way with us anymore. We're just friends now. But we don't tell people, so please keep it to yourself."

"Why are you telling me?"

"I just want you to know there's no conflict of interest here. In case, well…" His gaze shifted downward even as his smile grew. He looked like a teenager. It was darling.

"Thank you. That's considerate of you." Recklessly, she forged on. "And just for the record, I'm very interested in hearing more about the 'in case' business."

He met her eyes. Butterflies bashed about inside her chest.

"Come with me upstairs," he said.

"Are you serious?"

"I am. But follow a few seconds behind me."

"So no one sees us together."

He looked abashed. "Do you mind?"

She laid a hand on his arm. "I don't mind in the least. I know you're here for business."

The room he led her to appeared to be the master bedroom. It looked like something she envisioned royalty living in. Gil waited for her to slip in before he shut and locked the door. That done, he took her by the hand and led her to the far side of the room.

"I want to show you this painting," he said.

Although she knew little about paintings and fine art, she could tell this poster-sized, gilt-framed, Impressionist painting was a rare, exquisite one, dreamy and evocative. There was a lush garden setting, a patio table laden with food and wine, and in the periphery, a half-dressed couple reclining on a blanket, limbs entwined. The suggestion of sex, rather than an explicit portrayal of it, made the scene all the more alluring. They stood there, observing it in silence until Gil stepped behind her, his hands resting on her shoulders.

"Look at it," he murmured against her temple. "That's the closest image of paradise I've ever seen." His hands began to caress her bare shoulders. She was finding it increasingly difficult to focus on the painting, but managed to nod.

Gil's hands moved; she could feel him working the back zipper of her dress, down, down, until cool air touched the small of her back. His fingers slipped under her dress's shoulders, nudging them off her. In the time it took Lana to realize how the laws of gravity might work against her here, the dress slithered right off, landing in a puddle of silky material down at her feet. Her first instinct, like the time her costume had come undone onstage, was to follow it right down, lift it back up in a flash. But Gil held onto her shoulders.

"No," he whispered. "Lana. Let it stay."

From the corner of her eye she caught her reflection in a mirror on another wall. She saw the scared pale face, her mostly nude body. As a dancer she was used to semi-nudity. Most of the women had nothing to hide on top; they hardly even reacted when one of the male dancers entered their dressing room. But this felt different, scandalously so. In the Macy's dressing room she'd stuffed her white cotton bra into her purse because it had clashed with the black dress. Now, only her skimpy thong panties kept her from full nudity.

She saw Gil in the mirror and watched him watch her, a curiously erotic experience. His expression seemed to encompass pleasure, wonder, but sadness, too. He gently stroked her shoulders, her arms, before his hands fell to his side and he stepped around to the front of her. She stood there, swaying, unsure about what was expected of her.

Gil took a few steps back and sat on a chair. "Come here," he said.

Like something out of a dream, she felt herself move toward him. He reached out and drew her closer, his hands closing around her waist, sliding to the small of her back. He bent his head so that his forehead was resting on her upper abdomen. He didn't move, he didn't try to turn it into sexual foreplay. She could feel his breath sending warm waves of air across her belly. When he looked up at her and spoke it was with the awed solemnity of a young boy.

"Something's happening. I've never felt this way before. Never. Tell me you feel it too."

This was moving too fast. She wanted to reach out, grab at his arm, tell him to slow down, that the wind was pounding her face too hard, tearing her breath from her. It was all too much, too soon. Instead she heard herself replying, as if in a trance.

"I do."

"I knew it. Some things you can just feel."

He sighed, his shoulders relaxing, as if released of a heavy load. Shifting back onto his feet, he straightened slowly, hands moving higher up her back. He kept his head close to her body, his lips grazing her still-pubescent breasts, her neck, a spot just below her earlobe that sent an electric shiver through her. One hand came around to cup her face. She was trembling, not just in hungry anticipation of the kiss, but at the unexpected intensity of what had just transpired.

The jiggling of the room's doorknob jolted them both from their reverie. Another jiggle, followed by a knock. Lana panicked. Even Gil looked alarmed.

"It's okay," he whispered, clutching at her shoulders. "Tell him you're fixing your dress."

"I'm *what?*" she whispered back.

"You're fixing your dress. Say it. Quick. Casual like."

So she did.

"Oh. Sorry," she heard a voice say. The host's voice. "I was looking for someone else."

"I'll be right out. There was a pin digging into my skin," she added and Gil, still alert as a cat, nodded in approval. "I had to take the whole dress off. I hope you don't mind."

"No, no. Take your time. Lana, is it?"

The host had remembered her name. She felt like Somebody. "Yes, it's Lana."

"All right. See you shortly."

"Okay. And thanks!"

"No problem."

Ten minutes later she and Gil were back in the kitchen, trying not to stand too close. She was smiling dreamily into her Perrier and lime, thinking about the way they'd kissed and kissed just before leaving the room, once he'd helped her back into her dress and zipped her up. Her lips felt chafed and swollen now, her mind reeling every time she thought of what he'd said to her.

Something's happening. I've never felt this way before.

They'd agreed to play it cool so Gil could get back to business. It came as a jolt, nonetheless, when Andy Redgrave entered the kitchen a moment later and Gil turned his back on Lana.

"There you are," Andy was saying to Gil.

"Here I am indeed." Gil's voice sounded uncharacteristically hearty.

Lana didn't look up from her Perrier; surely her swollen lips and hastily reapplied lip gloss would reveal what she and Gil had just been doing.

"I was just talking with Ryan Dudek," Andy said. "He's interested in meeting you."

"Viatech's CEO? That's fabulous."

Again the hearty voice. Lana looked up and saw Andy's eyes now fixed on hers.

"Hello, Lana. Where's Alice?"

"I think in the living room, maybe," she stuttered.

"And the pin?"

"What?"

"The pin. In your dress. Gone now?"

"Oh, that pin. Yes, it's gone. Thanks. Sorry to be in your room like that."

He offered her one of his cool host smiles. "It's no problem. I like my guests to feel at home."

She pulled away from the counter, sloshing Perrier on her hand, but too jittery to care. "Well, I think I'll go find Alice."

"You do that," Andy said, already turning away from Lana to face Gil.

She hesitated. "Gil," she blurted out, which she immediately realized was the wrong thing to do. Gil didn't look at her.

Andy did.

"I'll tell Alice you're in the kitchen," she improvised. "If she needs to talk to you."

What a stupid thing to say. What a stupid girl she was. Out of her league didn't begin to cover it, next to Andy Redgrave, in this mansion of Andy Redgrave's, where it seemed as if even the portraits on the walls were now frowning down at her.

She left. Fled.

In the living room she found Montserrat and Alice, still, unfathomably, talking about music. She remained there, nonetheless, willing herself not to shrink when she saw Andy approach five minutes later, Gil by his side. Andy and Montserrat bantered about the night's recital, about how Montserrat, Matthew and their pianist partner had been simply using the performance as a rehearsal for one of their upcoming recitals. Lana tried to avoid looking at Gil, but the moment she gave in and snuck a furtive look at him, his eyes were on her. It was like that first meeting; she couldn't tear her gaze away.

Not after what had happened upstairs.

Alice's nudge was a rude awakening. Lana looked over and the others were regarding her in an amused fashion. "What?" she stuttered.

"Andy wanted to know if you liked classical music," Alice said.

Andy was studying her like before, but this time he wasn't smiling. "Um, sure," she managed.

She could feel confusion coming from Alice, who hurried to fill the awkward pause. "Of course you do, as a ballet dancer. All that Tchaikovsky, for starters. *Swan Lake, Sleeping Beauty, Nutcracker.*"

"Yes," Lana said. "All that. Definitely."

Andy looked over Lana's shoulder and beyond. "Ah," he said in reply. He nudged Gil, who'd remained silent. "There's a couple for you to meet. Paul and Laura Giordano. Their endowment handed over a generous contribution to the symphony last year. Shall I introduce you?"

"I think you know the answer to that one." Gil began to laugh, a low, conspiratorial sound.

"I do indeed." Andy turned to Alice and Montserrat. "Ladies, we must leave you."

"Gil, get to work," Alice mock-commanded, and they all laughed. But the smile dropped off her face the instant Andy and Gil walked away, Andy's arm now slung over Gil's shoulders. When she spoke a moment later, it was in a tone that chilled Lana.

"What just happened?"

Montserrat looked at Alice in concern. "What is it? What's the matter?"

Alice didn't answer her. She turned to look at Lana, her expression troubled.

Lana's heart began to hammer. "I don't know."

She didn't. Andy had just caught her gazing at Gil, and he'd heard her call his name in that certain way in the kitchen. He'd probably figured out that Gil had been in the bedroom with her. But that didn't explain the coldness now coming from him, not when he was looking so pleased with Gil.

Alice searched Lana's face. Forehead creased, she turned to Montserrat. "Nothing's the matter. It's just that we want to make sure Andy's happy with us. That he wants to work with us."

"But he looked happy," Montserrat pointed out. "With you and Gil both."

Alice tried to smile. "You're right. I just felt a little nervous there. No big deal."

This was how the next hour proceeded for Lana: Gil became Andy's best friend, his protégé, and Lana became invisible. No one spoke with her; no one even glanced her way. Gil wouldn't even try and catch her eye anymore. Instead he talked to Andy, focused on Andy, joined any discussion Andy was lording over. Meanwhile, Andy's polite disdain toward Lana morphed into an unspoken yet palpable hostility she could feel radiating from across the room.

She was no stranger to hostility. Look at how the other dancers had treated her when they saw the cast list for Program II. Her whole professional life, she'd produced this kind of reaction in others. But that was the dance world. The rules and hierarchies there were different.

A terrible thought worked its way into her mind. She'd been in the dance world for fifteen years. She'd learned to be a good observer, particularly of what was trying to remain hidden, in an environment that made no assumptions about gender attractions. Had they all been in the dance studio right then, the message Andy was giving off would read loud and clear. *Back off. You are poaching what has already been claimed.*

But this was not the dance studio.

She stumbled out of the living room, sought refuge in the bathroom. There, she splashed cold water on her face, trying to calm herself, but the suspicion planted in her mind wouldn't go away. She thought of Andy's eyes on Gil, the hand on Gil's arm, the proprietary nature of it all.

Gil owed her some explanation.

She wiped her face, her hands, slow and deliberate in her actions, as if that might allow her to approach her next task with equal control. Finally she left the bathroom to seek out Gil, whom she found chatting with Andy at the doorway of the study.

Gil spied her and looked alarmed. Horrified.

She faltered. And in that terrible moment, Alice swept in, sidled up to Lana. Gil sagged visibly with relief at the sight of Alice, which cut Lana even deeper.

"I think maybe Lana and I will head out now," Alice said to Andy, her voice light and flirtatious, as if proposing a run to the liquor store to buy more party booze.

Andy regarded the women in confusion.

Lana was confused as well. Alice had draped herself all over Lana, caressing her bare arm, pressing close to her. She threaded her fingers through Lana's long hair, as if they were lovers. Lana was too shocked to speak. Would the funhouse element of this night never end?

A smile spread across Andy's face. "Alice," he said, "you are a dark horse."

"Ever in pursuit of that perfect stallion," she quipped. "Or mare."

Her reply delighted Andy. He burst into laughter and like that, poof, he saw Lana again. He became once again the charming host, beaming, telling them goodbye, girls, glad they could both come by.

It happened fast, Alice's suggestion to Gil that she take his car and his agreement, his assurance that he'd find a way back to the city. Tomorrow. As the implication of this sank into Lana's mind, Alice's fingers dug into the soft flesh of her inner arm, a warning to keep her reaction to herself. They collected their belongings, bade Andy and Gil one last goodbye, then walked out of Andy's Hillsborough mansion and away from whatever was happening between Andy and Gil.

Chapter 7 – The Aftermath

They made their way down the steps into the now-chilly night air. Lana began to choke out a few strangled sobs. "Hold it in," Alice muttered under her breath. "People are watching."

The valets, spying them, sprang to attention. Alice pointed out Gil's car a quarter-block away and asked for the keys. "We'll go get it ourselves," she told them. "We need the walk."

The moonless night sky was dotted with millions of stars. It felt broader, more omnipotent than it did in San Francisco, lit by streetlights and never fully dark. A breeze sent the live oak leaves nearby rustling. Silence reigned, except for the *click-click* of their high heels on the asphalt and the throb of party music that receded as they continued on. She'd released her grip on Lana, but could tell the girl was trembling, taking little pained gasps of breath.

Lana was not the only one shaken by what just transpired. An hour earlier, Alice had been congratulating herself on a coup achieved without a single hitch. Then had come the mysterious interchange with Andy, but she'd thought no more of it until Montserrat raised the alert.

"I think Gil's young friend could use your help," she'd said. She gestured to Lana, who had a stunned look on her white face, like someone who'd just witnessed a crime and wasn't sure whether to report it or not. She looked so young, so vulnerable, lower lip quivering. Alice saw Gil and Andy nearby, clearly the source of Lana's dismay. She caught on fast. She bade Montserrat farewell and leapt onto the scene just as Lana was charging.

A bullet dodged. Just barely.

Close to the car, Alice unlocked the doors with the remote. Lana quickened her footsteps and slid into the passenger seat before Alice could get around to her side.

In the car, Lana was crying, shoulders shaking. "Why did you do that?" she asked between sobs. "Why did you make us leave? I needed to talk to him."

Alice didn't reply at first. She focused on adjusting the seat, the rearview mirror. "I was protecting Gil."

"Why? Are you two secret lovers or something?"

Alice snorted and glanced sideways at Lana. "Don't you wish it were that uncomplicated."

At these words, Lana seemed to shrink in her seat. She doubled up, clutching her midriff as if the thought had caused her physical pain. She didn't reply and Alice offered no further comments. Instead she started up the car and trundled down the narrow road, onto another road that took them back to the highway, back northbound toward San Francisco.

For the next ten minutes, neither of them spoke. Lana struggled to control her emotions, but from time to time issued a hiccupping shudder of grief. Alice, casting a quick glance over at her, felt the stirrings of pity.

"You going to be okay? Do you have someone to call, talk to?"

"No. No one."

Alice sighed inwardly. "Do you want us to stop for a cup of coffee, before I drop you off?"

"Do you mind?"

"Not at all," she lied.

Lana sniffed. "I'm sorry. About all of this."

"Oh, well, it is what it is."

"Anyway, yes, I'd like to stop. I don't want to be alone just yet." This made Lana start to cry again, but this time it was quiet, more like little mews of distress.

Alice stopped at a Denny's outside the city, where the rumble of highway traffic turned into a soothing hum once they were inside, seated at a brightly lit booth with red vinyl upholstery. They both studied the menu in silence until the waitress arrived. Lana, to Alice's secret amusement, ordered hot chocolate to Alice's black coffee. Lana seemed so much like a hot chocolate type, she decided. She probably wore flannel pajamas and bunny slippers. But the desolation in her eyes when she raised them to meet Alice's made Alice's amusement die away. Lana was hurting in an adult's way. Now was not the time to mock her little girl traits.

Their drinks arrived. She watched Lana down her hot chocolate, using her pinky to wipe the last of the whipped cream from inside the mug. Lana looked up at her afterward, almost apologetically.

"I'm feeling hungry. Would you mind terribly if I got a sandwich?"

"Why would I mind?"

"Well, the wait."

Alice settled against the cushioned back of the booth. "I'm in no hurry."

The club sandwich with a side order of onion rings and a chocolate shake came quickly. Alice accepted a refill on her coffee and watched, amused, as Lana tore into the food.

"Oh, the other females in the company must hate you," she commented. When she saw Lana's stricken expression, she hastened to add, "What I mean to say is, lucky, lucky you. For being able to eat like that, even after tonight's party food. And still be so thin."

The hurt look subsided into wariness. "My dad is a beanpole. I take after him."

"Like I said, lucky you. Do you have any idea how hard some dancers have to work to keep it off?"

"I think I do."

She didn't, of course. No one who was naturally thin and could devour such a meal with casual insouciance could understand how it felt to always be watching your weight, every pound, every ounce, terrorized by the slightest gain.

Alice had been one of those who'd struggled to keep her weight low through her dance years. In the first year of not dancing, she'd gained thirty pounds. She couldn't tell whether it had been dysfunction or the cessation of dysfunction that had driven it. Marianne, her stepmother, had been gently reproving, Alice's doctor thrilled. Nature had never intended for Alice to weigh 105 pounds. She had breasts now, as well, big round globes that shocked her to this day with their tacit but unmistakable presence on her body. Even her father took notice, asking Alice in a gruff fashion if she'd had "work" done on them, to which Alice had sputtered no, it was natural, thank you very much, Dad.

Lana finished her food quickly. "Can I ask you a question?" she asked Alice once the waitress had taken away the plate.

"About what?"

"Well, Gil."

Alice froze, ill-prepared to explain what they'd just left behind.

Lana seemed to understand her hesitation. "This isn't about that. It's about her. Julia."

"All right. Shoot."

"You know Gil pretty well, right?"

"Very well."

"So, he told me something. I need to know if it's true."

"Go on."

"He told me he and Julia are just friends. That there's nothing more between them."

Alice raised her eyebrows. "He told you that? Well, then again, I imagine he did."

"Is it true?" Lana sounded scared.

"Lana, it's not my place to discuss this with you."

"Alice, please."

Alice could hear her desperation. The poor girl really didn't deserve the fate she'd been served tonight. "Fine. Yes, it's true."

Lana's tense shoulders relaxed. "Thank you," she said softly. "I needed to know."

They sat, watching the people around them, all in various states of sobriety. "They've got a great setup, I have to say," Alice said. "It's a front for both of them, keeps the riffraff and the overeager Romeos at bay. Julia's got money, lots, and she's happy to lavish it on Gil to keep him close. He's there for her whenever she comes through town, a date for whatever event she attends. He's happy living rent-free in the Marina district, driving her nice little car."

"That red sports car is hers?"

"Technically it was a gift to Gil. But if they ever part ways, I sense he'll be expected to return it."

"I saw her with Gil last week. She looked old."

Alice frowned. "Typical twenty-year-old's response."

"I'm twenty-two."

"Okay. Well, Julia is forty-three."

"God. That *is* old."

This time Alice laughed, leaning back to allow the server to pour her more coffee. Once the server had left, Lana spoke again.

"Is it true you were a ballet dancer? With the company here?"

Alice regarded her in surprise. "Did Gil tell you?"

"No. Your friend Montserrat did."

Well. She hadn't seen that one coming. "Yes," she managed.

"What level were you?"

"I was in the corps for five years. Then a soloist for a year."

"Did it feel like a dream come true when you got promoted?"

An odd feeling rose inside her, the pleasure of the older memory that almost, but not quite, blotted out the pain of what later transpired. "It did. I'd been dreaming about it forever. It was a toss-up that season, I knew. Anders was considering both myself and Katrina."

"Katrina, the principal who's there right now?!"

"Yes indeed. Katrina, who went on to win the race."

"Wow." Lana studied Alice with new respect. "You were good."

Alice shrugged. "Good enough. I was getting anxious about being in the corps, though. As you probably know, if you're not promoted by six or seven years, odds are you never will be." Ironic now to think of how she'd fretted, the months before getting the news. Finally she'd gotten her promotion, and less than twelve months later, her dance career had ended anyway.

It was as if Lana could read the trajectory of her thoughts.

"Montserrat said that you'd had an onstage injury, and that was what ended your career. She told me to ask you for more details."

What on earth had Montserrat been thinking? But Montserrat had no way of knowing how unsettled Alice felt talking about her past losses. How could she? The two of them had always skirted around discussing their respective pasts—a true Catch 22.

"Yes," she told Lana. "I stepped into a piqué arabesque wrong and messed up my knee."

"Was it during a performance or rehearsal?"

"Oh, the real deal. In front of two thousand people. I don't do these things halfway. I fell and couldn't get up—my knee just stopped working."

"Did you tear a ligament or something?"

"Multiple ligaments. My ACL, MCL and meniscus. Oh, and I fractured my ankle."

"Dang. That's bad."

"It was."

Lana fingered her water glass. "I've only been out for eight weeks, with a bad sprain. I thought coming back after that was hard. Did you try? To come back, I mean."

"Of course I tried. Dance was my life. I wasn't going to give it up without a fight."

She felt curiously lightheaded as she spoke. She never talked about those days, made easier by the fact that her new friends in this new life of hers knew little about the dance world and wouldn't have known what questions to ask.

"I couldn't wait to get back," she continued. "But it was humbling, frustrating as anything. I was only supposed to be out for nine months, but I rushed things and reinjured myself, which required another surgery. So it turned into eighteen months off. And when I returned for the second time, oh, God. So much harder."

She shook her head and fell silent. Barre work had been relatively easy; she'd worked on that on her own, daily, in her apartment. Otherwise, though, so immersed in academics, writing papers, she'd forgotten how fast, how physically relentless the rest of company class pace was. Keeping up with the other dancers through grand allegro had been like riding a tricycle up a highway on-ramp, trying to merge with the Interstate traffic tearing past.

Her brain couldn't retain the adagio and petit allegro combinations thrown at the dancers, not like before, in the don't-think-about-it days. Her extensions sagged; her joints mutinied. She officially gave notice two months later, before Anders could lose all his respect for her and start nudging her toward the door. It had been a wrenching decision. But she'd put on a Willoughby front, lied and told everyone that the prospect of a college degree and an administrative career was more appealing to her now. They'd all bought it.

"Oh, poor you," Lana said softly. "Did your mom take good care of you during that time?"

Alice stared at her, jarred out of her reverie. "I'm sorry?"

"Your mom," Lana repeated. "At times like that, their support can really make a difference. My mom will hassle me about not helping her out enough, but those weeks I was out of commission, she was so supportive. It meant a lot to me."

Marianne had indeed been supportive through Alice's surgeries, her rehab and disappointing setbacks. But right then, her feelings of loss newly raw, all she could think of was Deborah.

Lana, looking less confident now, continued on nervously, unaware she was making things worse. "Or maybe that wasn't the case for you. My mom likes to totally get involved in my life. Sometimes it feels like too much. But I have to say, now that I'm far from her, I miss her. A lot more than I'd expected. Absence makes the heart grow fonder, huh?"

Lana peered at Alice expectantly, waiting for a reply.

This girl, who held the career Alice had lost too soon. This girl, who had the lifelong mother bond Alice had lost too soon.

Oh, the pain of the losses, even now. Sometimes it stole her breath.

She needed to be alone. She lurched up from the booth seat,

muttering something to Lana, about having to use the restroom, and how they needed to leave soon. She spoke harshly, not even bothering to wait for a reply.

In the bathroom stall, she slouched on a toilet and tried to compose herself, a few scalding tears working their way out in spite of her fierce commands to *not cry, damn it, you're in public*. She thought about Lana sitting there at the booth by herself, all pretty and fresh-looking even at this late hour. Lana, who'd had the nerve to drum up these memories, not knowing that Alice had told no one, not even Montserrat or Niles, about the aftermath of the injury that threw her world so off balance, the grief for her lost craft endless as she strived to realign herself.

She drew a deep, shuddering breath and held it as she straightened. She wiped the last errant tear from her face, exhaled and marched out of the bathroom stall, to the sink. Calmer now, she studied her face in the mirror. She forced a smile and the reflection Alice smiled back at her. She even managed to look grounded, sure of herself, confident and can-do.

Good. The Alice who mattered was back. One who did not need to discuss mothers or past careers and traumas with this Lana. Good riddance to the past, the tears, the emotions. Onwards, chin up, with a smile. A motto to live by.

Deborah would have been so proud.

After dropping off Lana at her apartment—what a terrible neighborhood she'd chosen to live in—she headed to her house, squeezing Gil's car in her driveway behind her own car. Home was a cozy little restored Queen Anne Victorian in the Castro, just off Market Street. She wouldn't have been able to afford her own house if it hadn't been for her family and their help.

One benefit of her accident was that it made her appreciate

family. When it felt as if her life had ended, there they were, her father and Marianne and even her brother, all contention aside, handing her the glue to put the broken bits back together. They saved her a second time after a bad breakup, at which time she declared a moratorium on romantic relationships and adopted a cat instead. Her father, in a combination graduation and thirtieth birthday present, made a generous down payment on the house she'd been dying to buy but couldn't afford. She saw it as a tacit admission by him and Marianne that yes, she'd missed the boat in the marriage department, but at least this way they could get her out of the rental market.

Once inside her house, she saw from the answering machine's blinking light that she had a phone message. She played it and smiled as Niles's voice filled the room. He was still up, working, and told her to call when she came in.

She punched his number into the phone and took a seat on the couch. Odette, her cat, came trotting toward her with a sleepy meow. Alice patted the spot beside her and Odette leapt onto it. "Hey, lover boy," she said into the phone when Niles picked up.

"Hello, beautiful. You calling from home?"

"I am."

"How was the event?"

"It was something else. Very impressive digs. The catered food was out of this world."

"And how'd it go with the business?"

"I'd say it went well. Except for Gil's date. Her presence, well, it sort of got in the way of the business angle at one point. Like, seriously in the way."

"Whoops."

Emotions now safely tucked away, she was able to talk about Lana dispassionately. "The poor girl. She's young, pretty, but was so out of her league there. Gil sort of blew her off by the end and she just didn't know how to deal with it all. I had to get her out of there before things turned bad. She was really upset, so we stopped at Denny's for coffee and a chat."

"That was nice of you."

"Oh, well, it's not like you were here for me to rush home to, anyway." She stroked Odette's silky fur. "So, what time can I expect your company tomorrow? Should I do the early yoga class, or are you coming up after lunch?"

"Well, the thing is." A tired exhale punctuated his reply. "I'm not going to be able to come up tomorrow after all, sweets. A whole section of this report, engineering's data on the presentation, blew up in my face today. I managed to get a hold of a few of the guys and we're meeting tomorrow in the office to get to the bottom of it."

Shit. *Shit.*

"Niles," she said, trying to sound reasonable, "you've been working all weekend already. Can't it wait till Monday morning?"

"Monday morning is when I'm supposed to be presenting these results to my boss. It has to be done before then. I hate it too. I really do."

She felt too crabby and disappointed to reply.

"Hey," he said a moment later. "You still there?"

"Yes."

"I'm sorry. I'll make it up to you."

"That's what you said Friday night when you cancelled. In fact, tomorrow was supposed to be the makeup for that."

"It won't always be like this. It's just…"

"I know, I know. 'Things are just busy right now,'" she mimicked. How tired she was of hearing that. How tired of everything she felt right then.

"I told you I'm sorry. I meant it."

She could almost see the determined set of his face. He was not the type to get deterred or derailed by someone else's opinion, even their disapproval. It was one of the many things she admired about him. He was no pushover. He knew what he wanted and he quietly pursued it, maintaining a sense of focus, of ethics and decorum in the process. He was nothing like Gil.

Thank goodness.

Sensing her moodiness, he changed the subject. "Gil's date, the dancer. Watching her seemed to unsettle you on Monday, after you'd been sent over to the studio."

"No it didn't," she said, realizing too late Niles was merely repeating to her what she'd told him on Monday night. Damn. Caught in her own lie.

"What I mean to say is," she continued, "it was a jolt, that's all. Like seeing a friend from high school and it's just been too long and you have nothing more in common, so it's uncomfortable. Like that."

"So being with her tonight has nothing to do with the fact that you're sounding a little, um, shrill right now?"

"I am not sounding shrill!"

Niles, to his credit, did not comment on the shrill nature of her reply.

"Look," she said. "I know what you're getting at. But the whole ballet dancer aspect of my life is ancient history. I'm over it."

"Are you sure?"

"Yes, I'm sure. Can we just fucking drop it?"

She'd never spewed out an obscenity or a harsh retort to him like that before. Another first between them.

"Alice," he said in that soothing, put-out-the-fire voice of his. "Do you want me to come up? I can be there in thirty minutes. I'd have to leave early in the morning, but I'll come up if you want me to."

The tightness inside her eased. This was what she'd been longing to hear. Except that he was offering it to placate her, not because it was what he wanted. This was not the way she wanted to woo him to her bed.

"No, that's okay," she forced herself to say. She apologized for the sharp tone, for the funk that had come over her, that had now passed. She was over it. She was fine. Perfectly fine. Sorry to have bothered him in calling so late.

"It wasn't a bother. I'm always glad to talk to you."

"Call me, tomorrow night?" she asked.

"Of course."

"And Montserrat told me to tell you not to pull any cancellations on her for her Monday night dinner party. She leaves on Tuesday for an East Coast tour."

"I promise you, this time I won't let you down. I swear."

"Okay. Good night."

After they'd disconnected, she sat there, stroking Odette's silky fur. What a load of dark adrenaline running through her. Unprecedented. Good thing it was a one-time occurrence, and fading away even now.

All was well. With a sigh she rose, gave Odette one last pat, and headed upstairs to bed.

Chapter 8 – Lana's Gloomy Day

She smelled the man before she saw him, as she stood at the counter of her neighborhood store, buying a muffin, banana and hot tea. It was the smell of the streets, a cocktail of unwashed clothing, urine, the sickly sweet smell of metabolizing booze. It was a difficult smell any time of the day, but on a Sunday morning it was particularly rank. She turned and saw the man, middle-aged, unshaven, brown hair in wild disarray, wearing an ancient, torn parka and tan trousers that were stained down the front with something wet. What, precisely, she didn't want to know. He took a few more shuffling steps and crashed into the potato chip display stand, which tipped precariously.

The store owner, a scowling Pakistani, shouted at him from behind the counter. The man backed up and took a lunging step toward Lana, who recoiled.

"I'm sorry, miss," he slurred with a grin, as if amused more than offended by her disgust, her unease. His beery breath wafted over to her in a great wave.

"Get out of here, sir," the owner said in a clipped, tight voice.

His son, coming from the back room, was more verbal. "What did I tell you just last week, Coop? Out you go. Stop scaring the customers. Shoo. Now!"

Lana watched the man shuffle out. He was one of the street people who congregated between her apartment building and the adjacent liquor store. She'd sometimes toss a few coins into the hat he'd set out but she preferred to steer clear and avoid eye contact. Conversation was out of the question; she wouldn't have known what to say to someone so down and out.

She paid for her items and took them to the back of the shop where there were a few scuffed Formica tables and chairs. She felt awful this morning; after last night's catastrophe she'd stayed up to watch late-night and late-late night-TV and had consequently overslept. She'd only had time to get dressed, throw what she needed into her dance bag and head out. The shop, fortunately, sold bakery-fresh bran muffins. She sat and ate her muffin, her banana, even though she was too nervous to feel hungry.

It was their first actual rehearsal for *Autumn Souvenir,* following the introductory rehearsal ten days earlier. Denis Rousselot, the stager, would be working concurrently with the two casts of leads. He wanted the second cast to be there, but to remain in back while he focused on Lana and Javier first. This in itself wasn't unusual; Lana had often been part of a second cast, relegated to the back. First cast, as well. But the prospect of the attention here, these days, with everyone assessing her critically, unfavorably, cut her breath short with anxiety. Denis was Paris Opera Ballet-trained, had spent the majority of his career there, and was accustomed to working with performers of the highest caliber. Would he, too, eye her critically, unfavorably?

But he'd chosen her, she reminded herself. He'd decided that she embodied exactly what Benoit Moreau, the French choreographer, now in his eighties, had intended. Denis had been part of *Autumn Souvenir's* 1988 premiere, handpicked and trained by Moreau himself. He'd performed the male lead a half-dozen times with the Paris Opera Ballet, and since retiring, had staged the production internationally twice that amount. He was as accomplished and terrifying as Anders Gunst in some ways. She dared not let either of those men, or her partner, Javier Torres, down.

Enough sitting and fretting; it was stressing her out. She wrapped up the last of her muffin, tossed out the banana peel, grabbed her tea and headed out.

Market Street was calm in the aftermath of Saturday night's revelry. The air slapped her face as she walked. It was fresh, bracing, the sun beginning to peer through as it burned off the morning fog. Her footsteps grew slower as she approached the WCBT building, quiet and all but deserted on a Sunday morning. Inside the building, just past security, she consulted the day's rehearsal sheet tacked on the bulletin board and saw that Denis was holding his rehearsals in the second floor studio. She headed over, her heart thumping louder with each step. Closer to the room, she heard voices. She peered in.

Denis was talking with the four female corps dancers who'd just finished their rehearsal with him. Ben was there, too, but on the phone, engrossed in conversation. She recognized Courtney and one of her close friends, Gabrielle, a tall dancer with wide green eyes that seemed too big for her face, lending her a permanently startled expression. They were easing off their pointe shoes while chatting with Denis. The accompanist was collecting her music, preparing to leave.

Otherwise, no one. She'd been expecting a crowd, and instead there was this. Denis looked up at Lana, perplexed. "Hello, what are you doing here?" he asked in his French-tinted English.

It was like something out of a bad dream. "I'm on the schedule," she said. "Javier and I. The two casts of lead couples, right?"

"Didn't one of the girls here call you? They were supposed to call you." He directed his frown to the women.

"I called Javier, like you said," Gabrielle said. "And he called the other couple."

"I did call her," Courtney said to Denis. "Her voice mail picked up. I guessed maybe she was already on her way here."

"Well, why didn't you call her earlier?" Denis snapped.

"I'm sorry, I didn't have her number on me. I had to go hunt down the roster and when I came back, you were shouting at me to pay attention. I called when I could." She flashed an apologetic glance at Lana. "Sorry."

Lana pulled out her phone and sure enough, a missed message. Likely when she'd been walking down Market, where the street sounds had overridden the phone's chime.

Denis turned to Lana. "I'm sorry to do this to you. This is a rarity, I promise. Something has come up and I can't remain for the second rehearsal. We'll plan on meeting on Tuesday afternoon, though, yes? I am sorry you had to leave your home on a Sunday morning for nothing."

"Oh, it's no problem. No problem at all," Lana said.

Disappointment engulfed her. She didn't want to go home. Not when all those terrible thoughts and the memory of what had happened last night were there, lying in wait for her to enter the room, where they'd swoop down and suffocate her. How ironic, that she'd been dreading this rehearsal, all but wishing it away, and now it was gone, with nothing to protect her.

She stood there, unsure of what to do next, even as everyone around her moved busily. Ben, still on his phone call, offered Lana a distracted smile and wave. The female dancers ignored her.

"All right, *je vous laisse, mes filles*," Denis said, shouldering his bag and picking up his empty coffee cup and joining Ben, who was now heading out the door, still on the phone. "I am, as you say, out of here. I'll see all of you on Tuesday."

"*Au revoir*, Denis," Courtney trilled. One of the corps dancers followed the two men out as Courtney gathered her things and turned to Gabrielle. "Ready?"

"Just about." Gabrielle finished wrapping the pink satin ribbons around her pointe shoes, tucking in the tips. She stowed them into her bag and eased into her sandals. "You joining us?" she asked the other corps dancer.

She smiled, pleased. "Sure, why not?"

Gabrielle hesitated and turned to Lana. "We're going out for a coffee. Do you want to join us?"

She heard the reluctance in Gabrielle's voice, the way the other two averted their eyes, busying themselves with arranging the contents of their dance bags. "Gosh, thanks," Lana said. "But I think I'll just head back home. Stop in on a friend who lives nearby." She envisioned Coop, shuffling over to his spot, his bedroll, by Lana's building. Her good friend Coop.

"Well, okay," Gabrielle said, and the relief from the corps dancers was palpable. "Have a nice visit with your friend."

"I will. See you guys in class tomorrow morning."

The street people were up and about by the time she returned to her street. A grizzled black man hunched in a grimy jacket called out for spare change in a voice that sounded accusing, almost like a challenge. Another man stumbled past, raving and muttering to himself about the motherfucker who'd pay, he'd *pay* for that, man, that *motherfucker* would *pay.* The last bit, shouted out as his eyes darted about wildly, caused the pedestrians to create a wide berth around him.

Coop, more lucid now, was standing by his bedroll in front of her building. He'd changed his trousers, she noticed, and combed his hair. He caught her glance and nodded at her, which she found disconcerting.

"It was a chilly one last night," he said to her. "That wind."

"It still is pretty chilly," she agreed. A burst of altruism came over her. "Can I buy you a cup of coffee to warm you up?" She gestured to the store he'd been kicked out of earlier.

He smiled. "I'd surely like that."

She bought the coffee and brought it out to him. Their hands touched in the transfer, his so rough, calloused and cold, they felt more like gloves than flesh. She pulled her own hands back quickly, bade him farewell. He thanked her profusely before settling into his nook, breathing in the coffee fumes, warming his hands on the cup.

As she trudged up the stairs to her floor, she was heartened by the thought that they'd established a sort of camaraderie. Maybe this would turn out to be the friendship that defined her life here. Not Gil after all.

The thought produced a dull, dreary ache.

Inside, she listened to her phone messages. Sure enough, the promised message from Courtney, left ridiculously late; how had Courtney thought she'd get it in time? She listened, as well, to the previous night's messages from Mom. The first one was polite confusion—had Lana gotten the time wrong? The second sounded wounded, that clearly Lana was having too much fun in her new life to remember her poor mother, who'd only been trying to help anyway. The third was Mom's voice, chilly with anger, telling her to call.

Lana called now, dreading the confrontation, but well aware that the longer she waited, the worse Mom would be. Dad answered and told Lana that Mom was at the grocery store. Lana, relieved, asked him to put Luke on the line instead.

Luke was Lana's favorite brother, smaller and slower to develop than his twin, Marty. The doctors kept assuring Mom he was still within normal standards on both motor and mental development, but he'd always required extra effort and attention. For Lana it had been a pleasure to lavish attention on him; he was the sweetest of the Kessler kids and never complained. For Mom, however, Lana knew Luke's developmental delays meant extra work, particularly when last year's kindergarten teacher suggested they keep Luke behind for another year, while moving Marty on to first grade. Mom, looking forward to more daytime hours without kids underfoot, had been crushed.

Luke entertained her, breathlessly detailing every little event going on in his classroom at school, his ever-expanding Lego Star Wars collection, his latest Pokémon card acquisitions. Then pure delight filled his voice. "Lana, guess what?! Mom just walked in!"

Lana squeezed her eyes shut. "Oh, goodie!"

"I guess you'll want to talk to her now, huh?"

"I guess I should."

"Well," Mom said coolly when she came on the phone a moment later. "Hello."

"Mom, I'm so sorry. Something came up."

"I guess."

"Please, I'm sorry. It was so unexpected."

"Where were you?"

"I was invited to a party at the last minute. With friends."

"But you told me you hadn't made any friends. You told me that, Friday night, about how lonely and homesick you were."

"I was. I am. But then this, um, new friend who was showing me around on Saturday, insisted I go to last night's party. Three of us did. We went together, me and this woman."

"And a man, I take it."

"Oh, well, yes."

"What was his name?"

"Well, my friend's name is Alice. That's the girl."

"I'm not dumb, Lana. I would have figured out that was the girl. I asked you what the boy's name was."

"Gil."

"Just Gil?"

"Gil Sheridan," she stammered. "He's from Chicago. Catholic, like us."

Lana, knowing her mother, continued to emphasize how she'd gone to the party with Alice, left with Alice, spent extra time with her afterward. In a burst of inspiration she brought up Coop, her new friend Coop. Who was a guy. They'd gotten a coffee earlier this morning, in fact.

She could almost hear Mom's brain ticking and whirring, looking for holes in the story. When Mom spoke again, she sounded suspicious. "You watch those boys. You're a pretty girl and that California liberalness—oh, I've heard all about it. You tell those boys to keep their hands out of your pants, do you hear me?"

"Mom!" Lana protested, her cheeks growing hot. "Please."

"You listen to me here, Lana. I know men."

"As it turns out, you're so far off the mark with Coop, you just don't know. He's this humble guy who only wants to have a quiet life and exchange conversation from time to time."

"So, this Coop. He's not the one who kissed you last night?"

"Mom! Of course not!"

Too late, she realized the correct answer should have been, *"Nobody kissed me, what on earth are you talking about?"*

For a moment neither of them spoke.

"That Gil character," Mom said. "I can just see him. Handsome, charming, making you feel like the only one in the room."

A chill came over her, that Mom had Gil so well pegged.

"Watch that type, Lana. They'll only break your heart." A heavy sigh followed. "Oh, I hate that you're alone out there, without family."

"This woman, Alice, you'd respect her, Mom. She's sort of no-nonsense and she really did watch over me last night. And, oh, Mom, guess what? I met her friend, a famous violinist, and she played last night in a recital with—you're not going to believe this—the cellist guy from the commercials. Matthew Nakamura! I got to meet them and talk with them. They're all friends with Alice."

"Well. Lucky you."

It grew quiet. Too quiet. She'd successfully diverted the conversation away from Gil, only to land here. The omnipresent knot deep in her stomach, dormant for so long, began to stir. "Enough about me," Lana said. "How are you doing?"

"Fine. I guess."

It wasn't the words; it never was. It might not even be the expression on Mom's face. She could be smiling, but Lana would know, the instant things shifted. It was as perceptible as the shift in the air when storm clouds swept over the sky and you could smell the moisture, feel the turbulence swirl around you, making your skin prickle in anticipation.

"Is it your back, or the kids?" Lana asked, trying to inject equal amounts of sympathy and cheer in her tone.

Mom issued a heavy exhale, one that managed to convey fatigue, exasperation, discouragement, and the burden of lifelong pain. "The doctor is saying I should take a thirty-minute rest every afternoon. What is he thinking? That I live a life of leisure?"

"Oh, Mom, it's my being gone, isn't it? Those afternoon breaks that you're losing out on now."

"Well, maybe so," Mom admitted.

"I'm so sorry I'm not around to help out anymore. I feel awful. And I miss you guys so much."

This seemed to cheer Mom up. "Well, we all miss you too. Apparently more than you miss us."

She bristled. "I think about you all the time. Last night was the first time I'd done anything social and fun since I arrived. You don't think I'm lonely the other ninety-eight percent of the time?" Her voice caught at these last words.

"Well, that's good."

"That's *good*?"

"What I mean to say is, that shows you love your family. That we're important to you."

"Of course you are. Was there ever any question? Do you think this is easy for me, being all alone out here?"

It was as if the full force of Gil's betrayal hit her all at once. Had it really only been yesterday afternoon that she'd been out with him, flying so high? Only to land so hard, so low. She wanted to climb under her blankets and cry.

"Honey," Mom said after a pause, "just remember what I told you. There's no shame in coming home, if all this proves to be too much. You just come right back to us."

How good it felt right then to hear the conviction in Mom's voice. "I'll be okay," she said. "I just need a quiet day, a good night's sleep."

"All right. But you call me, any time you're down, you understand?"

"I will. Thanks, Mom."

"You're welcome. Bye-bye, honey."

After a long afternoon of reading and napping, a dinner of grilled cheese and Campbell's chicken noodle soup (comfort food, Luke's favorite), Lana settled down for the night, finding solace in all the little rituals. Teeth brushing. Washing her face and applying moisturizer. Making sure she had clean tights and leotards for tomorrow, hand-washing a few for Tuesday. At the thought of company class, her heaviness lightened. This was the single best reality of her dance life: there would always be class. This reassuring sameness, day after day, year after year grounded her, defined her. And tomorrow afternoon there would be a rehearsal for the sprightly *Arpeggio,* with the partnered trios of dancers, some of whom were warming to Lana. That counted for something.

If it was the best life was going to hand her tonight, she'd take it.

Chapter 9 – Interviews and Interlopers

The thick fog that blanketed the city on Monday morning mirrored the subdued atmosphere in the WCBT offices. Employees shuffled in, heads bent, mumbling their hellos to one another in froggy voices. Coffees in hand, they made their way to their various cubicles and offices, the ensuing clatter of fingers to keyboard lackluster compared to the way it would sound by mid-morning. Alice, holed up in her tiny office, didn't expect to see much of Gil this morning. He tended to be elusive on Mondays, in and out of meetings and off-site. Given the weekend's drama and Alice's reproof when he'd come by to pick up his car, she sensed today he would be all but invisible.

She looked up from the report she was drafting to see Lucinda, the director of public relations, striding toward her office. Her heart sank. It was too early in the morning for Lucinda.

They'd known each other for years, since training as administrative assistants together, Lucinda in public relations, Alice in special events. Lucinda, already holding a college degree, had been promoted long before Alice, who'd been juggling part-time work with college classes. Even though Alice had obtained her own degree and risen up the ranks as well, Lucinda continued to lord over her with the overfamiliarity and scorn of a big sister, never mind that Alice was three years her senior.

"Sarah is out sick today," Lucinda called out without preamble. "She has an interview with a reporter from the *San Francisco Arts Times*. The reporter won't reschedule, she says this *is* a reschedule. No interview today, no feature article. I'd do it, but I'm booked all day."

Sarah was the director of special events. Apparently Lucinda still harbored the notion that Alice should be forever affiliated with that department.

"Sarah has her own assistant," Alice reminded Lucinda.

"She's too green. She's only been here four months and says she's afraid she'll get a fact wrong and get quoted on it. She has a point. So, you need to do it."

"Need to? Or you'd like me to? Because I've got my own work here, you know."

Lucinda gave an exaggerated sigh, hinting at the troubles that lay on her shoulders, troubles Alice alone was exacerbating.

"Alice. I need your help, please."

"Oh, all right, I'll do it."

"Thank you." Lucinda handed Alice a press release. "The interview is at ten o'clock. The journalist will meet you here." She tapped a finger on the press release, which Alice had set on the desk without looking at it. "Those are the details I'd like you to share with her. Stick to facts, not opinions. Do not bring up any of the dancers' names or quirks. Remember that the integrity of the WCBT and its dancers is at stake every time one of us speaks to the press."

"Oh, give it a rest, Lucinda. I've taken interviews before, you know."

"Well, just be careful. That's all I'm saying."

"Of course I'll be careful. Now, if you don't mind, I'd like to get through this report before that interview interrupts my morning."

Lucinda offered her a curt nod. "Fine. And, um, thanks."

The reporter arrived at ten, a pale, waif-like girl with sharp, intelligent eyes and expression that belied the waif persona. She introduced herself as Sam, offered Alice a firm handshake, and launched right into her questions. Alice steered each one around to the subject of the October fundraising event, the WCBT in general, to which Alice then offered staid, Lucinda-sanctioned replies, straight from the press release. The interview had all the charisma and spice of a bowl of Quaker Oats without the raisins and brown sugar.

Sam paused her onslaught of questions to peer around the office. Her eyes settled on a framed photo on the wall, an old publicity shot of Alice in an arabesque en pointe, taken from a dress rehearsal performance of the ill-fated *Tomorrow's Lament.* The photo was the sole nod to her dancer's past, doubling as a cautionary reminder of what happened when you didn't pay attention on the job. She'd almost forgotten about it, up there next to her college diploma.

"Wow," Sam said. "That's so pretty. So mesmerizing."

Alice smiled. "It is a nice photo, isn't it? It really captures the artistry of both photography and dance—the play of light against the black floor, the purity of body lines, the expression on my face."

"On your face," Sam echoed, puzzled. Her eyes widened. "Do you mean to say that's you?"

"Well, yes," she admitted.

"You were a dancer with *this* company?"

"Years ago." Alice gave an expansive little wave of her hand.

"That was another life."

"How long ago?"

"Eight years. And we all know how much things change in that time." Reluctant to revisit the subject that had brought her such distress on Saturday night, Alice seized on this new issue.

"The performing arts world and its audiences are really evolving. We've had to work hard and rethink the equation. How do you sustain interest in ballet in an era when so many other entertainment options exist now? I have to say, I think the West Coast Ballet Theatre has done a stellar job in capturing the pulse of the 21st century and capitalizing on it. Which is crucial."

Sam nodded and shot another glance at the photo. "So, if I might ask. Why did you switch to administration?"

Today her composure held.

"Oh, an injury forced me to reconsider my priorities. Through pursuing my degree, I discovered dance administration was a better fit." Alice angled her head toward Sam's notepad. "Anyway. Do you have any other questions for me? About the October event?"

"Whoops, sorry." Sam looked at her notes, checked off an item and posed the next question.

Ten minutes later they finished. Alice shook Sam's hand, escorted her to the elevator, and with a sigh of relief, returned to her own, safer work.

Monday evening was the dinner party at Montserrat and Carter's. She'd had the inspiration that morning to walk the two miles into work and take a taxi over to their place, so Niles could drive her home afterward. She hadn't, however, factored in the futility of trying to catch a taxi at rush hour. Taxi after taxi had whizzed past, full of attendees from nearby Moscone Center, which clearly had disgorged thousands of conventioneers around the same time.

Finally she arrived at their house, tired and stressed. Carter met her at the door with a broad smile. Montserrat's husband was much like Niles, minus the ponytail, and brown eyes instead of grey, but with the same breezy sense of humor and intelligence.

"You're late," he said, relieving her of the bottles of wine she was carrying. "And someone's been very insistent about seeing you."

Carter shut the front door and a moment later Niles was there, sidling up behind her. He wrapped his arms around her, whispered hello against her neck. The tactile pressure of his body against hers, the scent of him, made the tight, anxious knot in her loosen.

He gave her a squeeze, a soft kiss on the cheek. "I just met your friend," he said.

"My friend?"

"Lana, I think Montserrat said her name was."

She turned to face him. "I'm confused," she said slowly. "My friend, *Lana?*"

"Surprise!" Montserrat cried as she stepped out of the kitchen and into the living room. Alice pivoted around and there she was, right beside Montserrat.

Lana.

Everyone laughed at Alice's gape-mouthed expression, her stuttered words that she didn't expect to see Lana here, what a surprise, indeed. A timer went off in the kitchen and Montserrat hurried back in.

"Ladies, have a seat," Carter said. "Alice, what can I get you to drink?"

Niles patted the seat next to him on the couch. She sat, still in a daze. "Oh, whatever Niles is drinking."

"Coke," said Niles, gesturing to his glass.

Alice frowned. "Coke?"

He looked guilty. "I'm still sort of on the clock. Need to put in a few more hours of work tonight when I go home."

"Oh, Niles." Alice was too disappointed to say anything more.

Carter held up his own glass of red wine. "Alice, am I safe in assuming you'd prefer this?"

"Yes," Alice said. "Super-size me. Please."

Once Carter had poured her a glass, she left Lana and the men in the living room to seek out Montserrat's company in the kitchen. "Anything I can do?" Alice asked Montserrat, who was measuring the ingredients for her vinaigrette into a mason jar.

"Oh, thanks, but I think we're all set. Lana pitched in. She's quite the little helper."

"Um, I guess so."

Montserrat glanced at Alice. "You don't mind, do you? That I invited her?"

"Of course not," she lied. "It's just rather out of context seeing her here, in your house."

"She was over at the performing arts library—we saw each other in the foyer." Montserrat screwed the jar onto the vinaigrette mixture and began to shake it. "She was done with rehearsals for the day, so she'd been killing time all afternoon watching archived ballet performances and taking notes. Anything besides going back home. The poor thing seems rather out of sorts in her new life still. From the sound of it, she's made no friends except Gil and you."

"Whoa." Alice held up her hands. "She's not my friend. Not like that."

Montserrat's brow furrowed. "But when we talked last night you told me the two of you had a long talk on Saturday night."

"Well, yes. We did."

"Uh, oh. Did I get things wrong?"

"No, I told you it's okay."

"She was afraid you would mind."

"Why would I mind?"

"That's what I told her." Montserrat set down the jar and surveyed the kitchen. "Well, that's it for prep work. Let's go join the others."

When they entered the living room, Niles and Carter were each examining one of Lana's pointe shoes, turning the peach satin shoes this way and that. In spite of her grumpiness, Alice smiled.

"Oh, look at that," she said. Lana glanced up at her hesitantly. "You wear Freeds."

"I do," Lana said. "The guys were asking about them, and I had a brand-new pair here in my bag."

"I wore Freeds, too. Pretty much everyone in the company did." She moved over to Niles, sat and peered closer at the torpedo-shaped shoe in his hand. "God. It's been years since I've seen one of these up close."

"Does it make you nostalgic?" Niles asked.

"Not really. I had such a love-hate relationship with my pointe shoes. I don't think my feet were ever completely free of pain once I started dancing en pointe."

"I'd have to say the same," Lana confessed.

Niles tapped the side of the shoe on the coffee table. It gave a hollow *thwack* in reply. "Boy, it's no wonder," he said. "These are like plywood. I never would have guessed."

"You have to break them in," Lana said.

"How?"

In response, Lana reached into her dance bag and pulled out a ball-peen hammer. "Using this on them, or slamming them against a wall."

"Or sticking them in a doorjamb and closing the door on them," Alice added.

Lana nodded. "Sometimes I'll pour rubbing alcohol over the box while I'm wearing them, too. That helps break down the glue in the area around my bunions. At least temporarily."

"And these shoes, once they're broken in, how long do they last?" Carter asked. "I'll bet you go through several pairs a year, don't you?"

Lana and Alice exchanged amused, superior glances and began to chuckle.

"Okay, so I've proven I know nothing about ballet shoes," he said. "Care to enlighten me?"

Lana made a "you explain" gesture to Alice, who told the others how the shoes, once properly broken in, could last anywhere from twenty minutes onstage to a full night of performing. After that the toe, the spot that the full body weight rested on, got too soft and the shoe was only good for class or practice.

Niles shook his head. "That has to get expensive."

"Sixty to eighty bucks a pop," Alice said. "Although in a professional company you don't have to pay. What does the current contract give you?" she asked Lana.

"One hundred twenty pairs a season. Twice as many as I got in Kansas City. I'm in heaven."

This astounded the others. Carter leaned closer. "So, how does a dancer come up with that kind of money if they're not in a professional company?"

"You wear them a lot longer," Alice said. "Wince through the too-soft spots where your toes make contact with the ground. Pour shellac into the toe spot of the box to try and avoid that. Tell your parents you really, really need to buy another pair. Oh, the wars I had with my father when I was a teenager. I kept telling him the soft ones were hurting my toes, but I still had to make do with only one or two pairs a month."

She turned to Lana. "What about you? Were your parents that stingy?"

Lana abruptly shifted her gaze downward. Her shoulders rose and fell in a noncommittal shrug. "Oh, I found a way to get by."

No one spoke. Lana, realizing the others were waiting to hear more, looked up. "Well," she said, "the thing is…" She faltered.

This time the pause was distinctly awkward, as if they were all rehearsing a play and someone had forgotten their lines, important lines, lines that were required for the rest of the scene to make sense.

"Go ahead, Lana," Montserrat said. "We're all friends here."

Lana studied the ball-peen hammer she'd set on the coffee table. "They didn't have money for pointe shoes at all. We weren't poor, really, it was just considered an unnecessary expense, especially after my little brothers were born and there were six of us kids. So I had to earn it myself."

"By babysitting, or something?" Alice asked. "That's what I ended up doing."

Lana laughed, a hollow sound devoid of mirth. "Oh, I did that in my own house. Without pay. No, I, well, cleaned houses."

"You cleaned houses," Alice repeated carefully, and Lana nodded.

"I was doing it at home anyway, to help out my mom, and I learned how to do it fast. If I worked hard and was organized about it, I could do one right after school, before that afternoon's dance class." Lana spoke in a dogged fashion, still focusing on the hammer. "Another house I did first thing in the morning, once a week, before school started. Summers, I could pick my own hours. And that's how I paid for my pointe shoes. My leotards and tights. A car to get me to and from classes."

Lana, a cleaning lady. Alice didn't know what to say.

Montserrat did. She rose and went over to where Lana was sitting. "I did something very similar," she told Lana. "No financial support in the least from my parents. They thought taking violin lessons was frivolous. So, from an early age, I ran my own little laundry service. I came in, changed out the sheets, the towels, washed my clients' dirty stuff, ironed and starched their shirts."

Lana stared. "You're kidding."

"I'm not. Like I was telling you, we're not as different as you think."

Alice was speechless with shock, not just about hearing this facet of Montserrat's life, but that Montserrat had divulged more to Lana than she ever had to Alice. Much more. How could Lana have simply marched in and won over Montserrat, her own special friend, so quickly?

"Cleaning up someone else's mess," Lana said to Montserrat, "it paid great, but it felt demeaning. Especially knowing some of the other girls in my ballet classes had maids in their households. I was in the studio on scholarship and they knew it. I was a total outsider. If they'd found out about my work, they would've ostracized me even more."

Montserrat was sitting close to Lana, her arm around Lana's thin shoulders. "Working hard to support your craft is one of the most noble, powerful things you could have done. It will always define you and your artistry. Sure, it was hard, definitely humbling, but you should feel nothing but pride about it now. You alone made your success happen."

Lana offered Montserrat a tremulous smile. "Rich people," she said. "They just don't get it. They're all self-centered and spoiled."

Montserrat glanced at Alice and so did Lana. Her eyes widened. "Not all rich people are like that, though," Lana added hastily. "Some are really nice. The greatest."

"Nice try," Alice said, and the others laughed. Alice and Lana didn't.

"Alice has a great family," Niles said. "Good people, wonderful hosts. And, all right, they happen to live in a rather nice house."

"I'll second all of that," Montserrat said, laughing.

"They're here, in San Francisco?" Lana asked.

Alice nodded.

"What neighborhood?"

Why on earth was this girl making her feel ashamed? "Pacific Heights," she said, studying her wine glass.

"I know where that is," Lana said. "It's in movies and such. It's nice."

Another nod; she couldn't very well deny it.

"Did you grow up there, in that same house?" Lana asked.

"Yes." Alice set the glass down and met Lana's gaze.

"So, if I can ask. Did you have a nanny?"

"Excuse me?"

"What I'm wondering is, did someone besides your mom drive you to your ballet classes and pick you up? Like, did your family have hired help?"

The flash of spirit in Lana's eyes surprised her. The girl knew how to hold her own, after all. It was both affirming and disconcerting to observe.

"Yes," she admitted. "For a few years, my family had a nanny."

"I thought maybe so. You look like you grew up around wealth. I mean that in a good way," she added. "You're so elegant and polished and together." She offered Alice and the others a self-deprecating smile, a helpless shrug. "I'm jealous. I would have given anything to have switched places with you."

She could have replied in a variety of ways, most of which would have produced the same uncomfortable silence Lana's cleaning-lady admission had. But she was a Willoughby. Willoughbys didn't expose, or attempt to explain, those kind of things. "No," she told Lana. "Trust me. I don't think you would have wanted that."

An uncomfortable silence ensued anyway.

"Alice?" Montserrat spoke up. She caught Alice's eye. She knew this part of Alice's past; she and Niles both, but only Montserrat seemed to have figured out the chronology. "Maybe you want to…"

"No." Alice cut her off. No, she would not elaborate to Lana and the others why she'd had a nanny from age eight to thirteen. She would not rehash her young girl's trauma in order to solicit their sympathy.

"Sure," Montserrat said. "Okay." She nudged the appetizer tray in the direction of the others. "All right, people. Eat my fine cheeses and prosciutto," she commanded. "Do it, or there'll be no dinner served."

The tension eased. Even Alice could join the laughter this time.

But in spite of Montserrat's efforts, the rest of the evening seemed tainted for Alice. Every little breezy exchange, about families, careers that were exhausting in spite of your success in them, work that consumed you, seemed to offer the other four people a connection and a chance to chuckle, nod in commiseration. Everyone except for Alice. On the surface, she could fake it. After all, she had a career, the "much better suited for me" one outside of the other, destroyed one. She had the mom she even called "my mom" so it didn't stand out—she'd been doing that since age thirteen, with Marianne's permission and encouragement. But her spirits were working opposite of everyone else's, as if she were a pulley and by pulling her side down, she was hoisting everyone else's level higher and higher.

Lana, in contrast, grew more animated, encouraged by the others' interest and Montserrat's warm smile. Over coffee she told them about the WCBT's fall schedule. There'd be a pre-season series of local performances before heading out on a West Coast tour for three weeks. Upon their return, they'd start preparation for *Nutcracker.*

"Alice and I will have to come watch you perform," Niles said. He turned to Alice with an expectant smile.

Her reply was automatic. "I don't attend the ballet."

Niles looked confused. "Why not?"

"Because I don't do that anymore."

"But you work there. And now there's Lana to see."

"Sorry."

"Oh, come on. All women want to drag their boyfriends to the ballet, and here I am offering."

"I believe I've stated my position." Her voice grew sharp. "All right?"

Niles blinked at her, twice, then flashed the others a smile. "And that's my cue to go creep off and get Alice some more wine." He hesitated, looked at the empty glass, perplexed. "But wait. I thought I just poured you a glass, ten minutes ago."

"You did."

"Oh. I see." His confused frown deepened. "Sweets, you're not driving tonight, are you?"

"No. I took a taxi here," she bit out. "Thinking you might give me a ride home."

"Of course I will. I'd love to." He laid a hand on her thigh, massaged it softly and looked, really looked into her eyes. It felt like a life raft. She reached out and clutched his hand.

"You okay?" he murmured.

"Sure." She eased her grip.

"Okay. Good."

He turned to Lana, and to Alice's dismay, proceeded to offer her a ride home as well. "Or do you have a car nearby?" he asked.

Lana laughed. "Me? I can barely afford to live in this city, much less own and park a car."

Because only rich people had cars and private parking in San Francisco.

Here we go again.

"But I don't need a ride," Lana added, casting a nervous glance at Alice. "I can take a bus, no problem."

"Buses aren't too efficient in this part of town, after nine o'clock," Montserrat said.

"Well, a taxi," Lana said, but Niles cut her off.

"Absolutely not. Not when I'm headed in that direction to drop off Alice. You said you lived near the Civic Center?"

"On Taylor, close to Market Street."

Niles frowned. "That's the Tenderloin. Oh, we're definitely not letting you take public transportation back there."

Great. They'd pass her own neighborhood en route; what if Niles decided to drop her off first? She was not ready to watch Niles and Lana drive off together as she stood on her steps, alone for the night. "Um, Niles?" she asked, an edge creeping back into her voice.

"Alice," Niles said. "This is the Tenderloin we're talking here. Look at her." They all looked at Lana, so cute and delicate, sitting there on the couch, now squirming under their gazes.

There was no elegant way out of this mess. Except to drink more red wine. And more.

Twenty minutes later Niles looked at his watch. "Whoops. How did it get that late? I really need to get moving."

They all rose from the table. The room was starting to come at Alice in blurry angles. When she walked it was in a distorted, ponderous fashion, as if someone had affixed ten-pound weights to the bottom of each shoe while she'd been sitting.

At the front door, Montserrat studied Alice. "Everything all right?" she asked.

"Everything's fine." The words came out strident but slurred. Montserrat nodded, told her to get a good night's sleep, that she'd call her when she returned from her East Coast tour.

On the drive back toward the Civic Center, Niles glanced at the dashboard clock. "Ten-thirty," he muttered. "Damn. This is going to be a challenge." Alice kept silent, holding her breath until he'd driven safely past her street without turning. Lana, sensing tension, remained quiet as well, speaking up from the back seat only to offer directions to her apartment. Once they'd arrived, she slid out of the back seat quickly, thanking them both. Alice offered her a polite nod but Niles was more animated, smiling warmly, telling her no problem, nice to meet her. Even after they'd returned to traffic, he was still smiling over the exchange. "She's a cutie," he said.

Alice gave no reply and within moments, his preoccupation had returned. They drove the rest of the way in silence. He parked his car in her driveway and, to her relief, cut the engine and joined her on the sidewalk, taking her hand. Inside the house, Odette came padding into the entryway with a glad meow. Niles stooped to rub behind Odette's ears, murmuring his hellos before stepping away to use the bathroom.

Alice plopped down on the sofa with a sigh. The room spun and stopped, spun and stopped. Niles was here, she told herself. The rest would now fall into place. He'd make the spinning deeper inside of her stop.

Niles returned to the living room a minute later holding a can of Diet Coke. "You don't mind, do you?" he asked, raising the can.

"Of course not." She patted the couch cushion beside her.

He approached, leaned over and kissed her, but straightened right back up. "I'm off, then," he said.

She stared at him. "Wait. Not so soon."

"I'm sorry, sweets. I told you I'd need to get moving."

She rose with some difficulty, took the can out of his hand, setting it down on the coffee table before looping her arms around him. His arms slid around her waist, hands pressing into the small of her back. He squeezed her, gave her a soft kiss on the cheek. All too soon, he released her. She hadn't let go of her own grip yet, though, so he couldn't reach down and get the Coke can from the table, as seemed to be his intention.

"Niles," she murmured, pressing her lips against his neck. "Please stay."

"I can't."

He finally reached up and unclasped her hands from behind his neck. He gave them a pat, kissed her again, an impersonal little peck this time. Then he reached down and picked his can back up.

She hated this turbulence inside her, this desperate sense of ungroundedness. "Please. I really want you to stay a little longer." Her voice broke.

"Alice," he said, "this is such bad timing." He shifted from foot to foot, as if frantic with the need to keep moving.

"Well," Alice snapped, patience now spent, "it was pretty bad timing, as well, that Lana had to pick tonight to join us."

He paused. "What does Lana have to do with anything here?"

"Oh, forget it. Never mind. Just go."

He stood there, perplexed, hands out, elbows bent, as if expecting her to deliver her next comment in a ten-pound potato sack that he'd need to catch. But she said no more. He let his hands fall with a little slap against his legs.

"Fine. Fine. I'll stay. Let's go upstairs."

Like hell. She dredged up the last vestiges of her pride, lying there in a neglected heap on the floor, much in the same way their clothes used to do. "I don't think that's a good idea anymore." She marched, albeit unsteadily, over to the door and swung it open. "Good night."

He was still standing in the same spot, looking at her. "Look. I'll call you. Tomorrow it will seem—"

"No." Alice's voice cut through his words. Gone, the drunken slurring, the weepy, needy emotions. In its place was the Alice who'd always saved her when no one else could. Her inner bitch. A friend in need.

"No, Niles. Do not call me tomorrow. Do not call me until you are free. Work on your goddamned report. Achieve your goddamned checkpoint. Go on your business trip and wow everyone. But don't expect me to sit in the corner and wait for you."

"I never asked or expected you to do that." He looked sad.

The truth of his words cut through her.

"No. You didn't. I guess I overestimated my importance in your life." She drew in a ragged breath and before she could stop them, the terrible words slipped out.

"Maybe we're better off as just friends. So neither of us has to worry about the unreasonable demands I appear to be making on you."

Worse than the words was the fact that he didn't reply. No protest, no heated defense. Just silence.

Terrible silence.

He studied her grimly, his chin working. Without a word he

walked to the front door. She was unsteady; she clutched the door for support. Odette came up and mewed anxiously. They both gazed down at her.

"Alice," Niles began a moment later, but one look at her angry eyes made him fall silent. He leaned forward as if to kiss her forehead. She recoiled.

He exhaled, let his shoulders drop in an exaggerated "I tried" fashion. "Fine. We'll talk when I return. Because clearly there's nothing right I can do or say at this moment. Except wish you a good night."

"Good night." She offered him a curt nod, watched him descend the steps and make his way to his car. She shut the door, locked it, gathered up Odette, who'd been brushing against her leg. Clutching the cat, she buried her face in the silky fur, not even realizing she was squeezing until the cat meowed in protest.

What had she done?

What had she just *done*?

She could only think of one positive aspect of the disaster she'd just made of her precious, nurturing, too-good-to-be-true relationship.

Life couldn't snatch away from you what you'd already destroyed yourself.

Chapter 10 – Apology

When Lana arrived at her Tuesday afternoon rehearsal for *Autumn Souvenir*, the eight corps dancers were still rehearsing their parts. Denis saw her, offering her a quick, distracted smile and nod. She smiled back and claimed a spot in a corner of the room where she stretched, pulled out a pair of pointe shoes and began to put them on. They were in the smaller studio that day, which had a piano in the corner, a black, taped-down marley floor and a high open ceiling, the ventilation tubing still visible. She could smell the hazelnut coffee someone had brought in. It was a soothing smell.

It was the only soothing thing coming from the room, however. Denis did not seem happy. He'd shooed away the four male dancers, who now lounged off to the side, watching.

"Take it again, ladies, from your second entrance," Denis said. The accompanist cued their entrance but after sixteen counts, Denis slapped his hand down on the back of the metal fold-up chair he'd straddled. "*Non, non!* Gabrielle, what is that supposed to be? Autumn? You're giving me frozen winter, not winds of autumn. You must give me some air, some space under those feet in the petit allegro section. Again."

Lana could see by the obstinate tilt to Gabrielle's chin and the tension between her and Denis, that it had been a contentious rehearsal. Gabrielle glanced over at Lana and her expression grew even tighter. The four women danced the same passage again, and once again Denis stopped them.

"Lana," he called out. "Are you warmed up? Would you please show Gabrielle how to give me some air beneath her entrechats-quatre?"

He turned to Gabrielle. "You watch this dancer. She has what I'm looking for here. She is airborne all the time—that is what the eye sees. You? Your feet are heavy clumps of mud. That is what the eye sees with you."

As Lana rose, Gabrielle's lip began to tremble. "I can't believe you're doing this to me," she said to Denis.

Lana froze, bewildered. They were all a tableau of stillness, the other corps dancers, Gabrielle and Denis, gazes locked in a standoff. Lana looked from one to the other.

"Gabrielle," Denis said, "your job is to dance this part in the way I instruct you. Your other sadnesses, your difficulties, do not belong here."

"Excuse me, Denis, but maybe this is hard for me."

"This is not hard. Dancing with an injury, yes, that is hard. Dancing when influenza is consuming you, that is hard too. You are feeling sad? Aggrieved? This is a child's version of hardness."

Gabrielle said nothing. A moment later she began to sniff, dab at her eyes.

Denis scowled. "We have work to do here and I need cooperation, not resistance. Lana. Come over here."

"Fine," Gabrielle cried, "let her take that role, too. Let her take everything!" She swung around in an abrupt turnabout, ran over to her dance bag beneath the barre, grabbed it and fled from the room. The others heard the *clop-clop* of her pointe shoes on the hallway's linoleum, the hoarse sobs that receded as she made her way to the locker room.

The studio was silent. *"Merde!* Shit! *J'en ai ras le bol!"* Denis's curses bounced off the walls, reverberating through the room. "I am fed up with dancers who cannot leave their petty problems at the door. Do you think we have time for this? Do you?" He glared at the other dancers, most of whom avoided his gaze.

Javier appeared at the studio door, frowning. "What was that about?" He gestured with his head in the direction of Gabrielle. "Denis. Was she being difficult again?"

Denis heaved another disgusted sigh. He looked at his watch, told the seven remaining dancers they were out of time anyway, called out for the accompanist to return in ten minutes for the next rehearsal. He joined Javier in the hallway where the two of them began to talk.

The remaining dancers exchanged bemused looks, shrugs. The tension in the room now dissipating, they began to chat among themselves and collect their things. Courtney spied Lana and walked over to her.

"You don't know what's going on, do you?" she asked.

Lana shook her head.

Courtney glanced over at the open door where Denis and Javier were still talking. "Here's the thing," she said in a low voice. "It's just been kind of awkward. You being here, and Gabrielle in the corps of your ballet."

Gabrielle was one of the better corps dancers; Lana understood immediately. She drew an unsteady breath. "She was the corps dancer they might have promoted to soloist, if they hadn't given it to me."

Courtney looked at her in surprise. "So you did know."

"No. I mean, I had a hunch someone had lost out, but I didn't know who. And I've been afraid to ask."

"Well, now you know." Courtney shot another furtive look over her shoulder before continuing. "And further, just between us, it was nearly a done deal. The news that you'd gotten it was a huge shock to her. Because, no offense, we all thought you were going to be in the corps. The roster was pretty well set."

"With her as the new soloist."

Courtney gave a noncommittal shrug, as if reluctant to be the bearer of such uncomfortable news.

Right then, Lana wished the other scenario could have been the case. She would have had friends, support, commiseration. Gabrielle might have been the one earning the dark looks, the envious muttering that she hadn't deserved a lead role. Courtney could have been a friend, not some wary advisor of Lana's wrongdoings.

"I feel so bad." Lana clutched at the chiffon dance skirt she'd pulled from her bag. "And just now, Denis asking me to show her how to improve on the entrechats-quatre passage."

"I know, right? And it gets worse. I don't know if you knew this, but Gabrielle and Javier are dating. She's head over heels in love with him."

"I didn't know they were involved. Oh, God, thank you for telling me."

Courtney acknowledged this with a nod. "And I have to tell you, she's acting pretty insecure about things right now. Him being a principal and all. Now, she'd never admit this, but I have a hunch she's worried you're going to take this from her, too."

"I would never do that!" Lana stared at her, appalled. "Please. Tell her not to worry."

"I will." Courtney offered Lana an encouraging smile. "Anyway, don't give any of it a second thought. Gabrielle's very theatrical. You just focus on doing the best job you can. With one of our best male dancers. Dang. Lucky you!"

She did not feel lucky. Her own anxiety was doubling by the moment.

"Try and have a good rehearsal, regardless," Courtney said. "I mean, it's not like any of this is your fault."

Lana tried to smile back. "Thanks. And thanks for telling me stuff. Really."

She mulled over everything once she was alone in the studio, stretching out at the barre. Chagrin burned her face as she bent over and pressed it against her extended leg. Poor Gabrielle, who'd been polite to Lana since her arrival, perhaps not overly warm but not mean-spirited in the least. She'd even invited Lana to join them for coffee that horrible morning after the Cinderella night with Gil.

Gil.

Her other awkward, painful mess. It had been three days since they'd been together. It felt like trudging through a barren desert, the sun burning down on her, no water or shade in sight. She sensed he would contact her eventually and they'd talk. They were friends, after all. Buddies. In the meantime, she told herself sternly, he was doing her a favor. She'd moved out here to dance. For the first time in her life, it could be all about her craft and nothing more. She didn't need some sticky romantic entanglement mucking up the equation. She reached over her extended right leg, took her heel in her hand and straightened, lifting, tugging, bringing the leg alongside her upper torso until her calf pressed against her temple.

It was her less flexible side, and her muscles protested. Too bad. She tugged harder, holding the leg in place, the coolness of her calf against her hotter face, until the muscles relaxed and the tension began to feel oddly soothing.

This kind of pain she understood. Appreciated, even.

Denis and Javier returned ten minutes later, followed by a small crowd. If *Arpeggio* were like a democracy, three lead couples sharing equal billing and *Serenade* the communist worker-dancer experience, this was like being royalty. And not in a comfortable way.

There was the accompanist, an in-house assistant to take notes on the choreography, the leads for the second cast, the understudies. Javier had an entourage of his own, which included a photographer on assignment and a biographer (a *biographer!*) who followed Javier's movements closely and clung to his every word. Even Denis was deferential toward Javier, although Javier spoke to Denis with equal deference. They were two masters, simply at different places in their careers, and both acknowledged this.

Javier, Cuban-born and trained, was not just a stellar dancer, he was highly perceptive, intelligent, and picked up steps and nuances lightning fast. He could dance passages full out, after seeing them only once, marking them with his hands, his fingers. Lana herself was a quick study, she knew; it was one of the reasons she'd been so popular with Kansas City in the early years and had been promoted to soloist. She could learn a ballet in a matter of hours, if need be, and perform it well that night. She told herself she could hold her own here, against Javier, but even she saw the absurdity of her words, this overly confident little mantra. She was out of her league in this rarified realm, and the best she could hope for was to not make it too obvious.

They worked together, she, Javier and Denis, thirty-two-count increments at a time. Every time Denis said, "ready to move on?" Javier responded "yes" and Lana nodded, too intimidated to contradict. Chaîné turns, interwoven movements, step-steps into overhead grand-jeté lifts, everything articulated and intense. The lifts were astonishing with Javier as a partner. So were the pirouettes, the way his hands spun her in the perfect way, so they didn't slow down her own momentum or throw her off balance. He was a peerless dancer and partner. She wasn't sure whether this made her feel more relaxed or more rattled. And throughout, the memory of Courtney's words, the sense that she'd indeed stolen from Gabrielle and might still do so. Which made her freeze up at the wrong moment, mid-lift, which was immediately apparent to all.

"Stop," Denis commanded an instant later. "That didn't work. Take it again, please, from sixteen counts prior."

She and Javier paused, panting, and stepped back to the stage left corner. The accompanist started the music and they recommenced, but eight counts into the passage, Lana glanced toward the door and saw Gil.

Her back stiffened. Her face grew cold. She couldn't move.

"Pay attention, Lana," Denis, his back to the door, snapped. "Your cue. Stay on it. No, stop. Take it from the same spot again."

The accompanist began again. This time Lana stayed in focus. She directed her frustration, her hurt toward Gil into her movements, a chassé followed by an outside pirouette, stepping out of it into a high piqué arabesque. Javier pivoted her around in a promenade and Lana finished with a clean partnered pirouette.

"Better," Denis said. He turned, noticed Gil at the door and exclaimed in pleasure. She swallowed a sigh. It appeared that Gil, quite literally, knew everyone, even visiting choreographers. Denis gestured for Gil to come in and the two of them chatted for a minute.

"Lana," Gil called out afterward. "Alice wanted me to tell you that she'd be waiting for you, after you're done for the day. What time should I tell her?"

Lana regarded Gil in confusion. Why would Alice be waiting for her?

"I'll be done with rehearsals today at six o'clock."

Gil nodded. "I'll let Alice know." He held her gaze. "She said something about wanting to have a drink with you."

The message was unmistakable. They were not talking about Alice here. She'd be meeting Gil. Relief coursed through her. She drew a breath and affected a businesslike tone.

"Tell her I'll meet her out front at six-fifteen."

"Will do." He turned to leave, but first called out hellos and goodbyes to practically everyone in the room. He was like a politician in that way. It served one positive purpose, however: it dispelled the room's earlier tension.

Denis glanced down at his watch. "All right, you two step back," he said to Javier and Lana, "and we run it through with the second cast couple."

She'd never been so happy to take the back seat in a rehearsal.

At six-fifteen, Gil was there, waiting, in his red Audi TT Roadster. Correction, Lana told herself, Julia's Roadster. He opened the door from the inside. She caught it and spied, on the seat, a half-dozen white roses surrounded by baby's breath, wrapped in florist paper and tied with a diaphanous gold bow. They were beautiful, clearly from a florist shop and not just one of the ten-bucks-a-dozen type, clustered in buckets, being hawked by vendors around town.

"Oh, how pretty," she exclaimed as Gil lifted them from the seat so she could slide in. She hesitated. "Who are they for?"

"You, of course." Gil flashed her his most winning smile. "Who else?"

She refrained from reciting all the names that sprang to mind and instead accepted the flowers, burying her nose in them, which sheltered her from the awkwardness of speaking.

"How about a drink?" he asked.

"Sure. All right," she said, trying to sound as casual as he did.

She stayed focused on the flowers as Gil signaled and eased the car back into traffic. As he drove, he commenced his apology, the words coming out in a great rush.

"I am so sorry, Lana. Really. Go ahead and shoot me. You didn't know anyone there, and I got off in that business mode and I admit it, there were dollar signs in my eyes, weren't there? But that's no excuse. I feel sick about it all. That Andy, he was like a spoiled kid who never had to learn to share. When he wanted to talk, it had to be right then. Thank God Alice knows him like I do. I hope it didn't bother you too much, that she whisked you away like that."

He sounded like an actor in rehearsal. She offered no reply.

He fell silent and focused on traffic, the steep grade of Nob Hill, the taxis that tried to cut him off, the tourists driving too slowly. A right onto California, a left at Stockton, and a block later they pulled up at the front drive of the Ritz-Carlton, a hotel so fancy it looked like a palace. The doormen were dressed as formally as groomsmen at a wedding.

Once inside the lobby she stopped short. "I'm not dressed right," she told Gil.

"Sure you are. And we're just going into the lounge, besides. It's not fancy."

But it was. It felt like a luxury hotel's attempt at casual, at a sports bar. There was a big-screen television in one corner of the paneled room, but the volume was muted. The seats were leather and the tables a richly colored varnished wood. A server came up, Gil ordered a double Alberlour scotch and Lana asked for a Diet

Coke. The server hesitated for the briefest of moments, making Lana worry that such a plain option wasn't allowed, that it had to be a wine or liquor, but he nodded and turned away.

Gil sat back and flashed her another smile. Today he was wearing a blue shirt beneath a grey suit and the effect was spectacular, bringing out the vivid blue of his eyes. His smile, however, did not warm her as it had in the past. It made her wary.

Their drinks arrived quickly. Gil took a big sip of his scotch and carried on talking, in spite of the fact that Lana had remained largely silent. A few minutes later the concierge stopped by and he and Gil exchanged a joke about Friday happy hours *really* being happy here at the Ritz. When the concierge mentioned Andy Redgrave by name, Lana understood why she hated this place. It felt like a place he'd spent time in, which, apparently, he had. Which was why Gil was now slipping the concierge a few twenties.

Lana sat there for another few minutes, observing the Gil show. He never removed his mask of grace and wit and elegance, even after the concierge left. Disdain and something akin to revulsion filled her. She saw the slick character Mom had described, and Mom was right—Lana didn't need someone like this in her life. If this was the guy the other dancers at the WCBT coveted, they were more than welcome to him.

She rose, grabbed her dance bag.

Gil regarded her in surprise. "Wait. What's up?"

Anger mixed with adrenaline made her heart bang wildly in her chest, like a loose shutter in a storm. "I don't like the way this place is making me feel. And I don't like the way you're making me feel either."

She walked out.

Gil strode out after her, caught her arm in the lobby. Lana was dimly aware of the way some of the staff had paused to watch them, anticipating a dramatic scene. Lana wanted to snarl at them to mind their own business, but realized this *was* their business. She was the one who didn't belong. So she quietly told Gil to please let go, that this wasn't working. He released her arm and without another word, she turned and hurried out the front doors, being held open by doormen.

A taxi had stopped on the front drive, disgorging its passengers. She strode over to the driver, ignoring the valet, asking the driver if he was free. When he nodded, she hopped into the taxi.

She expected Gil to run out, stop the taxi.

He didn't.

Her spirits plummeted to the level of the sidewalk. *It's all for the best,* her pragmatic side consoled. *And at least you didn't make a fool of yourself over him. Well, much.*

"Where to?" the taxi driver asked.

She gave him her address and watched for the next ten minutes as the meter ticked away, spending more of her weekly bus budget with each minute. She thought of Gil, back there, probably having gone back to his drink. She thought about the roses she'd left in the car. The pretty white roses.

But Gil surprised her. Fifteen minutes after she'd returned to her apartment, she heard the buzzer, followed by the sound of his voice. Elation battled with dismay. Elation won and she buzzed him in.

"I had to pay for the drinks back in the lounge," he explained once he was in her studio. "I had to break a fifty and they took forever getting my change."

She offered no reply and he made no further excuses. Instead he sized up the room.

"Yes, I know," she said tersely. "It's a dump."

"It doesn't matter. You're the only thing in here I care about."

He looked at her, his blue eyes vulnerable and trusting, so like Luke that her anger began to fade. Reaching into a grocery bag he was carrying, he pulled out the roses she'd left in the car. With some reluctance, she took them from him. There was food in the bag too, which he set on the nearby table. Chinese food. Pot stickers, which he knew she loved. Moo Shu pork, another favorite. Fortune cookies.

"I didn't want to take the risk of hearing you say that no, you wouldn't let me buy you dinner," he said. "So I picked up some. Will you let me stay?"

It was harder to dislike this humbler, more honest Gil. She stood there, trying not to smile. "It would be a shame to waste the food," she said finally.

"It would."

"Okay. Feel free to stay."

"Thank you."

It wasn't ribs, but it was good. She began to relax. By the time they'd finished eating, they were once again swapping stories in a breezy, friendly manner. When Lana mentioned their last take-out meal together, the ribs, Gil was able to laugh at the afternoon's inadvertent adventure.

"Boy, that car," he said. "I love my Roadster, but it's way too temperamental in low gears."

"Julia's Roadster, you mean." The words slipped out.

He regarded her in surprise. "Well, yes. How did you know that?"

Her cheeks grew warm. "Alice told me. Over coffee, at Denny's."

To her relief, he seemed more shocked about the venue than the subject of their conversation.

"You went to *Denny's*? You and *Alice*?"

"We stopped in there on the way home from the party. To talk about things." She hesitated. "I was in a bad way that night," she said, and with that, it was out there. The real issue, not the glossy cover-up.

He looked stricken, chastened. "I'm sorry, Lana. I'm so sorry."

This time he seemed to mean it.

"That party. Us together in that room." She had difficulty getting the words out. "You told me you'd never felt that way before. You got me to admit it too. Was that just a game? See how easy, how gullible Lana really is?"

She focused on the table in front of her, the empty carry-out containers. Gil rose from his spot and sat next to her, reaching over to take her clenched hand.

"Lana. I meant everything I said. Afterwards, God, you can't imagine how torn I felt about not staying right there next to you. That Andy business was too important not to give it my full attention." He exhaled heavily. "Alice was right. I shouldn't have brought you along."

This last bit hurt, as if he'd chosen Alice over Lana. Alice, who'd likely play a bigger part in Gil's life than she ever would.

"I had to dance to whatever tune he played," Gil was saying. "I couldn't afford not to. But under any other circumstances, I wouldn't have allowed that to happen. Please believe me."

"All right," she said softly.

He moved even closer. Her body responded automatically, which bothered her. She felt too battered by the previous weekend's extreme high and low to offer him anything besides wariness. Gil seemed to read the situation. With a gentle kiss on her forehead, he rose from his seat and told her he was going to run next door to the store.

He returned ten minutes later, bearing candles, a tall glass for her roses and a bottle of port. Lana smiled and fetched them juice glasses. After arranging her roses in the tall glass, she sat on the edge of her twin bed, port in hand, and watched Gil. He was setting up candle stations around the room, saying who would have thought a liquor store sold candles? But there they were, right next to the condoms. Lana chuckled over this as she sipped at her port. It was a drink she'd never had before; it was velvety, heady and rich-tasting and seemed to offer a promise of good things to come.

Gil turned off the overhead light and the room was instantly bathed in shadows and golden flickering light. He poured himself a port, arranged the pillows along the length of the twin bed and settled against them next to Lana. They sipped, talked, allowed the dancing candle flames to hypnotize them, and only then did Gil set his hand on her thigh.

Instant high voltage.

He said her name once, a soft, cajoling "Lana."

Her hands, having hastily set down her glass, went to his shoulders and she and Gil were interconnected before she could even pronounce the word. His mouth covered hers, his tongue slid in, tasting of the port's spicy sweetness. Her fingers plowed through his thick dark hair as he edged her down onto the bed, pressing his weight into hers. Hands found bare skin, limbs tangled together. Her shirt came off. His too.

When he reached down to unzip her jeans, however, she stopped him with a muffled gasp. It was as if Mom had come in the room and was now standing there, beaming a flashlight down on them. Lana pushed him off and made her way up to a sitting position.

"I can't," she said between breaths. "My...my mom wouldn't approve."

The moment the words slipped out she felt mortified. She was afraid to see how he'd react. The guys she'd gone out with, the few she'd actually ended up having sex with, had always grown irritated when her straight-laced nature overtook her. And here she'd gone and mentioned her *mom?* But when she finally mustered the courage to meet Gil's eyes, there was a softness in them that surprised her.

"It's okay. It's more than okay," he said. "I admire it. That's what makes you so special."

She wondered if he meant it. She was no longer sure how to read him and what words of his to trust. But at least the awkwardness of the moment had passed. Enough for her to lean back toward him and seek out his mouth again.

This was a mistake, she knew.

A mess.

But what a sublime, exhilarating mess.

Chapter 11 – Alice all Alone

Never let them see your pain.

This, the ultimate mantra for any performing professional. Or perhaps only ballet dancers. Certainly, in sports performance events, things like soccer, an injured player became ennobled by making a spectacle of his injury, his pain. The cameras would pan in on him as he collapsed, rolled around on his back, clutching his ankle/thigh/calf, eyes squeezed shut, face contorted. And at the gym, somehow it was accepted, even looked upon favorably, to groan and make animal noises and faces when lifting heavy weights, as if this proved yes, they were indeed real athletes. Meanwhile, ballet etiquette: make it look as effortless as possible; maintain relaxed, elegant upper-body presentation regardless of what the lower body is doing; wear a serene smile, no matter how your feet/hamstrings/hips are feeling. Hide your pain and preserve the illusion. Or else.

When this mandate proved too challenging for Alice on Tuesday morning, she called in sick, took three ibuprofen and a Valium, and slept the entire day. The mantra sprang like a default into her mind as she entered the offices Wednesday morning and pasted on a determined smile. All it took, however, was one look at Gil, his goofy smile, so reminiscent of the one she'd worn after her first night with Niles, and her own smile dropped from her lips.

Gil, undeserving Gil, had won his special thing in the time she'd lost hers.

Her gut gave a vicious twist. She swayed and clutched at Gil's door frame.

"You look like shit," Gil commented. "You're still sick, I can tell. Go home."

She didn't need a second invitation.

Home provided no relief from her torment, however. She couldn't fight the hurt and she couldn't make it go away. She couldn't talk to Montserrat about it, who'd left for her East Coast tour. Calling Niles himself was forbidden, a sure recipe for disaster. In the end, there was only one place she could productively vent out her mood.

The gym it was.

The gym: an unpretentious, warehouse kind of structure, exposed beams on the second-story ceilings, a broad stretch of floor holding Nautilus equipment, Cybex Strength Systems, bikes, treadmills and racks of free weights. Pop music blared over the continual thud of various barbells and clanking weights, the buzz of conversations. Most people were like her, working out to keep in shape, but the floor was crowded with gym rats too, buff creatures of all ages, muscles bulging, who seemed to spend half their waking hours there.

She took the late-afternoon kickboxing class, which she tried to do twice weekly. Here, it was all about noisy boom-boom music and parallel position. She, who'd relished the advantages her naturally turned-out hips had given her in ballet, now struggled eternally with the mule kicks to the side, hips turned in, knees pointing straight ahead. She was the only one in the class who couldn't kick that way. She saw in the mirror, every dancer's best friend and worst enemy combined, just how stupid she looked. But this afternoon it didn't matter. She punched viciously at the air, she kicked and jumped until she was breathless and spent. By the end of the hour, sedated by endorphins, she decided life was tolerable.

Saved, by the gym.

She hurried back to the gym after work on Thursday, as well, striving to find the same comfort. Toward the end of her workout she noticed something out of the ordinary was going on, accompanied by a buzz of speculation. The word raced through the gym: there was some famous ballerina there. No one knew her name, no one there knew a thing about ballet, only that she was "hot" and "gorgeous."

Alice craned her neck and saw, with a sinking sense of disbelief, Lucinda, of all people, at the front desk, talking to the manager. Next to her was Katrina, principal dancer with the WCBT, the one whom Alice, in another life, had competed with and beaten.

Alice could only stare dumbly as the two of them, accompanied by the gym manager and the WCBT publicist, began walking through the gym, which created an even greater stir. Katrina, tall, willowy and blonde, didn't walk, she wafted. She was so thin, so milky-white, she looked like a different species next to the straining, grunting, sweating gym rats. None of the aging dancer showed today; she'd applied her makeup with great artistry and looked beautiful, fresh, much younger than Alice.

Lucinda tipped her head, murmured something, and Katrina nodded obediently, tucking herself in between the publicist and Lucinda. Alice resigned herself to the fact that it was too late to run and hide. Reluctantly she made her way over to their group. Lucinda recognized her first and smiled, pleased.

"Alice. So this is how you can eat all those muffins and ice cream bars and still look so good."

Lucinda had the unerring ability to toss out an inadvertent insult with any compliment she doled out. Then again, maybe they weren't inadvertent. Alice smiled back at her.

"Oh, that's me. A daily exerciser. Helps me cope with the stresses at work."

And the bitchy females I have to work around, she wanted to add. Instead she plucked at her too-small exercise shirt. Both the vee-neck shirt and the sports bra were too low cut and revealed too much. That she'd chosen to wear this old, overstretched outfit today only served to prove that the fates were having a good time with her this week, chortling over each new misfortune.

Katrina was even happier to see Alice, someone familiar amid this place so far from her own milieu. She offered Alice a warm greeting and asked what she'd been up to, outside the WCBT offices. In reply, Alice gestured around them. Katrina glanced around with the nervous, guarded expression of a covered-wagon pioneer surrounded by unseen Indians.

"So you really lift weights?" Her voice was hushed. "Alongside all these men?"

"Sure. Why wouldn't I?"

Lucinda cut in to direct Katrina's attention to something the gym manager was telling them. Apparently this was a dry run before a photo shoot the following day. This PR ploy of Lucinda's was part of an effort to make the dancers appear "just like anyone else," thus forging a connection with the elusive 22- to 30-year-old age group. It certainly was effective here; every male from that age and up could not stop staring at Katrina.

The gym manager called over two of the men, who, apparently, were to be in on the action tomorrow, serving as a backdrop for Katrina while she struck some everyday pose by the weight machines. The gym manager and the publicist conferred and the manager suggested having one of the guys lift her. One of them stepped forward eagerly and Lucinda pressed closer to Katrina.

"No one lifts the dancer!" she cried in the shrill tone of a little girl harboring her best Barbie from her playmates.

Alice couldn't hide her amusement. It was Lucinda's job to protect the dancers from the wrong sort of PR, to guard the mystique that was the WCBT. She didn't, however, appear to recognize that this was at odds with the very thing she'd set out to do in bringing a dancer out into public. Alice's hand towel slipped to the ground and she bent to pick it up. When she straightened, she saw that Katrina's eyes had dropped to her chest. The too-small sports bra and the shirt had apparently once again collaborated against her. Katrina raised her gaze.

"Alice," she exclaimed, "you have *cleavage.*"

Alice hid her sigh and instead offered Katrina a polite smile. "Well, of course. It was part of the severance package I negotiated with Anders, eight years ago."

Katrina regarded Alice, her face a tableau of elegant confusion until a moment later, her eyes widened and she laughed, a lilting, musical sound. "Oh, Alice." She laid a delicate paw on Alice's arm. "I've forgotten how funny you can be."

She herself had forgotten how easily entertained Katrina could be. Part of her seemed to be eternally frozen at the nine-year-old girl stage, the obedience, the gullibility, the sweet, somewhat confused smile. She was beautiful, like a fairy-tale princess, and still at the top of her game. Alice, looking at her, didn't know whether to worship, envy or hate her.

The ringing of her cell phone in her pocket jolted her. *Niles,* she thought. *Please, please.* She fumbled for the phone, her heart pounding so hard she could hear the whoosh of it in her ears, but one glance at the incoming caller's number dashed her hopes. It was her stepmother, Marianne, not Niles. Lucinda and Katrina were watching her, however, so she hid her disappointment.

"Ooh, goody," she said, with a coy smile. "Gotta take this call." She offered Lucinda and Katrina a farewell with a flutter of her fingers.

"Why, hello there," she cooed into the phone as she walked away from them. "I was hoping you'd call me."

"You were?" Marianne sounded confused but pleased.

"Well, yes. It's been a while." Once out of range from the others, her voice returned to normal. "How are things going?"

"Oh, busy days, busy days."

Alice found herself lulled by Marianne's chatter, its soothing, predictable cadence. A humorous encounter during her shift as a gallery volunteer at the Yerba Buena Center for the Arts. Adventures with the garden and the presence of rabbits. Considering signing up for the ceramics class her friend Lolly had. Alice murmured an affirmative reply from time to time but otherwise kept quiet. When Marianne finished her rundown she asked, with a laugh, why Alice was acting so complacent today. Was she fishing for a favor?

No favor, she told Marianne, she was simply glad to hear from her, that autumn seemed like a season for family. All of which she meant, she realized. She found herself proposing a Sunday dinner at the house, an idea that seemed to please Marianne as well.

"I'll make a roast. With some of those fingerling potatoes roasted in olive oil and rosemary."

"That sounds wonderful."

"Why don't you come over early, around five-thirty? And what about Niles—will he be joining us?"

"Oh, far too much work." She tried to laugh, which ended up

sounding more like a bleat. "It'll be just me. Shall I bring dessert?"

"That would be nice. Oh, I'm looking forward to this!"

"Me too. See you Sunday."

She made it through a lonely Saturday night by treating herself to pizza, Ben and Jerry's ice cream and juvenile classic comedies like *Dumb and Dumber* and *Wayne's World*, movies guaranteed not to make her cry, think of ballet or Niles. She stayed up late and slept in till noon on Sunday. Thus fortified, she made her way late Sunday afternoon over to the Willoughby house, a rose brick Tudor in hushed, manicured Pacific Heights.

"Mom? Dad? Anyone home?" she called out as she pulled open the heavy front door and stepped into the paneled entryway.

The word "Mom" came differently out of her mouth today. She hadn't paused to consider its definition in years, but in the last week, it had come up again and again, courtesy of Lana. Marianne, this woman who'd played the role of mother in Alice's life for twenty years now. Marianne, who'd been successful in finding that sweet spot of being a friend to Alice, not threatening in the least as a future stepmother. She'd been direct with Alice back then, when it became clear to all that a marriage proposal was forthcoming. "I could never replace your mother and I wouldn't presume to try," she'd said. "But I hope you'll let me be your friend."

Alice, almost thirteen, had been flattered to have this grown woman act so respectful, so caring toward her, and had agreed. What she'd left unsaid was the fact that she wouldn't have minded if Marianne had gone ahead and established herself as mother from the start, as she had for Alice's brother Sterling, four years her junior, who hardly remembered the healthier, larger-than-life Deborah. "The boy needs a mother," Alice had heard her aunts murmur among themselves, and then to Marianne. "Alice will be fine," they'd added. "You'll have no trouble there."

Which pleased Alice to hear, but in some ways, it nudged her to the periphery. She needed a mother, too. She'd dreamed of having a mother again, yearned for it with every fiber, a sick pang in her stomach that rose up every Mother's Day, every school event where other mothers came and stood on the sidelines, beaming with pride. But she'd fantasized about a softer, kinder, more loving mom. She didn't even need to be beautiful. Deborah had been beautiful, but she'd been a strict, unyielding mother with high standards and even higher expectations for her daughter. The years of illness, instead of bringing softness and warmth, brought fragility and terrible, life-shaking insecurity that went on and on. Alice had had a strong, domineering mother for eight years, a weakening one for two and a half, and then the two-year abyss of nothingness.

Ballet had saved her. All her teachers became, in a collective way, her second mother. Ballet was beautiful, feminine, like her mother. And, like Deborah, it had been both nurturing and demanding, harshly exacting even as she remained utterly wrapped up in her love for it. The women at her studio had treated her ideally after her mother's death, not with continual hugs and sad puppy eyes, but with affirmation and approval when she danced well for them. Firm, but caring. She'd felt it, responded to it. She didn't reveal personal emotions beyond the dazed, shaky first few months in the aftermath of her mother's death, which had been like a too-rough carnival ride that unceasingly battered and ungrounded her. But eventually she grew stronger. She clung to the memory of Deborah's words, her mantra, and became a true Willoughby, a ballerina in training, someone who could excel in adverse conditions, rise above the white-hot churning emotions and turn ballet's regimented, disciplined steps into art.

She'd succeeded; she'd excelled. And, as a reward for her hard work, her exemplary comportment, she got Marianne. A mother for Sterling, a friend for herself.

It could have been a whole lot worse.

A muffled voice replied to Alice's called-out greeting.

"I'm in here," she heard Marianne say from down the hallway. Alice followed the voice into the bright warmth of the kitchen and immediately felt better. Home did that to you. Sunday roasts did that to you. She sniffed appreciatively. "Mmm. Something smells good."

Marianne was busy poking at the contents of a pan inside the oven. "The roast," she said as she withdrew from the heat of the oven and closed the oven door. She smiled at Alice. "Well, don't you look lovely," she said, sizing up Alice's blouse and sweater.

"Thank you." Alice came over and dropped a kiss on Marianne's hot cheek, giving her arm an affectionate squeeze. "Mmm, you smell good too."

"Again, the roast."

Alice laughed as she set a white bakery box on the counter.

"Pull up a seat and tell me what's going on in your glamorous life," Marianne said. "Weren't you talking about attending some fancy party last weekend?"

"I did, and oh, it was something else." Alice perched herself on a nearby bar stool. "Very posh and fun. Montserrat sounded incredible. Gil was a charmer." She went on to describe the evening, edited for content, of course. Marianne nodded, all smiles; she knew and admired both Montserrat and Gil. They were People Who'd Made it Big, or, in Gil's case, someone on the upward rise Who Knew People. She chuckled over the story of how Gil had hunted down Andy Redgrave in the first place.

"That kid," she said. "He'll go far."

A timer went off and Marianne turned her attention to her roast.

Alice glanced through the archway that led to the living room, scrutinizing the room as if for the first time. Lana and Montserrat were wrong; she and her family were not rich, certainly not by Pacific Heights or Andy Redgrave standards. Yes, she'd grown up in comfort and relative privilege. Yes, there were expensive touches there in the living room, with its spotless suede sofa and chairs, sleek designer tables and lamps punctuating the space. But her father complained eternally about the money Marianne's interior decorating cost them, the exorbitant property taxes they paid, the cost of living in San Francisco. He kept threatening to move out of the city and down the Peninsula, where they could have a big yard and a four-car garage for the same money, a threat as empty as Marianne's promise that this redecoration would be her last.

"Where's Dad?" Alice asked once Marianne had returned to the counter. "And how's Sterling doing?" She wasn't particularly close to her brother, who was more about business than feelings, a younger copy of their business executive father, but in their affection for their stepmother they were united. It was easier to keep tabs on each other through the neutralizing filter of Marianne, who always managed to put a cheerful, optimistic spin on things.

"Your father is in the den and as for your brother, well, you'll be able to ask him directly. He and Olivia will be joining us for dinner. Oh, and she called and asked if it would be all right if her parents joined us as well. They're in town. I told her to tell them of course, always room for more family."

"Whoa, wait!" Alice regarded Marianne in dismay. "Couldn't you have told me you were going to invite them too?"

"I just found out about her parents two hours ago."

"Yes, but what about Sterling and Olivia?"

Marianne looked perplexed. "I spoke with them after I spoke with you. Why would you mind? You requested a family dinner."

"No. I said dinner *together*. As in you, me and Dad."

"Now what's wrong with your brother and his wife being invited?"

Alice's relaxed mood evaporated. A family dinner tonight would be a disaster. Chitchatting with her brother and his bland, incurious wife of three years took a certain kind of energy that Alice simply didn't have today. And the prospect of chatting with Olivia's parents drained her just to think of it.

"Well," she spluttered, "what if I didn't bring enough dessert?"

"What did you bring?"

"A chocolate mousse cake."

"Perfect. The Schneiders are bringing over a fruit and nut platter. Those two items will work wonderfully together." Marianne beamed at her.

"Oh, *fine*. I just wish I'd known. So I could feel prepared."

"Give Niles a call. I know you said he's busy with work these days, but he needs to eat, too. And his presence always does you good."

Alice took a deep breath. "Well, to be honest, the truth is, Niles and I are taking a little break."

"Oh, Alice." Marianne's easy smile faded. She stood there, bagged carrots in hand, and shook her head. "Why? Why does this happen to you? Lolly's daughter just got engaged, did you hear about that? She's got a fraction of your looks, your talent. Why don't things work out for you?"

Even Marianne, apparently, couldn't find a silver lining, a positive angle here. Which made Alice feel even worse.

"It's just taking a break," she said, furious with herself for how pathetic, how insecure the reply sounded. "He needs to focus on work. And, well, so do I."

"All right. And that's okay. It's good not to push things." Marianne began to shake the carrots out of their bag and into a roasting pan, intent on her task, as if the carrots were the better horse to bet on here. Alice, chastised, slid out of the chair and muttered something about getting herself a glass of wine. Afterward, glass in hand, she wandered into the living room and stood there, brooding, until her cell phone chimed from within her purse. Reluctantly she returned to the kitchen to retrieve it. No, not Niles. Of course not. But Gil, at least.

"Hey, Gil," she said into the phone.

"Hey, you. Am I calling at a bad time?"

"No, it's good."

She could feel Marianne's mournful reproof still emanating from her, in waves, like an oven set at 450 degrees with the door left open. She took her phone call out to the patio that overlooked the garden. Even in late September there were roses and the trellis was covered with vivid coral-colored bougainvillea.

"What's up?" she asked Gil.

"I have a question for you. But first, what's up with you? I can tell you're in a mood just from your voice."

She hesitated and found herself offering Gil an abridged version of the Niles disaster and the misguided attempt to find comfort here, at home. She sank into one of the padded wrought-iron patio chairs.

"And it's going to be a family dinner tonight, which was news to me until a few minutes ago. Spencer's in-laws, even. I just don't have the kind of energy required to work a crowd. Even if they're family. Wait. Especially if they're family."

"Doesn't sound like it would be a challenge for me."

"No kidding. You'd be perfect here—would you please come join us?"

He hesitated, which made her laugh. "I was joking," she said.

"Yes, but what if I did? Would that help you out, ease your social burden?"

"Oh, God, like you couldn't imagine. But just a minute here." Suspicion washed over her. "What's going on? Why did you call, anyway?"

"I need your advice on something. Maybe your help. I was hoping we could meet up for a few minutes this evening. If I came over for dinner, there you go, two birds with one stone."

Marianne loved Gil. She'd perk up immediately with the news.

"Hold on, let me ask the hostess." She rose and returned to the kitchen. When Marianne looked up, Alice gestured to the phone.

"Would it be all right if Gil joined us in place of Niles?"

"Oooh." Marianne's eyes lit with girlish enthusiasm. "That would be wonderful. Eight is such a better number than seven around a table, besides. Tell Gil we'd love that. I always enjoy his company."

Alice returned her attention to the phone. "You hear that?"

He laughed. "I heard that."

"You really want to join us?"

"I do."

"Well, damn. See you in about forty-five minutes, then?"

"I'll be there. I'll bring booze."

She disconnected, restraining the urge to laugh out loud. Relief coursed through her. With Gil here, assuming the burden of sociability, she'd be free to relax.

She pondered his original intention in calling her. He wanted something. He wasn't doing this just to be kind to her.

No matter. He'd just helped her out; she'd do the same in

return.

Gil arrived, bottles of wine in hand, right around the time Sterling and his wife Olivia and her parents did. He proceeded to render an Oscar-worthy performance all evening, winning over everyone, even her brother and father, who were prone to suspicion around pretty-faced theater types. Gil was a chameleon; he became what each person needed. He complimented Marianne several times over, drew out the reserved Olivia, set Olivia's parents laughing with a clever anecdote, and engaged Alice's father and Sterling in lively conversation. She even heard him murmuring to Sterling something about "those pansy dancers" and the frustrations of finding "real" men to conduct business with in the arts field.

Her brother nodded in agreement, approval. Alice tried not to choke over her wine.

He had them all hooked.

No doubt about it, Gil was a master of working people. It was daunting, even a little distasteful, how good he was. She was grateful they were forever aligned on the same team.

After dessert, she slipped away to use the bathroom, check her phone for nonexistent messages from Niles. Instead of returning to the dining room afterward, she stepped out on the patio. Gil joined her there five minutes later.

"Where'd you go?" he asked.

"I needed a breather from all that Mr. Personality show going on in there."

He glanced at her. "That's what you wanted, right?"

"I did, and I thank you. I owe you."

"You do."

"And you're going to call in the favor. Which is the real reason you came over tonight."

He tried to look injured. "What? It wouldn't be enough to help my associate out on a night that she was feeling down?"

"Try again."

He grinned. "You know me well."

"I do. What do you want?"

"Okay. Here's what I want—I'd like to rent your guest room."

"For you?" she asked in confusion.

Gil laughed. "Of course not me. Well. Not really. No, I'm talking about for Lana."

She stared at him. The words ricocheted in her head before coming out in a rush. "Oh, no. Absolutely not. I told you to keep me out of this. I've had enough involvement. Do you know what she *did* last Monday night?"

"You mean about her accepting an invitation to a dinner from your violinist friend?"

Gil's amusement served to cool her anger. He had a point. Really, what had Lana done? She'd brought up, yet again, the memory of things lost, however inadvertently. Had Alice spoken up, told her about losing her mother, maybe that would have shifted the tides entirely. Instead, she'd clammed up, claimed nothing was the matter, and look what that had brought. But the end result was hardly a crime she could pin on Lana.

"Whatever," she said. "What makes you think I'd consider this kind of arrangement?"

Gil rose from the patio chair and wandered over to study the flowers on the trellis. "Here's the thing. She's not safe where she's living. She's got a week-to-week lease, and I want her out as soon as possible."

"Don't you think that's a bit presumptuous on your part?"

He swiveled around to face her. The smile was gone.

"Alice. A man died outside her apartment early on Saturday

morning. A homeless guy. He'd bled to death from a knife wound. She heard the sirens, the commotion, went downstairs and saw it all—the blood, the sheet over the body, all the cops."

Alice stared at Gil in horror. "Were you there?"

"No, and I could kick myself for not spending Friday night with her. But she called me and I came right over and got her out of there. I didn't even want her returning today, but she was insistent."

"Gil. God."

"I know. And according to the liquor store owner next door, stuff like that happens in that neighborhood. Just another day in the Tenderloin."

"How does she feel about things?"

"She doesn't want to stay there but she's pragmatic, saying that if she needs to, she'll just continue to stay week-to-week. Apparently there's little else available right now. I spent the day today calling the classifieds, checking out units while she had her rehearsal and she's right, the pickings are slim at her price range. She won't let me help pay for something better. And it's not as if I can offer her my place right now."

"So. That's how this comes around to me."

"And, not to rub it in or anything, but you have to admit, with Niles not around…"

"What, that I'll get lonely and need someone to talk to, there at night? Give me a break. I like my solitude, I crave it. You're asking me to give it up."

For Lana, who'd poached both Montserrat's and Niles's attention, who'd found Alice's tender core and given it such a shake. But a homicide rendered everything else petty and irrelevant. She thought of the weeping, trembling girl who'd seemed so defenseless on Saturday night, leaving Andy's party, and knew there was only one right response. She sighed.

"Let me talk to her about it."

"I'll subsidize her share of any rent."

"Look. Just let me talk to her first, okay?"

"Fine." He pulled out his wallet, extracted a scrap of paper and handed it to Alice. "Here's her cell phone number."

"So. Do I get to ask a personal question?"

"Feel free to ask. I just might not answer."

"This business with Lana. Really, what's going on here? Is this just some good time?"

"No. Absolutely not." Gil's expression grew soft. "Alice. I'm in love."

She rolled her eyes. "Where have I heard this before? Like, less than six months ago?"

"Cammie? That wasn't love. I never said that was love."

"You distinctly said, 'I'm in love.'"

"Oh. Well, that was the horny man's way of saying 'I'm in lust.'"

"Ah. And that is different from this?"

He looked indignant. "Definitely. Lana and I talk. We relate to each other on a deeper level. Cammie and I—it was all about having sex. Getting drunk and having sex. Not that that wasn't fun, mind you. But really, it was a pretty shallow relationship."

"Imagine that."

"Actually, the truth is, I loved telling people I was screwing a lawyer. Everyone got such a kick out of that. I think I was screwing her long after I stopped liking her. Kind of like my contribution to society."

"I don't need any more details, thanks."

"You brought it up, not me."

"This Lana. She's a good girl."

"Do you think I don't know that? In fact, you want to know the truth? We haven't even had sex yet. There. That's how serious it is."

She studied him, so improbably beautiful and sexy as he stood there, hands at his sides, palms open, as if to show her how vulnerable he was.

"All right." She rose from the patio chair. "I'll call her."

"Today? Maybe now?"

"Gil. I'll call her. Tomorrow. Please let's just leave it at that."

"Okay. I'll let her know."

"You're not going back over there, are you?"

"Hell yes. I don't want her there alone. Unfortunately, though, Julia arrives tomorrow. I'll have to behave all week."

"What's Julia going to think of this new, enraptured Gil?"

He walked over to the table and swept the flower debris off the edge with a flick of one hand. Buds tumbled to the ground. "She won't complain. I meet her needs. What I do with the rest of my time is my business—we've both agreed to that."

"You play a lot of dangerous games."

"Don't we all?"

"No, we all don't."

Marianne appeared in the window and waved gaily at Gil.

"Whoops," he said, "shirking my duty."

As they headed back toward the French doors, Alice nudged him. "Hey, thanks. For tonight. I owe you."

"Of course you do. And I'm giving you the perfect opportunity to repay me."

She could only shake her head and laugh.

Chapter 12 – Lana Moves House

Serenade rehearsals were a throwback to her days in the corps de ballet, which she found both comforting and a little deflating. The WCBT had performed the Balanchine ballet last spring and for this fall's tour, all the dancers were keeping their same roles. The only change was that Lana and two corps dancers were filling in for the three corps dancers who'd left. Lana knew the choreography; all professional ballet dancers did. Since every Balanchine ballet was staged by the same group of répétiteurs from the Balanchine Trust—guaranteeing the same nuance, hands, head angles and intentions—continuity prevailed, allowing Lana to blend in quickly. One of the herd, one of the corps.

The dancer next to her for much of the time, Dena Lindgren, was a new corps dancer this year, although she'd danced the role the previous year as a company apprentice. She was young, diminutive, and looked like a student still. In fact, the first time Lana noticed her, during the ballet school's late afternoon class Lana still took, she'd assumed Dena *was* a student. Watching her during adagio and grand allegro, however, there'd been no mistaking her for a mere student. She was extraordinary, even by professional standards. Gil had mentioned that two dancers in the company, sisters, were from the Chicago area, and Dena turned out to be one of them. Around the other company members, she seemed quiet, subdued, and kept to herself, neither an insider nor an outsider. Rebecca, her older sister by three years, on the other hand, struck Lana as the consummate insider. She, too, was in the corps de ballet, another beautiful dancer, graceful and confident. Like Gabrielle, she was seen as potential soloist material, evidenced by the fact that she was included on the rehearsal list with Lana for *Arpeggio*.

But even though she and Rebecca were the same age and in *Arpeggio* together, it was Dena that Lana felt closer to. That is, until the end of that day's *Serenade* rehearsal. Charlotte, Courtney's friend, had cracked a joke at Lana's expense. Everyone around them, Courtney included, was having a good laugh. Lana tried to chuckle along with them, a good natured "yeah, I'll be the butt of the joke, but it was a funny one, so I'm totally okay with that!" Only Dena, standing within hearing distance, didn't laugh. Instead she frowned at Charlotte, followed by a flickered glance at Lana. It felt like a reprimand, not just to Charlotte but Lana herself. She wasn't sure, in the end, where she stood with Dena. Or, in truth, with any of them.

Arpeggio rehearsal came after lunch. Like *Autumn Souvenir*, the ballet incorporated a contemporary twist onto more traditional movements, but whereas *Autumn Souvenir* relied on an ever-flowing sense of movement from the body that was sorrowful, somehow, this one had a more joyful aspect, with clever interplay between the eight dancers, lots of leaps and spirited pas de basque steps. Today, she'd been paired with Boyd. Lexie, the company's choreographer-in-residence, was still experimenting with casting preferences, moving dancers in and out, testing out partnerships. Boyd was a corps dancer, but, like Rebecca Lindgren, he seemed to embody the confidence of a soloist already, or certainly one who knew he was heading in that direction. Sometimes it seemed to Lana as if she were the insecure corps dancer, and he, the seasoned soloist. Although not always in a good way. He offered suggestions to her that seemed more directive than opinion; he gripped her too tightly, without apology, during the overhead lifts, which left bruises on her thighs, her arms. But he smiled at her, wished her good morning each day, so she wasn't about to complain.

During today's rehearsal, Anders and Ben stepped in. Anders taught company class at least one morning a week and frequently dropped in on rehearsals, but this was the first time he'd arrived while she was dancing in a soloist capacity. Much different from being one of seventeen dancers moving across the floor. She and Boyd were immersed in one of their pas de deux passages when Anders came in, and it was only when the accompanist stopped playing that Lana noticed him. Lexie looked at him inquiringly and he made a "go on" motion with his hands.

"Would you like us to take it from the top?" Lexie asked.

"No, no. Simply from the arrival of these two." He gestured to Lana and Boyd.

She and Boyd had been taught all the steps, but still lacked the proper amount of time to fully own the moves, to integrate their respective interpretations. But luck was on their side and they moved through the passage with no mishaps.

When they finished and the accompanist stopped, Anders nodded. "Again, please. From the same place."

She and Boyd stepped back to their starting spot, casting quick, worried glances at each other, but the second attempt went just as smoothly. Afterward, as she and Boyd paused to catch their breath, Anders cocked his head and murmured something to Ben, who scribbled it down on a clipboard he was carrying.

Anders turned to Lexie. "From the top this time, perhaps?"

Anders watched them dance for ten minutes and without any further comment, slipped out. At the next break in the music, when Lexie focused his attention on the steps of another couple, Lana touched Boyd's arm.

"What did all that mean?" she asked. "Was it a bad thing that he didn't smile or tell us 'good job'?"

"That's just how he is," Boyd said, bending to massage his calf. "Sometimes you don't find out until later what he thought. Like when a new rehearsal listing is posted and you're not on it."

Lana felt queasy. Boyd looked up and offered her a confident smile. "Hey. All you can do is give it your best. And we did. I mean, I know *I* did. Let them do or say what they will. And besides, casting here is ultimately Lexie's choice, not Anders'. Lexie chooses his own dancers and decides what's working, what's not. He likes us. You can tell."

When rehearsal ended, she checked her phone for messages. There were two, one from Alice, confirming a tour of her house that evening, and the other from Gil. Listening to it warmed her spirits. Gil had been her hero since Saturday morning when she'd called him, in shock over seeing Coop dead, shock that held her in its grip until Gil swept in thirty minutes later, taking her away from all of that, insistent on spending the whole day with her, holding her close that night, at his place, as she cried. She wasn't sure how she would have gotten through the weekend without his support. And now he'd brokered this arrangement with Alice.

All Lana had to do was pass the test. With this woman who had every reason to dislike her.

She thought again of her flare-up at Montserrat's dinner, where she'd gone and challenged Alice on being rich, privileged, insinuating she'd had no real problems while growing up. Thinking of it, Lana winced. What the hell had been her problem? Talk about biting the hand that feeds you.

After the school's late afternoon class and a nervously consumed plate of Thai noodles, Lana headed over to Alice's house, a snug, pretty Victorian with elaborate moldings over the front porch and windows. Alice came to the door, ushered her in with a professional smile, and invited her to sit in the living room. They perched on seats there, both sitting straight and proper. Alice offered her a drink, which Lana declined. Awkwardness hovered until Lana spied a cat, sleek and silvery-grey, meandering into the room.

"Oh, how cute," she exclaimed, moving over to pet the cat, who arched and squirmed against Lana's hand, purring.

"Are you okay with cats?"

"Oh, sure. My mom's allergic to them, so we could never have one at home. This one's darling. What's her name?"

"Odette."

"As in Odette from *Swan Lake?*"

Alice nodded and offered her a faint smile. "I have to say, you're the first person to catch on to that."

"Obviously not ballet dancers, the others."

"No, they weren't." She rose. "All right, shall we tour?"

Alice pointed out features in the elegant living room, the formal dining room, the bright cheery kitchen.

"This is all really nice," Lana said.

"Thank you. A lot of space for one person, but when it came on the market, my father agreed it was a fabulous investment."

"Niles told me he lived in Burlingame, down the Peninsula. Is that kind of a long drive for you two?"

"Outside of rush hour it's not too bad." She hesitated. "So, Gil didn't tell you?"

"Tell me what?"

Alice ran her hands along the carved banister of the hallway's oak staircase. "Well, at this time, Niles and I are taking a little time apart."

"Oh, no. You broke up?"

"No. It's time apart, that's all. His work is a little too consuming for him to focus on anything else right now." A note of bitterness arose with the last words.

"But he seemed so relaxed and generous with his time, talking to me at that dinner."

"Yes. He did."

Something inside Lana shrank. "Oh, God. It was me. Being there, monopolizing the attention. I brought on the conflict."

"Don't be ridiculous."

"It is. I do this to people. I mean well, but I blunder in, and something gets ruined. Socially, I'm like a bull in a china shop."

"Yes. No offense, but I can kind of see that." Without waiting for a reply, Alice turned and ascended the stairs, leaving Lana to follow behind.

Lana knew she should stop the tour, apologize, leave. She couldn't possibly be welcome here, in light of this new information. How could Gil have failed to mention this part? But Alice was speaking again, telling Lana about the house's history, and while it wasn't a warm, confidential voice, it was cordial.

Besides, she didn't want to leave. She loved this house. The feeling only intensified as she checked out the rooms on the second floor. Everything was so clean and organized, so delicate and pretty. She'd never lived somewhere pretty before. The first bedroom that Alice showed her was an inviting shade of yellow, with an angled roof, a nook that held a plush easy chair, and on the other side of the room, a bed decorated with pillows and a gold and cream patterned comforter. The skylight drew in the pale hues of the evening sky. There was a faint scent of lavender in the air.

"Wow," Lana said, "this is a beautiful master bedroom."

She couldn't believe when Alice told her that no, this was the guest room and therefore would be hers. This room surely couldn't be surpassed, but when she saw the master bedroom a few minutes later, she understood. Textured ivory walls, a fireplace, silk curtains, an overhead light fixture that looked like a chandelier, gold-framed mirror, antique writing desk and chair. Alice misinterpreted Lana's gape-jawed reaction with a self-conscious shrug.

"I didn't choose all this formal décor. Whenever my mom redecorates, my house gets the old stuff. The periods don't match; this is eighteenth-century French and the kitchen is Early American. But the price was right."

"Omigosh, it's fantastic."

Alice reflected over this and nodded. "It's a nice place to come home to."

"I can imagine."

Alice led her back down the stairs and into the living room. "So," she said, gesturing for Lana to take a seat on the couch. "That's about it. Are you interested in moving in? For a short spell?"

The last words said it all. Lana felt her hopes, her good spirits, evaporate.

"I don't think it's the right thing to do," she muttered, looking at the carpet.

There was a pause. "You don't want to move in here?" Alice sounded incredulous.

"Well, yes. But no. Because you don't want me to."

She looked up and saw that Alice was finally looking at *her*, instead of over her shoulder, Andy Redgrave style.

"I'm sorry," Alice said.

"It's okay. I understand."

"No. I'm sorry I gave you the impression I don't want you here. Because, the truth is, I do. I'm with Gil. You need to get out of that terrible area. You're not safe there. And that's all that matters." She gestured around them. "There's room here, as you can see. You seem to be a considerate person, I don't imagine you'll be a noise problem for me."

"Oh, not noisy at all. Not me." She tried to keep her voice neutral even as her body began to tremble with excitement. "And it will be temporary," she said, and Alice nodded.

"So, if it really is all cool with you," Lana added, "I'd love to."

"All right. Welcome."

"That's it?"

"Well, yes. It's not like I've got a landlord to report to."

"But how much for weekly rent?"

Alice shook her head. "I'm not going to take your money, Lana. I know what dancers get paid, and it's never enough to live well in San Francisco. Consider this part of the company package."

"I can't do that!"

"Fine, you can chip in thirty bucks every week for the PG&E bill."

"That's not enough. I'll keep the refrigerator stocked too."

"Only if you want to."

"I do."

Decision made, they both rose. "When would you like to move in?" Alice asked.

"Um, any chance that I could do it right now?"

A smile broke through Alice's somber expression. She agreed

and even offered to drive Lana back and forth, to load her car with Lana's belongings. They stopped at a Safeway on the way to get empty boxes and plastic bags, which Lana filled frantically in the thirty minutes it took for Alice to run another errand.

Lana looked around the studio. She couldn't get out of this place fast enough now. All she could think about was seeing Coop's dead body, thinking of how he'd died, alone, unloved, overlooked. Tears stung the back of her throat. She could have, she *should* have done more. But she'd been preoccupied by her own life.

Alice returned, and somehow they managed to squeeze everything into the car's back seat and trunk. As they drove back toward her house, they chatted about the company, people Alice had known who were still there: Delores, Joe, Katrina. And, of course, Ben, who had been Alice's partner the night of her onstage accident.

"He was the greatest about it all, afterwards," Alice said. "One of the few dancers who knew how to offer comfort, encouragement, without making me sick with jealousy over their own good health. But maybe he sensed that he, too, would be in the same boat pretty soon."

"What happened to him?"

"Oh, he was battling some lower back pain for years, I think, but after one really bad episode he was diagnosed with a ruptured disk. An L-5 S-1, I think it was. There he was, still in his twenties, at the peak of his career, but they told him he would need major surgery and six months of rehab, minimum, if he wanted to keep dancing. Not to mention lifting women. And for the rest of his career, it would be an issue that would limit him. He shocked everyone by deciding to have the surgery, and terminate the dancing anyway. But he was pragmatic and can-do about it from the start. He'd always had strong administrative and logistics skills, and when he got an offer to co-artistic direct a new company a few months later, he took it. Anders wooed him back a year later, as a ballet master and his own assistant."

"I really like Ben," Lana said.

"Everyone does. He diffuses Anders' intensity."

"Anders still scares me," she confessed.

"He scares a lot of people. That's just him. He pushes Ben, too. I don't see how Ben takes it, but he does. With a smile and a good attitude."

"Sounds like he's a good friend to have," Lana said.

Alice frowned and worry shot through Lana. Had she said the wrong thing yet again?

"He's a good friend to *make*," she told Lana, who recognized the suggestion in the comment. But, oh, as if. Much easier for someone like Alice, who'd be shocked if she knew just how few friends Lana had made within the company.

They both fell silent after that, hostage to their own brooding thoughts.

Back at the house, though, Alice grew sociable again, helping her unload the items inside. When everything was settled, divided between Lana's bedroom and the kitchen, Alice glanced at her watch.

"It's early, but if you don't mind, I'm going to go into my room and have some quiet time. Just knock if there's anything you need, though."

"Oh, one thing," Lana said. "I need to call my mom and tell her my living situation has changed. I'll give her my cell phone number, but she might get suspicious and want to know the address of where I'm living and such. You know how moms can be. Would it be okay, maybe, if I gave her your home's phone number too?"

"Of course. I told you, make yourself at home. You live here. Give out this address and home number as yours. I'll jot it all down for you."

She strode over to the counter, scribbled out the information on a pad of paper, tore off the sheet and handed it to Lana.

"Thanks. I appreciate it. My mom will too."

"No problem," she said, an edge creeping into her voice. "I'll be in my room if you need anything more."

Alice disappeared and Lana swallowed, vowing to be less annoying, somehow. She moved around as quietly as she could, stowing her kitchen items in the pantry and back cabinets. In the bedroom, her few personal belongings fitted easily in the guest bedroom's maple chest of drawers and spacious closet. Twenty minutes later, she was finished. She called Gil first, leaving a message that all had gone well at Alice's, she was now settling in, and that she'd talk to him tomorrow.

Her next call would be considerably more tricky.

She perched on the edge of the pretty bed as the phone rang. Mom answered. She was still up; she was a night owl and rarely went to bed before midnight, which worked well for calls from the West Coast. They chatted for a moment before Mom asked how things were going in San Francisco.

"Well, actually, I've made a change in my housing," Lana said. "There was a little, um, trouble in the old neighborhood. And it turned out to be easy to make the change."

"Trouble?" Mom's voice rose. "What did you do?"

"Oh, not me. I wasn't involved in any way. It was actually a problem that took place outside my building."

"What kind of problem?"

"Well, someone kind of...died."

"What are you saying? Right out there, in front of where you live?"

"Yes."

"Dear God. A heart attack? A car accident?"

"No. He'd been stabbed."

The moment the words slipped out she regretted them. Mom didn't need the truth, she needed reassurances. How quickly she'd forgotten the rules of The Mom Game.

"So that's why I'm out of there," she added in a rush. "Far from there, now, thanks to the help of my friend, Alice. No chance of that happening again."

Silence. A moment later, Mom began to cry.

"Oh, Lana. Don't I have enough on my plate here? Now I have to worry even more about you."

Lana felt terrible. "But I moved, Mom. To someplace safer."

"Where? With who?"

"With Alice. Into her house."

"Lana! And you think I'll stop worrying now?"

"Yes. It's a real house, in a safer neighborhood."

It was as if Mom couldn't hear her. The sobs became louder, jagged breaths of air in between.

"You aren't safe and you have to come home. Now."

"Mom, stop. I'm fine."

"I can't lose another, Lana. I can't."

It was horrifying, like Mom was caught in the grip of some terrible hallucination. "My baby," she was moaning now, "my angel. How could I lose you?"

She'd done it; she'd conjured up The Memory. The worst thing possible a Kessler child could do, the ultimate gaffe. Remind Mom of Baby John.

"Mom," she tried to say now, "that was sixteen years ago."

"A mother never forgets, Lana. You may have gotten wrapped up with your own life, your own needs, but a mother never forgets."

More gasping sobs, a note of hysteria rising in them.

"Mom," Lana tried again, shaken now as well. "I'll be okay. This is a much better situation."

No answer, only those muffled sobs.

"Mom?" The fear grew. "Tell me you're all right. Where's Dad? Is he home? Let me talk to Dad."

"He's away overnight," Mom managed to say.

"Then Annabel. Is she home?"

A sniffle. "Yes."

"Let me talk to her, Mom. Please."

She could hear the *clunk* of the phone being dropped and for a paralyzed minute she didn't know whether that meant Mom had dropped to the floor herself, or if she'd merely gone to get Annabel.

The silent seconds ticked by, agonizingly slow. When Annabel came on the line with a "yo, sis," Lana was nearly tearful with relief.

"Annabel. Is she freaking out?"

"Yes, she is." Annabel did not sound happy. "What did you say to her?"

"I was just trying to tell her I'd moved to a safer place, and give her the new phone number and address here."

"I think it's safe to say your delivery sucked."

"I'm sorry, I'm sorry. I didn't see it coming."

"Too wrapped up in your exciting new life to notice it?"

"God, not you, too. Look. I'm doing the best I can out here. And right now I'm scared about Mom. You need to spend some time with her. Even if she tries to push you away. She needs someone to coax her out of this mood."

She could almost see Annabel's pretty face scrunching up into a pout, the careless rise and fall of her sister's shoulders.

"That's not my particular skill, as we all know."

"Annabel, I'm begging. Please."

A heavy, burdened sigh followed, which Annabel had perfected from years of listening to their mother perform the same thing. "You owe me," she said finally.

"I do. And I'll pay up. Those Ghirardelli chocolates you like so much?"

"The ones in their own little shiny wrappers that have caramel and mint fillings?"

"Yes. I'll send you a bunch as a thank-you. Okay?"

"All right. But don't you dare forget."

Without waiting for Lana's reply, Annabel hung up.

Lana set her own phone down and stared blankly at the wall. Her arms and legs were trembling with spent adrenaline. She rose and tried to organize some of her personal items, knickknacks and figurines, but she felt so jittery and clumsy she finally gave up. She returned to the bed, sprawled on it and lay there, too drained to finish organizing, too wired to crawl under the covers and attempt sleep.

She was furious with herself for the grand faux pas. The other kids were normally the ones who let the Baby John reference slip out accidentally, and it had always been Lana that Mom could turn to. Lana, who'd say the right thing, who knew just how to bring Mom back down, soothe her, get her out of her funk. Granted, the first gaffe had been hers, back when she was six and everything was fresh and raw for everyone.

It had been Christmas morning, the Christmas she'd discovered that there was no Santa Claus. This had become evident after everyone's sly comments of "Santa's going to bring you a new little brother or sister" had come to nothing. There'd been the excitement of Mom's pregnancy, touching her ever-expanding belly, then Mom's nocturnal trip to the hospital and Lana's first grade teacher so enthusiastic about it the next day.

The news was delivered to the classroom just before the end of classes: a baby boy had been born. But shortly after that all information became hushed, top secret, whispered from Dad to Aunt Kelly and to the neighborhood moms who stopped by their house the next day. The gist of it: no baby after all. Mom returned home from the hospital three days later without a baby. It was impossible to understand. Granted, Lana understood the words part, that her new brother had died, but what she couldn't get her mind around was how months of happy preparation could lead to such devastating emptiness.

The worst part was the dark, terrible grief coming from Mom. It filled every molecule of air, a black, toxic gloom that made it impossible to draw a full breath. Mom wouldn't talk, she wouldn't laugh, she wouldn't even cry. She still looked like she had a baby in her stomach, which Annabel innocently noted aloud, which made Mom squeeze her eyes shut while Dad hastily changed the subject.

Lana took it upon herself to bear the terrible disappointment nobly. On Christmas morning two weeks later as they sat around the tree and exchanged gifts in a curiously joyless manner, Lana reached over and patted Mom's hand.

"It's all right," she murmured. "I didn't need another little brother anyway."

Mom's eyes widened from the half-mast position they'd maintained since her return from the hospital. She reared back as if she'd been struck. Then she jumped up from her chair, the little ceramic bowl Lana had made for her tumbling off her lap. She ran down the hall, into her bedroom, door slamming shut behind her, and in the appalled silence of the living room, they could all hear her low keening moans. Not even crying, but something infinitely more frightening.

"Nice going, Lan," her older brother Danny commented. Lana felt too awful to even throw back a reply, a defense.

They all lived in that terrible grief-saturated limbo for another month, a ghastly period that filled Lana with such fear, she found it difficult to sleep, eat, or focus at school, until the day that Mom left and they thought they'd lost her, all that evening, the long terrible night.

That had been the bottom.

The blackest of black.

When Mom finally came back home—after they'd found her, after her long stay in the hospital that healed your insides, not your outsides—she didn't seem much better than the Mom who'd scared Lana with her zombie expression. But now there was counseling and "happy pills" and people coming by the house to check up on Mom and the kids as well, and somehow they hobbled through the next few months, all of the kids cowed into obedience, into getting along, not creating any discord. Which they managed for several months, a feat that Lana, to this day, found to be nothing short of a miracle. A collaborative effort. It worked, slowly but surely.

What they couldn't do for Baby John, they did for Mom. They brought her back to life.

She stirred from the bed, glancing at the clock on the nightstand. Ten-thirty. She rose, changed into a nightshirt, checked her phone to see if Gil had left a message. He hadn't; he'd told her he'd be out with Julia tonight. She could visualize him, having glanced at the incoming phone number, smiling to himself, maybe, but turning to Julia with a "oh, it's nobody—I'll let them leave a message" comment.

She turned off the lights and slid between the bed sheets. From the other room she heard the reassuring sound of Alice's voice, high and sweet, talking to her cat, and a corresponding meow. The bed was comfortable, luxuriously so. The sheets were a soft, rich cotton; who knew cotton could feel so silky to the skin? A feather comforter managed to feel both weightless and warm on her body. If it hadn't been for the conversation with Mom, she would have been reveling in the experience of this new home.

She thought of Mom and found herself resorting to prayer, the way she'd done as a little kid.

Please, God. Let her be okay. Don't let her go to that black place again. Whatever it takes to protect her, we'll do it. I'll do it.

Chapter 13 – Confrontation

Alice would have thought, given Lana's relocation, that Gil would act a bit more deferential to her at work. But at their weekly two o'clock meeting, during which she confirmed the Redgrave Foundation proposal's delivery, she caught on to how they weren't the "everything's equal" buddies she'd thought.

Their two o'clock meeting was a breezy, Thursday affair where one of them wandered to the other's office sometime between two o'clock and two-thirty, reclined in the guest chair as they updated each other on key client issues, sharing whatever good joke happened to be circulating. Sometimes they headed to the café to conduct it over coffee. They'd been known to step across the street to Murphy's to discuss business over a pint of beer.

Today, after Alice had shared the news about the Redgrave proposal, she leaned back in her chair and regarded Gil.

"So, you've been closemouthed, but I have to know. What really happened that night with him? You can trust me."

No conversation topic had ever been too bawdy for Gil in the past. The more scandalous, the bigger the smile on his face as he told the story, even when it involved him. The wealthy, widowed octogenarian who'd seduced him over drinks back at her place; the mother and daughter duo who'd had no problems sharing him; the famous actor, a buff, macho man's-man, who'd propositioned him one night. But now, to her surprise, a dull red flush came over his face and he frowned.

"That doesn't concern you."

"Yes, well." She paused to finger the papers on her desk before looking up at him. "I need to know if this is going to be a problem at any point."

"Problem, like what?" He enunciated each word carefully, with disdain.

"Like, um, the wrong kind of interest?"

The disapproving, "mind your place" frown deepened, her cue to drop the subject.

She needed to know. She sat there, smiling politely at him, waiting.

Finally he replied, in a dignified fashion. "Our interest in each other is professional only. Aside from that momentary, drunken deviation at the party, the sole component of my relationship with Andy and the Redgrave Foundation is business."

"Oh. Okay. That's great to hear."

She offered him a big, stupid smile, made a mental note to never bring it up again, and they moved on to the next client issue.

Lana was the cause of the change in him. Alice had known from the start that something like this would happen. What she hadn't known was how personally involved she'd become, how ambivalent her feelings would continue to be toward this pretty, talented, lonely girl, who, unfathomably, seemed to like and respect Alice, no matter how prickly she acted.

There was not one thing to complain about in regards to Lana living with her. She was neat, polite, helpful and unobtrusive. Something about the whole situation unnerved Alice, however, saying nothing for the nocturnal presence of Gil, who'd slip in late after Alice had gone to her room for the night. He'd head out just as quietly in the early hours of the morning. Seeing him at work a few hours later, all fresh and shaved and smiling, felt awkward.

Everything felt awkward, off kilter.

Montserrat called her that afternoon, to her considerable surprise and joy. Alice knew how the autumn months were for her friend; it was prime concertizing season, with back-to-back engagements through much of the period. But Montserrat had found time to call. Better yet was learning she was in town, if only for a day and a half more.

"Carter told me about you and Niles," she said in a voice so warm and contrite it made Alice's throat constrict. "I'm so sorry I wasn't there for you. You were so weird that night, I should have known something was up and called you."

"It's okay," Alice told her.

It was. Because she had her best friend back, albeit temporarily, who was now insisting that Alice stop by that night after work for a glass of wine. Alice happily agreed.

Montserrat was on the phone when Alice arrived. She opened the door to Alice's knock, blew Alice a kiss and offered a "make yourself comfortable" gesture, before shifting her attention back to her phone caller. Alice went into the kitchen, poured herself a glass of wine and returned to the living room, settling in on a corner of the couch. Montserrat talked for a few more minutes, alternately listening while she leafed through documents and sheet music on the nearby table. She wandered into the kitchen as she finished up her call.

As soon as she hung up, she called out a hello to Alice. There was the soft clinking of glass, and a moment later she showed back up in the living room with her own glass of wine and a bowl of olives.

"Sorry about that," she said. "I thought I was answering a question or two but it turned out to be a full interview." She set down the bowl on the table between them and with a happy sigh, eased herself into the oversized armchair adjacent to Alice.

"It's always so nice to slip in a few days at home in between tours. Some musicians would rather avoid the extra travel time and just spend a free day in the next city, but this is what I want. Home. Sitting in my own comfy chair." She allowed her head to fall back against the pillows.

"And a glass of wine," Alice added.

"Oh, yes. A glass of wine is part of the equation. As is a visit from my dear friend." She lolled her head over to smile at Alice. "How are you?" she asked.

"Right at this moment, I'm good."

"Glad to hear that. So, what's new, besides this bad news of our Niles getting himself too involved in work once again?"

"Well, I have a new housemate."

"Another cat?"

Alice laughed. "No. Is that all you think I'm capable of housing?"

"Well, I'm just saying, from a cat's perspective, it's a great place to move into."

"No, this is a roommate of the human persuasion."

Montserrat looked puzzled. "I've only been gone for ten days. Who'd you conjure up so fast, and why?"

"You're not going to believe it."

"Who?"

Alice was enjoying the suspense. "Let me give you a hint. You know her."

She watched the confusion work over Montserrat's face, the

way her eyes widened in surprise only to narrow immediately afterward as if to rule out the idea, until she finally looked up at Alice.

"Not Lana," she said, more as a statement than a question.

"Yes, Lana."

Montserrat sputtered comically like something out of a cartoon. "Well. I didn't see *that* coming."

"Trust me. Neither did I. That's Gil for you, though."

"Care to explain?"

Which Alice did. Afterward, Montserrat gave an approving nod. "Good for you. Really. That was a big gesture."

"Yes, it was rather big. It's just now sinking in how big."

"You and Lana."

"Or shall we say, me and Lana and Gil."

"So, the two of them obviously worked everything out."

"I'll say."

"Oh, that's good to hear. She looked like a little lost lamb when I saw her at the performing arts library that afternoon."

That afternoon, less than two weeks ago, when Alice had still had her secure, functional relationship. A pang of hurt shot through her. "Well," she said, "she's a survivor."

"I agree. I must say, it's been a pleasure getting to know her. It's exciting, really, observing a hardworking young woman who's on the cusp of actualizing as an artist." Montserrat paused, swirled the wine around in her glass and regarded it thoughtfully. "She reminds me of myself at that age. All focus and determination, but at the same time, quite rudderless, deep down."

"Ah, but I wouldn't know about your past, would I?" Alice strove to keep her voice light. "Aside from what I learned the night of your dinner party. When you and she were confiding in each other."

She immediately regretted the words, their petty insinuation. Worse was the pity that came over Montserrat's face.

"Oh, Alice. She's just a girl. Don't feel threatened by her."

A surprise resentment welled up in Alice. She didn't welcome Montserrat's easy smile just then, her smooth dismissal of her past as something Lana was privy to, but not Alice.

"Maybe I'd like to know more about you."

"Trust me, there's nothing pretty about my past. Nothing worth listening to." Montserrat leaned over, selected an olive, and popped it into her mouth.

"Why don't you let me be the judge of that? You've heard about my childhood, after all."

"And I loved hearing about it." Montserrat extracted the olive pit and tucked it into a napkin. "Especially the happily-ever-after when Marianne turned all of you back into a family and kept it going that way. I loved imagining it, in that pretty house of your family's."

"Why? What was so bad about your youth?"

The same nervous undercurrent that now permeated her house seemed to have followed her to Montserrat's living room. Alice could feel it around them, swirling and uncoiling, like cigarette smoke.

"Honestly, it's not that dramatic," Montserrat said. "I've told you how my parents were, all wrapped up in their acting, dragging me all around Europe like a piece of luggage. Emotional neglect is probably the worst I can pin on them. But I was a levelheaded kid and I learned from an early age to fend for myself. Playing the violin? My idea alone. When they told me it was impossible, that they couldn't pay for lessons, I made it happen. Every goal I achieved from then on was through my persistence and diligence alone. That's why I feel like I can relate to Lana, even though her circumstances sound quite different."

Montserrat settled back in her chair. The room was silent as she took a sip of her wine.

"And so you went on to London's Royal Academy of Music for four years and played your way to international acclaim?" Alice asked.

Montserrat paused, for the briefest of instants, before nodding.

"Hard work alone got you there, huh?"

"That's it. Endless hours of work and practice. No glamour in that story."

She was lying. Alice could tell.

"So, your conservatory days. Were your parents living there in London too?"

"No. They alternated between Paris and New York during those years."

"How did you get by?"

This produced a small frown. "I was eighteen, Alice. I'd supported myself for years with my laundry business. By fourteen I was able to charge for music gigs—weddings, parties, events. I knew how to live on a tight budget; I'd done it all my life."

Alice straightened from her relaxed position on the couch. "Did you make good friends?"

Montserrat looked uneasy. "I'm not following this. You want to know what, precisely? Yes, I had friends there. A few. But conservatory is not intended to be a social experience. You're there to work hard, learn music and technique from world-class teachers, and perform whenever possible. What else do you want to know?"

Where did it come from, this dark, distressing urge to challenge, to take down such an artist? Was it the pinnacle of admiration or the pinnacle of envy? Or perhaps the two met, there at the very top, and there was no difference.

"Tell me about your good friends back then," she insisted. "Your most intimate friends."

Montserrat's brown eyes had grown bright; color had crept into her cheeks. She'd never looked more lovely. She'd never looked more trapped and uncertain.

Good.

Montserrat rose abruptly and left the room. She returned a minute later, bringing with her the bottle of wine, pouring each of them more without speaking. Afterward she sat back and met Alice's eyes. Gone was the trapped, afraid look. In its place was a chilliness that sent a jittery thrill down Alice's spine.

"Let's see. Is it Len Stevenson you want me to talk about, Alice? For whatever reason God only knows."

"Who is he?"

"Who do you think? The intimate friend from conservatory days you seem so keen to hear about. Ah, Len. A true friend in need. Do you want to know how much he helped me? I'm thinking you do, or you wouldn't have brought this up."

Montserrat didn't wait for her to reply.

"Len was the owner of the Vuillaume back then. He was a very wealthy, well-connected arts philanthropist and patron. He asked me if I'd like to test it out and borrow it. For the duration of my career. This was a pretty heady proposition for a twenty-year-old to hear. As you see it here in this room right now, you can probably guess the answer. Of course it came with a price. Let me tell you all about that price, Alice."

Montserrat's eyes were flashing now. Alice knew the trapped, uncertain expression was now on her own face and that Montserrat was taking equal grim pleasure in being the one to put it there.

"A young woman's virginity carries a premium at the bargaining table. Good thing I saved mine for the right occasion.

And after that? The Tourte bow, mine for the asking. Imagine having to shell up 25,000 quid for a bow on my own and yes, that would be pound sterling and not U.S. dollars. What's a blow job or two, or six, between friends? And how to put a price on the introduction to Judith, my New York manager? Handles only the best, only by referral. Then there were the calls to some big-name conductors. Cigars and chocolates sent alongside a demo CD to presenters who pretty much control the concert circuit. You think, for a second, a nobody like myself could have made that kind of action happen?"

Alice's mouth opened but no sound came out. She shut it, chastened. Montserrat took another gulp of wine, picked up the bottle and slopped more wine into each of their glasses.

"Len became very important the season I finished up my conservatory studies, when I was competing in the Royal International Violin Competition. That's one of those big, prestigious, career-launching competitions, and it was held that year, right there in London. The stress of it, the pressure to excel were just unbearable. I made it to the finals. The night before my final concerto performance, after fourteen hours of practice—par for the course throughout the entire fourteen-day competition— my nerves were so fraught, I was close to a breakdown. Len took one look at me, made me set down the Vuillaume and go out with him and his wife to dinner. Drinks beforehand, drinks during, drinks after. Stupid idea, yes. That's stress for you. Back at their home, Len dropped his bomb, telling me that unfortunately they might have to sell the Vuillaume, that they had an interested buyer offering a price they couldn't refuse."

Alice stared at her. "That bastard! How could he? And why?"

"In retrospect, I think he was worried that I'd outgrow him and the need for the Vuillaume, which, after all, wasn't a Strad. Big competition winners attract lots of sponsors, who like their names and instruments affiliated with winner musicians. But, then again, Len knew how much the Vuillaume meant to me. And we both knew it was his to sell.

"As you might guess, I was pretty upset. I was also very drunk. The timing of his announcement couldn't have been worse. But of course he knew that; he'd planned it that way."

"Montserrat. God. What did you do?"

"I begged him to reconsider. I told him I'd do anything, anything to keep the Vuillaume safe with me."

Prudence told her she'd heard enough, but a lurid sense of curiosity got the better of her. "How did he respond?"

Montserrat's eyes flickered from her wine glass to Alice and back to her glass. "He invited me to show him and his wife 'anything.'"

The insinuation became clear.

"With both of them?"

She was sounding like Lana, she realized. Montserrat rewarded her with a condescending smile.

"Yes, Alice. Both of them. Particularly useful when one of them wants a moment captured on video. Or when the other prefers girls to her hairy overweight husband. Goodness. The tricks and positions I was taught that night. Can you imagine?" She flashed Alice a look of scorn. "Silly me. Of course you can't. Anyway. I let them play their games. And the next morning, I felt so wasted, so hung over and full of misgivings, I wanted to die. But hey, not on the agenda. Because I had to perform my concerto that night. It was the Sibelius Violin Concerto, a marathon, even on the best of days."

Here she seemed to lose her bravado.

"That final performance was nothing short of surreal. Who

knows where I pulled all that energy from? It was like pure despair. Like I'd reached the end of my rope. Which, in truth, I had. If I'd lost the competition, an open door to professional freedom would have shut in my face. But even that would have been tolerable compared to losing my Vuillaume. That would have been like having a limb cut off."

She glanced over at Alice. "Are you familiar with the Sibelius?"

"I've heard it. But I don't know it well," she admitted.

"The second movement is so haunting, so intense. You hear the brass from the orchestra slowly building, and there you are with your violin, desperately trying to… I don't know. Stay alive. Survive against the odds. The pain of it—I felt like a bird in the dead of winter, knowing I would die, because the cold was just too much to overcome. But you know what? I'll bet that bird keeps singing until the instant before it dies. Because what else can you do if you were born to sing?"

She laid her head against the pillow back of the chair. Alice, sickened by the story she'd just forced out of her friend, kept quiet. Silence hung over the room, opaque and cloying, until Montserrat spoke again.

"I don't think my body, my psyche, could handle a repeat of that night. But it won me first place. And I kept my Vuillaume."

They both turned to look at the Vuillaume, nestled in its case on the side table, the case opened to reveal Montserrat's bows and a few tucked-in, fading photographs.

"Does he…" Alice began, and faltered. "Does that man own it still?"

Montserrat snorted. "God, no. I'm out of that prison, thank goodness." She reached for the wine bottle and sloshed more wine into each of their glasses. "No, the West Coast Musicians' Guild owns it now."

"Who is that?"

"A consortium of three investors, one of them being the team of Carter and myself. We own thirty-four percent."

"How did this come about?"

A smile crossed Montserrat's face, the first one in a while.

"Actually Len did himself in. He got greedy. When Carter and I got engaged, he had the nerve to try and scare me again. There was a potential buyer, a very interested buyer, he told me. Maybe he was thinking he could blackmail me. No chance of that—I'd told Carter the whole story already. Carter was so incensed by the new threat, he immediately set to taking care of things. He got Matthew on board and together they devised this little plan. Carter and I publicly made an offer to Charles Beare in London, who was conducting the transaction. Len, of course, saw our names and rejected the offer. Then another investor with an infinitely more reputable name stepped in and offered two thousand over the Vuillaume's asking price. Since there was no real buyer to begin with, Len leapt at the offer, certain he was destroying me. Even after he found out the buyer represented the West Coast Musicians' Guild, which planned to loan the Vuillaume to me, he thought he'd gotten the upper hand."

Montserrat chuckled, shaking her head. "Silly, fuckwit Len."

"Wait." Alice sat up. "So you're saying the Guild is composed of three investors. You and Carter teamed up, Matthew, and who else?"

Montserrat regarded her expectantly. "Oh, come on Alice. You're an intelligent woman. A West Coast musical instrument investor with a reputable name—you mean you can't figure that part out?"

"No," Alice replied, mystified.

"Didn't you ever wonder why I was performing at Andy

Redgrave's house that night? Did you think it was some nice coincidence set up to please you?"

Alice was too stunned by the implication to take in the fact that Montserrat's words had contained a barb directed at her.

"Andy Redgrave owns part of the Vuillaume," Alice said slowly.

Montserrat nodded. "Thirty-three percent, as does Matthew. Which makes Carter and myself the majority shareholder, with the ability to overrule any decision to ever sell the violin. And any one shareholder's decision to sell his shares must meet with a two-thirds majority vote. Carter and Matthew are lifelong friends; Matthew won't ever turn on us. The Vuillaume is as safe with me as it will ever be, seeing as we'd never be able to buy it outright. Not after paying for its insurance and our own mortgage. A violinist has to decide, own a house or own a prestigious violin. Only a lucky few can afford to do both."

Alice thought back to Andy's words at his party, the "how do you like the Vuillaume?" comment. She'd replied, certain she knew more about the Vuillaume than Andy did. Instead, she'd been preaching to its part-owner.

"I can't believe you never told me this," she said to Montserrat.

"Why?" Montserrat retorted. "What makes you so entitled, that you should have been privy to that information?"

This time the barb was more evident. The two of them regarded each other uneasily, aware that some shift had occurred in their friendship, an opened Pandora's box that allowed ill feelings and hidden resentments to come creeping into the room.

Why hadn't she seen all this coming? Why hadn't she just let everything be?

There was a jingle of keys at the front door and a moment later Carter stepped into the entryway. Montserrat leapt up and scurried over to fling her arms around him. Carter slid his arms around her waist, puzzled but pleased.

"And to what do I owe this burst of affection?"

"I just want to show you how much I love and appreciate you," Montserrat murmured into his neck.

"Um, have you ladies been consuming a little too much wine, perhaps?"

Montserrat and Alice both laughed, a little too loudly, too cheerfully, as if to convince each other that they were done with the heavy stuff, that life was about laughter and good company and good wine.

Alice rose from her seat. "I should get going."

"No, no, don't leave yet. But let me go get Carter a glass so he can join us." Montserrat hurried off to the kitchen. Carter remained standing in the living room, shuffling through the day's mail. He smiled over at her.

"How's it going?"

"Not bad," she lied. "How about you?"

"Good, good."

She knew she should steer away from the subject, but like a semi-reformed alcoholic who'd accidentally stumbled into a bar, the temptation proved too great.

"Niles in country still?" she inquired lightly, to which Carter shook his head.

"He left yesterday afternoon for Taiwan."

"Did you see him before he left?"

"For a few minutes on Monday evening, when I brought over my adapter kit. It was late, he was still working."

The questions flew through her head. *Was he happy? Did he look tired? Did he mention my name? Did I blow it with him?* She wanted to reach out and pluck at Carter's sleeve, touch his arm, as if that somehow might impart the essence of the missing member of their party of four.

"Did he say anything?"

"Like what?" Carter looked puzzled, then guarded. "Should I have been trying to find out something?"

"No, no. Of course not. Don't be silly. It's just, oh, nothing."

"He was in that zone of his," Carter said by way of explanation.

"Oh, sure. That's why I told him the two of us should just hold off on things, as well."

"Good call."

The red wine in her stomach gave a great lurch. Before she could speculate about the possible meanings behind Carter's two-word reply, Montserrat returned, bearing a glass and a plate of cheese and crackers.

Montserrat was in a good mood now, her high spirits infectious. She persuaded Carter to sit with them, and for Alice to have one more glass of wine. Conversation grew light, entertaining, as they argued about what constituted a good beef bourguignon and whether it was truly necessary, as Montserrat was insisting, to boil beef bones for eight hours to produce a good stock.

Finally Alice excused herself to use the bathroom. On her return, she spied Montserrat and Carter, now in the kitchen, standing close. Carter's hands were on Montserrat's hips, his face buried in the crook of her neck. Montserrat's hands were moving up and down Carter's back, having slipped under his shirt. Carter raised his head and the loving look he and Montserrat exchanged, the palpable aura of their affection, made a lump form in Alice's throat. It was so intimate, so exclusionary. She felt a recognition somewhere inside her, an "ah, so that's what true love, enduring love looks like." It made her feel both happy for her friends and more achingly alone.

She slipped into the living room, finished the last of her wine and called out in a loud voice, "Well, I'll be going now!"

A whisper from the kitchen, a chuckle. A moment later Montserrat and Carter appeared in the archway, dazed smiles on their faces. Alice knew the minute she left they'd make a beeline for the bedroom.

Montserrat pried herself from Carter's side and gave Alice a hug. "Thanks for coming over," she said.

"Thanks for inviting me."

"Any time. When Niles comes back we'll have a beef bourguignon cook-off."

Neither of them made reference to the earlier conversation.

Enough damage had been done already.

Chapter 14 – Lana Needs Coaching

Lana was vacuuming Alice's living room floor and enumerating the reasons why it was a good thing, or at least a productive thing, that Gil had left town for the weekend. She'd be able to catch up with sleep, with tasks. Come down from the week's hard work and ramp up for next week's opening night. And it wasn't Andy Redgrave he'd left town with, after all. It was Julia, the lesser of the two evils.

"It's only for two nights," Gil had told Lana over the phone. "I'm sorry, love. It was a last-minute decision, Julia being capricious. She wasn't ready to go to New York just yet, and suddenly Los Angeles and the Beverly Wilshire seemed like the perfect solution for her. Only, with an escort."

Gil sounded gloomy about not being able to stay in San Francisco with Lana on her last free weekend, but duty called, he admitted. Once he began to describe the hotel, however—did Lana know that this was the hotel *Pretty Woman* was filmed in?—and the suite Julia always insisted on, she could hear his undercurrent of excitement. Whether or not he wanted to be there, she sensed, he was going to enjoy it.

But Lana would never be far from his thoughts, he told her. Not after this week together.

They'd made love finally, a dizzying, thrilling experience that had kept them up long past midnight the first night, touching each other, reveling in the closeness, the deep satisfaction of bare skin against skin, body parts clicking into place just right. Afterward, lying there next to him, stroking the length of his bare backside as he slept, she'd wondered how she could have ever let Mom persuade her this was wrong. They'd used protection. Gil had been wonderful and caring, before *and* after. She'd never felt so sheltered, so nurtured by one person before. The next day when she saw him in the café, they'd acted breezy and casual around each other, as they'd agreed was best, but when he met her gaze and held it, she knew he was taking this as seriously as she was. That night when he came over, and the following night, he proved it all over again.

The flip side was that he was gone for the whole weekend. She decided that nothing felt quite so empty as the emptiness that had temporarily been filled by something perfect. She could rationalize all she wanted, but in the end, her body missed him with an ache she would have found impossible to imagine, only two, three weeks earlier.

A tap on the shoulder sent her airborne with shock and fright. She swiveled around to see Alice there behind her, hands on her hips, regarding Lana in amusement. Lana switched off the vacuum cleaner.

"Boy," Alice said. "You were in your own world. I was practically shouting your name."

"I'm sorry," she stuttered. "I was lost in thought. Vacuuming always puts me in a sort of trance."

"So I see. Tequila might do the same thing, with considerably less effort involved." She surveyed the room. "How did you ever find the vacuum cleaner?"

"I didn't mean to go snooping around in your storage closet or anything. It's just that I was feeling sort of restless and wanted to put my energy to good use, and I saw the vacuum there."

"Oh. Well, thanks for cleaning. But really, stuff like that isn't necessary."

"It's no problem. My mom would always tell me, be a good guest and keep your host happy." She prepared to turn the vacuum back on but Alice held up a hand.

"Lana," she said, and hesitated. "I'm not expecting a 'clean in exchange for rent' kind of setup here. I want to make sure you know that."

The cleaning lady thing. Lana felt a blush rise up her neck and stain her face.

Alice looked uncomfortable as well. "Excuse me. I'm going to go start my dinner prep," she said, and headed to the kitchen.

Lana finished the vacuuming and put away the cleaner as quietly as she could, before going into the kitchen. Alice was there, chopping vegetables for a salad, a glass of wine beside the lettuce bag. She surveyed Lana and took a sip of wine before speaking.

"Gil abandoned you this weekend, it sounded like."

"Yes. L.A. The Beverly Wilshire with Julia. I guess she didn't want to go there alone so she begged him to join her."

Alice grimaced. "Is that what he told you?"

Lana thought back to the conversation. "Well, I don't know if those were his exact words. Just that she wanted to go and he was going along to keep her company, to be nice."

"Nice," Alice repeated. "Yes, it was 'nice' of him. Particularly since he was the one who persuaded her not to go back to New York so soon. And since he was the one to suggest the Beverly Wilshire and make the arrangements."

Lana regarded Alice, appalled. "But he made it sound like she was dragging him out."

In response, Alice only shrugged.

"How do you know this?" Lana asked.

"Because the wall that separates our offices is thin and I heard him make both calls."

It felt like someone had driven a fist into her stomach. "But why?"

Alice's expression softened. "I'm sorry, I shouldn't have said anything. Really, it didn't sound like some sneaky business, anything for you to get worried about. It was just Gil being Gil. But, I have to say, sometimes I get tired of listening to the way he works people. He puts so much energy into positioning them right where he wants them, making sure he's on their good side at all times."

"You mean like Julia? I thought the two of them were fine with how things were. That it was a convenience thing. Why would he feel the need to invite her away for a weekend?"

"Preventative maintenance, if I had to guess. I've got a hunch she's caught on to you two."

"How would she know? He says she never asks when he comes and goes."

"Lana, he's come over here three out of the past four nights and stayed long past socializing hours. Don't you think that's maybe just a tiny clue?" She shook her head. "He's got to be careful here. He likes his free rent, his pretty little car, but she's not stupid, nor is she that desperate. But if he invests a few nights into making her feel special, important, he can continue to play both sides."

Alice gave an irritable wave of her hand. "Can we drop the subject of Gil's behavior? It's going to make me lose my appetite."

"Sure. Sorry." Lana tiptoed over to the counter adjacent to the sink. There were a few scattered items from her own meal that she quickly popped into the dishwasher. While she was at it, she picked up the soaking saucepan Alice had used earlier for morning oatmeal and began scrubbing it clean. Alice's voice cut into her activity.

"I'll get to that."

"Oh, it's no problem. I'm right here, I'll take care of it." Lana continued scrubbing. "My mom always tells me, when I'm in a cleaning groove, I shouldn't stop, I should just keep powering on. Of course, she profits from that, huh? That part is a little annoying. I'll bet your mom wasn't like that."

"Stop it!"

Lana shut off the water and turned to regard Alice in confusion. Alice didn't look grateful for the help. She looked angry.

"Stop cleaning my house," Alice said. "And Stop. Bringing. Up. Our moms." The last sentence was exaggerated, bit out.

The awkwardness was terrible. Lana didn't know what to say.

Alice shoved away the knife and cutting board, ignoring the chopped carrot circles that rolled off and tumbled to the floor. "Look. I don't mean to be rude. But I just want to prepare my food in peace. Alone. Can you give me that?"

Lana felt tears rising, like nausea, in the back of her throat. She could only nod in reply.

Alice grabbed her glass of wine, only now noticing the carrots she'd sent to the floor. With her free hand, she stabbed a finger in their direction.

"I'll take care of that later," she said to Lana, her own voice trembling. "Please do not clean it for me." With that, she left the kitchen, hurried up the stairs. A moment later Lana could hear the thump of her bedroom door shutting.

She stood there in the now silent kitchen, still frozen into place. Then the tears began. She crept up the stairs and made it to the safety of her own room before the deluge commenced. She headed straight to the little tub chair that felt like a pair of arms holding her close. Whenever she sat in it sideways, legs tucked in, it gave her that precise feeling, these two strong arms, like Gil's but not. Gil, who was spending the night in a fancy hotel tonight with the woman he still publicly referred to as his girlfriend. Gil, who'd extended the invitation to Julia, not the other way around. She curled up in the chair, squeezed her eyes shut and cried.

Five minutes later a tap sounded at the door. Lana froze, mid-sob, horrified. "Yes," she called out in a high, phony voice.

"Can I come in?"

This was Alice's house; of course she could. "Yes," Lana managed. She knew she should straighten up, pretend to be fine, but she couldn't move from her huddled position.

Alice entered, saw her and stopped short. "That was the chair I had in my bedroom all through my teens. And the way you're sitting is exactly what I would do."

In response, Lana could only sniffle and offer a hiccup.

Alice came closer. "I just wanted to say I'm sorry. My impatience was about me and my stuff. It had very little to do with you."

"Thanks for saying that."

"It was rude of me."

"This is your home."

"That's no excuse." She sank to the bed and sat facing Lana. "Look. The mom thing. I owe you an explanation. You see, when I was a kid, I lost my mom."

"Like, lost her in a crowd?" she asked stupidly.

Alice's expression didn't change. "No. She died."

She stared at Alice in horror. Oh, God, how many times had she brought up Mom? Asked Alice whether her own mom was the same, simply as a way of making conversation? Dozens of mom references. Dozens of gaffes, over and over. Could she have been any more of a bull in a china shop?

Before she could begin to stutter her way through an apology, Alice lifted her hand.

"Wait. It's not some ghastly tragic story that's haunted my life. You are not irreparably damaging my psyche by bringing up moms. Marianne, my stepmom, has been like a mother to me since I was thirteen. I couldn't have asked for a better second mom. I've called her 'my mom' for years. Decades. Really, I'd even stopped thinking about it until recently. Until..."

Here she hesitated.

"Until I showed up," Lana finished.

Alice paused to ponder this. "You might be right."

"I'm sorry," Lana whispered. "I'm so sorry."

"Oh, it's not you. I think it's just what happens at my age." Alice spoke slowly, her expression pensive, as if she were figuring this out for the first time. "The stuff you thought you'd successfully run from, well, damned if it doesn't show up at your front door. Literally, in this case." She chuckled, good mood restored, but Lana only felt worse.

"Anyway," Alice said, "I don't talk about it much—the truth is, I'll go out of my way to avoid discussing it—but I thought you should know. I've had an atypical experience in the mother department. And I've never considered this before, but maybe I'm a little envious of you and your closeness with your mom."

Oh, if Alice only knew.

Alice rose but made no motion to leave. Instead she angled her head and studied Lana. "Are you okay? Did I say the wrong thing?"

"No," Lana managed.

"Well, what's going on, then? And don't tell me you're fine. Because you're not."

In response she could only shake her head.

Alice sat back down. "Tell me."

"I'm scared," she said. A great sob escaped and suddenly she was crying to Alice, babbling how she felt so ungrounded and worried, about her own mom's welfare, about how it no longer felt like Kansas City was her home, but neither did San Francisco feel like home. And Gil, so reliable at times, so flaky other times, like this weekend, so how much could she count on him? And the way she kept annoying Alice; what would she *do* if Alice kicked her out? She'd have nowhere to go. She'd end up just like Coop.

Alice looked sad. "Were you really thinking I'd kick you out? Because you made me irritable?"

Lana wondered if admitting to the truth would hurt or help her case. But Alice had taken her silence as an affirmative.

"Oh, Lana," she said softly. "I would never, never do that. I may be prickly, but I'm not a monster. I'm on your side here, even when I don't act like it." She gazed down at the comforter, tracing the nubbed pattern with her finger. "I'm sorry. I wish I could be a bigger person about this all. Sharing a house. Having functional relationships. It just doesn't come easily to me."

"You've been the greatest to me," Lana said. "Really."

A dubious expression crossed Alice's face. "Well, that's considerate of you to say. But anyway, know that this is your home for as long as you need it. Until you find some place you like more."

Lana refrained from telling her she'd probably never find a place she liked more. She didn't want to frighten Alice, who'd just bought her some time with her soothing words.

"So," Alice said. "You've got a week before you start performing. How are rehearsals going?"

"Okay, I guess. I'm only dancing in the corps in the first

program, which I suppose is good because it's less pressure on me. But aside from that, in class and around the other dancers, I feel, I don't know."

"Yes?" Alice encouraged.

"I feel so alienated," she whimpered. "Like no one likes me."

"Oh, sweetie." Alice moved over to the ottoman by Lana's chair. "It just takes time. The first season with a new company is mostly about getting into the groove."

Lana drew deep breaths to keep further tears at bay. "And I'm worried that *Autumn Souvenir*, the ballet for Program II, isn't going well. And the répétiteur has only got two more rehearsals with us before he heads back to Paris."

"Who are the other two demi-soloists with you in *Autumn Souvenir?*"

"I've got just the one partner. Javier Torres."

Confusion crossed over Alice's face. "Wait. That would make you the lead pas de deux couple. Not part of the demi-soloist trio."

"Right."

Alice's eyes grew round. "Oh, boy. That's big. Wow. That'll put you on the map here."

"Only if I do it really well."

"You're right," Alice admitted, which sent a jittery rush of anxiety through Lana's gut.

They sat there for a long moment, Lana unspeaking, Alice offering soft "wow"s to herself, as if still processing it all. "Okay," she said finally, in a stronger, take-charge way that immediately calmed Lana's nerves. "Tell me what the problem is."

Lana drew a deep, cleansing breath. "It's like I said. There's this undercurrent, this feeling that we're not getting along. I mean, it's not obvious. The opening pas de deux is fine. The variations and the coda are fine. It's that adagio in the middle. We've got the steps and basic intention down. It's just that there seems to be an impasse over the dynamics in one of the lift passages, that has everyone frustrated. During group rehearsal sessions, the second cast leads are practically jumping, there behind us, in their frustration, like they're sure they could do it better. They're both principals—I'm sure they could, too. And even the répétiteur is showing his frustration with it. With me."

"Who's the répétiteur? Any chance it's Denis Rousselot?"

"It is."

Alice looked pleased. "Oh, that's good to hear."

"You mean you *know* him?"

Alice began to chuckle. "Yes, I've worked with him. Great guy, even though he likes to get all Paris Opera Ballet and shout at his dancers." She gave the ottoman a pat. "Tell you what. I've been bad about not ever stopping by to say hi to him. Maybe I'll drop in on your next rehearsal. That is, if you want. Sometimes a fresh pair of eyes can provide some new perspective."

Lana's relief increased. "That would be great. You don't mind? The next rehearsal is on Sunday afternoon. Two o'clock, for two hours."

"Okay. Maybe I'll swing by around three."

"I can't tell you how much I'd appreciate that."

Alice rose. "Well. Here's to my first visit to a Ballet Theatre rehearsal in eight years."

It all went as planned. Even without Alice, the first hour of the rehearsal ran smoother. The entire cast of thirteen dancers was rehearsing together for the first time and the added presence of the demi-soloist trio and the corps dancers took a little of the pressure off Lana, made her less aware of the Cast II leads and the understudies, watching her critically. Yet sure enough, when it came time for the tricky partnered lift passage, the unease arose.

As if on cue, Alice appeared at the door.

Denis was delighted. "*Mais non, c'est pas possible. C'est toi!* You little bitch," he exclaimed, arms out, striding toward her. "Twice now I have been here staging work, these eight years, and they tell me you are right here, in the same building. But you don't stop by to say hello to your old friend, Denis?"

He'd enveloped Alice in a hug even as he spoke, bestowing kisses on her cheek before pulling back to regard her critically. He announced that she looked wonderful, that being *plus grosse* suited her, that she was *belle come une femme maintenant, pas comme une fille.* Lana supposed it was a compliment and not the insult "gross" sounded like, because Alice was pink-cheeked and smiling and even—God, who knew?—responding in careful French, which made Denis' smile broaden.

"Oh, you are most decidedly the college graduate now, yes. The educated career woman. *Bien fait, ma fille.* And now here you've returned to your old place of stomping. What brings us this good fortune today?"

"To see *you,* of course, Denis. Well, and, at the same time, to stop by to see my housemate here," she said, gesturing to Lana, which caused heads to turn her way. Alice peered closer at the corps dancers and gave a little cry of recognition. "Delores! And Joe! Familiar faces, oh how great."

More hugs, exclamations of pleasure, and now the older dancers and Denis were all talking at once and Lana learned how Joe had been a newbie the year of Alice's accident, but Delores had been part of Alice's circle of corps dancers in her early days and oh, the number of stories they could tell you about those early Anders years. And Ben, too. Before his back problems, when he was still dancing, burning up the stage, teasing the ballet masters before he switched camps and became one himself. What a shame he wasn't here right now, enjoying this little reunion.

Alice turned and surveyed the other dancers. She squinted at Courtney. "You look familiar," she said, a note of coolness creeping into her voice. "I think we once chatted. In the restrooms on the administrative level."

"I'm not sure," Courtney stammered. "You don't look familiar. It might have been someone else."

Alice hesitated, then offered Courtney a quick, uninterested smile. "Maybe you're right," she said. She turned back to Denis. "*Alors*, Monsieur Rousselot, I hope you'll allow me to sit and watch. Maybe share my humble opinion on a few tricky passages Lana might be struggling with."

"Oh, yes." Denis nodded vigorously. "Thank you, *thank* you. This is a fine idea."

He and Javier discussed and agreed upon the most troublesome spot, the very one Lana herself had worried about. Denis cued the accompanist to start the music sixteen counts prior. Lana and Javier waltzed their way to the center, Lana bourréed her way into a prep, a partnered pirouette turn. Afterward, her leg swung back into an attitude, Javier promenaded her around and lifted her out of the attitude, up over his head. *Whoosh*, like an autumn leaf picked up by the wind. She slithered down the length of his body. He caught and sustained a hold on one leg, stretching it into a 180-degree extension. One more gravity-defying toss upward, propelled by the extended leg, before he dipped her into a fish dive and lifted her back up.

It was not bad. It was not, however, performance-ready. Lana knew it; they all knew it. From the corner of her eye she saw the dancers in the second cast exchanging private looks, head shakes.

"Well, Alice?" Denis asked. Lana bent over, trying to catch her breath, hands on her thighs, face down. The corps members banded off to the side, murmuring to each other.

"It's too rigid there in the middle, isn't it? It's like Lana isn't trusting Javier."

Denis issued a big, theatrical exhale. "Thank you, Alice! She won't believe us. She thinks we're picking on her."

"Lana," Alice said. "Here's my take. It's like you're closing yourself off to Javier as you slide down. It's not physical so much as mental, I think."

Lana pondered this, sighed and nodded.

Alice turned to Javier. "And *you're* intimidating her."

Javier and Lana protested at the same time that he was not.

Alice shook her head. "I see what I see. Lana, try this." She paused to do a few stretches, adjust the yoga outfit she was still wearing from her morning class. Afterward she held out a hand to Javier, a command, really, and Javier took it.

"You're close, here, see?" She bourréed, positioned herself and executed a surprisingly sharp double pirouette. "Then the promenade. And the grand jeté lift."

There was a ripple of laughter as Alice slapped down Javier's attempt to lift her fully overhead, with a quip that she wouldn't subject him to the torture of her extra thirty pounds over Lana.

"Now, when he brings you down," Alice called out, "*cling* to him. Not with your arms or legs, but your body. Like your torso is Velcro'd to him. It's like being in love. The thought of separating, even for a minute, is enough for this, this *thing* inside you to seize up. So, you see, it's something in your core that tries to stay. It's not the arms at all."

Alice demonstrated the slow slide down Javier's chest one more time, this time with the music, dancing it full out.

It was uncanny to watch. Lana could feel the intensity in the air, the magic between Javier and Alice. For a moment, watching them, she could almost believe the two of them were in love. There was something so sweet and yet desperate about the way Alice adhered to him. Javier hooked her leg and raised it high; Alice could still manage a good extension, Lana noted. She'd lost none of her ballet dancer's grace. He dipped her, held her close, tenderly, before releasing the leg and his grip around her waist. It was beautiful to watch. It made Lana want to cry.

The spell broke a moment later when the music ended and Alice became just Alice again, readjusting her top, slapping Javier on the shoulder, telling him he was a sport, working with an old mare like her. She stepped back from the center. Denis cued the accompanist and Lana and Javier took the combination again.

This time it was so much better, so smooth, so right, that afterward everyone burst into applause. Denis looked almost tearful in relief, and even Javier was smiling as he told Lana the change was significant, that the weight redistribution had made everything fall into place.

They ran the adagio and coda movements straight through, acclimating to the presence of both corps dancers and soloists in the same performing space. The second cast, set up behind them, took their turn with the corps dancers as well. Denis looked up at the clock finally and exclaimed that their time was up and wonderful rehearsal, everyone.

As the women eased off their pointe shoes, Alice and Delores started joking around with Denis about a long-ago bet they'd had, that Alice had lost and never made good on. Alice insisted the time had come to pay up and that they should go out for a beer. Right then. The chance might not come around again.

"Denis, call Ben," Alice said. "Tell him he has to join us too."

Denis whipped out his phone, punching in numbers. A

moment later he was grinning, telling Ben there was trouble in the rehearsal room, some riffraff that needed to be dealt with. He listened, chuckling at Ben's reply.

"The culprit's name is Alice Willoughby," he continued. "Yes, you are so right. Too long, *n'est-ce pas?* We are all going over to Murphy's. I believe your presence is now mandatory." More laughter, and he pocketed his phone a moment later, smiling.

"*Allons-y, tous,*" he said. "Let's go drink."

Denis insisted Javier join them, and Alice turned to Lana.

"You're game, too, right?"

Lana shook her head. Gil was back; Gil who'd explained his way out of the "misunderstanding" of who'd invited whom to L.A., and now wanted to take Lana someplace special. She was supposed to meet him in twenty minutes.

Alice caught her eye. "Now, Lana," she said in a mock-scolding voice, "what could possibly be more important than *us?*" She held her arms out wide, as if encompassing the whole room, the whole of the WCBT. She was smiling but Lana saw the warning note in her eyes. She understood this was not an invitation Alice was offering her so much as an assignment, to get to know these long-established dance people better.

"We won't take no for an answer," Alice said.

She meant it.

"Maybe I can make a phone call," Lana said. "Delay my plans for an hour."

"I think that would be a splendid idea," Alice said. "Make it two hours."

The teacher had spoken.

The student complied.

Chapter 15 – The Article

Monday brought with it a curious reversal of moods between Alice and Gil. Alice was breezy and cheerful, buoyed by her time spent with Denis and the dancers. It had felt good to help Lana. It had felt good to be told her assistance made a real difference. There'd also been the subversive thrill of seeing the alarm on the pretty corps dancer's face. In spite of her comment to the contrary, Alice knew the girl had recognized her, not just from the restroom but from the snippy look she'd tossed out at Alice the day she'd gone to observe company class. It had given Alice a delicious sense of satisfaction to prove to the girl that she, too, could dance, that she was not just some administrative drone who could only gaze wistfully at the talent.

She popped by Gil's office to say hello once he'd arrived. He offered her a preoccupied, "leave me alone" smile. She ignored the hint and rested her weight against his door frame.

"So, Pretty Boy, how was your stay in the Beverly Wilshire? Say hi to Julia Roberts while you were there?"

"Oh, that's clever. I've never heard that one before."

"Did your Julia take you shopping? Hand you the credit card and tell you anything goes?"

He heaved an exaggerated sigh. "If you're through, I've got

work to do here."

She made no motion to leave. "Okay, I'm sorry. I'll stop with the *Pretty Woman* jokes. Seriously, how was your weekend?"

"Long. Painfully long. Except for the last part of it."

"That would be the part where you met back up with Lana."

"Yes. And thanks to you, my time with her was cut even shorter."

"No one was holding a knife to your throat to make those weekend plans, you know."

He frowned. "You told her, didn't you? That I was the one who suggested the getaway to Julia."

"Um, why was that wrong? When it was the truth."

"I would have thought you'd cover for me."

"Gil. In order to cover for you, I need to be apprised of the full situation. And besides, this wasn't a work-related issue. I don't have to lie for you on my personal time."

"There would have been no lying involved in the least."

"Ah. Just a little evasion."

This brought forth a distinct glare from him. He was in one of his prissy moods, Alice sensed. But she had news to change that. She waved a business letter at him.

"This just arrived. It might interest you."

She laid it down on his desk, a letter from the Redgrave Foundation. They'd read the WCBT's proposed request for $250,000, the letter stated, and prior to the final decision they wished to arrange a meeting and site visit. She watched Gil read it. A smile bloomed on his face.

"Andy told me this part is mostly a formality," he said. "He even brings the foundation's letter of agreement with him to the dinner meeting so it can be signed by both parties right there if he chooses."

He read the letter again. "This is very good news."

"It is indeed."

She could feel his good spirits returning, filling the room with optimism so heady, it made her feel like she'd just taken a whiff of some intoxicant that would soon cause her to burst into giddy laughter.

"Record turnaround time on a proposal, to boot," she said.

"He told me he'd fast-track it once he got it."

"He certainly lived up to his word."

"This'll put us back on forecast for next year."

"All thanks to your hard work."

Gil smiled at her, with genuine warmth this time. "Our hard work. Couldn't have done it without you."

"Thanks."

They smiled at each other and like that, they were fine again, great friends, an unbeatable team.

Tuesday morning signaled the end of Alice's good mood. She overslept, there was a long line at Starbucks, they skipped her order and on the second pass, got it wrong. When she entered the main lobby from the street, the door caught on her heel, making her stumble. As she hobbled toward the elevator, she heard the female security guard ask her colleague, "Is that her?"

"Yeah. Kinda clumsy, though," he said, and they both chuckled.

She puzzled over this on her way to her office. A few more curious glances cast her way made her wonder if there was a terrible stain on her blouse, or perhaps a smudge of cocoa dust on her face. She stopped by the ladies' room and peered into the mirror. Nothing.

One of the administrative assistants was washing her hands at the basin next to Alice. She smiled at Alice.

"I didn't know you *danced,* danced," she said. "With the company here, I mean."

Alice nodded, mystified.

"Well, I think that's just great. Really. It's very touching."

Something was going on and Alice didn't have a clue what it might be. It was as if a year, not an evening, had passed since she'd left the offices, a year in which something very profound had happened to her, only she didn't know what. A hint arrived ten minutes later when she received a phone call from Lucinda.

"You're late," Lucinda snapped. "I thought you came in at eight o'clock."

Alice glanced at the clock. 8:17 a.m. Still before Gil, before official business hours. She swallowed a sharp retort and instead told Lucinda that she was here now.

"Stay there. I'll be right over," Lucinda said and hung up before Alice could ask her just what this was all about. A minute later she arrived, carrying a copy of the newest *San Francisco Arts Times,* which she slapped down on Alice's desk.

"Dance section," Lucinda told her, her expression a mixture of fury and triumph.

Alice leafed uneasily to the section. And there she was, poised in an arabesque en pointe. Dear God.

It was the eight-year-old *Tomorrow's Lament* publicity photo and further down the page, a photo of two dancers in the ultra-contemporary *Paradigm for Six* ballet. Between the two photos—which were oversized, glorious, taking up a quarter of the page—was the article, entitled, "Moving Forward: Changing What no Longer Works."

The first thing one notices about former West Coast Ballet Theatre soloist Alice Willoughby, the article read, *is her brisk professionalism, her commanding presence that hints at the grace and artistry of her former craft. The thirty-three-year-old is the associate director of development, but during her tenure with the West Coast Ballet Theatre Association, she has taken on many roles. Rising from apprentice to the corps de ballet and ultimately to soloist level, Willoughby's promising career was tragically cut short following a debilitating injury in 1997. Forced to reassess her career goals, the determined dancer shifted her attention and her abilities toward the administrative side of the game, starting as an assistant and working her way up to her current position. Flexibility, so important in a dancer, becomes a philosophy, a business model that has spelled success for both Willoughby and the West Coast Ballet Theatre, as the institution commences its pre-season performance schedule and prepares for its annual black-tie October fundraiser.*

It continued on, from Alice to the WCBT, to today's group of dancers and back to Alice. Her spirit and drive that was so symbolic of the art of ballet in the 21st century in general, its challenges, the constant need to reassess, ask what wasn't working and how to change it. How the WCBT, under the direction of Anders Gunst, managed to do just that. But it was not until the final paragraph that the October fundraising event received further mention. And only at the end of the paragraph did Lucinda's name appear as the public relations contact. Sarah, as the special events manager, was not referenced at all.

Alice wanted to shrink into a tiny ball and roll herself under her desk, staying lodged there until five o'clock. Maybe past then. Maybe she'd just shack up for the week under her desk.

"What did I tell you?" Lucinda had the high brittle voice of an elementary school teacher who'd been at the same job way too long. "What did I specifically tell you?"

"You told me not to say anything bad. And I didn't." Alice

pointed to the article. "I had no idea whatsoever that she was going to pull this. She never gave me any clue that this was going to be about anything besides the upcoming events."

"Did you tell her these things about your past?"

She hated that she had no defense here. All she could do was protest that even though yes, she'd said these things, she'd considered it all to be off-topic, just chitchat.

"Don't you know anything? She's a *reporter*. She sniffs out stuff like that, it's how she develops her hook," Lucinda said. "There's no such thing as 'off-topic' conversation. From the moment you shake their hand, it's on the record, even when they try to tell you that something's off the record. It's never off. Honest to God, I regret the day I let you give that interview."

Rage billowed up in Alice. "Maybe I do too. Maybe, just maybe, I was more interested in doing *my* job that day, not your job, not Sarah's job. Try and remember that next time you pawn another department's work off onto me."

Lucinda's eyes glittered with hostility. "Well. I'll let you get back to your work again." She pivoted around and headed toward the door.

"Wait, don't you want the paper?"

Lucinda looked back at her. "Why don't you keep it? A souvenir of your glory days to go show all your friends. Which was what you wanted all along."

The breath left Alice's lungs in a great whoosh. She was so angry she couldn't speak. Which was not a bad thing in retrospect, because the things she might have otherwise shouted out at Lucinda might have gotten her into trouble. Instead she sat, seething.

Obsessed by her former "glory days." Was that how she was perceived here? How long had Lucinda been waiting to say such a thing to her?

Her eyes settled on the framed photo on the wall. The very same *Tomorrow's Lament* photo. At least Lucinda hadn't noticed. She rose from her chair, strode over to the wall and yanked the picture down. So much for the reminder to pay attention at all times while on the job. She shoved the framed photo face-down in the bottom desk drawer.

The day was ruined. Every time Alice stepped out of her office she felt the stares, heard the whispers. In the break room, someone had pinned the photo and article in its entirety on the bulletin board. Gil, to her relief, was more amused than angry about it, as if Alice had displayed poor choice in attire at an important function.

"What the hell," he said when she sought him out to explain. "There's no such thing as bad press. Lucinda's just getting all excited for nothing. Guess that's part of her job. Create a buzz whenever possible. But no media buzz lasts forever, much as she'd like it to."

Gil had a point. By Wednesday, the comments and jokes had become routine. By Thursday they'd subsided. There were more important things going on; it was the company's opening night for Program I, what they'd be taking on tour. The marketing and special events departments were hosting a pre-performance reception, which Alice begged off, claiming a pounding head. Gil excused her under the condition that she'd join him and other key administrators at L'Orange, a posh bar-restaurant, following the performance. Charlie Stanton, the WCBT's executive director, had booked a private alcove adjoining the dining area, for him and Anders to more comfortably mingle with the WCBT's key clients and friends.

Alice agreed to Gil's proposal. They both knew that no amount of cajoling or threats would get her to sit through an actual performance.

At ten-thirty that night she took a taxi back to the Civic Center and met Gil in the lobby of the theater. Together they waited for Lana to remove her makeup and change into street clothes. Alice knew Gil wanted to time their entrance at L'Orange as a trio on purpose. Once again, Alice was to be their front.

Tonight, however, she didn't mind. Lana, appearing a moment later, looked sensational in her black party dress, her Ferragamos. She'd let her hair down and it was a shiny brown shimmer down her back. Some eyeliner still remained from her stage makeup, lending her a sultry, sophisticated air. She looked like a rising star, Alice decided, as the three of them entered L'Orange.

She was not the only one who thought so. Lana was creating a stir and, even more charming, she didn't even seem to notice. Instead she was wide-eyed with admiration over the restaurant's cosmopolitan ambiance, the wrought-iron stairway curving up to the second level, the sleek taupe walls interspersed with exposed brick.

L'Orange, post-performance, was more of an event than a source of meals. Michael's alcove was crowded with people and the party had spilled out to the main area, making the whole restaurant feel like a nightclub, a New Year's Eve party. Gil had asked Alice to make sure Lana didn't get lost in the shuffle of the boisterous crowd. He needn't have worried. Alice led Lana around and everywhere they went, people wanted to know who she was, congratulate her on a fine performance, even though they likely wouldn't have been able to pick her out, there in the ensemble of *Serenade* dancers. Alice introduced her to board members, administration, influential patrons. She saw Mark Haverford, a WCBT donor, better known for his flirtatious, womanizing behavior than his financial generosity. He was staring at Lana. Two minutes later he was by Alice's side, tugging at her arm, insisting on an introduction.

She looked up and saw Gil, across the room, frowning at her. She ignored him and introduced Lana to Mark. Lana was being her sweet, polite self, and Mark was falling over himself in his eagerness to get her a drink, have her sit down next to him, get to know each other a little better, and was she seeing anyone? No time for anything but her ballet? Ah. Well. Too bad. But commendable. But here was his card, should Lana change her mind.

Alice saw Gil, trying to make his way back over to them, but the crowd seemed to be moving against him. Tonight Gil was the one who was forced to fight for Lana's attention and compete with the others. It was the opposite of the night of Andy's party, a fact that Alice found entertaining. Gil finally returned to their side and flashed Alice a reproachful look.

"I told you to look out for her," he said to her once Mark Haverford had been shooed away, replaced by two elderly ladies eager to tell Lana of their own bygone ballet days.

"I was looking out for her. You'll note she's been by my side since we arrived."

"Mark Haverford? How could you? No woman is safe around him. And you introduced them. I saw you."

"Gil. She's twenty-two, not sixteen."

"She's taken, in case you haven't noticed."

"Right. Taken, by Julia's boyfriend."

Gil scowled, but held back further comment.

Lana's hand on his arm a moment later seemed to diffuse his anger. She murmured to Gil that, if possible, she'd like to have a seat and eat a real meal. Gil, being Gil, managed to procure them a private table in the restaurant area within minutes, ahead of the people still waiting to be seated. A waiter materialized, took their order and hurried away. Alice asked Lana how she thought the performance had gone.

"I think it went okay," Lana said and cast an inquiring glance at Gil, who nodded.

"You were incredible, utterly gorgeous. It was amazing to watch. Alice missed a good one."

"Gil said you never attend performances," Lana said to Alice. "And I remember your telling Niles the same thing. Why not?"

Gil snorted with laughter but made no comment. Lana looked expectantly at Alice, who gave a self-conscious shrug. "Oh, I don't know; it just gives me the hives. Sitting there, after so many years of having done it. I guess I burned out on it all."

"Alice can't be the star of the show anymore," Gil joked, and Alice made sure to laugh with him.

"No, that was you, Gil. As the actor onstage that people couldn't take their eyes off of."

His eyes narrowed, but he tossed out the same hearty laugh. "I only wish the reporter had interviewed me instead of you. I've got a couple great publicity shots I would have loved to see in print again."

Lana looked like a spectator at a tennis match, eyes swinging from one person to the next. "That was a nice article, Alice," she offered, which made Gil guffaw again.

Alice couldn't fake a smile any longer. "You told me you didn't have a problem with that, Gil."

"I don't."

"I had no idea she was going to do that. I told you. I wasn't out to advertise my past."

"Well, hey. I say it's great. So your past got advertised. It was a great pic. Good for you."

The food arrived quickly, an appetizer plate with cheeses, pâté, fruit and nuts, along with a crock of French onion soup for Lana. Gil ordered another glass of wine. Alice was drinking Perrier tonight, which seemed to annoy Gil, as if she were being purposefully difficult, not celebrating Lana's big night in proper style.

"I'm just not in a partying mood, I guess," she said.

"You're out of practice. Haven't had a date in a while have you, old girl?"

He chuckled and nudged Alice's arm in an attempt to show her that he was jesting, all in good fun. She decided the Mark Haverford business had angered him more than he'd let on.

"I think you forgot that my boyfriend is on an international business trip."

"Oh. He's still got boyfriend status. Sorry about the mistake there." Gil studied his glass of wine, pretending to ponder this. "So. I'm curious. What does 'time apart' mean, anyway?"

She told herself not to give him the reaction he was so clearly itching for.

"Time apart means he works hard and I work hard. And when he's free, we'll meet up again."

"What, no phone call in the meantime?"

Her patience snapped. "No, Gil. No phone call. He is hard at work. He's probably in meetings all day from the time he leaves his hotel room to the time he returns after a business dinner. It is a working hotel. It is not the Beverly Wilshire. He is not a toy-boy, catering to someone else's whims."

Gil looked stunned, perhaps the first unguarded reaction he'd ever shown her. Then contempt washed over his face, cold, pure contempt.

She'd elicited a lot of reactions from him, but never this. It was terrible. He said nothing. He didn't need to. It was reminiscent of being disciplined by Deborah as a small child. Death by silence, by The Look.

"You might want to visit the ladies' room, Alice," he told her, his voice chatty, relaxed. "Your face is suddenly looking quite red. Splotchy. Maybe there's something you can do about that. Or maybe it's just an aging has-been dancer thing."

The rage. The terrible, consuming rage.

She could feel Lana shrink beside her.

"How considerate of you to have pointed that out to me," Alice said to Gil. "Someone has obviously trained you well." She rose, took her purse and forced herself to amble, not stalk, toward the ladies' room.

In the bathroom, her limbs shaking with anger and adrenaline, she stared at her face in the mirror. Her face was indeed a fright, with its blotchy, scarlet cheeks and too bright eyes.

This would not do. Deborah Willoughby's spectral presence was like a giant wagging finger of disapproval in her face.

She ran the cold water and splashed it on her cheeks over and over until she began to cool down. She took her time patting her face dry, practicing her yogic breathing exercises, until she felt composed enough to rejoin Gil and Lana.

Gil and Lana both smiled at her, a forced cheerfulness. She didn't bother to sit back down.

"I think I've done my work for the night," she told Gil. "I'm going home."

"Oh, don't go having a hissy fit. Sit down and have another drink. Look, I'm sorry. I was rude and I apologize. Okay?"

He recited this in the bored monotone of a nine-year-old boy being told by his mother to apologize, or else.

"Good night, Gil. Good night, Lana." She picked up her wrap, tucked her purse more tightly under her arm.

"Alice, wait." Lana looked distressed.

"She's fine," Gil told her. "She gets this way sometime. Maybe it's PMS."

Without another word Alice walked away, ignoring everyone, everything but counting the moments till she could be alone. Outside she hailed a taxi and clambered in the back. Finally, peace, blissful Gil-free silence.

Odette greeted Alice inside the house ten minutes later. "Hi, kitty," she murmured. "We're safe now, away from that terrible butthead boss." She squatted down to pet Odette, who tipped over, offering her belly for Alice to stroke as well, purring like an engine once Alice got it right. Finally Alice rose, locked the front door, switched off lights and made her way upstairs.

She was in bed with a novel, Odette at her feet, when Lana and Gil returned. She stayed in her room, vowing to ignore them. Five minutes later she heard the front door shut again, followed by footsteps on the stairs, a tentative knock at her door.

She sighed, rose from the bed and opened the door.

"Hi." Lana smiled at her. "Um, I just wanted to let you know I was here."

"Oh. Fine."

"Well, good night."

"He still here?" Alice gestured with her chin toward the living room.

"Gil? No. I sent him home."

"Why?"

Lana squirmed. "Because it felt right. Or maybe to show you some support."

"What's that supposed to mean?"

"There at the restaurant, I could tell that what Gil said really hurt you."

"Well, you're wrong. I'm fine. I just had a headache and Gil was getting on my nerves. You missed out on getting laid for nothing."

She made a move to shut the door but Lana was in the way now and she wouldn't budge. Alice pushed harder at the door; Lana still didn't move. Odette, sensing tension, leapt from Alice's bed and darted out of the room.

Lana caught her gaze and held it. "I'm not oblivious, Alice. Maybe he is, but I'm not."

It became a stare-down of sorts. But Lana was more persistent than Alice would have expected. "What's the real reason you don't go to ballet performances?" she asked.

"Why the hell do you think?" Alice snapped.

"Because it hurts to watch what you lost?"

Had Gil been the one to say those words, they would have carried a jeering element. But this was Lana. In reply, Alice offered her a curt nod.

"That's what I figured," Lana said softly. "And I totally get it."

They pondered this in silence for a moment. "I wouldn't make a very graceful ex-dancer," Lana said finally.

Alice grimaced. "None of us do."

Us.

Lana nodded. The hurting thing inside Alice subsided the tiniest bit.

Lana stepped away from the door. "Anyway. Thanks for coming to the restaurant like that. I really appreciated your company. But I'll leave you alone now."

"Thank you. Good night."

Fifteen minutes later Alice, still wide awake, gave up on reading. Lana hadn't merited her terse retorts. Certainly not tonight, of all nights. She slipped out of bed, put on her robe and went into the hall. Noting a wedge of light coming from the ajar bedroom door, she tapped at the door and peered inside. Lana was already sound asleep, hair spread out on the pillow, one arm flung over her head. Odette was on the bed with her, by Lana's blanketed feet, curled up in a C. She lifted her head when Alice came in but lowered it, shutting her eyes, pressing against Lana's leg.

"Traitor," Alice grumbled. She crept over to the nightstand to turn the lamp off. Before clicking it off, she paused to study Lana. She looked so young, so innocent. An unfamiliar feeling passed through Alice, a mix of tenderness and unease, some vague disquiet at the thought of the Gils of the world, the Mark Haverfords, Montserrat's Len Stevenson, indulging in what they could get from a young girl, her beauty, her freshness, her easy trust. She was fiercely glad right then that she could offer Lana her home, this sanctuary, away from potential predators.

Perhaps this was what a mother experienced when regarding her sleeping child.

Or better yet, a stepmother. One like Marianne, who'd surely paused like this to check on the young, sleeping Alice from time to time.

The thought stopped her cold. What, after all, had that been like for the childless Marianne? Suddenly sharing a home with an impressionable, vulnerable girl whose real mother was absent from the picture, and here you were, unfathomably being seen that way, as a maternal guide. All these unfamiliar feelings arising, coursing through you, that you weren't quite sure what to do with.

The answer was simple enough: you offered them all you could. Because they needed it.

It was like seeing Marianne in an entirely new way. And Lana, too.

Too much introspection. She gave herself a mental shake, reached over and clicked off the light. "Sweet dreams," she whispered, as she made her way out of the room and back to her own.

Chapter 16 – Lagging

No one expected Anders to stride into company class the morning after opening night and teach. It was a rude awakening for Lana, spent after the adrenaline rush of opening night. *Serenade* had been lovely and exhilarating, a thrill to perform. The group of them in their soft, flowing palest blue tulle skirts, Tchaikovsky's glorious music, Balanchine's clever geometric patterns, the audience's hushed appreciation of the closing tableau, one lead dancer, the Waltz Girl, held aloft by four men in a backward arch, elegant and still as the masthead of a ship, as the ensemble bourréed in two parallel lines behind them. It had been pure art in movement. She'd loved dancing it; she'd never felt closer to the other dancers, to the company as a whole.

But this morning Anders moved and spoke impatiently, as if irritated that their bodies might feel sluggish this morning. During barre, he was especially aggressive on the tendu and dégagé series. Sixteen counts, a soutenu turn to the other side, lightning-quick dégagés with a pirouette thrown in, soutenu back to the other side, eight here, eight there, then all of it split-time.

It was madness, more dismaying than exhilarating, as Lana struggled to keep up, stay alert and repeat the fiendish combinations he threw at them. At the start of class she'd harbored an idle fantasy that Anders might meet Lana's eyes, stop in his tracks even, to tell her she'd done a splendid job the night before, that she was a welcome addition to the company. None of this, not even a glance cast her way. Which, given the way she was forced to fudge some of the trickier combinations this morning, wasn't a bad thing in the end.

After barre, she exchanged her soft leather ballet slippers for pointe shoes, wincing at the blisters on her toes that had torn open last night, the way the sweat now rushed in to sting them. It was poor form, in truth, to not begin company class wearing pointe shoes, but she'd thought she could get away with it. Another reason why it was just as well Anders hadn't noticed her. Although she had a hunch he'd registered her pointe shoe omission. Very little seemed to escape his notice.

The worst was her big toe: the open wound was not healing and each day it was red and angry, blood soaking through the Band-Aid every time she danced en pointe. The only solution, Lana knew, was to stay off pointe for several days and let it heal properly, which was an impossibility. Going en pointe daily, hourly, was the reality of her work. She would therefore simply grit her teeth and buy more Band-Aids.

The dancers moved to the center of the room. Lana hated the feeling of having pointe shoes on this morning, with her big toe so inflamed and throbbing, but she knew better than to display any sign of discomfort. Worse, the shoes were brand new, without having been hammered or softened in any way. Her feet in them felt numb and clumsy, which explained why, when hurrying to the back of the room after completing the first jump combination, she accidentally kicked over a cup of someone's coffee.

A horrified silence came over the group as the creamy mixture, a Starbucks latte, flowed over the wood floor. There was a flurry of activity as people yanked their own items out of the way amid grumbles and exclamations.

Anders was furious. He strode over and stood there, hands on his hips.

"Who did that? Who knocked it over?"

The others, to their credit, avoided casting blame on Lana. She raised her hand and his frown deepened.

"You're a dancer, not an ox," he snapped. "Why this clumsiness? And what are you doing bringing coffee into class?"

"It wasn't my coffee." Lana's voice was barely above a whisper.

"What is that? Speak up." When Lana repeated her comment, he looked around.

"Whose coffee is this?"

Everyone had been reduced to cowering like children. Katrina raised her hand timidly.

"Shame on you. For shame. And you, a principal. You should be setting an example for the younger ones. Not this slop. This crap. Now clean it up. The rest of you, back to center. This is not a vacation. Focus. Now where's my second group? Move, people!" He strode back to the front of the room.

Someone had brought over paper towels and Lana bent to help Katrina wipe up the coffee. Katrina said nothing but flashed Lana a reproachful look. Lana felt herself shrink. For the rest of the class, she cowered in the back of whatever group she was in, still dancing full out, but trying to remain unobtrusive.

After class, as soon as Anders departed, Lana dropped to the floor and unlaced her pointe shoe ribbons, yanking off the heel end as fast as possible. The pressure around the front of the shoe's box eased. Pain mixed with relief as sweat sank beneath the torn skin. She sighed and shut her eyes, but a moment later she heard a murmured message move through the group: a revised rehearsal list had been posted in the hallway.

She joined the others making their way there too and scanned the list. Some of the lead roles for *Nutcracker* were being rehearsed. Sugar Plum Fairy and her cavalier. Arabian Dance. Snow Queen and King pas de deux. Lana's name didn't appear, and she reminded herself, sternly, there were over a dozen dancers with more seniority and rank than she had. They couldn't use everyone for these roles, and this was early rehearsing, anyway. More ominous, though, was the rehearsal list posted for *Arpeggio*. There'd been changes.

Her partner of the past few weeks, Boyd, was out, Lana saw with shock. Replaced by the likeable Sergei, a soloist, but still, it was unnerving. And one of the other female soloists was out. Replaced by Gabrielle. That was how quickly one's favor changed. The thought unnerved her, horrified her.

Reaction from this posting was different from the time Lana's name had appeared as the female lead in *Autumn Souvenir*. No glares sent her way this time. Gabrielle gave a little squeal and jump of excitement. She spied Lana nearby and hurried over. "We'll be rehearsing together now, it would seem," she said. Her tone was casual but her eyes sparkled.

Lana tried to echo her enthusiasm. "I know, isn't that great? Congratulations on making the *Arpeggio* rehearsal list."

Gabrielle beamed. "Well, as we all know, it's not casting. Yet. But *Arpeggio* is a lot of fun. Lexie's one of my favorite choreographers. I can't wait to bite into this!"

Courtney approached, smiling, happy as well, and Lana told herself to focus on the positive. She was still on the list. Gabrielle and Courtney were being friendly, chatting with Lana as the three of them walked down the hall at the same time. When Gabrielle saw Javier, she cut off her talk with a quick "see ya!" and bounded over to him. Courtney chuckled as they continued walking. "She's psyched," she said to Lana.

"She is."

"Hey, great job last night, by the way."

"Oh. Thanks."

Courtney seemed to understand that the morning's class, not to mention the new rehearsal list, had troubled Lana. "Hey," she said in a softer voice. "Don't sweat the other stuff. Anders blowing up at you, Katrina getting mad. Dancing in the corps last night and not as a soloist. And, well, that you're not under early consideration for one of the big roles in *Nutcracker*."

So Lana hadn't been the only one to notice. But Courtney was being warm, cordial to her, so she tried to respond in kind.

"Thanks. I appreciate your saying that."

Courtney returned her smile. "No worries. Honest, none of it means a thing."

After grabbing lunch, Lana called Mom, which she'd been trying to do regularly since the frightening incident. Annabel had assured her that Mom was fine now, snappish and irritable, but fine. Conversations with Mom herself were tricky, though. Lana couldn't bring up the Baby John relapse, because to do so might trigger another relapse. Another family game of theirs. Ignore the skeleton that got pushed back into the closet, never mind that you were leaning against the door to keep it in there. Lana chose her words carefully, trying to read into each response Mom made, guess what mood she was in.

Today Mom was complaining about her bad back, about the way the younger boys were arguing so much of the time, and how Annabel and Scott were no help at all.

"It was opening night last night," Lana offered.

"Oh. That's nice. How did it go?"

It bothered her that Mom sounded distracted, unimpressed. "It was okay," she said, allowing a note of injury to creep into her tone.

"I wish we could be there to see you."

"I wish you could be too." A lump rose in her throat. No family in the audience, ever. What a depressing thought.

"And how are those fancy new friends of yours?" Mom asked.

In the previous conversation, she'd asked about Coop, to which Lana had evasively replied that she didn't get back to the old neighborhood much. "Some friend you are," Mom had said, to which Lana had held her tongue.

Today Mom tried to weasel new information out of Lana about Gil. Lana, forewarned, knew how to say the right things now, focusing on the truth, that Gil and Alice were close, so sometimes Lana saw Gil at Alice's but he had a girlfriend he was living with. And how Gil was friends with almost everyone at the WCBT, besides.

A snort from Mom. "Your type wouldn't hold that kind of guy's interest anyway."

More holding of the tongue.

She targeted her attack next on Alice, searching for issues of possible contention, trying to drum up points to illustrate why Lana shouldn't be trusting Alice. When Lana produced no complaints, Mom muttered that Alice sounded just as slick as that Gil character. What was Lana's backup plan? Surely she didn't think this Alice woman would continue to be nice to a nobody like her. Not when she had friends like Lana described, the celebrity musicians and the billionaire.

"I need to go," Lana finally said, exhausted from not being able to blurt out what she was truly thinking and feeling.

"All right. You have a good day. And a good performance tonight."

Mom sounded cheerful now, downright happy. Which was a good thing. A cheerful Mom was a safer one.

If only it didn't have to be at the expense of Lana's own energy.

Her fatigue and diminished spirits seemed to be reflected in her performance of *Serenade* that night. She didn't make any big mistakes, but her timing seemed off at one point during a quick-moving passage. Here, even the tenth of a second mattered. She got back on track quickly, but the gaffe seemed to taint the rest of her efforts. Once offstage, Dena Lindgren gave her hand a reassuring squeeze, which told Lana that her uneven dancing hadn't gone unnoticed. The other performance and the dress rehearsals had been impeccable; she supposed it was no surprise that one night didn't measure up to the others. It was not a big deal, she told herself as she stood in the downstage wings awaiting their next cue. It was all part of the live performing game.

Gil, meeting her after the show, took note of her subdued spirits. "I know what you need," he told her. "A taste of something completely different. A singer I know is performing late tonight, at a low-key club that serves food till midnight."

Lana didn't want to go to a club. What she wanted was a shower, her fuzzy bathrobe and a quiet meal, but Gil seemed so eager about his idea that she couldn't bring herself to say no.

The place was, as he promised, low-key. In fact, it was downright dingy, dimly lit, redolent of old beer and wine. But the seats were comfortable, Gil found them a table in a quiet corner, and she was able to order food.

The singer, Lana had to admit, was worth watching. She had a low, husky voice, deep-set eyes and prominent cheekbones, her face framed by a haze of tangled blonde curls. Her sequined dress revealed a modest cleavage and a thin frame not unlike that of a dancer. Her movements were sinuous, mesmerizing. There was a mysterious allure to her that Lana couldn't put her finger to. She noted the others, almost exclusively men, maintained equal rapt attention on the singer.

When the set was over and the woman had taken her last bow, she spied Gil and smiled. She stopped first to speak with a table of men near the stage, but afterward came to Gil and Lana's table.

Lana's heart sank. Gil looked thrilled. His face was bright with something akin to mischief as he introduced the two women. They shook hands, exchanged polite greetings, and promptly ignored each other. Gil and Jewel chatted for five minutes, Gil's arm slung over Lana's shoulders, fingers caressing her arm.

Gil asked Jewel if she'd consider showing Lana her room upstairs.

Both Jewel and Lana rose in their seats at the same time. "No thanks, Gil," Lana said, followed by an emphatic bob of agreement from Jewel.

"No, no," Gil protested. "Lana, this is something you've really got to see. As a performer, you'll be so impressed. You can't imagine some of the pictures Jewel's got on her walls."

"No, Gil." Jewel wagged her finger at Gil, a gesture that came off as half-scolding, half-flirting. "Not a chance I'm taking you up there. Not after what you did last time."

They both laughed.

Lana tensed. How, she wondered, did this new development fit into Gil's idea of doing "something special" for her tonight?

"Aww, come on," Gil was saying to Jewel in a coy tone. "Lana needs to see this."

Lana touched Gil's thigh. "You know, I'm tired, Gil. And I'm sure Jewel is too."

Jewel gestured to Lana and nodded.

"I won't take no for an answer." Gil pulled out his wallet and extracted a twenty, setting it on the table next to Jewel.

Jewel didn't pick up the bill. "This isn't about the money, Gil."

"What about that time I saved you from Butch? Have you already forgotten that?"

Jewel's nostrils flared. She regarded Gil solemnly and shook her head. "You know, if I didn't love you so much, I'd hate you."

"I know that. And that's why you're going to do me this favor. I really want Lana to see a different angle of the performance world. And Jewel, you are the jewel."

"Oh, dammit, sweet talk will get you everywhere." Jewel grabbed at the twenty and tucked it into the cleavage of her dress.

"Five minutes," she said to Gil. She turned to Lana, motioning for her to follow.

Lana knew the easiest way out of the whole irritating scenario was simply to do what Gil was acting so insistent about. Gil looked at her unhappy face and squeezed her hand.

"I'm sorry. You're ready to go home, aren't you?"

She nodded.

"I'll pay up and we'll leave once you get back."

Jewel was looking impatient, so Lana rose and followed her through the club, past the back curtains, down a hall and up a flight of narrow stairs, miserably aware of the sexy side-to-side sway of Jewel's hips.

On the second level, Jewel opened a door at the end of the hall and beckoned Lana inside. The room was small, decorated like a living room, a smell of stale cigarette smoke in the air. Jewel flipped on a set of track lights that highlighted one of the walls. Lana turned and stared.

The entire surface was crowded with performance pictures, publicity shots, black-and-white portraits, half of which featured the beautiful Jewel. They were sensational. There were other framed photos as well, featuring men, one man in particular. Theatrical poses, spontaneous ones, the man in formal attire, the man standing with flashy celebrity types, arms around each other. Jewel and the man must be a team, Lana decided. And yet they were never together. Out of the corner of her eye she could see Jewel standing there by the door, smoking a cigarette, watching Lana.

"You look beautiful in these," Lana said, which Jewel acknowledged with a bob of her head. "And he's gorgeous. Who is he?"

Jewel leaned over to retrieve an ashtray from a nearby table. She tapped her cigarette ash into it before replying. "'He' is Joel."

"You two look alike. In fact, your names sound alike."

"You're a quick one."

Lana finally caught on. She understood why Gil was so entertained by Jewel, why he'd wanted Lana to see the pictures. Jewel was Joel. She turned to look back at the beautiful woman and there was no mistaking it. Jewel had an Adam's apple.

Jewel was a man.

Which threw the situation downstairs into confusion as well. Gil hadn't been flirting with a woman down there at all. He'd been flirting with a man. She didn't know whether to be relieved or appalled. She could only stand there and stare at Jewel, jaw agape, trying to process it all.

Jewel chuckled. "I'm good, huh?"

"You are," Lana managed. "You're incredible."

Jewel reached up with her free hand, removed a few hairpins and yanked the golden curls off her head. And like that, Jewel became Joel, a beautiful man in makeup, wig in hand. She—or rather, he—took another drag of his cigarette and scrutinized Lana again. The smoke drizzled out of his nose, like a dragon. "You don't look like Gil's type," he said.

First Mom and now this Jewel. What did either of them know of the Chicago boy, the Gil who held her close at night, who'd told her he loved her, that she'd changed him, that this was Something Special for him?

"Oh yeah?" she finally said, crossing her arms and affecting a similar pose. "Neither do you."

Jewel—or Joel, Lana reminded herself—looked taken aback. Then he began to laugh.

"*Touché,*" he said.

"I'm ready to get back to Gil," Lana said.

"Honey, I'll bet you are."

She was quiet on the drive home, pondering the way Gil had been beaming, having offered this "gift" that, in truth, had made her queasy. Seeing the affection Joel had displayed for Gil, leaning closer to accept Gil's kiss on his cheek, the girlish goodbye hug, a long one, and at the end, Joel squeezed Gil's ass. Gil had laughed, but hadn't look horrified or uneasy. All Lana, watching, could think of was that carefully tucked-away Andy Redgrave memory, the moment just before Alice had pulled her away, and how comfortable Gil had looked next to this man who'd been clearly coming on to him. A warning arose within her, Mom's lecturing voice all the way.

You do not know this guy. You think you do, but you don't.

And this, even bigger, in a voice neither Mom nor herself, or at least not the suggestible, compliant Lana. This was the Lana who'd sent Anders the tape, the one who'd told him "yes."

This is not *why you sacrificed your security and came out here. Watch yourself.*

Chapter 17 – Reversal of Flirtation

When Alice entered the house late the following Wednesday afternoon, a sweet, buttery aroma greeted her. She inhaled deeply, smiled and made her way into the kitchen, where Lana stood at the stove, stirring something in a pot. She looked up in surprise at the sight of Alice. "Uh, oh," she said, "Am I late or are you early?"

"I'm early. Yum, what do I smell?"

Lana looked sheepish. "It's melting butter and marshmallows. I'm making some Rice Krispies treats to bring in for Dena Lindgren tonight."

"Who's that?"

"One of the corps dancers who's helped me acclimate in *Serenade*. She's stepping in for Katrina tonight."

"Oh, no, did Katrina get hurt?"

"Her tendonitis was flaring up and Anders didn't want her to risk aggravating it, not on a closing night. He'd rather she rest up for Program II."

"That's wise. So, what's the understudy's name again?"

"Dena Lindgren."

"Hmm. I've met a Rebecca Lindgren at a social function. Any relation?"

"Sisters. Dena's three years younger."

"Wow. Well. A big night for her."

"I know." Lana gestured to the pan. "That's why I wanted to bring in something for afterward. And these only take, like, ten minutes to make."

"What fun. I don't think I've had Rice Krispies treats since I was a kid."

"Want me to cut you out a piece before I go?"

"Tempting, but best to save my calories for tonight." Alice opened the refrigerator and pulled out a Diet Coke.

"Business dinner, right?"

"Yup."

"Gil told me you two had a big one."

"Yes indeed. Time to reel in Andy Redgrave."

Lana put down her spoon and turned to look at Alice. "The two of you are having dinner with Andy Redgrave?"

"We are." She watched Lana eyes widen with surprise, uneasiness. "What? You mean Gil didn't tell you we were meeting Andy?"

"No. I guess he didn't mention that detail." Lana sighed. "Here we go again."

"Don't worry, it'll be purely business tonight. Gil's boss, Charlie Stanton, will be there."

Lana picked the spoon back up and focused her attention on the contents of the pot. She opened her mouth as if to speak, but closed it. A moment later, the words came out in a rush. "What do you think happened? That night, with Andy?"

"Lana. Don't torture yourself." Alice focused on popping open her can. "Whatever happened that night is not going to repeat itself here."

"But what if this kind of thing is, well, in his nature?"

Alice looked up in surprise. "Why on earth would you think

that?"

"Okay. Here's the thing." Lana switched off the stove burner. "Last Friday night after the performance, Gil took me to this show he loves, this beautiful woman singing, and she came over, totally flirtatious, and you know Gil, he was eating it up, offering it back. Only ten minutes later, I come to find out that 'she' is a 'he.' A drag queen, a gorgeous one. But a gay male, as well. So was Gil flirting back with a woman or a man?" She looked miserable.

"Oh, boy." Alice began to chuckle. "Trust Gil to come up with a unique scenario for you."

Lana didn't laugh with her. "Gil was so comfortable with all the flirtation and Jewel's caressing. They seemed to know each other well. Do you suppose Gil sort of…leans that way? Or gives in easily to the obvious invitations? Which—why be in denial?—we both saw happening that night."

Lana's voice was shaking by the end; Alice knew what it had cost her to get the words out. "Look," she told Lana, "I can offer speculation, I can offer reassurances. But the truth is, you need to hear the answers from him. Come right out and ask him. Just throw it at him, out of nowhere, and see how he reacts."

"I can't do that!"

"Sure, it would be awkward. But you'd get answers."

"Maybe I'm not ready to hear the answers." Lana seized the box of Rice Krispies and began to shake the contents into the melted mixture in the saucepan. Little Rice Krispies flew everywhere. "You know, my mom keeps telling me I'm making some big mistake, getting involved with him. And sometimes I wonder if she's right."

Alice watched Lana stir the mixture and spoon it into a greased pan. She herself had spoken with Lana's mother a few times, and each time, the woman had sounded suspicious, somehow disapproving, even as she thanked Alice for hosting her daughter, and was Lana there, right now, and if not, why not?

"Can I offer a personal observation?" Alice asked Lana.

"Go ahead."

"Your mom's sure a big influence in your life, I can tell."

"She is."

"Which means she's got an awful lot of power over you." Alice tried to keep her voice relaxed, unthreatening, but she could feel tension seeping into the air. "And I've watched you sometimes as you're talking to her. You sort of hunch over, as if you're anxious, or cowed by her. But she doesn't strike me as the harsh, authoritarian type either. It's clear the two of you are close and love each other deeply. So, I think I'm missing something. Something big."

Lana focused her attention on patting the Rice Krispies treats into the pan. Only after she'd finished did she speak.

"Okay. You shared your private mom story with me, so I guess I should share mine. Here's the thing." She drew a deep breath and when she spoke, she directed her words to the pan. "When I was seven, my mom tried to end her life by crashing a car she was driving. She'd lost a baby six months earlier and just couldn't bear to live with the pain of it all. The police found her, sixty miles from home, near a steep bluff she'd planned to drive off, into the river below. She'd swerved at the last minute and crashed into the trees instead. They rescued her, and when she came home from the hospital six weeks later, we all banded around her. Our aunts had told us that if we kids did our part, if we were loving and helpful, we could save her. And they were right. We did it. When she started smiling again, it felt like a miracle."

She looked up at Alice. "I'll do anything for her to keep that darker stuff at bay. Some of my other siblings can be slack-offs. So I made it my role in the family to be my mom's helper in any way I can. Well, you can imagine what a bad call it was for me to leave Kansas City. It was the worst thing I could have done to my mom."

"So, why'd you do it?"

Lana's chest began to heave, as if she'd been running a race. "Because I was dying inside. I saw it all, where I was going with my career. It was stagnating there in Kansas City. I could feel it and it was like suffocating. So I sent that audition tape."

For a while neither of them spoke. Lana began furiously wiping down the stove, the counter, scrubbing at the pan she'd just used. The hiss of the water filled the air, making it impossible to talk. The silence, once she'd turned off the water, seemed abrupt, expectant.

"Your poor mother," Alice said softly.

"I know."

"But poor you, as well."

Lana shook her head. "No. I don't see it that way at all. Lucky me. I had a mother who came back from that terrible, dark place. The rest has been a small price to pay."

"But didn't you hear what you said? You just said, 'I was dying inside.'"

"Oh. That's just what came out of my mouth. Of course I wasn't dying." Lana's eyes darted about, looking for something else to clean.

Alice leaned closer. "You've spent your life in pursuit of an artistic career. You're an extraordinarily talented dancer. Normally it's the family and home life that revolves around a kid of such prodigious talent, not the other way around." A thought took hold in her mind. "So. Your mother has been fine since that year? No big relapses?"

"Nothing too big, thank God. She gets difficult around the

anniversary of his death, during the holiday months. And it was a little iffy when she was expecting the twins. When they were born, both healthy, everyone heaved a sigh of relief. Of course that doubled the workload for my mom."

"Which is to say, for you as well."

"It was a labor of love."

"So. You said she was 'difficult' around the holidays. But not 'depressed.'"

"Yes. And?"

"That sounds more manageable than depression."

Lana snorted. "You bet it is, and I'm proud our efforts have paid off in that way."

"But here's the thing. Maybe, just maybe, after all these years and no sign of a serious recurrence, she's relying on your help and support because it's there, as much as she needs. Or wants. And all she has to do is act like it's all too much once again—and I can just visualize the tone she uses, because I've heard it. Like a martyred but peeved voice. And boom. You respond to it, lightning quick."

"I left her with a huge load to bear." Lana's tone grew defensive. "It was very hard for her to see me go."

"I wholly believe that. You made her life so much easier, you probably accommodated her in every way possible. That had to have been nice. And now you're establishing a life of your own, like a person your age is supposed to do. You're thriving, away from her. I'll bet that threatens her. And I worry that she might try to use that against you. Manipulate you."

"Stop it! Just stop it right there." Lana held up both hands. "My mother has suffered so much. Chronic back pain aside, she's delivered seven children. She watched her baby die. The pain was so terrible it nearly killed her. She's devoted her life to raising her children. And here you are, acting suspicious about her motives."

She started to say more but her voice trembled. She looked up at the clock on the wall.

"I'm late. I have to go."

"Lana, wait." Alice reached over and tried to touch her arm, but Lana eluded her. "I'm sorry, I spoke out of line. I was just hypothesizing and I missed the mark."

"You sure did." Lana's angry eyes met hers. "Now if you'll excuse me, I've got to go."

She grabbed the pan of Rice Krispies treats, her dance bag and ran out of the kitchen, up the stairs, as Alice stood there dumbly. She took a sip of Diet Coke and shook her head.

The mom thing again. It was destined to be an eternal minefield between her and Lana, bombs exploding right and left. How had something so well-meaning turned out so poorly?

She heard the guest room door upstairs closing and a moment later Lana scurried down the stairs with a tossed out "good bye." The front door slammed before Alice could reply.

Just as well. She would have only said the wrong thing again.

Dinner with Andy, his associate, Gil and Charlie Stanton, was a surreal shift in mood, a formal affair in a formal restaurant, fine food and a stilted ambiance. Andy's associate, one of the foundation executives, directed question after question to Gil and Charlie, which they answered carefully, correctly. Andy remained largely silent, eyes ever observant. After twenty minutes of listening, Alice felt bored and grumpy. She blamed Gil for it. Gil, in a snippy mood of his own, who'd told her on the drive over that she was to clam up tonight and let him and Charlie do all the talking. She'd asked him why her presence had been required in the first place. He replied, somewhat testily, that Andy himself had requested it, telling Gil a business dinner with all men was taxing and besides, he'd taken a liking to Alice and her caustic wit. Gil's sideways glance after sharing this last bit of information told Alice that these days, Gil was not sharing Andy's appreciation of her wit.

"And no off-color jokes tonight," Gil had added. "Not in front of Charlie and Andy's associate."

"Thank you for saying that because I wouldn't have been able to figure out that one on my own," Alice had said, ignoring the frown the comment produced.

Following aperitifs, first course arrived, a pan-seared *foie gras* with port-soaked cherries. Then it was a mixed greens salad with a champagne vinaigrette, topped with warm goat cheese and caramelized walnuts, followed by a Normandy corn bisque drizzled with truffle oil. The five of them made quick work of the first bottle of wine, a Sonoma Valley chardonnay with smooth, buttery undertones that Andy had chosen. Alice would have been enjoying the meal if not for the presence of Gil alongside her, prim as a schoolteacher, choosing his words and actions carefully tonight.

She sat, in clam-up mode, as Gil's gaze wandered over the restaurant. Just over Alice's shoulder he saw something that made his eyes widen. He said nothing at first. Only after the soup bowls had been cleared and Charlie, Andy and his associate had fallen into a discussion about sailing, did Gil lean toward Alice.

"So," he said. "Hear from Niles yet?"

She allowed a tired sigh to escape before replying. "I think you know the answer to that. I'm not even sure he's back from Asia yet."

"Oh, I'm going to guess he is."

"If so, I'm sure he's busy with work. And the jet lag."

"Not out wining and dining pretty girls."

She frowned. "What on earth are you going on about?"

He made a little pivoting gesture with his fingers. Baffled, Alice looked around. There sat Niles, having dinner in the restaurant.

It was like seeing a nun in full habit seated in a biker bar. A naked man in the women's dressing room. It was so very wrong.

Niles was here.

And not alone. Across from him sat a pretty young woman, a slightly older version of Lana, same creamy, unblemished skin and demure features, but with lighter hair and a bigger chest. A real knockout. Alice felt sick.

"Oh," she said, willing herself to sound pleased. "That must be the family friend he said was planning to visit. I'll just go say hi."

Alice forced her numb legs into action, pushing the heavy chair back, rising and strolling over to their table. Niles looked up, stunned. Under different circumstances, she might have found his expression entertaining. He tried to rise from the table, but got caught between table and un-budging chair. He looked like a toddler in a high chair, flailing against his restraints.

Alice raised a hand. "No. Don't get up. I just came by to say a quick hello. Before I go back to my men." She congratulated herself on her light, flirtatious tone, one that told Niles she'd been having the time of her life since he'd been gone. Before he could speak, she thrust out her hand to the girl.

"Hi, I'm Alice, a friend of Niles."

The girl was indeed like Lana, in her sweet, bumbling hesitation, the way it took her a moment to get out an eloquent sentence. Her name was Christine and she was a friend of Niles' sister. She was in the area looking into graduate school programs, staying with Niles for a week.

Which meant she was sleeping under the same roof as Niles. This pretty girl. Alice maintained her mask of pleasant reserve as she next asked Niles about his trip, which he said was a success, but tiring. He reached out as he spoke to grasp Alice's fingertips, resting on the edge of their table, but she snatched away her hand, startled, as if burned. He hesitated, but resumed his flow of conversation.

"Christine checked out UC Berkeley today. And University of San Francisco. Yesterday afternoon, when she arrived, it was Stanford."

"How nice," Alice said. "And did you like them?"

"Oh, yes," Christine said. "This is a wonderful area. I just love it."

Stanford, Berkeley. The girl was smart, too, as well as attractive. Great.

"And where are you from?" Alice asked.

"Southern California. Pasadena."

"There are some excellent schools down your way, as well."

The girl nodded. "I'm considering some of those too."

"Oh, good." In more ways than one.

Alice saw Niles looking over at her table. She glanced over her shoulder to find Gil and Andy looking their way, Gil with an amused smirk, Andy with his mysterious half-smile.

"Your men beckon," Niles said.

"They do," Alice agreed, affecting a cheerful weariness, the fatigue of the party girl.

Niles lifted his gaze to hers and her defenses faltered. She drank in every little detail of his face, the tiny scar on his cheek, his full lips, the way his thick eyelashes framed his grey eyes, eyes that could send her into a frenzy of desire. But there was apology, not seduction in them tonight. Maybe even—please, God, no—pity.

"I'll call you," Niles said.

Nobody pitied her and got away with it.

"Don't make it too soon, though. I might be a little caught up in work for a spell. This is a big deal we're closing in on. Big.

Might require a little extra effort on my part." As if to add a certain innuendo, she gave Christine an affected wink.

Niles looked over at Andy. Handsome, impeccably dressed, billionaire Andy. She could almost see the implication, the possibilities, register in his mind.

Good.

"All right. We'll be in touch."

"Yes." She turned to Christine. "Have fun while you're here. Enjoy the area." *And leave my boyfriend alone.* Only maybe that wasn't what he was anymore.

She returned to her table, where she could still feel Gil's amused scrutiny, burning into her shoulders. To her relief, the waiters arrived with their main courses. She busied herself with her grilled salmon and fennel, accepting Andy's offer to pour her more wine, a lush, velvety Chilean cabernet this time. After he poured he studied her more closely.

"Let me guess," he murmured. "A conflict of interest over there."

She shrugged. "So to speak."

"With one but not the other."

"I think you're on to the situation."

Andy looked over at them and back at Alice. A mischievous grin crossed his face. "Let's show them. I'll make her jealous."

Her.

He thought Christine was the one she desired. He thought she was a lesbian because of the way she'd acted toward Lana the night of his party. The shock of it, the inadvertent humor made her emit a sharp bark of laughter, one she immediately tried to stifle with her hand over her mouth. Gil frowned in her direction. Andy looked delighted.

Alice couldn't see Niles and Christine, but Andy could, and he began to orchestrate his moves based on their attention. He was enjoying himself. So was she. His attention, contrived as it was, made her feel more sexy and alluring than she'd felt in weeks. He angled himself toward Alice, his expression bright with interest; he laughed longer than necessary at her witticisms. His hand came up to touch her arm from time to time. When he got up to take a phone call in the reception area, he trailed a few fingers along the length of Alice's arm before stepping away. It was both disconcerting and hilarious.

Gil and Charlie had noticed. Gil looked furious. Charlie looked confused.

Andy returned just as his associate was preparing to leave, apologizing for his early departure, one last function to attend. Andy agreed to stay and share a third bottle of wine, which put him in a more relaxed mood, more entertained by their company. Correction, Alice told herself. By her company, and their flirtation charade. There were no hints of homosexual interest tonight, that was certain. Lana needn't have worried about Gil and Andy. At one point Andy half-rose, leaning in toward Alice, letting the warmth of his palm slide up her arm and continue on to the nape of her neck. He leaned in like he was going to kiss her, which threw her thoughts into a tailspin, but instead he only murmured into her ear.

"They're leaving. And she's trying very hard not to look over here at you."

Niles was leaving, seeing all of this. It took everything in her power not to turn around and look, to catch one last glimpse of him. Niles, whom she missed right then with an acuteness so strong it was like swallowing a knife. One of those Swiss Army knives with multiple sharp edges and poking features. Niles, who hadn't called, who appeared to have taken her friends-only pronouncement seriously.

Andy dropped his hand, sat back with a chuckle, and like that, the game was over. He was a better actor than she'd realized. So was Gil. She didn't catch on to his fury until they met in the hallway outside the restrooms later, as she was leaving the ladies' room. He was there, leaning against the wall, but sprang up when he saw her and grabbed her arm.

"Just what the hell were you doing out there?" he demanded.

"Um, I was eating dinner with my boss and his boss and clients."

"I know that. Don't play innocent."

She shook her arm free from his grasp. "We were joking around."

"You were flirting with him."

"Gil, he thinks I'm gay. That's what's doubly funny about the situation. He wasn't making the moves on me any more than I was on him. We were both just acting."

"Well, it wasn't funny. Or appropriate. This is business."

She bit back the dozen angry retorts that arose. There were endless opportunities to bash Gil here, from his own behavior at Andy's party, to Lana's most recent story about him.

"I am returning to the table now," she said, in the exaggerated fashion of a preschool teacher talking to a difficult child. "And you? Why, your face is all splotchy, Gil. Maybe you should go splash some water on it."

He didn't move. "That's what this is about, isn't it? You're pissed off still about what I said that night at L'Orange. Even though I apologized right away. And a second time, the next day."

"No, Gil. I accepted your apology. This is about Andy and I exchanging a harmless joke. Go back out there. Look at his face. He's having fun. And you and Charlie were boring him."

"Don't tell me how to do my job."

"Oh, I forgot. I'm in clam-up mode. Sorry, boss. Will recommence clamming up."

"Yes. I think that's a good idea."

Back at the table, over coffee, Andy told them that he'd rather save the rest of business talk for the office and his site visit the next day. The implications were clear: no signed letter of agreement that night.

Alice avoided looking at Gil afterward. She knew how disappointed he must be; he'd wanted to leave the restaurant with the grant a done deal. Gil acted jovial and breezy as the four of them left the table and made their way outside, but Alice could feel frustration radiating from him as they waited for the parking attendants to return with Gil's and Charlie's cars. Andy had called his driver to pick him up.

Charlie's car arrived first and he left, bidding them all a good night. The other two cars pulled up to the curb a minute later. Gil extracted a few bills from his wallet to hand to the valet as Andy's driver got out of the car and exchanged a few words with Andy. Gil glanced at Alice.

"What are you waiting for? Get in the car."

"I'd like to say good night to Andy."

"You've said enough, trust me."

She didn't budge. He looked at her and his eyes narrowed. "Do you want a ride or not? Or would you rather walk?"

"I think there's a third option here. It's called public transportation."

"Fine. Get your own ride."

"I will." On impulse she called out to Andy. "Oh, Mr. Redgrave. Would you be a sweetheart and give me a ride home?"

A smile broke across Andy's face. "Alice, it would be my

pleasure."

Gil clutched at Alice's arm as she took a step in Andy's direction. "You are not going with him."

"Watch me."

She tried to yank her arm free, but this time his grip was strong. "If you do anything to put this account in jeopardy," he told her in a low voice, "I'll fire you."

He was serious.

Andy was looking over at them, a puzzled expression on his face. She struggled to draw a deep breath, remain calm. "Andy, tell me something," she trilled. "Am I putting this account in jeopardy by going with you? Because my boss has informed me that I'm out of a job if that happens."

Gil's fingers, digging deeper into her biceps, transmitted his rage. There would be bruises there tomorrow. And she would get an earful.

Andy began to laugh. "Absolutely not. Gil, I wouldn't have thought of you as being that harsh. Why would you want to risk losing such an invaluable associate? Or clearly you don't want to lose her, judging from the way you're hanging onto her arm."

Gil released his grip with a "ha ha, aren't women a hoot?" chuckle. "All right," he said to Andy. "She's your problem."

"Oh, Gil," Alice cooed, "I'm not a problem, I'm the *answer* to your problems. Haven't you told me that?"

"You two," Andy said. "You're quite a team." His driver had come around to open the back passenger door and now Andy was standing there, waiting to get in. "Alice?" he asked.

She needed no further invitation. She skittered over and slid in before Gil could say another word. She heard Andy saying good night to Gil and a moment later Andy was in there next to her. The closing door shut out the sounds, Gil's toxicity. She was trembling, adrenaline still racing through her system. She wanted to scream. She wanted to cry.

"Thank you," she managed to Andy, afraid to say anything more for fear her voice would break.

"You're welcome."

To her relief he said no more. She turned her head and watched San Francisco flash past. On Union Street, they drove past bars, restaurants, happy, carefree people. Gradually her rage subsided and she became more aware of Andy beside her, the hint of his cologne, the sandalwood notes, his energy. He was like a cat, reposing yet ever watchful. He seemed to sense when her attention had returned to him.

"Can I ask you a personal question?" he asked.

"Go ahead."

"Are you and Gil lovers?"

At this she had to laugh. "No," she said. She turned to look at him. He stared back, his pale blue eyes unblinking.

"Why does he act so territorial?"

"That's a good question. I ask myself that often."

"He's a funny one sometimes, that Gil."

"Hilarious. Sometimes I simply burst into laughter at work, just thinking of him."

If Gil were around he'd give her a smack aside the head for her sarcasm, her flippancy toward such a power broker. But Andy only smiled. "Or maybe it's you. You're the funny one, Alice. You're a real breath of fresh air."

"Some would argue frigid air."

"Sub-zero," he agreed.

"Arctic. December Arctic air, in the middle of a storm, with a driving wind."

She started to laugh, both appalled and thrilled by how the

night had turned out. Andy began to laugh with her and suddenly it was like the night of his party, minus Gil. They were on a high, reveling in the humor, the unpredictability, the bizarre nature—to her, at least—of this moment. She felt wondrously free of all constraints, from Gil's influence, from Niles's, even. Niles, who'd gone home tonight with a beautiful woman, who'd be sleeping under the same roof as him for the next week. It was no surprise, therefore, that she found herself considering Andy's offer for a nightcap at his San Francisco apartment before going home.

"Gil would kill me, you know," she said. "He'd come at me and choke me with his bare hands."

"Not if you hand him a signed letter of agreement."

This made her fall silent. As if in reply, Andy twisted around and pulled the document out of a leather-bound folder. He leafed through the pages of the thick vellum paper. The only sound was the scritch of his pen as he scrawled out his signature on the bottom of the second and fourth pages.

"There you have it, Alice," he said, collecting the papers and handing them to her. "That should make your boss think twice about strangling you."

She took the letter and its duplicate and studied Andy.

"You, too, are a funny man."

He shrugged. "Just restless."

She tucked the documents into her purse, dazed by their significance, their power.

"So," Andy said. "The nightcap?"

"Yes. I'd like that."

Andy's Russian Hill apartment was surprisingly austere, one of those ultra-chic residences that defined itself not so much by its furnishings but by its lack thereof. Cream walls, beige carpets, track lighting, invisible speakers, with a plasma screen television and plush suede sofa and armchair the only nod to hedonism. Glass cases showcased antique vases, soft light beamed from beneath their respective glass shelves so that the vases seemed to hover in air, buoyed by an unearthly force. Andy kept the lighting dim, which perpetuated the feeling that this night was nothing more than a surreal dream. She wandered over to the sofa and sank into its softness as he poured them both a Courvoisier.

He handed her the drink and headed over to the stereo system. "What would you like to hear?" he asked.

"Classical."

"That's a given. Era?"

"Late Romantic, maybe."

"Chamber music or orchestral?"

"Concerto. Violin concerto." She hesitated. "The Sibelius."

He swung around to regard her. "Interesting choice. That's one of my favorites."

"I really don't know it that well," she confessed. "But it's one of Montserrat's signature concertos."

She fell abruptly silent, remembering how Andy owned part share of the Vuillaume, and therefore, peripherally, Montserrat. She felt a strange sense of possession rise up at the thought. Did she, too, want to own part of Montserrat? Did that make her no better than Len Stevenson, in the end?

But she didn't want to discuss Montserrat with Andy. It was her special friendship and she'd already lost some of it to Lana. She couldn't bear to part with anything more.

Andy, to her relief, made no comment about Montserrat or the Vuillaume. "The Sibelius it is," he said.

He slid in the CD, dimmed the lights further and joined her on the sofa. They sat there, side by side, and listened. She felt oddly privileged; she sensed he didn't often invite people up to silently ponder the Sibelius in semi-darkness. It was not a gentle, Mozart-esque piece of music. It was not pretty so much as alluring, haunting. And all she could visualize was her beloved Montserrat, a girl Lana's age, struggling through the most important performance of her life, having sold her soul, not to mention her body, the night before.

The first movement was epic, dramatic, like a full concerto in itself. The second movement, the lush *adagio di molto*, was beautiful, bittersweet. Just as Montserrat had said, it seemed to encompass a wintery longing for something nameless that could never be found. She could almost feel it, the challenge that Montserrat had endured that night, performing the concerto in her exhausted, traumatized condition.

Could she have done what Montserrat did? Gone over there and straddled Andy, while wanting only Niles, grieving his indifference? Unzip Andy's trousers and lower her face to his lap, take him into her mouth, not out of desire but out of obligation? And Andy was an attractive man. Montserrat's benefactor, from the sound of it, had been no Andy Redgrave. Hairy and overweight, she remembered Montserrat saying, probably decades Montserrat's senior.

Could Alice do that?

No.

Could she fathom it, what propelled people like Montserrat or Gil, comprehend where their journeys and challenges had taken them?

No.

This thought cut her unexpectedly. Or perhaps it was the music. She felt bereft, as if she'd lost something precious, or seen something stark and unforgettable that would forever redefine her life. Feeling the beauty of art right there alongside something unspeakably dark, and discovering that the two coexisted. That they were necessarily intertwined.

How fitting that a Finnish composer should have so aptly illustrated the beauty of light amid so much dark. Listening to the music's lament, her throat constricted. She felt one tear slide down her cheek, a lone rebel, leaving a cool damp trail behind as it made its way to the corner of her mouth, where she licked it away.

She wondered what Andy thought when he heard the Sibelius, and why it was one of his favorites. It was doubtful that it soothed him; it was not that kind of music. Perhaps it stirred his soul, or compelled him with its contradictory beauty. Or perhaps he was just a bored billionaire who liked elegant music with an edge.

Another tear slid down. She was glad it was dark.

The concerto ended and silence fell over the room.

"Another?" Andy's voice floated over to her. He hadn't raised his head from its spot on the couch's back cushion.

"Yes, please."

He didn't clarify whether he meant Courvoisier or another concerto. It didn't matter. Tonight, they were equally intoxicating.

Chapter 18 – The Wake-Up

Although the Program I run had now ended and in less than thirty-six hours Program II would open, the buzz on everyone's lips that morning before company class was Dena and her astonishing performance the previous night. She'd drawn a crowd backstage, fellow dancers alerted to the drama. When an understudy takes on the lead role with only a day's notice, after all, anything can happen. Rebecca Lindgren had stood beside Lana in the wings through the performance, her body tense, watching every move her sister made, sighing with relief whenever Dena managed a particularly tricky passage, or completed clean triple pirouettes.

Dena had excelled in every way possible. She'd been on fire, and, further, she'd been enjoying herself. Lana could feel it, the way Dena's enthusiasm ratcheted the energy and quality ever higher, the audience responding to it all. At the end, they'd gone wild with applause.

After the final triumphant curtain call, Dena, calm and controlled up to that moment, had walked up to her sister, said, "Oh, Becca," in an anguished voice, and burst into tears. Rebecca had pulled Dena in for a fierce hug, murmuring, "You did it. What did I tell you?" It had been so touching, observing their closeness, this built-in support system these sisters had. Lana had thought of

Annabel, her sneers and defensive posturing, their distance, and felt a twinge of envy for all Dena seemed to have.

But like any Cinderella story, the clock struck twelve and one returned to the real world. This morning Dena was subdued, not jubilant, warming up quietly in a corner, back to being a first-year corps dancer. When barre began, so did the work, every dancer focused on technique, their taxed bodies, working out the kinks, the aches, the reluctant muscles. This was their chance to fine-tune their machinery after four performances and a new set of five performances commencing the following night. And this was merely a warm-up to their three-week, three-city tour, their holiday season. The WCBT offered thirty performances of *Nutcracker* through the month of December. Rehearsals would start the Monday after they returned from tour; there would be three casts for the production, multiple new roles for Lana to learn and perfect. It would only get more challenging from here.

The increasing pressure was apparent everywhere. Gabrielle, always on the emotional side, seemed even moodier than usual today. In the studio dressing room after class Lana heard Gabrielle's voice rising in dissent. "Oh, give it a rest, Courtney," she said, loud enough for Lana, approaching her locker, to hear. "God, I get so sick of you sometimes." She stalked off, passing Lana without a word. A row away, Courtney and Charlotte, heads together, were grumbling to each other. When they saw Lana, they stopped talking.

"Don't mind me," she told them. "I just need to grab something from my locker."

"So." Courtney gestured in the direction of the now-departed Gabrielle. "You heard that."

"Well, not what you were talking about. Just Gabrielle's end bit."

"Her lovely, calm farewell." Courtney exchanged wry glances with Charlotte.

"Is everything okay with her?"

"Oh, she's just being Gabrielle," Charlotte said, with a dismissive wave of her hand.

Courtney stepped toward the aisle that led to the exit and looked around. Satisfied, she turned back to Lana. "Actually, there's more." She and Charlotte exchanged another one of their private looks. Charlotte nodded, a *go ahead* gesture.

But before Courtney could speak, they heard April's voice.

"Is Dena Lindgren in here?" A moment later, April appeared. "Have you seen Dena?" she asked them. "Anders wants to talk to her."

"No, it's only the three of..." Courtney started to say, but fell silent as Dena appeared from the back row of lockers. As Dena passed, Charlotte said, under her breath, "Eavesdrop often?"

Dena offered her a polite smile. "Don't worry. Your gossip goes in one ear and out the other. I didn't retain a thing."

No reply. Courtney and Charlotte kept quiet as Dena and April made their way out of the locker room. Afterward, they both exhaled.

"Was that, like, a totally bitchy comment, or what?" Courtney asked.

"No kidding," Charlotte said. "One success and she thinks she can talk that way to senior company members."

Again, both of them stopped, glancing uneasily at Lana.

It was getting irritating. "Stop tiptoeing around me with what you say," she burst out, and to her surprise, they laughed. The tension in the room eased.

"So," Courtney said. "Where were we?"

"Gabrielle," Charlotte said.

"Do you want to hear about Gabrielle?" Courtney asked Lana.

She felt flattered to be included in on gossip. "Sure. Go ahead."

Courtney lowered her voice. Charlotte leaned in, and so did Lana. "The truth is," Courtney said, "I don't think things are going well with her and Javier."

"Oh, no. I haven't noticed. They seem fine," Lana said.

"Well, she's going to hide it, of course, especially from you. If you went over and asked her about it right now, she'd act like she didn't know what you were talking about. But actions speak louder than words, and after I saw what I did yesterday afternoon."

She let the words trail off.

"What? What did you see?" Charlotte asked.

"She was in the back hallway, next to the café, talking with someone."

A frisson of unease traveled up Lana's back. "Who?"

Charlotte stifled a laugh. "Oh no."

"Everybody's favorite male friend," Courtney told Lana.

"Gil." The name caught in her throat.

"Bingo," Courtney said. "They were just talking, but I have to say, they were standing awfully close. I didn't want it to look like I was listening in, so I just turned and went the other way. But I'll tell you what, when I saw her twenty minutes later, she had a much bigger smile on her face."

Charlotte seemed to find this hilarious. She was spluttering with laughter. Lana felt sick. Courtney took one look at Lana and contrition replaced her own grin.

"Oh, shit, I forgot you were good friends with him, that you really like him and stuff. I totally put my foot in my mouth there, didn't I?"

"God, Courtney, you're awful," Charlotte exclaimed, still laughing. "Why didn't you think before talking?"

"It's all right." Lana forced a casual expression. "I know what Gil is like. Everyone does."

Courtney relaxed. "Oh, good. You see that about him. You know, I have to say, I really kind of pity his girlfriend Julia. She's up against so much."

"No kidding," Charlotte added. Her phone chimed, and she pulled it out of her bag, glanced at the screen. "Boyd's waiting for us," she told Courtney. "We gotta run."

"We do." Courtney turned to Lana. "We'd invite you to join us for lunch, but Boyd's the one taking us out. And he's still a little irritable about getting dropped from *Arpeggio.*"

"Oh, sure," Lana said through numb lips. "No problem. Enjoy."

"Thanks. See you later in rehearsal."

Forty minutes later, she was leaving the café by way of the building's lobby after lunch when she spied Gil, standing outside with another businessman in front of the WCBT building. Gil was listening in rapt attention to something the man was saying. A moment later Gil began to laugh. He clapped the man on the shoulder, who shifted so that Lana saw his profile.

Andy Redgrave.

Gil glanced up and saw her. Quickly he returned his attention to Andy, keeping his eyes locked there, ignoring Lana. It was terrible, like Andy's party all over again. A rush of cold washed over her, followed by aggravation, even a perverse sense of the comedy of the situation at hand. Gil and Andy, Gil and Gabrielle, Julia, Jewel, the countless others in the company whose lust-glazed eyes followed Gil's every movement—would the list ever end?

But she didn't have to meekly accept it, watch Gil conduct his flirtations, his manipulations as she crept away, letting it undermine her confidence.

Enough of playing victim.

She headed over to the front double doors and marched right outside. Gil looked over at her in alarm. It was indeed a perfect duplicate of his reaction at Andy's party, only this time she wasn't going to allow it to stop her.

"Hi there," she exclaimed, walking up to the two men. Andy turned to face her, puzzled. Gil began to stutter a hello, but Lana ignored him. She thrust out her hand to Andy.

"I'm Lana Kessler. I met you at your party, about a month ago. I was there with Alice."

At the mention of Alice, Andy's puzzled expression cleared.

"Yes, of course I remember you. How are you?" He shook her hand.

"Oh, great. Never been better. I'm a soloist with the company here, you might remember my telling you. And Alice tells me the three of you"—here, a careless gesture toward Gil without glancing his way—"have been working together."

"Yes," Gil started, but Andy spoke over him.

"Yes indeed, with an agreement signed, sealed and delivered. Alice will be my main contact now, in fact." He studied her closer. "The two of you are still...friendly?"

"Oh, my goodness, yes. In fact," she said, lowering her voice in a conspiratorial manner, "I've moved in with her."

"Really!"

"Yes, really!" Lana beamed at him. She wagged a finger at him in a mock-disapproving manner. "And if I'm not mistaken, *you're* the reason she got home so late last night."

Andy laughed. "Guilty as charged."

She could see Gil trying to send her a message with his eyes, but she ignored him. He did not want her there; he did not want her speaking to Andy, mentioning Alice or anything at all.

Too bad. She was doing this, she decided, for Alice, who'd helped her so much, to whom Lana had been unspeakably rude to the previous evening. Alice, another victim of Gil's manipulation. Not to mention his hostility: he'd left two messages on the answering machine last night for Alice, the latter one stating, "You bitch, you'd better not be sleeping with him. Call me the minute you get home." It had shocked Lana, hearing the harsh message, particularly since he'd left a message on her cell phone at roughly the same time, in a sweet, loving tone.

"And I must say," Lana continued, "I wasn't the only one wondering what she was doing out so late, was I, Gil? I heard the messages you left her." She turned toward him, her and Andy both, and watched his mouth open and close in surprise. An instant later his eyes lit with relief as he gestured to the curb.

"That looks like your driver pulling up," he told Andy.

"Well, I'll let you boys say your goodbyes," Lana told Andy in her best Courtney imitation. "I just wanted to stop and say hello."

"Thank you," Andy said, smiling back just as broadly. "Nice talking to you again."

"Bye, Gil," she sang out. "See you around."

She turned and headed back toward the lobby. Yes, she'd be seeing Gil around. Soon. Because she could tell she'd made him very angry, which was a shocking, disorienting feeling. It frightened her, jolted something deep inside her, something that had thought it was safe.

Gil didn't disappoint; he strode into the lobby two minutes later and came right up to the corner she'd planted herself in.

"I just want to know what that was all about," he said, trying to keep his voice controlled. "Why you had to go barging in like that. Do you realize he just signed a letter of agreement for a quarter of a million dollars? That's how much we're getting from him. And you could have put it at risk."

She angled her head at him as if in confusion. "If you'd already received his signature on an agreement, how could my greeting him have put things at risk?"

He glared at her. "Jesus. You sound just like Alice. What's gotten into you?"

"Alice, who once again had to enlighten me on the details of your plans last night that you conveniently omitted. The part about the two of you meeting Andy for dinner."

"Look. I didn't want anything to distract or upset you before a performance."

"Well. Thanks for your consideration. It's a shame you can't have the same consideration toward Alice."

"I do."

"Oh. Like on the message you left on her machine last night?"

A dull red flush rose to stain his cheeks. "That message was for her, not you. Do you make it a habit of listening to her messages?"

She could feel her own cheeks growing warm. "With her permission, yes. My mother calls and leaves me messages there. As proof I'm living where I say I'm living."

The muscle beneath Gil's jaw ticked. "Alice behaved inappropriately last night."

"How so?"

"She was flirting in a ridiculous manner with Andy over dinner."

"Don't you see how comical that accusation is?"

"Why?"

"Why? Because of the way *you* were acting, that night at Andy's party."

There. It was out.

His expression grew cold. "That was business, Lana. Business that produced today's awarded grant."

"Oh, I think there was more than business going on." Her voice shook, as did her whole body.

"What has that bitch been telling you?"

"Who?"

"Alice, that's who. What lies has she been feeding you?"

It was as if she were speaking to another Gil, a cruel, unlikeable one. She leaned closer and spoke in a slow, clear tone.

"Alice didn't have to tell me anything. I saw it, that night. Did you think I was blind? I saw that look in Andy's eyes and the acceptance in yours."

"This conversation is ridiculous," he spluttered. "You're overwrought, I need to go prep for my next meeting, and I think the best thing for us to do is—"

"Over*wrought*? Did you really just call me overwrought?"

He stopped. "I'm sorry, that was a cliché. A stupid guy response. You're not overwrought, you're…" He gestured with his hands like a magician trying to conjure up a less inflammatory word.

She *was* overwrought. Not about her dance, her career, as she should be, but about a guy. Someone who couldn't muster the courage to call her "my girlfriend" in public. The realization chilled her. What had she allowed herself to get drawn into? Alice was wrong; it wasn't Mom she'd handed too much power over to, it was Gil.

He was still trying to justify himself, his words, his own anger. "Just stop it right there," Lana interrupted. "I'm sick to death of these games. The others are welcome to you. I want out."

He stared at her, stunned. "Are you trying to break up with me?"

"Is that even possible, when I'm not even 'your girlfriend'? But to answer your question. Yes."

The reality of her words seemed to wash over them at the same time. Gil's next words echoed her thoughts.

"You can't do this. We're not ending things here, Lana. Not over some little dispute."

"No, Gil. What I can't do is live like this."

She turned around and walked away. Ran away. To the ladies' room, where he couldn't follow. There, she ran the water, splashed it over her face, tried desperately to retune her brain.

Tonight was the final dress rehearsal with orchestra for Program II. *Souvenir* was better than it had been, but it would take everything in her to excel in it. She'd willingly give it all that, and more. Because this was the only world that mattered for her. Her place of safety.

She repeated this to herself like a mantra as she dried her face, her hands, studied her pale face in the mirror.

She was safe. She needed only focus on dance.

When she walked out of the restroom and saw Gil, leaning against the opposite wall, she exhaled in impatience. She felt like telling him this wasn't the Ritz, that she wasn't looking to be talked out of her decision. She didn't need to be rescued.

He didn't say anything. He merely regarded her with mournful eyes, and she knew he wasn't going to let her off easily.

"Will you just sit with me for a few minutes?" he asked.

She sighed and nodded.

She followed him to a less public spot, a bench in a far corner of the hallway. The place, perhaps, where Courtney had spied Gil and Gabrielle in their cozy exchange. They sat. She was wordless, and it was a while before he spoke.

"I just want to know why you would want to break up with me

because I left an angry message on Alice's machine," he said finally. "Or because Andy Redgrave was being a flirt that night. Talk to me. Please."

"Jewel. Andy. Gabrielle. Where do you want to start?"

"Jewel?" His confusion seemed genuine. "I'm not following."

"Gil. He—or she—was caressing you, hugging you, all but humping you while I stood there, watching."

He relaxed, even chuckled. "It's all part of the Jewel act. All for show, and everyone who knows her knows it. That's the friendship, weird as it is. Nothing more to know, or see."

"Fine." Her heart began to hammer wildly. "Andy. That night."

No confusion here. Gil hesitated, plowed his hands through his hair before looking at her. "Look. That's not going to be an issue again. He knows I don't go that way."

"Did he know, that night?" She could hardly hear her words for the way the blood was whooshing through her veins, clogging her ears, her throat.

He studied the linoleum floor. "He found out."

Oh, the ugly scenario that had surely transpired. Andy, holder of so much power. Telling Gil to kneel before him, bow his head and pay homage to the king, so to speak. Or Gil would have offered to do so. Begged. Anything for that account.

She didn't need to watch Gil squirm through a detailed recounting of what actually happened, or, worse, offer a prettier, made-up one to better suit his audience. Neither of them would profit from that. "Is it ever going to happen again?" she asked him instead.

"Never," he said to the floor.

"Does he know that?"

His gaze rose to meet hers. "Yes."

The effort required to ask these questions, visualize what she'd long pushed out of her mind, drained her of words, of spirit. Gil looked equally depleted. They sat there in silence, letting the subject waft away like a bad smell.

"So, that's why you're trying to break up with me?" Gil said finally.

"Oh, Gil. That was just two examples. There's Julia. And today I heard about Gabrielle."

"Who?"

"One of the dancers?" she supplied.

He looked perplexed, yet again.

"Someone told me she caught the two of you together the other day in the hallway, all close and cozy."

He gazed at her as if waiting for a punch line to a joke he hadn't really caught.

She sighed in impatience. "Whether you remember it or not is beside the point. Or maybe that *is* the point. There are so many you don't even remember names."

She shut her eyes. It was easier that way.

"I don't want to be involved in these guessing games. I don't even want a boyfriend. That was never my goal. Dancers don't date. They dance. In a way, I feel like this whole thing has been about you getting what you want. In fact, that defines your whole life, doesn't it?"

"Lana, please, it's not like that anymore."

Silence.

"Lana. Look at me."

"No."

She could feel him slipping from the bench and hunkering down next to her, pressing against her thighs. She opened her eyes and met his gaze.

"I'd do anything for you," he said. "Tell me what you need and

I'll do it."

The answer seemed to rise up from within her. "I need space from you."

He hesitated. "I can appreciate that. This is all terrible timing, I know, with the opening of the big ballet tomorrow night. I'll give you that space." His tone changed; it became canny. "But I told you weeks ago that I'd help you find a more permanent living arrangement. That was my job. It still is. Why don't you let me take you out, for a few hours on Saturday or Sunday afternoon?"

His eyes were still soft, coaxing, but in his manner she could feel the same pressure he'd applied to Jewel. He got this way, so caught up in what he wanted, that he'd just push on, bullishly, determined to get it at any cost, regardless of the other person's feelings.

It turned her off like nothing else. It made rejecting him that much easier.

"Oh. That won't be necessary, after all," she told him.

The softness receded. "Why?"

"Alice has invited me to stay there, at her house, through the end of the year."

"Wait. She did? Why?"

"The company is touring soon. Alice pointed out how silly it would be to pay rent for the time I'm gone. And after that the whole *Nutcracker* season—the craziness of it, the way all you want to do when you're not at the theater or the studio is go home, sleep and try to stay uninjured. She understands that. And her house is an easy commute to the theater."

"Alice isn't the one who really cares about you here."

"Oh, yes she is."

Gil's eyes grew hard. "So. Alice gets your company, you get your space, and I'm pushed to the periphery, until you say the magic word."

She held her ground. "Yes. That's how it has to be. That, or a clean breakup."

Her body tensed, waiting for the awfulness sure to come. But Gil surprised her.

"Okay. It's a deal. I'll give you the space you need. You mean that much to me." He rose, unsmiling. "But if you'll excuse me now, I need to go. I've got a three o'clock meeting with Alice."

Something inside her faltered. Her goal had been to support and defend the person who'd helped her so much, in the hope that it would help Alice in return.

It might have done just the opposite.

Chapter 19 – Alice's Very Bad Day

Alice was putting the finishing touches on a correspondence when she looked up to see Gil standing by her door. "You're late," he said with a frown.

"Late for what?"

"Our three o'clock meeting."

Their Thursday "show up whenever it's convenient" meeting. She smiled politely at him.

"It's five minutes to three, Gil."

"My watch says 3:02."

He looked as petulant as a little boy, lips pursed, arms folded.

"I'm sorry, I'm not ready to meet yet," she said. "I've got something important to take care of first. I'll join you in your office the minute I'm done."

He scowled, nodded and disappeared.

She sighed. Yet another mood swing on his part. He'd stormed into the office at eight-thirty that morning, probably to berate her for her behavior the previous night, for not returning his nocturnal calls. When he'd caught sight of the letters of agreement on his desk, topped with a big, obnoxious bow, however, his mood had cleared immediately.

She finished and saved her computer document, filed her nails for five minutes. Only then did she rise and make her way over to Gil's office.

It was not a good meeting. He questioned her about her log sheets and call reports. He nitpicked at her written summary of the WCBT's most recent Form 990, used to assess compliance with the tax laws and detailing how the Ballet Theatre spent its money. Frowning, he asked why the output on proposals was low and she pointed to a stack of papers on his desk and said that once he'd approved those, it would put her fifteen percent over her monthly goal.

She asked about how the meeting with Andy—largely symbolic since the letters of agreement had already been signed—had gone.

Andy was a touchy subject. Gil had wanted to know what had transpired the previous night. Alice told him they'd gone back to his place, but would say nothing more. No need for Gil to know they'd spent two hours merely listening to violin concertos in the darkness. The innuendo of it all was infinitely more exciting. An added bonus was the way not knowing had irked Gil.

"It went fine. He left happy." Gil focused on his pad, and drew a line through one of the items.

"And?" she prompted.

He said nothing.

"I'm sorry, I'm missing something. Did the ball get dropped in any way? Is Charlie Stanton not happy?"

"No. Everything is fine."

"So what's the problem here?"

He peered down at his button-down oxford shirt, brushed at an invisible imperfection. "Long story short? Lana just tried to break up with me."

She couldn't believe it. Jubilance filled her, which she immediately tried to quell.

"Gil, I'm sorry. What happened?"

"She saw Andy and me talking. Came right up and started chatting with us, like everything was fine. But afterward, when she and I were talking, she freaked. Over the Andy business, over a rumor about me and someone else, even over Julia, even though we all know Julia's no threat to her."

"Um, regarding Julia. You really don't see any reason why such a compromised situation should bother Lana?"

"What? I'm being up front about it. It's a tricky situation, but it's all working out."

"Gil. Maybe you need to rethink your success here from the woman's perspective."

"You're feeding those kind of thoughts to her."

"I'm what?"

"You heard me. She wasn't herself today. All this talk about needing her space, this sudden need to challenge things that were just fine. It was vintage Alice-speak. What are you having there at your place? Little coaching sessions for how Lana should act and speak?"

She drew a deep breath. "The irony here, Gil, is that you are the one who pushed us into this closeness. You've been orchestrating our relationship all along. Asking me to spy on her in the studio, leaving me to rescue her the night of Andy's party, begging me to let her move in. I think you've acquired a very convenient memory about these things."

"Stop talking to me like you're the boss here."

Jesus. Twenty-nine-year-old males and their sensitive egos.

"Yes, you're my boss," she said, keeping her tone bright. "And I've tried hard to accommodate you and your needs, which, in the aforementioned circumstances, I've done. So now I'm trying to figure out how I've suddenly become the villain."

"You're butting in where you shouldn't be."

"My housemate's welfare is not a work-related issue. I don't have to offer you deference there. Why shouldn't I try and help, advise a vulnerable, impressionable young woman? And I've shown discretion, to boot. When I think of the things I *could* have been telling her about your sleazy escapades of the past."

He stabbed a finger at Alice. "It's that attitude right there that's coming through. You're poisoning her mind. You're injecting your opinion, over and over, into this equation. Your bitchy, suspicious opinion."

"I'm telling her the truth. Tell me, Gil. Tell me what isn't true here." Their voices had risen. She didn't care.

"And you're trying to live through her success. The dancing you can't have anymore."

"That is such bullshit and you know it. Everything I've done has been to help either you or her."

"You're jealous, then."

"I am not jealous of her."

"No. You're jealous of me. That she's in love with me." His face lit up, as if he'd just found a fifty-dollar bill crumpled in his pocket when he'd thought he was broke. "You want her for yourself. That's what this is all about. You've gone dyke on me, haven't you?"

She was so angry, she could hardly speak.

"You fucker!" she sputtered. "You son of a bitch. I could slap a discrimination suit on you right there. Or whatever it is. Defamation of character, harassment. Inappropriate language."

He rose and slammed his hands on the desk so hard the pencil jar rattled and tipped over. "Inappropriate language? And you think you can get away with calling your boss a 'fucker'? Huh? Mess with me, Alice, I'll mess with you."

"Oh, right. Mister Tough Guy. What are you going to do, Gil?"

"I'll fire you."

"Just try it."

"All right. You're fired."

There was a dizzying, tunnel-vision moment as they stared at each other, as if neither could believe what he'd just said.

Gil recovered faster. "You're fired, Alice."

He didn't mean it. He couldn't.

"Oh, right." She injected as much scorn as possible into her response. "Just try explaining *that* to Andy."

He matched her scorn. "Andy doesn't give a shit about you."

He does too! she wanted to cry out. *He likes me!*

"We would have never gotten those party invitations if it hadn't been for me," she burst out instead, well aware that she was bringing the argument down to the schoolyard level.

"Oh, that's right. You and your holier-than-thou great-grandfather."

"Great-*great*-grandfather."

"Whatever! Your magical upper-class family name. Well, guess what? You wouldn't have had it in you to see this account to fruition. You're a nobody in this scheme."

She shot him a poisonous glare. "Since the business portion of this meeting is clearly over"—she made little quote marks in the air over the word "business"—"I think I'll just make my way out of here now. I've done enough work for the day, bringing in that signed letter of agreement for $250,000."

"Go ahead and leave. Pack up your office before you go. I fired you, remember?"

"What's the point in packing up when I'd just have to bring it back? After you've called me to apologize and begged me to return?"

"That's not going to happen, Alice."

What frightened her the most about his last words, which echoed around in her head as she marched over to her office, shut down her computer, grabbed for her purse and jacket with icy, trembling fingers, was the calm way in which he'd spoken. His rage she could handle. Words spoken in a low steady voice were something different entirely.

He couldn't have been serious.

He couldn't do that. Not on the day of their biggest triumph together.

She left.

He didn't try and stop her.

Somehow she made it out of the building, into her car, through traffic, into her home, her haven. It felt strange in the middle of the afternoon on a weekday, the sun casting rays of dappled light into her living room, setting dust motes aglow. She sat on the couch, but sprang up a moment later and began to pace.

Montserrat. She'd be a good, understanding listener. She'd call Montserrat.

She called the house and Carter picked up on the second ring. "Oh, good," Alice said with an exhale of relief. "You're there. What are the chances Montserrat's there too?"

"She is." Carter sounded guarded. "She's packing for a trip. She leaves in a few hours."

"What good timing on my part." She could feel her shoulders, all her tense muscles, beginning to relax. "Can I talk to her?"

Carter hesitated. "I have to be honest here, Alice. Is this something that can wait? She's got a big performance tomorrow night with the Baltimore Symphony Orchestra. And, well, she was pretty upset after your last visit here. It wasn't a bad thing, she told me, but I could tell something you two talked about really shook her up. That kind of thing can mess with her concentration. I don't want to risk the same thing happening, not before Baltimore."

"Oh." She was momentarily thrown. "Sure."

"So, I hate to do this, but I feel like I need to watch out for her."

He sounded as miserable as she felt.

"Um, sure," she managed.

"She'll be done performing on Sunday afternoon. You can call her any time after that."

"Okay, sure." She was sounding like a parrot, she realized. "Just tell her I said hi, and good luck."

"Will do. And, hey. Thanks."

"No problem. Glad to help."

After she hung up, she stared bleakly at the wall and drew a deep, shuddering breath.

Niles. She had to risk it; she was desperate to talk to a friend right then.

She called his work number, her heart thudding. Soon it was thumping so loudly she was afraid it would override her speech, her hearing.

"Niles Rowley speaking."

His clipped voice, the implied impatience even when he didn't know who it was, made her feel faint.

"Niles." She had to pause, clear her throat and repeat herself. "It's Alice."

If he was surprised or nervous to hear from her, his voice didn't betray it.

"Alice. How are you?"

She'd planned to tell him the truth, to unleash her woes, but his cool tone made her reconsider. "I'm fine," she said instead. "Great."

"Glad to hear it."

He offered nothing more.

"When did you get back from Asia?" She tried not to sound accusing.

"Sunday. The same day Christine arrived."

"Ah. Party boy."

"Hardly."

She realized, belatedly, if she wasn't going to share her bad news with him, the most obvious subject to discuss would be their recent encounter.

"I was surprised to see you last night," she said in what she hoped was a casual voice. "That was a fancy restaurant."

"It wasn't a date I was on, if that's what you're getting at. Christine paid. She wanted to go to a nice restaurant in San Francisco before she left, and thank me at the same time for a week of free housing."

"She seems very considerate."

"She is. And your dining partner seemed quite considerate as well. Attentive."

As she was searching for the best reply, he spoke again. "So. Did you go home with him?"

Of all the questions he might have fired at her, this was one she was the least prepared for.

"Niles. It's not what you're thinking."

"You didn't answer my question. Did he take you back to his place?"

Silence.

"I thought so. I could tell."

She found her voice, her wits. "Look. Let me explain."

"Answer me one thing. Has this been going on since before I left? Because it looked like the two of you were very good friends."

"Niles. That was Andy Redgrave. Gil's Andy Redgrave."

"Oh. Well. It all makes sense now."

"Nothing was going on. It was a charade. He's a business client, nothing more."

"And you just happen to make house calls."

"Look. At his place we listened to music. Nothing more. He saw I was upset and offered a diversion. The same thing at the restaurant—he noticed that seeing you upset me. Did *that* variable ever creep into your mind? That it devastated me to see you there, with another woman?"

"You didn't show any pain or insecurity." He sounded suspicious. "Not one bit. Watching you laughing with that guy, leaning into him, all I could think was that it was over between us and you'd moved on just fine."

"No! That wasn't the case in the least. I was just protecting myself by acting cool."

"I don't think you realize how effective your use of coolness as a weapon is. That goes for last night and that night at your house as well. When you told me not to call you."

"Niles. I'm sorry. That hadn't been my intention, either time. Please. I don't want it to be over between us." Her voice trembled. "God, if only you knew how I've been hurting."

"But I didn't know, did I? You failed to transmit that message to me."

"Niles. Please believe me."

He didn't speak for a moment. He sighed, a tortured sound. "Look. I'm sorry. I need some time here to straighten things out. In my head. And Christine's still here."

She understood, in a rush of glacial clarity, what he was choosing not to say.

Something had happened between him and Christine last night. She could just see it, that pretty young girl roping her arms around Niles's neck, wishing him a good night, sweet dreams, telling him she appreciated his help, his company, so very much, and was there anything she could do in return? Some comfort, perhaps?

She wouldn't have thought she was the jealous type. But this cold, sick feeling washing over her, this territoriality, choked the words right out of her. Had Niles been looking for a fitting punishment for her, he'd certainly found it.

Even he seemed to realize this. When he spoke next, his voice was gentler.

"Look, I said I'd call you when I was free, and that's still my plan. Christine leaves on Sunday morning. I'll call you after that, okay?"

She prided herself on the fact that she'd never cried in front of him. She wasn't going to start now.

"Sure. Whenever it works for you. I'm here."

Lana came in an hour later and looked stunned to see Alice there, sitting on the couch, beer in hand. She gaped at her and in response, Alice lifted her beer bottle in Lana's direction.

"Why aren't you at work?" Lana asked.

"Oh, work. That." She took a swig of beer.

"Alice. What happened? Something happened between you and Gil, didn't it? Oh, God, I blew it again. I got you into trouble."

In response, Alice only shrugged and offered a polite belch.

"Tell me."

"Oh, only that Gil tried to fire me."

Lana's eyes grew wide. "What are you saying?" she gasped.

"You heard me."

"What do you mean, he 'tried' to fire you?"

"Well, he said, 'You're fired.' And I laughed in his face."

"And what did he do? Take it back?"

"Hardly. No, he stood there like some sheriff in a bad Western and held his ground with a mean look on his face. All that was missing was spurs and a six-shooter." The image made her laugh. Or perhaps that was simply the three beers doing their job. "I told him I was leaving and just walked out."

Lana looked uneasy. "So, he didn't un-fire you?"

"Well, no. Not yet."

"Alice. This is serious."

Alice gave an expansive wave, brushing aside the terror that was growing with each passing hour. She'd been so sure he was just trying to call her bluff in walking out. Gil was the one bluffing, she was positive. Right at this moment, she could almost visualize him, standing there, hand on the phone, ranting to himself, saying he would *not* call her first, that he'd make her stew in her fear a little longer.

As if on cue, the phone rang.

"I'll bet you money that's him." Alice said. "See, I know him. This is just one of his games. We'll argue some more, we'll make up and by tomorrow it will be like nothing ever happened."

She struggled to her feet, went over to the machine and pointed at the incoming call number. "There you go. It's a WCBT number." She peered closer. "Except that's not Gil's number."

She let the answering machine pick up the call.

"Alice, it's Lucinda. I just heard the news."

Alice and Lana exchanged uneasy glances as Lucinda's voice filled the room.

"I just want you to know that I think what Gil did was wrong. He had no right. You've shown so much loyalty to the WCBT, and for it to end like that? I wanted you to know that if you want to contest it, I'll back you up."

She felt sick. She picked up the phone while Lucinda was still talking.

"Oh! Alice, you're there?"

"Yes, I'm sorry, I was slow in getting to the phone. But you're saying you heard that Gil…"

She couldn't even say the words.

"That he fired you? Yes."

"How did you hear that?" Maybe Lucinda had just been nosy, she told herself. Overhearing their argument, eavesdropping on her nemesis to see what trouble she could stir up.

"He told me. He's telling everyone, Alice. He was on his way over to HR to document it, in fact."

"He can't fire me!" Alice cried. "He has no grounds."

"I know, that was my thought, too. I don't care what disagreement you were having today, you did not deserve that. I say you contest it. Like I said, I'll back you up. I mean, you have *history* here." Her voice quivered with indignation.

Alice somehow made it through the rest of the conversation, mind awhirl, thanking Lucinda for her support. She wasn't sure which was more difficult to believe—that Gil had actually fired her, or that it was Lucinda who was so fiercely standing up for her.

It was turning out to be a very bad day.

She hung up and stared at Lana.

"He did it," she said in a dazed voice. "Gil fired me."

Chapter 20 – Falling

Luke called Lana after company class on Friday while Lana was finishing the last of a granola bar snack. At the sound of his high, uncertain voice, a rush of fear clutched at her heart.

"Luke! Sweetie, hi. Is everything all right?" She balled up the wrapper, threw it away, and left the dancers' lounge to talk in a more quiet spot.

"Yeah. I just wanted to talk to someone and remembered you told me I could call you. Except that you have your class where you can't talk, so I waited. That was right, huh, Lana?"

"It was. What a big boy you are to call! Is Mom there?"

"No, she's gone."

"Is Annabel there with you?"

"No. I'm all alone." His voice quivered with a mix of pride and unease.

"Goodness, you *are* a big boy." She tried to sound casual, not alarmed. "Does Mommy do this often, leave you alone?"

"Only when she really has to. It's okay. I know I'm never supposed to answer the door or the phone. But sometimes I get lonely. So I'm glad you were there."

"I'm glad I was here for you too."

He chattered nonstop for the next few minutes before the

conversation turned to Christmas, even though it was still only September, and how he already knew what he was going to ask Santa for.

"Ooh, what is it? Can you tell me?"

"Well, I shouldn't," he said gravely. "Because I might jinx it."

He was dying to tell her, she could tell. After much hedging, she got it out of him.

"I'm going to ask for you to come home." He sounded proud, convinced he'd solved a tricky issue once and for all.

Lana squeezed her eyes shut. "Oh, sweetie, you can't do that."

"Sure I can."

"Luke? Santa doesn't do stuff like that. He brings presents."

"Oh, he does *everything*. He's Santa. And besides. A grown-up told me I could."

"Who told you that?"

"Mom."

Indignation rose up in her. "Luke, I can only talk for another minute, because I have a rehearsal. But the minute Mom comes home, tell her to call me, okay? So I know you're safe and someone's in charge of you again."

He agreed and hung up on her without another word, phone etiquette having yet to work its way into his six-year-old mind.

Lana glanced at her watch. Time to head over to the theater. The first cast of *Autumn Souvenir* had stage time for a rehearsal in ten minutes, a run-through for some final checks on lighting. As she was organizing the contents of her dance bag, her phone trilled again. She grabbed at it hastily.

"Mom?"

"Lana. Hi, honey. How are things?"

"Mom, why was Luke alone?"

"Oh, now don't you start on me. It was only for thirty minutes and he's a responsible kid."

"Mom, he's six years old."

"And I've been raising kids for twenty-four years, Miss Know-it-all. Is that why you had me call you?"

"No."

"Good."

"No, the thing is, Luke seems to be under the impression he can ask Santa for me to come home."

Mom chuckled, her defensiveness gone. "I know. Isn't that sweet? He sure misses you."

"But what's going to happen on Christmas Day when I'm not there?"

"Well, you'll just have to make sure you're here."

"That's not so easily done. I'm a little far to just 'drop by.'"

"Oh, I know, you're far and you have your show going on and such. But this is Christmas Day we're talking about, Lana. You've never missed a Christmas here. No one has. Not ever. And we all agreed that this was the kind of thing that made our family special. So, I realize you can't come much earlier, and will have to leave right after, but we'll just make do."

"Mom, I can't. We perform the day before Christmas and the day after. There's no way I can work around that."

"You tell them you can do one day's show and not the other. You take the red-eye flights both directions. You make it happen, honey."

"Look, I'm new in the company. *Nutcracker* is huge—I can't just call in sick and pop back in two days later. I have to be here at all times, except for Christmas Day. And one day is just not enough time to get to Kansas City and back."

There was an ominous silence from the other end.

"Mom? I can't do anything here if you don't speak up."

"I can't believe what I'm hearing you tell me, Lana. That you're not going to even try and come home to be with your family on Christmas."

"Maybe I can make it for New Year's Eve. How about that? I'll be done with *Nutcracker* and it will be so much less complicated."

"And would you just like me to change the date of our Lord's birth? Just change it around to accommodate your selfish whims?"

"This isn't about me! This is about my job. Ballet isn't some hobby to try and work around my 'real' life, like when I was a kid. Why can't you get that? Why aren't you letting me devote myself to it the way I need to?"

"Because sometimes life just doesn't work out that way!" Mom burst out. "Not everyone gets to carry out their dreams, their perfect worlds. Some don't get to at all. Some don't make it past their first day of life. And that creates a big, terrible hole for the rest of us. The rest of us who care about family, that is. The things that matter. Things the family has lost, that will never, never come back."

Mom began to cry, sobs that started off small and grew in intensity.

Lana had done it again.

She glanced at her watch in a panic. She was going to be late for rehearsal, this last one for *Souvenir*. Tonight was opening night. The timing here couldn't have been worse.

"Mom, I'm sorry. Please don't cry. Please. Don't do this. I'm begging you."

Mom managed to speak through her sobs. "Then tell me you'll come home." A noisy gulp for air. "To us. On Christmas Day."

Something in Lana snapped.

"Stop doing this to me," she cried. "Stop backing me into a corner, scaring me, so that you can...*manipulate* me."

Alice's words. Alice's scenario.

Alice had been right.

"I'm not going to come home on Christmas Day," she told Mom. "And that's how it's going to be. You're just going to have to live with that."

The sobs had stopped. In their place was a cold voice, seething with anger, terrible in its indictment.

"Fine. You made your decision, Lana Marie Kessler. You'll deal with the consequences."

The rehearsal, run by Ben, was only intended to be an onstage mark-through, for lighting to work on cues with the dancers in place. Lana, however, chose to dance full out. There was no other way she could deal with the sick anxiety brewing inside her.

She knew she was distraught, and that distraught equaled distracted. She knew she was putting herself at risk. So when she fell, coming out of a turn, she wasn't shocked as much as resigned. There was even a sense of rightness, of satisfaction, that consequence should so neatly follow poorly thought-out action.

She hit the floor hard with a bone-jolting *bam*. She lay there, too stunned to scramble up and continue, thoughts swirling through her head at a millisecond's pace.

I'm hurt.

It's Alice all over again.

Maybe Luke will get his wish after all.

She heard the "God, is she all right?" whispers amid a dawning realization that while the fall had hurt—she'd banged her head, producing stars, like in the cartoons, little spirals and asterisks of blue and pink—it hadn't broken or torn anything.

This wasn't Alice, after all.

"Lana?" Ben called out. "Are you all right?"

She managed to sit up. The other dancers and Ben were frozen in place, waiting for her reply.

Was she all right?

No. Nothing in her life was all right. Tears rose and spilled out, which she wiped away angrily, trying to pretend like they were just sweat, but more kept coming out.

Tears had bonded her to her fellow dancers in the past. She herself had been quick to comfort and sympathize with others who'd wept out their frustration, their pain. But that was not going to be what happened here. Because once she called out in a high, unsteady voice that she was fine, after a collective exhale of relief, one of the male corps dancers began to laugh. Courtney joined him, and another, and even Javier.

They were laughing at her.

These people who'd judged her, made her feel out of place, from the day of her arrival.

Not everyone was laughing, however. Delores hurried over to Lana, face creased in concern, bent and laid a hand on Lana's shoulder. She glared at the others. "This isn't funny. Lana could have been seriously hurt."

"Yes, but she wasn't," Javier said, walking over to her. "And that makes all the difference." He offered her his hand. She took it and he lifted her to her feet. When she'd risen, he stepped closer, wrapping his arms around her. "That was a beautiful, impressive, and, yes, hilarious fall. Do you forgive us for laughing?" he asked, and reluctantly she nodded.

Ben, after confirming Lana was fine, stepped away to speak with the lighting director. The other dancers used the break to recount their own big-fall stories. Javier repositioned himself behind Lana and began to massage her shoulders. "Are you really all right?" he murmured into her ear.

She melted into the soothing pressure of his hands as they kneaded her tense muscles. "I am. Thanks."

"Good." He continued to massage her shoulders, her arms, as the others spoke.

"My most embarrassing fall was during *Nutcracker* last year," Courtney was saying. She turned to Delores. "Remember, during 'Land of Snow'?"

Delores nodded. "It was those snowflakes. They'd gotten so dusty and slippery by the twentieth performance. I remember, it was like a minefield onstage during the final few shows."

"Alice told me all about her fall," Lana said to Delores, who nodded solemnly and shared the story with the younger members who hadn't heard the details.

"I remember the night," Delores said. "Poor Alice. But the crazy thing is that she and Ben improvised so well, you would have thought it was the actual choreography if you didn't know the ballet."

"Katrina and I had a night like that two years ago," Javier said. "*Ay*, I wouldn't want to do *that* again. She was out for the next six months."

"All right," Ben called out. "One more time from the top." He paused to scrutinize Lana. "You don't look good. Sit. We'll run it with your understudy."

Her throat seized up. "I can do it," she croaked out.

Ben shook his head. "It's not worth the risk. You hit your head; what you need is rest."

"Please, Ben, I'll be fine."

"Lana," he said. "This is just a run-through for lighting. We're not taking your role away tonight. Just sit and rest up."

He turned to Lana's understudy who was yanking off her leg warmers, her sweatshirt, and told her in a lower voice, "But you're on alert for tonight."

Lana numbly made her way her way to one of the folding chairs at the front of the stage. She sat and watched her understudy dance her part and wondered if her life could get any worse.

Bad question.

When the rehearsal ended, the dancers disbanded for lunch, followed by another rehearsal for most of them. Ben told Lana to go home, rest up, a direct order from Anders. Lana stopped in her dressing room to try and call home. *Please, Mom*, she prayed as the phone rang. *Please be home and talk to me.* The answering machine picked up; all she could do was leave a message.

She left the building, stopping a few blocks away for a bowl of soup, away from the café, away from the chance of seeing Gil, because if she did she'd melt into him, despite his firing Alice, and never let go. She didn't need Alice to tell her that would be a mistake. No Gil. Not right now.

After lunch, she tried calling home again.

No answer.

She walked slowly the rest of the way to Alice's. Inside the house, to her surprise, Alice was right there, holding the phone out to her.

"Perfect timing," Alice said. "It's your father." She looked worried.

Lana went cold.

She knew it was bad by the way Dad kept assuring her it was good news.

"She's fine, honey," he babbled. "Mom's absolutely fine. She had a little fender bender on the way to picking up Marty from school, but there's absolutely nothing to worry about. She and Luke are fine, not a scratch. Both a little shook up, that's all. But I just now heard your messages on the answering machine. You sounded worried—boy, you sure do know your mom." A nervous chuckle here. "You must be telepathic. But it's all over, everyone's home and safe. Nothing to worry about."

Her mouth had gone dry, her lips papery. "Where did it happen?"

"You know that curvy stretch in the road that if you take it too fast it gets tricky? Well, it got tricky on her. She said she must have been distracted."

"Dad. That's the opposite direction of the school. What was she doing there?"

"Well, honey, I don't know," he said in a bright, bland voice, a "we aren't going to talk about this because we're all fine now" tone. Dad was good at that tone. He'd had sixteen years to work on it.

He droned on in this manner for another few minutes, words that flowed through Lana's ears and out before her overworked mind could process them.

Your mother had an accident. With Luke in the back seat.

Lana had caused it.

She alone was to blame.

She hung up after extracting a promise from Dad to call her the next day, tell her how everyone was doing. Then she went numb and checked out.

She slid down the wall until she found the floor. The ringing in her ears muffled the outside world, like having cotton wadded in her ears. It felt good, soothing. But Alice didn't like it. Lana could tell; she could register Alice trying to engage her, but she felt too heavy, too sleepy to care. Even turning her head to talk to Alice felt like too much of a burden.

Alice wouldn't go away. She kept posing question after question until finally Lana had to answer. She was a guest in Alice's house, after all.

"Yes, I can hear you," she told her.

"Good. So. It sounds like your mom's all right."

"My dad says so."

"Lana. Then why aren't *you* all right?" She squatted down to Lana's level and took Lana's limp hands.

She had no answer for this.

"I'm so, so sorry, Lana," she said. "I feel terrible, like I pushed you to challenge your mother, and this is what happened. I owe you and your family a big apology for that. But listen to me." She gave Lana's hands a little shake. "You need to push this away for the moment. It'll be there tomorrow for you to address. You have a performance tonight."

"I can't dance tonight."

"I'm sorry, what?"

"I can't dance tonight. I already know that. So does my mom."

"Why are you saying this?" Alice sounded frightened, very un-Alice.

"I can't do it, and she knows it. It's like she's got this crystal ball and she's watching me. I fell in rehearsal today, after we argued. It's like she willed it. It's like she sucks something essential out of me. I can feel it right now, like it's seeping out of me. I can't do it."

She drew her knees up and rested her forehead there. "Ben has my understudy on alert for tonight. It's as if he saw what was happening too."

"Lana, you don't throw a performance. Not like this. Not for this reason."

She had no reply. It was too much effort.

Alice didn't move. Her perplexed look faded.

"This happened in Kansas City, didn't it? This is why your

career there stalled."

Clever Alice, who saw everything. She raised her head to meet Alice's eyes.

"What does it matter now?"

"It matters now because we're not going to let it happen again." Alice's voice rose with each word. By the end she looked downright angry. She stood and held her hand out to Lana. When Lana didn't reach out, Alice gave an impatient sigh.

"Come on, don't make me haul you up. And don't think I won't. I lift weights, you know."

Alice ran a hot bath for her and made her a glass of chocolate milk. "Now upstairs you go," she commanded, handing the glass to Lana. "Afterward, some rest in the bedroom with the shades pulled. Some light dinner. And when it's time, I'm driving you to the theater."

Lana gave a wordless nod and trudged upstairs. Once in the tub, she lay there, the heat of the water sinking into her muscles, relaxing her, which, unfortunately, woke her thoughts back up.

It was happening again. A choice: family or career.

Alice had pegged it.

It hadn't felt like much of a choice that night, two years ago. The twins were four, and a handful. Dad was traveling, Luke had an ear infection and was screaming. Mom was weeping, turning the boys over to Lana the minute she walked in the door at four o'clock, but even with Lana, Luke was inconsolable. Scott came into the house, took one look, reared back and darted right out again, ignoring Lana's cries to come back, she had to leave for the theatre soon.

The time for her to be at the theatre grew closer and closer. *Tick, tick* of the clock, competing with Luke's wails. Annabel came home finally, but began to shout that she would *not* stay alone with everyone crying, panicking, which now included Lana. Their voices rose, the boys screamed, Mom's sobs increased from behind the closed bedroom door with an extra-loud "Oh, I just want to *die.*"

Somehow Lana gave in, the way she always did with Mom and Annabel, despising them, despising herself, calling over to the theatre where Theo was, already deep into logistics with the stage manager. Theo, who'd fought for her, who'd gotten her noticed by management, promoted, even under consideration for a promotion to principal.

He was furious. Incensed. Lana couldn't tell him the truth, that her mother was acting suicidal. No Kessler would ever admit to that. She couldn't even use Luke, because she'd been warned about putting family before the company. So she lied. Stomach flu. Her voice wobbled and she knew at least that part sounded convincing. She was not well.

Silence hung on the other end of the phone. When Theo spoke, his voice was cold with anger as he told her to get her ass in, to dance sick.

She told him she couldn't.

Another long silence.

"No more, Lana," he said finally. "I give up on you. Once again, this is about your family, and don't try to tell me otherwise. Your priorities are skewed. You will not make it any further here, talented soloist or not."

"Theo, please! I didn't plan this."

"I've backed you. I've fought for you. And this is how you thank me."

He hung up on her in a rage.

Lana began to cry again. She reached for a tomato sauce-crusted dish towel and mopped at her face before going to tell Annabel she was staying home. In response, Annabel glared at her.

"Don't go looking at me like you think I owe you some grand apology," she said through her tears. "You just watch. We'll both stay and Mom will thank you and not me. Do all of you think I didn't have plans tonight? Maybe not as important as *Lana's*. But plans."

"Fine. Go."

Annabel's red, mascara-smeared eyes widened with hope. "Are you serious?" she stammered.

"Oh, just go."

"I will." She smiled at Lana, edging her way toward the door. "I don't need a second invitation."

With that, she turned, grabbed a jacket, her purse and in a matter of seconds had left the house. Lana heard the sound of her car starting up, the *putt-putt* of it receding as she drove down the street.

Capitulation carries with it its own curious relief. Once you stop trying to exert your own individual will against a greater force, once you give up on a notion, an endeavor, no matter how cherished, and say *oh, well*, it gets easier.

The comfort of no escape. Even the boys had stopped crying so hard.

Lana sank into a chair and Luke scooted right over, climbing into her lap. She buried her face into his soft hair and let the tears fall silently. Family, she reminded herself. Family was the noblest investment of all.

She sat in the tub now, soaking, her thoughts churning. Her beloved Luke, whose life Mom had put at risk today.

Mom had done it on purpose.

The truth of this hit an instant before the guilt for thinking such a thing did.

Mom had done it to prove to Lana she could. Even with Luke in the back seat. Mom would forever deny it, but Lana knew.

The rage in her built, a subterranean thrum, ever increasing, until she felt like she was going to puke her guts out, only it didn't come from her stomach, it came from somewhere deeper inside her.

She hated her mother.

Hated her.

The mantra grew legs, vocal cords, climbed out of her. She stepped out of the tub, wrapped herself in a towel. She held another one to her mouth and let a scream tear out of her.

"I hate you! I hate you!"

The sound bounced off the walls and made her ears ring, in spite of the towel. She didn't care. She felt free, for the first time, to scream out how she truly felt.

"I HATE YOU!"

The wild, unhinged feeling of it all. Like steering a car off the road, uncaring of the precipice below. Uncaring of the consequence.

There was the sound of pounding footsteps approaching, stopping outside the door. Alice was there, calling her name, jiggling at the door handle. Before Lana could turn the knob, Alice burst in.

The two of them regarded each other, frozen, Lana still clutching the muffling towel that clearly was not as effective a muffler as she'd thought.

"Are you all right?" Alice asked.

"Yes."

Alice looked around, perplexed. "But I heard you scream."

"I guess I did."

A wry half-smile crossed Alice's face. "I can't say soaking in a hot bath produces that reaction in me."

A laugh burst out of Lana, a lone sound, like a bark, that morphed into a choked sob.

"I hate her," she said to Alice.

"Who?"

"My mom. You were right about her. You were absolutely right." She began to cry again, but softer this time. "She crashed that car to prove a point."

"You don't know that."

"Oh, but I do. I know my mother. Anything to prove her point. Prove to her daughter what results from crossing her."

Alice hesitated. "Families are tricky," she said gently. "All that love and familiarity make you vulnerable. They know how to entrap you, get you where it hurts. Your mom is doing stupid things right now, but it's because she's afraid. This is new for her, your independence. It's huge and scary."

She could offer no rebuttal to this.

Alice glanced down at her watch. "Okay. Go rest for an hour. Relax."

"How can I? After this mess with my family?"

Alice considered this. "Let me deal with your family. I'll call your dad right back. I talked with him for a spell already—he seems like a reasonable guy. I'll tell him I'm going to be the intermediary for a while, that you need to focus on your performing and that any issues or dramas should come through me first."

"My mom won't accept that."

"Oh yes she will."

"You don't know my mom."

Alice drew herself up haughtily. "Your mom doesn't know me."

The thought of Alice confronting her mother was enough to make a weak smile break across her face. Alice noticed, and smiled back. She began to walk out of the room until Lana's voice stopped her.

"Alice? Can I ask you for one last favor?"

"Anything. Anything that helps you tonight."

Lana told her.

Alice winced. "Oh, Lana. Anything but that."

"Alice, please. It would mean everything to me."

Alice squeezed her eyes shut. There was silence, except for a mew from Odette, trotting over for a scratch behind the ears. Alice opened her eyes.

"All right. For you, I'll do it."

Chapter 21 – Facing the Truth

She dropped Lana off at the theatre at 5:30 PM, enough time for Lana to squeeze in a session with the company massage therapist, as per Alice's mandate. "You know how to pick up the tickets at the will-call window, right?" Lana asked her as she edged out of the car.

Alice laughed. "Oh, I think I've practiced the drill once or twice in my life."

Lana winced. "How stupid of me. I forgot who I was talking to."

"No, no, not stupid. This is important, I get that. Don't worry about a thing."

"You know you really should have invited Niles."

"No way. Not after yesterday's conversation."

She'd told Lana all about the conversation, and about calling Montserrat and having Carter rebuff her. There seemed to be no need to maintain any sense of distance or decorum between them anymore, given the dramas of the past two days. Alice leaned over the passenger seat now to gaze up at Lana.

"Hey. You going to be okay?"

Lana nodded. "Thanks. For everything."

"No problem. See you after the show. Oh, and merde."

Merde, the French word for "shit," the dance world's equivalent to theatre's "break a leg." You didn't want to tell a dancer to break a leg. Because she just might.

Once Alice had guided the car back into traffic, she hesitated. She had time to kill, but she didn't want to hang around the area, so close to the WCBT building. She didn't want to risk seeing Gil.

She'd heard from him finally. She'd anticipated a call all morning long, a "what are you doing at home, couldn't you tell a joke when you saw one?" rant. Instead he left a message in the afternoon, telling her she needed to come in and clear out her desk by Monday at the latest, and to schedule her exit interview for the same time so she wouldn't keep coming and going from her former place of work. And to please pass on to him any recent correspondences with the Redgrave Foundation, since he'd take over as Andy's contact.

This last bit hurt more than she'd anticipated. She wouldn't be working with Andy Redgrave after all. She would have enjoyed it. He would have breathed new life into her professional world. It felt like a door shut in her face.

But even this had been rendered petty by the call from Lana's father and the terrible story that unfolded. What kind of mother crashed her car merely to prove to her daughter that she had the power to do it? Worse, with Lana's little brother in the back seat. The thought of such coldhearted vindictiveness chilled Alice to the core.

Marianne. She wanted to talk to her stepmother. Drink in her calm, rational nature, her affection, warmth and wisdom.

It was Friday, Marianne's afternoon for volunteer work at the Yerba Buena Center for the Arts. The complex was less than a mile away and they were open late on Fridays. When a street parking space opened up midway between the theater and the arts center, free parking for the night, she grabbed it.

Marianne, manning the information desk along with another volunteer, looked pleased to see her. "Hey there, pretty lady, what's new?" she asked.

"Well, let's see." Alice relaxed against the counter. "Aside from attending the ultimate power business dinner with Andy Redgrave, drinks alone with him afterward that produced a signed contract for a quarter-million-dollar grant, seeing Niles with another woman at the very same restaurant, Gil's maybe having fired me, my roommate's mom crashing a car with a child in the back seat as part of a power struggle with poor Lana, oh, I'd call it a fairly mundane week."

Marianne chuckled. "Which is why it's a good thing you arrived just as I was about to take a break and stroll around the gardens. Let's go."

Outside, over the green expanse of landscaped lawn that comprised Yerba Buena Gardens, they walked as Alice elaborated. Through it, Marianne listened, wincing and shaking her head from time to time. "Your poor roommate," she murmured.

"The worst thing is that I encouraged her to stand up to her mom rather than just meekly follow her dictates. To do what was right and important for herself, not just her mom. And then this happens."

"I'm assuming you didn't know the mother would be so vindictive."

"I did not. Although I could tell she was a controlling type. She loves her daughter, that's obvious. But it's on her terms, and don't you dare cross her. A big, terrible love."

They stood there, taking in the sight and sound of the garden's water fountain, a shimmering waterfall, twenty feet high and fifty feet wide, splashing water into the shallow pool below.

"My mother. Deborah," Alice said, startling herself. How odd, jarring, to be saying these words to the mother she'd known much longer, much better. "She wasn't like Lana's mother, not by a long shot. But she was strict, uncompromising, and when she got angry with me, she'd grow so cold and distant. I'd always comply, in order to get her approval back. Her love." The memory sprang to mind so vividly, it made her feel dizzy, disoriented. "She terrified me. And then she got sick and it all became so much more complicated."

"You had a big challenge back then, kiddo," Marianne said softly.

Emotion welled up within Alice. She turned toward Marianne. "I don't think I've ever spelled out to you how much I appreciated your arrival in my life. Your support. Back then, I never said a word about it."

"You didn't need to. I understood how things were."

"No, but I should have spoken up. The way you saved me. You were there and if you hadn't been there, I'd have been so…"

She was shaking. Her hands had balled into fists. She swung away from Marianne and focused on the water.

"Alice," Marianne said. "Thank you, sweetheart. That's a lovely thing to say."

"No, it's *not* lovely. It's gritty and it's real. And I resent that, as a Willoughby, I'm not supposed to talk about stuff like that, get emotional about it."

Silence. Even awkwardness.

"Alice." Marianne spoke gently. "I'm not sure what you want from me here."

Alice's spirited manifesto, so quick to arise, dissipated just as quickly.

"Oh, don't mind me. I'm just in a weird place this evening."

"Gil will call you, make amends," Marianne said. "He's not that foolish. You'll have your job back by this time next week, I'm sure of it."

She was about to tell Marianne that the job loss was secondary right then, eclipsed by the prospect of attending the night's ballet, confronting the old, deep pain, when she realized it would be just more of the same confusion.

Willoughbys didn't show their pain. Or discuss it.

Marianne was no Deborah. But she was still a Willoughby.

Therefore Alice only nodded, made murmurs of agreement. Marianne smiled at her, and in this calmer, more agreeable fashion they returned to the information desk so Marianne could get back to work and Alice could confront the gremlins that lay waiting for her, at the ballet.

She'd been in the California Civic Theater lobby for plenty of work-related client functions, but she'd always slipped away on performance nights as their clients went to their seats. It felt strange to be the one now entering the double doors, working her way through the murmuring crowds to find her seat. The last time she'd done this, she'd been on crutches, hobbling around during her rehab, unable to dance, unable to stay away.

She'd waited until the last minute to take her place. Once seated, she consulted the program and nearly groaned aloud. Lana's was the third ballet on the mixed program bill. The first one was a ballet that featured none other than Katrina. All feelings of nobility toward helping Lana faded. She didn't need to see her former competitor perform the opening piece. There was no dancer she would less rather watch. But the lights were already dimming; it would have been poor etiquette to try and slip out now.

A rippling of applause greeted the arrival of the conductor, and moments later, the music began, the curtain opening to reveal a group of assembled dancers. The ballet began, a neoclassical standard choreographed by Anders several years earlier, twelve ensemble dancers and one lead couple. In her pale, silky costume, Katrina looked beautiful, ethereal. She was an audience favorite; she had been for years now. She waltzed, spun, shimmered, lifted by her partner as effortlessly as if she were made of nothing more than chiffon, air and sinew.

It hurt to watch. She'd always known it would. It created a curious fluttering in her heart, like a caged bird had come to life inside her, only it was stuck in there, trying to flap its way to freedom.

The ballet went on and on, the flutters now more like hammer blows. Katrina completed a triple pirouette by striking a développéd arabesque pose, which seemed to defy gravity and the turn's speed. The move was so perfectly rendered, the final pose so long-lasting, the audience exploded into applause. A contraction of pain wrapped itself around Alice's heart and squeezed.

Dear God. She was going to cry.

A Big Cry.

She shut her eyes through the ballet's final movement, dug her nails into her palms, but it didn't stop the tears from escaping. Elbow on the arm of the seat, she shielded her eyes with her hand as if caught in the grip of a terrible headache. The moment the ballet ended, as the crowd roared its approval for Katrina and her partner, Alice rose and pushed past knees and feet, issuing apologies as she stumbled out of her row and up the aisle to the doors. She arrived just as the doors swung open to admit latecomers. She lunged through the people, her sobs now audible, which made everyone regard her in alarm.

It was intermission. Within a minute the lobby would fill with chattering, energized patrons. She raced across the lobby, taking the stairs up two levels, to the smallest, least used ladies' lounge, where she locked herself into the corner stall and cried.

And cried.

This world, this craft, had meant everything to her. She'd lost it, and only Lana could fully appreciate how much it still hurt, how deep the loss went.

That's because you never told me, Alice, she could almost hear Niles say. *You didn't trust me enough to try.*

Niles. She desperately wanted to talk to him right then. She'd say it all now; she'd come clean, exposing this wretched side, this troll under the bridge, that wouldn't go away.

Before she could change her mind, she reached for her phone with shaking hands and punched in his number. To her unutterable relief, he answered his phone.

"I'm so sorry to bother you like this," she said in a wobbly voice. "I know you're probably doing something with Christine right now."

"Well, yes. We're in the city, actually. Having dinner."

A knife of pain shot through her. She almost hung up.

"You don't sound good," he said. "Where are you?"

"I'm at the ballet."

"The *what?*"

"The ballet. And there's something I didn't tell you yesterday. Gil fired me."

"He didn't." He sounded disbelieving, even suspicious.

"He did."

"When?"

"Just before I called you."

"Sweets." Concern replaced the suspicion. "Why didn't you tell me?"

"There were other things to talk about. And I thought he was bluffing. But he wasn't."

He drew a breath. "Whoa. Let's back up here. What does this have to do with your being at the ballet right now?"

"I did this for Lana. She needed the support tonight."

"You're talking about the Lana I met?"

"Yes. She's my roommate now. Well, more than just a roommate."

"No! When? How?"

He sounded as incredulous as Montserrat had been.

"Long story. The point is, she was in a bad way earlier, at the house, and begged me to be there for her tonight. And so I came." The gremlins returned, climbing up to claw at her heart, clog her throat, destroy her composure.

"But you know what? It's as painful as I was afraid it would be. I knew it would crush me inside, make me cry, and it did." As if to illustrate her point, the tears returned, noisy sobs that appalled her, particularly as they increased in intensity.

He said nothing. She couldn't believe what a mess she was making of things.

He didn't speak again until after she'd quieted down.

"Alice." He sounded sad. "Why didn't you tell me, before all this?"

"I suppose I thought I should be bigger than all of it," she said through the last of her hiccuppy sobs. "Leave the past in the past, and all."

"This has nothing to do with being 'bigger.' I'd rather know about your anger or pain over something from the past, before it comes up and affects us in the present."

"I'm sorry. It just doesn't come easily to me. To my family."

"Try."

"I am."

"You are," he agreed. "And I, for one, really appreciate it."

In reply she offered an inelegant sniff.

"Okay," he said in a brisker tone. "Let's focus on what we can do for you right now."

Inspiration seized her. "Lana gave me a pair of comp tickets and I've still got the second one. I know it's late and all, but you could come here. See her perform, too. I could leave the ticket at the will-call window."

"Hmm," he said, and the line went quiet.

Oh, please, oh please.

"Hold on a minute. I have to get back to my table."

Through the pause, Alice heard the clink of silverware against plate, the return of muted conversation. She visualized the scenario. He and Christine, having a romantic dinner together. With his hand over the mouthpiece, he was saying, *She's hysterical. Should I humor her or say I'm too busy tonight?*

Just as the tears began creeping to the surface again, Niles came back on the line.

"Okay. Tell me this. Will they allow me in if I show up in thirty minutes?"

"Yes," she stuttered. "Lana doesn't perform till the third ballet. There's still the second ballet to go and second intermission."

"I should be able to make it. But I don't want to rush Christine here."

She had to push past the jealousy and tell him sure, no problem. Any effort on his part would be great. Lana would love it if he could make it. Really love it.

They both knew it wasn't just Lana who would love it.

"All right," he said. "I'll do my best."

Chapter 22 – The Performance

The green room of a theater was like the waiting lounge of a train station, a resting place for dancers en route to the stage. The room didn't have to be green; in fact, they rarely were. Some were fancy, others utilitarian. But it was, at all times, a safe haven for the dancers before and after performances. Lana, since arriving at the theater, had tried to keep herself in a safe place, visualizing Alice there by her side, murmuring words of support, gentle admonitions when her attention strayed to destabilizing thoughts. In the dressing room, she'd applied makeup, corralled her long hair into a tightly wound bun pinned into place, put on her costume. Beneath the filmy skirt she wore sweatpants, and slippers over her pointe shoes, to keep her body warm following the massage and her own warm-up onstage. The second ballet was now in progress; she had another thirty minutes to wait. Good time to hunker down in the green room and sew ribbons onto pointe shoes.

Once in the room, she exchanged smiles with Dena Lindgren, who'd performed in the first ballet and was relaxing, studying the notice board affixed to the wall. Lana took a seat on the couch nearby and began sewing. Five minutes later, Courtney approached.

"Great minds think alike," she said to Lana, grinning, holding up her own pointe shoes with loose ribbons. "Can I join you?"

Lana smiled back. "Please do. Misery loves company."

"This damned task never ends, does it?" Courtney plopped down next to her. "Little did we know that as professional ballet dancers we'd be part-time seamstresses as well."

"One of the job's many perks," Lana said. Courtney's appreciative chuckle, the camaraderie, warmed her. The following comments, less so.

"You seem better now than you were after you fell."

The terror of the day's events flickered over her. She could almost hear Alice's voice, telling her to ignore it, not pay it any mind. "Yeah, thanks, I feel stronger," she told Courtney.

"That's good to see." Courtney focused on pushing her needle through the pointe shoe's soft fabric siding. "Still. I'll bet you're feeling kind of anxious about what happened."

Before Lana could respond, and in truth, she didn't want to talk about it, Dena called out from her place at the message board.

"Lana!" she said. "Come here. There's something you need to see. Right now."

Dena's voice was urgent, almost shrill. Courtney frowned in her direction. "What, she can't see that we're talking?" she grumbled.

"Come here, please," Dena said, and her eyes conveyed to Lana a baffling sense of urgency.

"God," Courtney muttered under her breath, "what a little princess."

"I'll just go see what she wants," Lana said. She laid down her shoe, ribbon and threaded needle, and walked over to where Dena was standing. Dena was still sweaty from having danced, her Pancake foundation smeared where sweat had worked a path through it. Her false eyelashes made her eyes more theatrical and expressive than they normally were.

"Look at this," Dena said with a too-bright enthusiasm, and pointed to a notice that was advertising a pair of stereo speakers for $200.00.

Lana's head whirled with confusion. "Why are you—" Lana began, but Dena interrupted, speaking in a low voice.

"I should stay out of it," she told Lana, "but I can't. Courtney and Charlotte are working you. Hazing you. I've overheard them in the past, feeding you these little false truths, trying to shake you up. Just ten minutes ago I heard them talking. Laughing. It wasn't a kind laugh. So." She gestured Courtney's way. "Take everything she says with a grain of salt."

Lana stared at her. "No," she protested. "You've got it wrong."

"Do I?" Dena asked.

Charlotte, maybe. But Courtney? She'd been kind. Helpful.

"Yes." Lana gave a vehement nod.

"Okay." Dena looked uncertain, but when she spoke again, her voice became jovial. "All right, then, bad call on the speakers. Never mind. Just didn't want you to pass up the chance at a bargain. I could have sworn I heard you say you wanted some."

"Nope, sorry." Lana mirrored her hearty, loud tone. "But thanks for letting me know."

They exchanged charged looks.

"Thanks," Lana repeated. "I appreciate the heads-up on them."

"My pleasure."

Not possible, she thought, returning to the couch. She and Courtney were becoming friends, of sorts, just like she and Dena were.

Or was it all a ploy?

She didn't know what to say, what to think. She sat back down on the sofa, feeling queasy.

Courtney smiled at her, lifting up a pointe shoe, the two pink satin ribbons now firmly affixed. "One down, five to go."

"You're fast." She picked up her shoe, ribbon and thread.

"You'd have been fine if Dena hadn't interrupted you." Courtney glanced over her shoulder, and Lana saw, too, that Dena had disappeared.

"Dena can be kind of pushy," Courtney said. "Bullish. I suppose it's a little sister inferiority complex kind of thing."

Lana offered a noncommittal shrug.

"Anyway, like I was saying before we got interrupted, do not worry for one minute about that horrible fall happening again." Courtney focused on sewing as she spoke. "It won't. Not a chance. You know what they say, bad rehearsal, good performance." She paused, her brow furrowing. "Well. Then again, I guess the night of my fall during *Nutcracker* last year kind of went against that rule. It was uncanny, that I should do the same thing twice, but—"

She stopped herself in a theatrical, practiced way, her eyes widening. "There I go again, yapping when I should have just kept quiet. I'm so sorry. You didn't need to hear that."

Oh, but she did. Lana's stomach gave a twist.

Dena had been right.

Courtney, whom Lana had trusted. Courtney, who'd "advised" and "consoled" her a half dozen times, all in the same confidential fashion, always something that planted insecurity or fear.

All the serenity she'd cultivated over the past few hours drained right out of her. Even Courtney seemed to understand that she'd just delivered a bigger punch than intended.

"Lana?" Courtney looked worried. "I'm sorry. I should have kept my mouth shut."

"You're right." Lana met her gaze and held it. "It was a big mistake."

One small consolation: Courtney didn't know what Lana had

just discovered. She made a decision right then to keep it that way. No confrontation, no revealing her awareness of the plan to undermine Lana's confidence at every turn. Let Courtney assume the clueless role, wondering why her jabs no longer held much power.

Oh, the manipulators of the world. Mom and Gil, Charlotte and Courtney. How sad it was, and thank goodness for people like Alice and Dena, who cut through the bullshit and told you things you didn't want to hear, doing it for your own good, not theirs.

"Anyway," she told Courtney. "No harm done. Your story is just that. Your story. It has nothing to do with me."

Courtney looked uncertain.

Lana didn't much care. She shifted her focus to the sewing. When Courtney rose a few minutes later, Lana bade her a cheery goodbye, a "see you onstage," without ever looking up.

She had more productive things to focus on.

Intermission was last-chance-to-warm-up time for the dancers, each one immersed in their own personal pre-performance ritual of jumping, stretching, push-ups, jogging. All too soon came the amplified voice of the stage manager.

"Dancers, three minutes to curtain. Those not in the next ballet, please clear the stage."

Lana and Javier made their way to center stage. She was preoccupied with drawing deep breaths to keep her stage fright at bay. An interesting thing, the stage fright. For some dancers, it went away after years onstage. For Lana, it had always been there, manageable but real, if only for a moment. Dry mouth and icy fingers, trembling limbs, a pervasive terror that she'd forget the steps, which she'd never done, but nonetheless remained a threat until she was immersed in the dance.

"Dancers, one minute."

They took their opening poses. She remained standing, as Javier lowered to one knee by her side, a will-you-marry-me position. Her fingers rested on his shoulder.

"Hey," Javier whispered, and she looked down at him, in the semidarkness. "Merde," he said, and squeezed her cold fingers.

"Thanks," she whispered, and the fright lessened. "Merde to you too."

"Dancers, ten seconds to curtain."

Showtime.

The curtain rose. The music began, a solo cello, sonorous, nostalgia-laden. Their opener was thirty-two counts of languorous pas de deux, then Javier lifted her from behind and it was time to move. Time to conquer the passages that had dogged them throughout rehearsals: the first tricky combination; the troublesome bourrée series; the leap into Javier's arms where he caught her and she appeared to hover, mid-air, frozen in time.

The movements grew quicker, more defined, autumn leaves stirred up by the wind. On came the corps dancers behind them. Javier and Lana leapt off. Twenty seconds, spent panting in the wings, a swish of water for her dry mouth, a dip into the nearby Vaseline jar to lubricate her teeth to keep her lips from sticking. Onstage again, leaping, running, flying, a dizzying pace of piqué turns, and another passage that had once troubled them. Two minutes later they arrived at the sequence where Lana had taken her spill earlier in the day.

No spill.

Offstage they went, turning the ballet over to the demi-soloist trio for the next five minutes.

The adagio was at the ballet's core, the slowest, most romantic movement. Autumn souvenir. Memory of what was now past, or was passing. Regret, nostalgia. Tonight she added sorrow to the list. Sorrow over Mom's actions, over Luke's pain and vulnerability. Courtney's deception, Gil's manipulation and the way she still felt so helplessly, hopelessly drawn to him. She let the sorrow work its way through her movements in the adagio, and Javier responded to her internal cues. He was far and away the best partner she'd ever danced with, anticipating her needs, providing a steady hand without ever gripping too tightly. It was a powerful force, this support. "It's all about trust," Alice had said that day she'd provided help, and she'd been right. Lana would have trusted Javier with her life.

Time for the Big Scary Lift passage, the one that had dogged her for weeks.

It went perfectly. Never better. She could almost hear Alice's voice.

You see? There. It works.

Alice, out there right now, watching her. No audience member's presence had ever been so rife with significance, nor meant quite so much to her.

The last movement was all about motion, swift and articulate, no time to think or ponder. All the rehearsing hours, the committing to muscle memory, paid off here. Javier was on fire, and she followed his lead. She felt dazed, almost giddy, afraid to even consider the success of this night's performance for fear of jinxing it.

The explosion of applause at the end of the ballet shocked Lana with its intensity. Back in the wings, Javier swept her into a bone-crushing hug.

"We nailed it," he crowed. "Every last bit!"

They were both saturated with sweat, drunk with endorphins and euphoria as the stage manager cued all the dancers for a curtain call.

When they returned from their first bow, she could see Ben, across the stage, standing in the stage left wing. Anders was next to him, arms folded. Not clapping. He gave a brief nod, turned and said something to Ben, before stepping away to speak with someone behind him. Impossible to tell from his face what he'd been thinking. But Ben caught Lana's eye and thrust his arms in the air, overhead, thumbs up. He was grinning.

Anders had liked it.

Ten minutes later, in the green room, Lana still hadn't stopped trembling. She chattered with the other dancers, accepted the congratulations from audience members who'd been allowed backstage, but only when she saw Alice across the room, gazing around in a tentative manner, did something in her relax.

She stopped short, peering closer.

Alice had been crying. Her eyelids were puffy, her eyes red, the makeup on them smeared. She seemed dazed, exhausted. She looked, to Lana's eyes, a little like Lana must have looked earlier tonight. But an even greater shock followed when Niles, of all people, came up behind her. He was holding Alice's hand, kissing her temple, as Alice leaned into him, her eyes flickering shut. When she opened them, she spotted Lana, straightened, a broad smile replacing the fatigue on her face. She strode toward Lana, who hurried over to her. They met halfway, crashing into a hug.

"You're here," Lana said, voice trembling. "Thank you so much. This meant everything to me."

Alice pulled back, beaming through her tears. "You were beautiful. So beautiful it broke my heart."

Niles came up from behind, stammering about how much he'd enjoyed it, how great it had been to watch her. He and Alice took turns explaining how Alice had called him just an hour earlier, how he'd shifted his plans, shot over here, and here he was, only now he had to dash, back to the other girl.

"Go," Alice laughed, wiping the last of the tears from her face. "The other woman calls."

Niles drew her in for one more hug, his lips brushing against her forehead. "Sunday night?" he asked her, and she nodded. "I'll call you before then."

"That would be nice," she murmured.

Lana had never seen Alice look so happy. Ever. Watching her watch Niles depart produced a bittersweet pang, made her wish things were as clear and uncomplicated with her and Gil.

Gil, who, if Dena's theory continued to hold true, hadn't been flirting with Gabrielle after all. Just another one of Courtney's fabrications.

Once Niles had disappeared from sight, Alice glanced around, her expression growing wary. "I think I'm going to head out of here, too," she told Lana. "Are you going out, or coming back to the house?"

"The *Souvenir* cast has been invited to join Anders and his group over at L'Orange. I'm sure everyone would enjoy seeing you there, too. Would you consider joining us?"

Alice shook her head. "Sorry, but tonight has drained me of everything I have. Besides, I'm not ready to discuss with anyone the fact that I might no longer be a Ballet Theatre employee." She looked stricken as she said the words, as if the truth were just now sinking in.

"Alice, Gil couldn't have meant it. It's impossible. Please, let me call him."

"No," Alice said. "It's between him and me. You stay out of it. You've got enough on your plate right now, anyway."

Mom. Of course.

"You told me, on the ride over here, that you had an idea on how I could most effectively deal with the situation," she said to Alice.

"I did. To be discussed later."

"Will you tell me now?"

"Nope. Not tonight."

"Why not?"

"Because this is your night to celebrate your huge achievement."

"When, then?" Lana persisted.

"Maybe Sunday afternoon, after your matinee performance."

"I'm holding you to that."

"Fine. Now go party. I'm going home. To my safety zone."

On Sunday, minutes after Lana had returned home from the matinee performance, she sought out Alice, who sighed, nodded, and shared her plan. She'd been right to wait; it was shocking, painful to hear. Alice explained gently that it was the only way Lana could break this terrible cycle and free herself.

"This is helping me? This is helping my family?" Words failed Lana and she began to cry.

Alice sat by her side, feeding her Kleenexes. Only after Lana had calmed, did Alice try and speak again.

"You can do nothing, of course. That's the easiest option. This current crisis will all blow over, and nothing would change. But that's just it—nothing would change. You'd live in the shadow of knowing it might happen again. And in time, that would keep you from flying as high as I know you can go."

Lana felt panic rise up inside her. "I can't do it," she cried. "I can't."

"Then don't. You certainly don't need to make a decision or a move today. Just ponder the option."

"You have no idea what you're asking me to do."

Alice looked sad. "You're right, I don't. Not a clue. That's why I'll leave it in your hands and not bring it up again."

Lana had Sunday night to ponder it, a quiet night, no performance. Alice had gone to Niles' place for the night. Lana sat and watched movie after movie, only taking half of it in. She could have turned to Gil for support, advice. He would have loved to hear from her. Given his contentious relationship with his own mother, however, she didn't think he could understand her agonized indecision.

Monday morning she woke early to a quiet house. She went downstairs, fixed herself a cup of tea, and managed not to look at the incriminating sheet of paper Alice had set on the kitchen counter after they'd talked.

She lasted forty-five minutes before she gave in. She picked up the paper, which held three sets of names and phone numbers.

Kansas Social and Rehabilitation Services.

Kansas Protection Report Center.

Child Protective Services.

She couldn't do it.

She wadded the page into a ball, shoved it deep into the trash and went upstairs to take a shower. Five minutes later she came down again, shower untaken. She reached back into the trash, past the damp coffee grinds and orange peels, searching until she found the crumpled ball. She pulled it out, smoothed it out.

Stormed out of the room and went back upstairs.

Cried. Railed.

Came back down.

Picked up the phone and called.

Chapter 23 – A New Chance

The call from Gil, the call Alice had been expecting, came seventy-two hours later than she'd anticipated. But it came.

He'd left a message on her cell phone and a duplicate back at her house, which she discovered upon returning home Monday morning from Niles' apartment. "Oh, Jesus, Alice, help me. Name your price," he said on the message. "I apologize, on my knees. I was so out of line, I'm a jerk, I'm an asshole, I'll give you all of that. Only please, please, call me back. Better yet, come in. Please. Let's talk. Do *not* go to the HR office. Come straight to me. Are you there, listening? Alice? Call me, ASAP. Please."

She called him, more out of curiosity than concern. She expected him not to pick up. It was Monday, after all, with his erratic hours, wandering in late, in and out of meetings. But he picked up on the second ring, crying out in relief when he heard her voice.

"Oh Alice, I'm in deep shit. Please, please be kind to me here."

"What on earth are you going on about? Your message made no sense."

"It's Andy. He heard about your leaving."

"My *leaving*? Gil, call it what it was. You fired me."

"Okay, semantics. He heard. And it's not what he wants. And

now he's threatening to invoke that three-day clause if I don't get you back in your position. Right away."

Her head spun. "Andy said all this?"

"Trust me. I wouldn't lie to you here."

"Can he do that? Invoke that clause?"

"It's fine print at the end of the letter of agreement. Three business days to pull out if the factors are irrevocably altered. He says he wants to work with you on this account, not anyone else I hire. Not even *me*."

Gil sounded as if he couldn't believe the last part.

Neither could she. A chuckle slipped out of her. "Wow. Damn."

"Please. Can you just come in? We'll hash out the rest later."

She relished this moment of control, the pause that so agonized this person who had let her agonize for days. Then she decided to ease up on him. She was the one getting laid now, after all.

"Give me an hour."

"Okay, that's great. And, hey, thanks."

Her return to the WCBT offices ninety minutes later—she was late, she didn't care and Gil didn't comment—felt surreal, askew, like stepping into a funhouse version of her job.

Gil issued her into his office, all smiles and courtesy, offering her a seat, a cold drink.

"Of course I wasn't serious about going through with firing you," he said. "How could you think that? Sure, I was pissed off. Very much so. But Lana would never speak to me again if I went through with firing you. Besides, what would my grounds have been?"

He spoke fast, throwing all this at her in a mildly accusatory manner, as if this were all Alice's fault, that he was getting ready to fire her all over again for being so obtuse as to not know he'd been bluffing about firing her.

"It's almost lunchtime," he continued. "Should we go get something to eat? Why don't we go off-site? Stop by Human Resources afterward to make sure everything's smooth?"

The other administrators, when they saw the two of them together, were wide-eyed and silent. Only Lucinda beamed at her, giving her a little "you go, girl" nod of her chin. Her good friend, Lucinda.

This was indeed a funhouse day.

Following a bite to eat, the two of them visited Human Resources, where Gil had them tear up the grievance report he'd filed on Alice—not quite the firing he'd boasted, but nonetheless inflammatory and probation-worthy. Gil made a big show of apologizing to Alice again, enough for her to tell the HR director that no, she herself did not feel compelled to file her own grievance report against her boss for his self-admitted egregious behavior. They were fine, Gil and Alice assured her, putting on big phony, professional smiles for her and each other.

Back in their offices, Gil asked if she wanted to go across the street to Murphy's later, for an afternoon meeting over beers. She didn't. She felt drained, curiously sad. That specialness, the cozy team spirit they'd shared for three years was gone. Maybe for good.

Once upon a time, they might have even been able to discuss it, brainstorm on how to get it back. No more. Instead, she told him she was feeling a little disoriented from all the upheaval, and if it was all right with him, perhaps she'd just head home, call it personal time off if she needed to, and start fresh early the next morning.

Gil nodded. "Just go, no need to call it PTO. But would you mind giving Andy a call from here? Tell him you're still gainfully employed here, and such."

"I can do that."

Andy, when she spoke with him, made no comment about what had transpired, only asking if she could stop by his Hillsborough house the next morning, for a logistics meeting over coffee. She agreed, and informed Gil of her plans.

"No problem," Gil said. "Absolutely no problem. Give Andy as much time as he wants."

"Okay. Well, then, see you tomorrow."

"One last thing." He hesitated. "Tell Lana I'm thinking about her. How's she doing?"

She knew Lana had asked him for time apart, and the irony was surely not lost on him that he'd mocked Alice for having had the same setup with Niles. Remembering her own pain, she decided to go easy on him.

"Truth is," she told him, "she's going through a bumpy patch with family back home. Her mom's scaring her, intimidating her, but being passive-aggressive about it. It's really tearing Lana apart."

"God. The poor thing."

His care and interest were genuine. She found herself thawing further to tell him about the car crash. He looked horrified.

She nodded. "I know. Lana was in a pretty bad way Friday afternoon. It's a good thing I was home. She really needed someone to help her through it."

"They told me you went to her performance that night."

Who were "they"? So she'd been spotted. In reply, she only nodded.

"To support her?"

She paused. They were entering dangerous territory.

"Yes," she said, vowing to herself that if he said one cutting thing, offered one snarky or derogatory comment, she'd walk out of the room.

But Gil surprised her.

"Thank you," he said.

"For what?" she asked, wary.

"For taking care of her."

The two of them sized each other up uneasily.

"That's all that matters to me, Alice," Gil said. "Whether you believe that or not. I love her, and I want her to be happy. Feel safe."

"That makes two of us."

Laughter outside the room, two workers joking, eased the tension inside Gil's office.

"Anyway," Alice said, "she's muscling her way through it. Keeping focus on her dance, resting, staying uninjured."

"Could you, maybe, tell her how much I care? That I understand and appreciate the challenge of family problems, and for her to call me anytime, anytime I can help."

He looked so serious, so somber. It was like knowing two different Gils.

"I'll do that," she said.

"Thank you. I'd appreciate it."

Amazing to behold, this other Gil, she mused as she headed toward the elevators to go home five minutes later. Granted, professionally, she still thought he was an asshole. But through Lana, he was revealing himself to be vulnerable, wholly human, surprisingly compassionate.

No, not necessarily a better boss. But a better person.

Tuesday morning she headed down the Peninsula to her meeting with Andy. The Redgrave mansion looked different in the weekday morning light, more austere, almost like a posh private school. She ascended the front steps and knocked on the door. A moment later his housekeeper greeted her and led her back to the conservatory, a sunny room enclosed on three sides by glass and filled with flowering plants and vines. It was like being outside, with all the benefits of the indoors. It smelled like gardenias. A young man was serving Andy croissants from a proffered baking tray as Alice entered the room.

Andy acknowledged her with a nod, a cool, "Good morning, Alice. Join me for a bite?"

The croissants smelled heavenly. She accepted one, along with a cup of coffee.

A Vivaldi guitar concerto played softly in the background, piped in through invisible speakers. Andy didn't speak as he ate his fruit salad. She was getting used to this facet of his personality. He couldn't have been more different from Gil, who liked to chatter, establish some warm, friendly bonhomie before allowing any silence to fall over the conversation. Alice felt comfortable with Andy and his silences. They brought calm into the room.

Only after he finished his fruit salad did he speak.

"Alice. Tell me a joke."

She sipped her coffee reflectively and gave a little nod.

"Okay. There's this lonely old woman sitting in her living room, pondering her lonely life, when all of a sudden a fairy godmother appears in front of her and tells the old woman she will grant her three wishes. 'All right,' says the old woman. 'First, I'd like to be really rich.' And poof, the furniture and accessories around her turn to gold. The old woman smiles and says, 'Okay, I want to live in a big castle.' Poof, it happens—they're suddenly in a room that looks like something out of Versailles.

"'And your third wish?" asks the fairy godmother. Just then the old woman's cat wanders through the living room. 'Ooh,' the woman says, 'can you change him into a handsome prince who loves me?' Voila, it's done. The cat is now a tall, incredibly gorgeous man. He offers the old woman this sexy smile that just melts her. He comes right up to her and whispers in her ear, 'Bet you're sorry you had me neutered.'"

She liked the way Andy reacted, the twitch at the corners of his mouth, the delight in his eyes, his otherwise composed demeanor.

"Thank you," he said.

"Any time."

He chuckled a moment later as he tore another piece off his croissant. They continued eating in a relaxed silence, enjoying the music, the morning sun spilling into the room.

"So," Andy said finally. "I had the pleasure of meeting your partner once again."

For a moment she thought he meant Niles. "My partner?"

"The pretty girl you brought to my party."

"Oh, *Lana*."

"Yes. That partner. The one who told me you two were living together." His brows knitted. "Is that not the case?"

She laughed; she couldn't help it. "Okay, I have to be honest. Here's the thing. Yes, Lana and I are living together. I invited her to move in shortly after your party. But, I'm not gay, Andy."

To her relief he didn't look angry, merely expectant, waiting to hear more.

"That night at the restaurant—that couple?" she continued. "It was *him* I was eyeing. Not her."

"Well. That made two of us."

She laughed again, pleased that he'd divulged such a candid opinion. Gil was wrong. Andy did like her. And he trusted her. "Anyway, that guy is my boyfriend. Although, that night, he was close to being a 'was.'"

"And so the 'almost was' is now safely an 'is?'"

"Yes. He's very 'is.'"

"And this suits you?"

Her face grew warm. "Very much so."

"Well. Good for you. Sex is good for the complexion." He regarded her from over his coffee cup. "Nice color to your cheeks today."

The warmth of her cheeks grew into a fire.

"Why, Alice. I do believe I've made you blush."

She was too flustered to come back with a witty retort, which seemed to entertain him further. "All right," he said, leaning back in his chair. "Let's talk some business. But first, tell me. Are you glad to have your position reinstated?"

At moments like these, she was reminded how tricky Andy could be, how quick to disarm and subtly attack.

"Um, yes," she replied carefully, which made him shake his head in amusement.

"This is off the record. This is not a test for which you need to provide the right answer."

"Oh, Andy." She allowed a note of exasperation to creep into her voice. "How could it be otherwise? You're the power holder here. Ask me to jump and I will. Ask me if I like my job and I'll say yes sir, thank you."

"Here's the reason I'm asking." He sat up, eyes more alert. "There's a development position at the San Francisco Symphony just opening. I'd like to know if you'd have any interest in it."

She couldn't believe what he was saying.

"When did this come about?" she asked, trying to sound casual.

"I heard about it on Friday."

"But you had a conversation with Gil on Monday morning. Why strong-arm him into reinstating me when you could have just mentioned the job to me directly?"

He grimaced. "Maybe I wanted to remind Gil who the real boss is in this equation."

She felt it again, a flash of insight mixed with unease, that neither she nor Gil truly knew Andy. Foolish Gil, to have thought there'd be no consequences for choices he'd made over the past few weeks.

"All right. Tell me about the job," she said.

"There's been some change of staff at the symphony. My key contact in development there has moved on. They want to put a junior staff member in his place. I can't stand the guy. He's an ass and I don't want to work with him. Maxwell asked me to think about whom I'd consider a better fit."

Maxwell, Alice knew, was the director of development there. She'd met him and found him to be both likeable and impressive. His was a position of status; the symphony ran a much bigger development operation than the WCBT. She wouldn't be able to touch associate director for years. She'd most likely be taking a pay cut.

But it was the symphony. *The symphony.* She tried to keep her expression neutral, aware that now it was Andy watching her, the way she took a leisurely sip of coffee before replying.

"Keep talking," she said.

"You'd be reporting to Maxwell and dealing a lot with me. A few other accounts as well. But I tend to be the squeaky wheel."

"With reason. You supply them with a lot of oil."

A shrug was his only reply.

She couldn't keep her excitement at bay any more. She began to laugh. "Gil would kill me. Tear me apart."

"You say that a lot, you know."

"I do, don't I? And I don't have to."

The thought of leaving Gil to go work at the symphony

astonished her, shook her, but in a not altogether unpleasant way. "You're fully serious here?" she asked.

He studied her, his pale blue eyes now bright with animation, almost like Andy on cocaine. "I am. Of course, I'm not the decision maker. You'd have to go through the usual routine there. Résumé, application, a few rounds of interviews."

"Sure. Of course."

"But they'll have your name on the table, and Maxwell will know it meets with my approval."

"Thank you," she stammered. "I'll get on it." Fearing a trap, she added, "Of course I won't let that get in the way of servicing your account at one hundred percent effort right now. Here at the WCBT. We value your financial and professional support there above all."

He chuckled.

No trap, then. And she'd probably just made herself sound idiotic.

The young server returned with an urn of coffee, offering refills. Andy nodded, sat back to let him pour, and the two of them exchanged comments about the day's weather forecast.

Alice sat back as well, relaxing into her seat, her mind whirring with all the information she'd just been fed.

A new job. A new start.

That Andy Redgrave. A good one to have in her pocket.

Gil had reeled in a good one.

Chapter 24 – Preparing to Fly

She not only survived opening night of *Autumn Souvenir*, she'd excelled. That was what people were saying. Relieved couldn't begin to describe how the review of Friday night's performance in the *San Francisco Chronicle* made Lana feel. The reviewer had described her dancing as "fresh, lyrical, nuanced" and had declared her "a powerhouse, a welcome addition to the West Coast Ballet Theatre's roster of talented dancers." Javier's performance had garnered praise, too, as had two of the principals in the night's earlier ballets. Two other soloists were mentioned, as well. And Dena Lindgren was noted as "someone to watch."

Lana had read and reread the review, alternately thrilled and terrified. Would this be yet one more thing to alienate her from the other dancers? But in the end, Javier's support and endorsement, of both her and their performance together, carried a lot of clout. And, further, the grumbling dancers had found another target for their antipathy: Dena, who'd replaced Gabrielle on the rehearsal sheet for *Arpeggio*. The two Lindgren sisters were now rehearsing it together, along with Lana. She saw Lexie's nod of satisfaction during the rehearsal, once the three of them had completed a trio passage. He liked the fit.

Lucinda in public relations called her into the office on Thursday after company class. *Dance Magazine* wanted to schedule an interview, she told Lana, and an online periodical was asking for a photo shoot. Lana was now to be included in media-related events during the company's tour stops in Santa Barbara, Los Angeles and San Diego.

Lucinda handed her leaflets, public relations memorandums, then proceeded to educate her on how to interview, how to answer questions and present herself, even how much makeup and what kind of outfits she should wear in public. When Lana squirmed over answering more personal questions, Lucinda told her to get used to it, that everyone else would want to know everything about her. She was hot, on the radar screen, and the WCBT planned to capitalize on that. Did Lana have a website, a social media platform? How did she feel about public speaking?

"Oh, and there will be an *Arpeggio* publicity photo shoot," Lucinda said, reading off a memo. "You and the two Lindgren girls. When you three are back in town."

"Um, a publicity photo shoot?" she repeated. "For, like, brochures? Promotional stuff?"

Lucinda peered at Lana over her reading glasses. "That's what a photo shoot usually implies." *You dimwit,* her expression seemed to add, but she remained silent.

Lana struggled to take in this last bit of news. Her, Dena and Rebecca, representing *Arpeggio* to the public, forever affixing their identities to the ballet. "But," she stammered, "um, casting hasn't been decided."

"I don't think you need to worry about Lexie and Anders making a mistake here. And this was a directive from them." She glanced down at her notes. "Next. Let's talk about your habit of saying 'um' a lot."

"Um, pardon me?"

"Yes. Like that."

Ten minutes later she stumbled out of Lucinda's office, only to encounter Gil. The sight of him produced twin bolts of fire and unease, which shot through her and left her weak-kneed and hesitating over her words. Even Gil seemed unsure of himself. Their conversation sounded stilted, contrived, as if they were being recorded for public viewing later, a WCBT training video, on how to avoid romantic entanglements at work and how to deal with them once things got messy.

But her anger toward him had cooled since he'd un-fired Alice, since he'd delivered the tender message through her. In truth, she missed him terribly. Well. The non-dancer part of her did, the sensualist she'd become in his arms, his bed, ever craving his touch, the smell of his skin, the taste of it. The dancer understood that this was the price you paid to remain true to what mattered most.

They chatted. He accompanied her to the elevator and when the door opened, disgorging a few administrators, he reached over and touched the small of her back, his fingers grazing her hip as she moved away from him, into the elevator. It sent an electric shiver through her. She saw, from the glance they shared, just before the door closed, that it had similarly affected him.

He was honoring his end of the bargain, handing her the power to dictate the terms of their relationship. No gesture could have been more crucial, more appreciated. It assured her that from here on out, she had the ability to call the shots in her personal life.

Mom's terrible hold on her wouldn't have to ever repeat itself.

When she'd called the Kansas Department of Social and Rehabilitation Services on Monday to report Mom's behavior, she'd spoken calmly until the worker asked her relationship to the perpetrator. Her throat had closed up and she'd begun to cry.

The woman on the other end had been kind. "You're proving how much you care for your mother by doing this, not the other way around," she'd said through Lana's sobbed out story. Lana answered the questions the woman posed about Mom, about Luke, about the family, despising herself for what she was doing to the Kessler family. Only the fact that she'd given them her phone number, name and address kept her from hanging up.

The woman told her a case worker would follow up some time over the next two to fourteen days. Lana explained how she was leaving town the following Monday, and it would help if they could make the initial contact before she left town. She knew Mom would call her afterward, ranting. She needed to be in a stable place when that happened.

Today was Thursday; she hadn't heard from Mom yet.

She knew she would.

The call came midway through lunch break. The conversation lasted ten minutes. It was the worst thing Lana had ever had to endure. Mom was hyperventilating, spewing words of rage.

"My own child, accusing me of this! I can't believe it. I just can't believe it."

"Mom. You crashed a car with Luke in it."

"I was distracted!" she shrieked, noisier and more plaintive than Lana had ever heard her. "And you told them, *you told them* that I'd left Luke alone that day."

"You did!" she cried, her stomach churning.

"That was a family issue alone!"

"No. It's a Kansas law."

"You're a self-centered, ungrateful child. A child, that's all you are. You know nothing about parenting, about being a mother, taking care of a family. You waltz out of town, take up with fancy friends, and suddenly you've got the world figured out."

"Please don't be this way, Mom. Please."

"Don't you 'please, Mom' me. You little monster."

She couldn't believe her mother would call her that. All those years of being dutiful daughter, mother's helper, taking it all without complaint, meant nothing.

"I told Annabel," Mom was saying, "I told her California would taint you, turn you ugly, against your family, but I had no idea—"

"I did what I did for our family," Lana interrupted.

Mom snorted in contempt. "Don't make me laugh."

Lana lost all patience.

"You were a threat to your child," she said in a cold, hard voice. "I'm a grown one; I can fend for myself. But if you *ever* involve the little boys in one of your issues again, I'll call SRS a second time. I'll go against you, Mom. Don't think I won't."

"You, you…"

Mom couldn't even speak, she was so outraged. When the words finally came out, they were shrill, staccato.

"You have shamed this family beyond words, Lana Kessler. Don't ever bother coming back here. You hear me?"

With that, she hung up on Lana.

She stood there, phone in hand, reeling, bent forward, as if Mom's voice had reached right across the miles and punched her in the stomach. She made her way on wooden legs through the hallway, seeking out the quiet corner where Gabrielle hadn't been trying to flirt with Gil last week, and where Lana had tried, instead, to break up with him. She hunkered down on the bench, trying to stifle her sobs, as the hysteria rose in her, threatening to spill over.

Don't ever bother coming back here. You hear me?

She was huddled there, weeping, trying to be quiet about it, when, to her horror, someone approached, and all she could think was that it was Courtney and it would be shame on top of pain on top of having been deceived by a fake friendship. But it was Dena, who rushed over when she recognized Lana.

"Oh, God, something's happened. Are you hurt? Is someone else hurt? Was there news from home?"

She couldn't possibly explain, and even if she could, Dena wouldn't be able to relate in the least. Lana had seen the Lindgren girls' mother; she was lively, engaging, pretty, the kind of mother all girls dreamed of having. Mom was a freak next to the woman. Lana could only shake her head after each question, wave Dena away.

"Just go. You wouldn't understand. Please, *go.*"

Dena took a step back, turned halfway as if to leave, but hesitated.

"Lana. Gil's right there in the café. I saw him less than a minute ago. I'm friends with him, and I know you are too."

This made Lana look up.

Gil would get it. He'd had his own mother problems. Back that first day of meeting him, she'd been appalled by his mom story, wondering what terrible thing he'd done to produce such ire and rejection from her.

Gil might be the only person on earth to understand here.

"Should I get him?" Dena asked.

"Yes," she told Dena, who sped away.

Dena was fast. Or Gil was. Or both. Moments later, two shadows appeared at the other end of the hall. Within seconds, Gil was seated on one side of the bench, Dena on the other, Lana sandwiched in between.

"Lana?" Gil took her hand. "What's happened?"

"Do you remember," she said to Gil in a voice too high to be calm, but it was the best she could do, "back when you told me that story, about your mom, freaking out over something you said, or did? And her telling you—" Here she ran out of voice, courage. She studied the floor, her slippered feet next to Gil's shiny black dress shoes.

"Yes. Is this about your own mom?" Gil sounded more urgent. "Lana, what did she say?"

"I betrayed her in the worst of ways, Gil. She put Luke at risk and I turned her in for it. I broke the family vow of 'unity above all'. I told the authorities what she'd done, and in turn, she told me never to come home again."

The tears followed, a childlike wail that tore through her, and that was the end of explaining.

How odd, times like this, when the people you've known and trusted forever become so vicious, and it's the others around you, maybe your closest friends, maybe not, who know exactly what to say, what to do, how to soothe, how to help you heal. Gil and Dena took turns offering words of consolation and advice, sharing their own stories.

"There is nothing that can break your bond of family, Lana," Gil said. "Not if you want it. Your mom's angry, but she can't unmake you her daughter. She can't make your home suddenly not be your home. She can't un-love you. She might threaten it, but she can't."

Gil's words, his indignation, began to soothe the raw, raging thing inside her.

"Alice said my mom's resorting to all this because she's scared she's losing me."

"Alice is right."

A chuckle broke through her tears. "I'm going to tell Alice you said that."

His serious expression relaxed into a grin.

"Okay, so I did. Only under dire circumstances, though."

Dena snickered. Gil wagged a mock-reproving finger at her. "My admission doesn't leave this room, Squirt."

"It's a hallway."

"Fine. This hallway."

With less tension in the air now, Dena and Gil began to banter back and forth. When he called her "Squirt" for the second time, Dena grimaced.

"You said you'd stop calling me that, once I became a full company member."

"Oops. Sorry. Old habits die hard."

"Sure, I understand. They say it's an aging thing, when you can't change your habits."

"Touché, Squirt."

More laughter, followed by an easy silence.

"You two know each other well," Lana commented.

"That Chicago connection," he said. "Isabelle, Squirt's mother, took me under her wing when I first moved out here. Made me dinner and made me feel like a member of the family."

"Which means," Dena said, "that Rebecca and I didn't stop arguing just because he was there at the table too."

Lana looked at her in surprise. "You two argue, wow. I'd been thinking you were the model family. The perfect mother, the perfect sister."

Dena found this hilarious. "I can't wait to tell them you said that. You ask the two of them, and I'm demon spawn. Always disagreeing with them, looking for a fight, there to tax them."

"No!" Lana exclaimed. "Not you."

Dena leaned over to catch Gil's eyes. "You're my witness. You hear what Lana's saying."

"Oh, no one would call you demon spawn, Squirt. We'll just say you're the family firecracker. You keep the Lindgren family interesting."

Dena nudged Lana's shoulder with her own. "See the reputation I have, even outside the family? Tell me I'm not trouble waiting to happen." She was smiling, though, seemingly pleased by the image.

Dena was a lot more interesting than Lana had realized. And compassionate, to boot.

Gil consulted his watch. "Whoops, I'm about to be late for a meeting."

He rose. So did Lana. He turned to her and hesitated.

He hadn't made any overtures a good friend wouldn't have. Holding her hand, slinging a companionable arm over her shoulders, giving one a little squeeze when the three of them were laughing over a joke. Now his eyes were pleading. Begging.

She took a step closer and slipped her arms around his waist. Immediately his arms went around her, holding her close, which felt as delicious and luxurious as slipping into a hot bath. She nestled her face in the crook of his neck that still smelled spicy-fresh from his shaving lotion. His hands worked her back. She drew in a deep, cleansing breath. Another. Another.

She pulled away finally, but he held onto her hands and met her eyes.

"I want you to know this, and Dena's here as my witness," he said. "Julia knows about you, about us. Everything. I told her I'd move out. Give her back the car. Whatever she deemed appropriate, because the bottom line is, you come first from here on out."

She sucked in a breath, staggered by the news.

"I'm not saying this to encroach on your space," he continued. "I'm going to keep honoring that." He gestured to Dena, who'd risen as well. "You two go on tour soon. I'll be thinking of you every day, all day. Because I love you. But I can wait. Through *Nutcracker*, through the holidays. I'm like family. You can ignore me, reject me, but I'll always be there."

He paused, winced. "God. I'm not coming off sounding like a stalker, am I?"

The comment was so unexpected, the three of them began to laugh.

"I'm going," Gil said, while they were still chuckling. "I'm officially late."

A moment later he'd hurried off, but his words, their impact, still hung in the air. Dena grinned and shook her head. "That Gil," she said.

A whiff of suspicion took hold in Lana's mind. "Do you suppose he planted that last bit, about the stalker, in there to lighten the air, make his exit easier?"

Dena stared at her. "Who cares? It was the rest that counted. And the rest—omigod. You're the luckiest girl alive."

Uncertainty battled with euphoria. "Do you really think he meant it all?"

Dena's nod was vehement. "Without a doubt. I know Gil, and that was honesty."

What a day for life-changing pronouncements. It put her in a daze, like the time she fell in rehearsal, only without the pain.

"We'd better get moving," Dena said, glancing at her own watch. "*Arpeggio* rehearsal in five minutes."

"The three of us together. You, me and your sister."

"Yup." Dena looked happy.

The memory of Lucinda's words floated back into her mind.

"Hey," Lana said as they made their way down the hall. "Wanna hear some exciting news?"

"Sure."

Lana lowered her voice. "I was in with Lucinda this morning. There's going to be a photo shoot when we come back from tour. For *Arpeggio.* They want the three of us in that trio variation."

Dena's jaw sagged. She stopped walking. "They usually cast the dancers they feature in publicity shots," she said.

"That was my hunch, too."

The two of them eyed each other, not sure whether to be loudly jubilant or quietly, cautiously, carefully elated.

"It's going to happen for us," Dena said.

Lana bit her lip and nodded.

"Oh, shit," Dena added. "I am so not going to be popular here."

"Ditto. Tell you what. We'll be not-popular together, okay?"

"It's a deal."

Laughter bubbled up, as though one of them had just told the funniest joke ever. They laughed until tears welled up in their eyes that they had to wipe away.

"We're going to be late," Lana said finally. "We really have to fly."

A smile spread across Dena's face that seemed to mirror Lana's own buoyance.

"Watch us fly, world," Dena said softly.

And together, they took off.

Acknowledgments

My thanks must always go, first and foremost, to my family for supporting me in my countless writing endeavors. Second, heartfelt thanks to my agent, Anne Hawkins, who was the one to say "why not a ballet novel?" What evolved from that simple suggestion turned not only into two novels, but an entire shift in direction of my writing, that nourishes and thrills me, immersing me in today's dance world as a blogger and reviewer. The shift has also sent me back to my own dance performance days, for which I hold eternal gratitude to Kristin Benjamin, friend, mentor and artistic director of the Kaw Valley Dance Theatre. I'll always appreciate the way you supported me, challenged me, and made me realize how high I could fly if I set my mind, body and spirit to it.

Books that enriched and educated me through the writing process of this novel include Toni Bentley's *Winter Season: A Dancer's Journal*, Steven Manes' *Where Snowflakes Dance and Swear: Inside the Land of Ballet*, Janice Ross' *San Francisco Ballet at Seventy-Five*, Kyle Frohman's *In the Wings: Behind the Scenes at the New York City Ballet*.

Thank you to all my writer buddies through the eight years of this novel's evolution, including Tara Staley, Kristina Riggle, Kelly Mustian, Carolyn Burns Bass, Kristy Kiernan Graves, Grace

Harstadt, Karen Dionne and the Backspace writers' community. Thanks for early support of my novel-writing career goes to John Dalton, author, teacher and advisor, whose words and positive attitude encouraged me to persevere, through novel after novel after novel.

Thank you to my readers and supporters at The Classical Girl. You are the reason I'm attempting this madness in book form. Thank you, to early readers of this novel: Kathleen Hermes, Donna Zimmerman, Sue Novikov, Alise Driscoll. A late-in-the-game thanks to fellow author and former dancer Grier Cooper, whose own ballet novel motivated me to publish mine once and for all. Thank you, Lauren Baratz-Logsted for your excellent editing and enthusiastic support. To James T. Egan at BookFly Design, kudos for creating the perfect cover. To ballet teacher Vicki Bergland at the International Academy of Dance, thank you for giving me the opportunity to continue the art and craft of ballet in such a supportive, pleasant environment.

Finally, at the risk of duplicating my words, I again offer my thanks, love and gratitude to my family. Jonathan, for all that you are, and all that you've taught me. Peter, for your unfailing support and faith in my ability to follow my dreams and make them happen. And to the entire Mertes family, my parents and seven siblings. Thank you for being you, and making me become uniquely and stubbornly me. I love you all.

Coming in Fall of 2015

OUTSIDE THE LIMELIGHT
Ballet Theatre Chronicles – Book 2

A brain tumor diagnosis forces a prodigiously talented dancer to consider a life outside ballet, just as aging and physical degeneration have forced her fellow dancer sister to do the same, even as she sinks deeper into an affair with the company's artistic director. Told in alternating point of views, OUTSIDE THE LIMELIGHT chronicles the sisters' forays into the unfamiliar world of medicine and academia and non-dancer relationships, as they strive to discover what is worth fighting for, what is best letting go of, and what should be shouted out to the online world.

Visit The Classical Girl (www.theclassicalgirl.com) for news and excerpts as the date draws closer.

26006311R00222

Made in the USA
Middletown, DE
17 November 2015